MW01139139

"THE ALBATROSS: CON
scope of worldbuilding with sm
epic that is immersive and engaging."

— Aimee Jodoin for *IndieReader* ★ ★ ★ ★ ½

"This isn't Star Trek. It's dark, it's gritty, it's interstellar war. Anyone who enjoys thoughtful, intelligent sci-fi will enjoy this. It's always compelling and it's always well-written."

— *Wishing Shelf* Book Reviews ★ ★ ★ ★ ★

"Connor Mackay has elevated alien fiction with this action-packed space novel . . . a high-stakes adventure, filled with all the expected alien trappings and intense battle scenes.

— Nicky Flowers, *Indies Today* Editorial Reviews ★ ★ ★ ★ ★

"Engaging battles, beautiful science-fiction and otherworldly encounters are what readers will find in the pages of The Albatross: Contact. Mackay easily keeps readers engaged . . . Brimming with humor, action, and the uncertain contact with extra-terrestrial life.

— *Literary Titan* ★ ★ ★ ★ ★ **Gold Book Award Winner**

"The huge cast of brilliantly portrayed characters, awesome interstellar settings, and spectacular technology make for an irresistible hard SF novel. This is a winner."

— *The Prairies Book Review* ★ ★ ★ ★ ★

"This is science fiction at its best . . . packed with gritty dialog and scenes so vivid I felt like I was watching a movie."

— *HUGEOrange* Publication Review, **Editor's Pick 2020 Award Winner**

"Engaging from the start and with Samuel Taylor Coleridge's "The Rhyme of the Ancient Mariner" as the pivotal element—the world-building, universal ethical issues and characters' personal conflicts are riveting to read and add depth to the well-paced plot."

— Lit Amri, *Readers' Favorite* Reviews ★ ★ ★ ★ ★

"I loved that this book handles the very real topic of the cost of war on those in the military while presenting the topic in the guise of an action-packed, alien fighting plot line . . . I can't wait to read more."

— *LoveReading,* **"Indie Books We Love" badge recipient**

THE ALBATROSS

CONTACT

BOOK I IN THE ALBATROSS SERIES

CONNOR MACKAY

FriesenPress

Suite 300 - 990 Fort St
Victoria, BC, V8V 3K2
Canada

www.friesenpress.com

Cover and book design by Geoff Soch

ISBN
978-1-5255-6727-8 (Hardcover)
978-1-5255-6728-5 (Paperback)
978-1-5255-6729-2 (eBook)

1. FICTION, SCIENCE FICTION, ADVENTURE

Distributed to the trade by The Ingram Book Company

TABLE OF CONTENTS

PART IV: (WILL – SARAH – ARTHUR)

THE ALBATROSS: REQUIEM (PROLOGUE)

To Family—Blood, built, and lost.

PART I

(WILL)

The ship was cheered, Merrily did we drop
Below the kirk, below the hill,
Below the lighthouse top.

—"The Rime of the Ancient Mariner"
by Samuel Taylor Coleridge

PROLOGUE

The Beginning is The End

Ash fell from the sky like waves of sleet, blanketing everything around us in a dreary grey sludge as it mixed with the thin mist of rain, the lighter particles dancing chaotically between the oppressive drops of moisture. The muck was slimy and gritty in our hair and on our skin and seared our already emotion-stricken eyes, but there was no avoiding it. The sound in the distance, like a horrible torrent of water and broken timbers crashing over boulder drops and into headwalls, echoed in our ears and spiked the hair on the backs of our necks.

We all stood in stunned silence, staring out from our overwatch position. No words were spoken, and no words would have been enough to describe the sight or allay the mountain of shit we all felt. No hymn or prayer could stem the bleeding sorrow. Nothing screamed or struck could have tamed the rage fighting its way to the forefront of our hearts and minds.

As the blood curdled in our veins, several of the squad sat or knelt in the mud, despair crippling their legs. Strength forged in countless battles crumbled with the ruins of the world around us. Something was so profoundly different here. This wasn't Stormwater or Cerberus or Forge or Prima or any of the other places we'd shed blood. This was our world. This was home.

As if the Fates felt it necessary to rub an ironic "fuck you" in our faces, a singed pamphlet floated to my feet, kicked up from under a burnt-out car by a light gust. I picked it up before the mire could claim another victim, the solar nano-paper flickering and distorting slightly, and read the blurred line at the top: "Earth Welcomes Home Our Brave Union Forces! We've missed you these last 187 years!" Below it was a moving 1940s war-bond-style cartoon of a human family waving up to three silhouetted alien vessels arriving in orbit, trailing phosphoric beams through the stars. The first three... The doomed three...

Gritting my teeth, I passed the sheet to one of the few remaining members of my original team, the only guy with whom I shared a past before the stars. Examining the page, his brow furrowed, and he curled some saliva in his mouth, spitting off to the side. Looking back up at the landscape, his lips tightened into a firm line, and he crumpled the flyer, tossing it away. The hellish orange glow reflected in his eyes.

Kneeling, I pressed my hand through the ashy tar and scooped up a handful of cool dirt underneath. I stared at the dark earth in my fingers for what seemed an age before letting it cascade to the ground in clumps. When I finally stood again, the doubt, fear, and sorrow were gone, leaving behind something much darker. The blue fire of the biotech coursed through every fiber of my body and shone like a torch.

A moment later, one by one, everyone else lit up their tech on either side of me. Bright technicolor beacons in the dark.

Home sweet home.

CHAPTER 1

Hi. My Name is Will.

THWACK!

Shit. Well, I sure felt that one. Blood dripped lazily from a small cut above my left eye, the swelling already taking hold on the corner of my forehead. One of those instant goose eggs where it felt like the only relief would arrive with a puncture to release the pressure and a cold beer pressed against it.

Getting to my feet, I swung a sloppy haymaker toward the brute with the shoddy politics, letting him know I was still in the fight. Allowing me to create that distance was his first mistake.

WHACK!

Nope, never mind. Apparently, his Neanderthal buddy hit like a truck too. The ground was hard and cold as I made contact. Rolling onto my stomach, I pressed myself up from the grimy tile floor, my body making a sticky Velcro sound as I peeled up. I glanced behind the bar at Frank who was—big fucking surprise—unimpressed.

Frank was fiercely loyal, an imposingly solid block of a man and a good number two in a fight—when he fought. Unfortunately, he was also usually one of those "calmer heads prevail" types unless absolutely necessary. Due to the nature of this specific brawl, my provocative language—which had inspired it—and the fact that none of Frank's bar property had been destroyed had me leaning toward his lack of involvement. Unless they really started kicking the shit out of me. So, as I dusted off my hands from my recent visit to the pavement, Frank just crossed his arms and shook his head.

"You know, Frank, wouldn't kill ya to mop the floor from time to time."

"Well, Will, wouldn't kill ya to keep your mouth shut for a change," he retorted without missing a beat.

I turned back to the two MAGA fuckwits in front of me, putting my hands up for the next round. "Touché. OK, last chance guys. I'm willing to let you walk out of here un-whooped if you just admit that your president is actually a fucking Oompa Loompa or…a Martian. I'll accept either. Now, I'll admit they're not my best barbs, but they'll do for now."

Frank exhaled with a sigh, and I grinned over at him.

Cro-Magnon numbers one and two smirked at each other before turning back to me and coming in for another dance. Talk about one-dimensional. No sense of humor at all. Relying on a roughhousing rebuttal, I guess. I was definitely not sober, but I let on that I was drunker than I was, a strategic waver in my step as I jockeyed for position.

"Don't break my shit!" Frank said from behind the bar as the first new swings were swung. Luckily for me, I was no slouch in a tussle, but unluckily, I was drunker than I thought.

Wasn't my finest bout, but I got the job done with no more than a handful of new bruises and scrapes and a wad of coarse brown paper towel from the bathroom stuffed up my right nostril—my left never bled, the result of a broken nose during hand-to-hand training with Frank during boot.

I plunked down on the well-worn and slightly torn vinyl cushion of my barstool and stared at Frank. Still shaking his head, he poured a beer and set it in front of me. Leaning on the counter, he looked left and then right, scanning the bar. No tumbleweeds, but there might as well have been. "Get that out of your system?"

"Yep."

"Last two guys in the bar…"

"Good thing I drink enough for two guys then."

"And pay enough for none."

"It's always about money with you, Frank."

He shook his head and began doing an inventory of his spirits behind the bar.

"You know, I was just defending your black ass," I said with a shit-eating grin.

Frank chuckled but didn't turn around. "Defending me, huh? Don't remember hearing them say anything."

"Well, I just assumed by their stupid hats and...stupid faces they were thinking something slimy."

"Well aren't you just a white knight," he said.

I laughed, slapped the bar, and returned to my beer.

It was a quiet dive, somewhere between Moe's from *The Simpsons* and Cheers from...*Cheers*. Darkened windows with off-putting green slats that let in only the minimum amount of light. Pale-yellow floors from beer spills and probably piss stains in the tiles and grout. Hand-me-down features from the previous owner, which Frank had attempted to scrub away but then had quickly realized they'd just need to be replaced or covered. Each table was made sturdy by a combination of folded coasters and the odd wooden shim under an edge of their circular bases. Three TVs were placed throughout the bar, each built into old custom 1970s faux-grain millwork, which Frank might've splurged on to replace had they not weighed a metric fuck-ton and by some magic still happened to work reasonably well—or at least Frank knew the quirks. He was not one to thrive on new tech. The joint was hell for those who had and a haven for those who had not. Exactly the kind of place an ex-SOF guy could afford fresh out of the service with decent credit and exactly the kind of place he needed to get things right in his head after receiving the shit end of the stick. A quiet oasis in a small southwestern town in the middle of nowhere. Perfect for the two of us. Whether Frank liked it or not, we were a package deal.

I drummed my fingers on the bar, fidgeting in the mental swirl of boredom. "You know what day it is?" I asked.

Frank looked up at me through the mirror behind the rows of spirits but didn't turn around. His amber eyes narrowed slightly, and his lips tightened into a line. "Yeah." He held the stare for a moment and then turned around and reached under the bar. After pulling out the sapphire bottle of Johnnie Walker Blue, reserved for this day, he set two shot glasses on the counter. He poured the light, honey-colored liquid into the glasses and slid one toward me. Lifting his glass Frank held it up between us. I did the same. We didn't clink shots, but we shared a nod and took the drink in silence. The scotch was smoother than I felt. It was wasted in a shot, but that wasn't the point.

Frank set his glass down and stared at it. "Hell of a day."

"Yep."

"You know I—"

"Yeah, that actually wasn't an invitation to talk about it." I switched back to my beer and took a deep drink.

When I lowered the mug, Frank was glaring at me. "You're not the only one who—"

"Hold on a second." I brought the beer back up, tilting my head back in an exaggerated chug as I finished it. When I brought the empty mug back down, Frank had resumed his inventory. I saw his downturned face in the mirror. His jaw was clenched, his brow furrowed. Normally, when Frank was irritated, I'd do the only sensible thing and irritate him more until he snapped or let it go. This was different. I couldn't bring myself to do it.

I looked over to the side of the room, the light filtering through the window slats in dusty beads. *She* passed there between the shade and the glow, smiling as she wandered, the beams slicing through her form. I felt my foot start to tremble on the stool rung and tried to stop it, but as soon as I did, I started fidgeting with the handle of the beer mug. I gripped it tightly and closed my eyes. I held my breath for a moment and then exhaled slowly. When I opened my eyes, she was gone. I needed to go too.

I patted one jeans pocket, then the other one, then the ones in the back, then the pocket on my cotton shirt. I looked up at Frank. "You got my keys?"

He held them out without turning around.

"Give 'em here."

He tucked them into his pocket and didn't respond.

"I'd like my keys back, Frank."

"Nope."

I felt my rage heating to a quick boil, like only alcohol and history could induce. A hot flush spread around my neck and into my cheeks. "I need those keys."

"You sure don't."

"I'm doing it tonight, Frank."

Frank turned and stared at me. "Not in my parking lot you're not."

"Why the fuck would I need my keys if I was gonna do it in your parking lot? I obviously would have driven somewhere dramatic, like the desert...or a Walmart parking lot."

Frank blinked several times and then shook his head. "You're drunk, Will. You're not getting your keys back tonight." We shared a hard stare. There's a wordless look people get when they've seen war or loss that says, "I'm serious. Don't fuck with me," more potently and deeply than your average Joe. Thing is, Frank wore the exact same expression. He stepped closer, leaning on the bar. After a moment his gaze softened. "This ain't the way, man." I looked away. Frank's gentle hand could be nauseating. "At least let me try to get you some money—"

"Fuck you, Fra—" Before I could get all the words out, Frank cuffed me hard along the side of my ear. The less-gentle hand of Frank. His glare intensified from compassion to frustration, and I shot an icy stare back at him.

"You're a mean drunk, Will, and you already lost one fight tonight. Grow the fuck up."

I wanted him to hit me again, to give me an excuse to swing back, to fight the world. But then I released the breath I didn't realize I'd been holding, and it allowed the briefest of revelations to sink in. I could've sworn at Frank for the next hour, taken a shot, stood up, and pissed on the bar, and Frank wouldn't have loved me any less. Sure, he'd be irritated as fuck, but his short spark of anger was the glass of water on a sleeping man's face, not a malicious attack. And if I really did try to fight him, it wouldn't go well for me. I could take him sober, but it'd be close. Now he'd make a fool of me, and what's worse, he'd probably do it without even really hurting me. That was the worst part. Rather than press my luck and potentially have my other nostril collapsed or my ego bruised further, I looked away.

One of the great benefits of having a big mug of beer in front of you is it's an easy hideaway for your rage and heartache. And that's just how I used it. Well, I brought my mug up, remembered it was empty, then set it down and reached over for the half-finished beer that one of the caveman dickheads had left behind. I buried my face in the frothy gold, picturing my fist in Frank's face. The man who I loved like a brother. Goddammit, I could be an asshole sometimes. Also, yuck. Of course those assholes drank light beer. I stared off into the corner of the room, avoiding Frank's gaze. Out of the corner of my eye, I saw him nod and then turn back to his inventory, leaving me to the numb silence and the turbulent wanderings of my mind.

The brains of survivors rifle through a mental scrapbook during silent moments. A slideshow of flashing lights scorched with faces and voices, laughter and tears clawing in the quiet. Alcohol can lose the book upon the shelves, slow the turning of the pages, or make each one a visceral, reanimated spirit that plagues your every moment until a dreamless sleep occasionally resets your timecard. At that moment, my non-fictional spirits were starting to peek out from their dark corners, walking again through the dusty beads of light.

We sat there in silence for several long minutes, my grasp on my emotions eroding slowly with the booze.

"Hey, I've been going to this group thing the last couple months," Frank said, still facing the back wall but stealing glances at me in the mirror.

"Oh yeah?" I mumbled, rolling my eyes.

"It's not a vet thing. Just a place for people who've—"

"I'm gonna stop you there, Frank. I'm not interested." I downed the last gulp of beer and slammed it on the bar with a loud "Aaaah" of satisfaction, gesturing to Frank for another.

Frank reluctantly took the mug and refilled it. "You should try talking to someone, Will."

"I talk to you."

"You don't even have to talk if you don't want to. You can just come and listen. Hell, I didn't say anything the first month I started going."

I saw how much he cared. I knew how much he cared, and I knew he was probably right. But I also knew I wasn't there yet. Apparently, I knew a lot. So, I just stared back with the ignorant gaze of someone who knows better than everyone else and gestured again for my drink. "I'll take a new beer please, barkeep."

Frank gave me the all-too-familiar head shake and then slid me the beer. "Just think about it, OK? And this is your last beer." I saluted him with the mug and took a deep drink as he picked up a tray of glassware and walked over to the ancient dishwasher. I watched him for a few moments before turning back to the company of my demons.

The lights flicked off as Frank locked the bar and prepared to head up to his apartment above the establishment. Swaying slightly, I sat on the cot in the back room, which I'd been sleeping on for the last several months.

Frank leaned into the room. "You good?"

I stood up uneasily and walked toward him with my arms out, going in for a hug. "Come here, Frank. I love ya, man. I'm sorry about before."

Frank looked skeptical that I had turned a corner again in the same night but didn't reject the gesture and hugged me warmly. "Get some sleep, Will," he said, his hand on my shoulder.

I pulled back with a smile and a cheesy finger pistol, confirming it was sleep time. I went back to the cot and lay down.

"Night," Frank concluded with a slight linger in the doorway. Moments later I heard him open the door to the upstairs and thump up the steps.

I sat up slowly on the bed and pulled my tightly clenched fist out from my side. Had to squeeze hard so there wouldn't be any space for the jingle of metal on metal. I opened my hand and stared down at my car keys, swiped clean out of Frank's pocket.

I was standing too close to the hot glow, but I didn't care. If it decided to explode right then, I'd be in trouble. The Molotov smashed through the backseat window just like in the movies, and it ignited in the backseat just like the movies, even engulfed the whole cab like the movies, but I knew it would take a couple of minutes to get to anything really volatile. So, I took in the heat and the memories. I let the spirits dance around me and the wreck. *He* stood just outside the glow, eyes shimmering like spectral jewels.

The burning fabric, plastic, paint, and vinyl spit up tarry black smoke in big billowing plumes that disappeared into the darkness. The smell was acrid and harsh and made my eyes water, but I couldn't turn away. The orange and chemical-green glow of the flames was hypnotic and laced with false promises of peace.

The car was a '65 Mustang that I'd rebuilt with my dad back in high school. A labor of love and bonding that had taught me more about life than fixing cars—look how much good that did me. It was a beautiful ride dipped in satin black with chrome accents around the windows, mirrors, grill, and classic rims. It had seen its share of miles and first times (boomchickawawa, among others). I had driven it to prom, to college, and to the funeral. I had also driven it to the recruiting office, to training, my wedding, the hospital, to our home, and then to more funerals. I even drove it on the day. This day. Every time I looked at it, every time I drove it, the scrapbook of memories flipped open again and again until the pages became too heavy to turn, and I was just tired. So damn tired. Dragged down by the drowning anchor of memory.

That was the main reason I decided not to let Frank tag along. Some people store memories in more than their minds; the sentimental folks who link love or hate to little trinkets and vehicles, unable to separate the nostalgic reincarnations. I'm like that. An endower. Frank is not. Either he'd say to go ahead and do it, forcing me to withdraw in a stubborn rebellion at his seemingly callous nonchalance about the issue's difficulty, or he'd encourage me to make a buck off it, which I also felt was emotionally impossible. He wasn't cold; he was practical (at least he'd be happy to hear I only stole his well whisky for the Molotov). A good soldier that way. His stock was always placed in the present, in people, not things. When the people were gone, they were gone. Or so I imagined. Which is fair, I guess, even if some of us felt the people lived on in totems. Maybe it didn't make sense, but it did to me then, and I'd take any break from the feelings that I could. Frank had every right to be there with me, every reason, but it was my selfish moment. I needed to do it on my own.

I walked back a few paces to the bottle of Jameson's (another liberation) sitting on the pavement, unscrewed the cap, and took a healthy swig. The heat of it lapped over and into me, the fire and the whisky sauntering through my blood. I closed my eyes and took a deep breath, exhaling slowly. I didn't want to feel anything. Didn't want to give it more power than it already had, but I couldn't hold it in any longer. Sinking down on the concrete of the vacant parking lot, I stared into the flames, quietly breaking down. I *really* didn't want to feel it all, but I did.

I dug my old snub-nose revolver out of my pocket and held it in my palm. A silver-and-black Ruger GP100 .357 Magnum. It wasn't a very big gun physically, but it carried the weight of life in it. Soul baggage. I pulled a single round out of my other pocket and stared at it for a long time. Then I reached over and released the cylinder, letting it fall to the side. Holy shit. I had absentmindedly, irresponsibly, been carrying it around with three bullets in it the whole time. Yes, a good example of why firearms and fire water don't mix. I slid the bullets out of the cylinder and held them in my hand, closing the cylinder with a snap of my wrist. I rolled the ammo in my palm for a minute or two.

Finally, I pitched the three neglected rounds into the burning wreckage. The sole remaining bullet I set aside on the concrete. It was a dud. A dark keepsake. Centerpunched and left wanting. The second round had done the trick.

"Get a hold of yourself, Will," I said gruffly, clearing my throat. There was a time when I'd wanted to die. Wanted to do it myself. Wanted it more than anything. I had thought the haunting scrapbook was demanding it of me, calling me to join its pages. But "conscience does make cowards of us all," I guess. Or rather love. When I'd come close, the book's ghosts had lashed their discontent to the forefront of my mind. In the corners, *her* smile had faltered and then faded into a devastating look of disappointment that broke my heart. It wasn't until the weapon was safely stowed that I saw her eyes shine again. Her happiness, my torment. Besides, when I really thought about it, I wouldn't take the way out that *he* had.

I looked up into the star-filled night sky searching for answers that wouldn't come, wondering if anything I had done was the right thing. Wondering what the world wanted from me. Wondering why the Fates had decided to fuck with me so goddamn much. I gazed for long, unmoving minutes at the silent celestials. The odd shooting star flashed across the sky. *Just being a dramatic little bitch, Will.*

A sudden ringing filled my ears, the kind you hear in silence or in the aftershock when something has gone BANG, and you're losing frequencies. Despite the loud crackling of my burning car, everything seemed to have muted and gone still. I stood, trying to pop my ears, and stared into the darkness beyond my glowing ring, searching for anything unusual, some sign of whatever phantom was causing the chill to run up my spine. A slight prickling on my arms brought my eyes down. Goose bumps had perked up, and all the hairs stood static-electricity straight.

Then, as if on cue, three blindingly bright green lights appeared over-head. They streaked through the black in a flash, like a satellite falling back to earth and skipping along the atmosphere. Then they came to an unnaturally abrupt stop above the horizon. They hung there like streetlights miles high as their initial emerald brilliance calmed to a strange, otherworldly glow. Motionless and menacing.

I stared with my mouth open for a long moment before a wave of heat brought me back to the ball of fire in front of me.

BANG! BANG! Whoa. BANG! The bullets ignited and popped off in haphazard trajectories out of the car's back seat. I ducked instinctively. The shots whistled past as they vanished into the night, one echoing alarmingly close.

"Jesus," I muttered, staring wide eyed. I shook my head and blinked several times, then looked back toward the mysterious lights. They still shone above the distant foothills.

"Goddamn."

CHAPTER II

Hurry Up and Wait

"This is fucking crazy." A sentiment that echoed with annoying frequency and with a buckshot of different tones. Some took the life-changing appearance as a reason to sober up, but most decided to double down. I prided myself on consistency, so I maintained my general state of mild to heavy inebriation to deal with the current situation. Frank also soldiered on, as he does, maintaining his steely composure and making sure to keep the taps flowing. Thank the good lord baby Jesus for him. I do know that Frank pulled his rifle out of lockup and kept it loaded upstairs, though, just in case the reckoning descended upon us. Practical, like I said.

Everyone was uneasy but talkative and cheerfully sardonic, the way small-town folk shake off the trials and tragedies felt by a place where neighbors all know and support each other. It was one of the reasons Frank and I liked the place—people cared about each other but stayed out of each other's way, save for the gossip in roadside diners and the gentle jeering that spoke to a compassionate curiosity over prying prickishness.

In the larger cities, almost immediately riots and looting had taken place as people expressed their fears in the most constructive way they could think of—stealing shit. The "practical" ones pilfered the stores for supplies to stock their homes and shelters in anticipation of a long hunker-down or guerilla war against the visitors, and the others figured if these were the end times, they might as well go out with a massive flat-screen. Violent crimes were still pretty low, probably because people believed if everything turned up tulips, the petty shit would be mostly forgiven in the mob haze of panic, but the heavy-grade stuff wouldn't get the same pass. Goes to show the self-serving nature of people—that we can collectively orchestrate an excuse to act out our lesser angels.

Frank's and my neck of the woods never saw much excitement even during wildfires and dust storms, so UFO arrivals didn't clock much either. Not like we were that far from Area 51 either. But the local flavor consistently turned up to drink booze and chat about the crazy goings-on in the world outside, as if we were in some distant, forgotten bubble. Probably about the only time Frank actually made some money at the bar.

For the first few weeks, business kept up like that. People came in to share in the mystery and intrigue of our silent guests in the sky. To drink away their fear and uncertainty and boast about what they'd do if the aliens hadn't come in peace.

As the weeks turned to months, the programming on the television returned to a somewhat normal routine, since nothing had happened, and we were apparently not being *Arrival'd*. Scientists and governments studied them around the clock with little to no luck at learning anything substantial. Speculations flew from one crazy idea to the next in a world that had now experienced life beyond our solar system. At any given moment we could still find some station running a new hypothesis or day count, but more and more the aliens faded into the background of our lives; a steady tension that people began to equate with long delays in traffic or the headache that lurked just on the edge of a migraine. They were always in sight, always in mind, but so far had little bearing on our daily lives.

Over the months all the cliché factions of the human spirit began popping up around the globe—cults, religions, and survivalist groups. Even a shadowy terrorist organization made its way onto our feeds, claiming it stood for human supremacy or purity or some shit like that. They were particularly colorful pieces of work. Like most illegal "movements," if you want to give it that much credit, they began small—graffiti, vandalism, effigies, online forums. But over the months, their radical following elevated their tactics to kidnapping, murder, and bombings. In the fanatics' minds, their violent passions were necessary, believing that the world would hail them as heroes when the lines in the sand were finally drawn. They called themselves the OnSpec, which stood for "Only Species," which apparently was too long of a title. They claimed their acts of terror against the cultists and new-world religions that prostrated themselves beneath the ships were justified because they were clearing the field of potential collaborators when the invasion came, or so their shaky iPhone warehouse videos claimed. The group's xenophobic slogan, "Humans first. Humans only. We are the OnSpec," adorned attack sites and back alleys across major cities around the world. Bunch of fucking lunatics if you ask me. Especially considering the fact that, though their message was "pro-human," the only things they'd terrorized were humans. Dipshits.

In time their manifesto was littered across all the platforms; words of hate and nationalism made global. It also contained detailed plans for when the aliens finally arrived, scenarios factoring in a faux peace or invasion. Basics in tactics and mass mobilization, firearms handling, survival skills, and so on. I'd flipped through a few pages on some trash website, not for any sort of sought or empathized conviction but rather due to curiosity about the crazies' minds. Read like an angsty teen lashing out against his parents—juvenile and radical. Something bred of unbridled fear and passion without the intelligence or life experience to back it up. As much as I wanted to slough it off as some flash in the pan, it was worrying to see how widely the voice had travelled. Some asshole in his basement making waves. Hope was it'd peter out if our guests ever decided to actually come down for a friendly "Howdy, partners." Or, if it came down to it, they'd provide some fodder for the real militaries when the guns started shooting. Either way, dickheads with radical fixations of hate get tamped down eventually. Didn't see them being a problem for long.

Somewhere around four months after they arrived, I decided to mix things up. I switched stools in Frank's bar. I didn't love the new one yet, but I'd work it in—get my new ass groove going. We were in the middle of a brutal heat wave, and I leaned against the bar with my cold beer mug pressed against my forehead. The fans in the corners of the room were working overtime. They didn't cool down the space much, but at least they moved the air around.

The familiar squeak of the door's hinges sounded the arrival of someone new, and I saluted with my beer without looking back. Took too much energy in that heat to make extraneous moves. "Welcome to Frank's bar, where it's one degree cooler than outside," I announced with a sarcastic grin and a chuckle to myself.

Frank didn't turn around from refilling bottles. "Dick," he said. One of Frank's regulars, an older guy named Larry, walked over and sat a few stools down from me. I glanced over mid-swig and did a double take.

"Jesus, Larry. What the fuck happened?" I asked, noticing the bruises on his face, his split lip, and his swollen bloody nose.

Frank turned and saw him as well. "Whoa. You OK, Larry?" he asked. Larry nodded, wincing from the obvious pain in his body. He was no spring chicken, a man made of leather and tobacco, and he looked worse than I did after my last brawl.

"Caught a couple kids vandalizin' the store," he said, tenderly stretching his neck. Larry owned the hardware store in town and was a good man, salt of the earth type. "Could I get a beer?"

"Couple of kids did this?" Frank asked, turning to pour Larry a pint. He set the cold beer in front of Larry, who took it and drank deeply before replying.

"Yeah. Little punks was spray paintin' my wall. Told 'em to stop. Told 'em that stuff they was writin' was garbage. This's what I got for it," he said, taking another drink.

We sat in silence for a few moments. Then I turned to him. "Want us to go kick their asses?"

"Christ, Will," Frank said, shaking his head.

"What? Larry's an old dude. Figured by 'kids' he meant like fifteen to eighteen range. I didn't think he meant, like, *kids* kids."

"I'm sittin' right here—"

"I'm just messing with you Lar—"

"And you want to beat up some teenagers, Will?" Frank asked.

I weighed it with my hands and thought about it for longer than I probably should have, alky brain and all.

Frank rolled his eyes and turned back to Larry. "Did you recognize them?"

Larry shook his head. "No. Must've been passin' through. Had a jeep I didn't recognize either."

"Get a plate number?"

"I wish. Only glimpsed it from the ground after they'd kicked the hell outta me." Larry shook his head and winced again from the pain. Frank dug out a bag and scooped some ice into it, then passed it over to Larry, who bowed his appreciation and held it over his cheek.

"Well, shit. I'm sorry, Larry. You need a hand painting over the graffiti?" Frank offered.

"Appreciate that, Frank, but I'll manage." Larry nodded gratefully, sculling the rest of his beer. Frank automatically poured him another one and set it on the bar. We sat quietly and drank for a few moments.

"Oh! What'd they graffiti by the way? Big dick or something?" I asked, a stupid drunken giggle escaping me.

Larry glanced slowly at me and then back to Frank. "We are the OnSpec."

At six months, still nothing had happened. Reports continued to detail the efforts of researchers attempting to penetrate the secrets above. Scans, telescopes, re-tasked satellites, shuttles, and other efforts at contact all came back negative. No radiation was emitted, and no particles, waves, or sounds, at least that we could detect. As far as the world knew we were witnessing magic or some sort of worldwide mass hallucination or hysteria, a theory that got thrown around more than once. Dust and debris was observed to deflect off the hulls, and they did block and reflect light, but other than that, we couldn't come to any concrete conclusions about them. I mean, I figured it'd be impossible for 7.5 billion people to be imagining the same intergalactic travelers sitting in space, but I guess they needed "solid evidence." The only somewhat intriguing new information was that a multinational operation was to be undertaken in the next few weeks for a more invasive approach at studying them (whatever that entailed).

Those were a long six months. I gave up drinking once for about two days and then decided life was probably definitely maybe too short not to have some happiness, so I started drinking again. That and that by the third day the detox was making me hate life more than usual. The group of old boys and girls who had originally flocked to Frank's in the early weeks of the arrival had dwindled to a small speckling of hard-cores who basically had nothing better to do and no loved ones calling them home. I only had Frank, so I wasn't giving up much being at the bar, and the company and curiosity kept me from the turning pages of my little scrapbook of torments.

A little drunker than usual, I finished my beer and stared into the bottom of my empty mug. I instinctively patted the chest pocket of my old, slightly ratty Hawaiian button-up shirt. Huh? I looked down, not trusting the consistency of my flailing fingers. The bright reds, blues, yellows, and whites of the background and flowers on the shirt made my eyes blurry. The familiar imprint of a photograph was missing. In a moment of panic, I dug my fingers into the pocket and felt around, and then scanned through my other pockets. I stood up, or half fell, from my stool and looked around the tilting off-balance floor. "Frank. Frank! Where's my picture? You see my picture? I always have it."

Frank walked down the bar toward me, having just served the only other patrons, a couple en route to somewhere shinier forced to stop for the evening.

"Frank!"

"Hey, what's up? What's wrong?"

"My picture. You see my picture?"

"Oh yeah, yeah. Hold on." Frank turned to the register behind the bar, dug out a creased old photograph, and handed it back to me. "You dropped it last night. Found it on the floor."

A wave of relief washed over me as I took the picture in my hands. The most beautiful woman and little girl in the world stared up at me from the faded white border. I had to choke back my breath to keep it all in. "Fuck, man, thought I lost it for a minute there." My voice wavered slightly as I threw a nervous smile at Frank and wiped the sweat from my forehead and under my eyes, the photo shaking in my hands.

I felt Frank staring into me. "I love that photo of them," he said.

"Yeah."

Maria's dark hair flew wildly around her face, and she laughed and smiled, holding squirming six-year-old Evelyn, barefoot in the Mexican sand. I remembered the salty mulch smell of the ocean and seaweed washed upon the shore. Fragmented driftwood mixed with the ivory-gold beach, getting caught between our toes. I felt her soft skin against my dry calloused hands.

"I remember when you guys took that trip. They couldn't believe how blue the—"

"Hey, what day is it?" I asked, clearing my throat.

The abrupt shift stopped Frank, who stared at me, his nostalgic smile fading away. I could tell he was debating whether to push the visit a little further down memory lane or let it go. After a moment of contemplation, he exhaled and went with the flow. "Thursday," he said.

"No, since AD?"

Frank picked up the remote to the bar television and flipped to the consistent "arrival information" channel. The bulletin read, "September 7, 2020 – Day 190 since Arrival Day (AD)."

"This is getting fucking ridiculous. Like, invade us or something already," I joked, further burying the emotion welling up inside.

Frank chuckled with me before we both stopped short, and our jaws hit the floor as the report on the news switched abruptly to a shot of the Washington, DC, skyline under a blanket of low cloud. Slowly and silently a massive ship with smooth, brushed-steel-like panels covering its flawless surface descended through the clouds. Its hulking figure cast a long shadow across the famous landmarks of the nation's capital as it sailed over the city. The ship wasn't one of the main vessels we'd seen on the news from the many space reconnaissance missions but a smaller expeditionary craft. Its windowless hull was seamless save for some sort of propulsion-system ports emitting a greenish-blue blur, like the ripples in a glass of water next to a subwoofer. *Oh great, first American they're gonna meet is our assclown of a president.*

The two other TVs in the bar flickered and jarringly switched their programming, each displaying the same scene with cut frames over Ottawa, Johannesburg, Sydney, Berlin, Moscow, Vancouver, Rio de Janeiro, Cairo, Beijing, Tokyo, Nairobi, and a few other major cities worldwide.

Frank and I stared in awe as the alien ships crept to a deadly stop in the air above the eyes of the world. I did not love how similar the move looked to *Independence Day*.

"Well," Frank said, "that's fucking crazy."

CHAPTER III

Everything Here

BANG!

The shot tore over the wide desert plain, kicking up a concussion gust of sand as it flew. It whistled through a hand-drawn target on a beer box set up around 500 yards away, making a near-perfect hole through the center. Frank shuffled up onto his forearms and pulled back the bolt of his rifle, ejecting the empty cartridge. I lay back in a lawn chair next to him beneath a ratty patio umbrella. I was wearing dark sunglasses, sipping a beer, and cradling one of our old military spotter scopes that we had liberated after our service.

In the days after our guests finally decided to show themselves, every soul on Earth was fixed to their television sets, computers, or phones or loaded up in vehicles making a pilgrimage to one of the several major landing sites across the globe. The doldrums that had preceded the visitors' appearance on terra firma were over as their arrival stirred the planet's citizens into frenzied curiosity. Millions flocked to behold the mighty extraterrestrials, and news reporters were reenergized with a narcotic-like zeal as the stations went back to their twenty-four-hour-a-day binges.

What began as a tsunami of fear when they had first descended through the clouds had turned into joy and amazement when governments around the world announced that, by some miracle, it was not all doom and gloom. Our leaders and the media were preparing us for a worldwide address by the aliens' highest representative to explain why they had come. Though no one, save a few high-ranking government officials around the globe, had seen the visitors, we were assured that they had come in peace and that amazing things were soon to occur. It all seemed a little too good to be true, but we tentatively awaited the news nonetheless. Still didn't stop the nuts from stockpiling supplies and weaponry though.

Frank and I decided to airgap the frenzy by getting out of the bar and blowing off some steam. Brand-new world every day it seemed, and I didn't mind a break from it.

"Will."

"Yo."

"Little high and right, wasn't it?" Frank asked, glancing over at me.

"Uh…" I finished my beer in a big swig and raised the scope, peering down range. "Sure," I said, lowering the sight and staring up through the shadow of the covering into the bright sun.

Frank stood up in frustration and snatched the scope from me, glaring through it toward the mark. "Pretty good, actually."

"See? Told ya," I said, wagging my finger.

Frank glanced at me with a *What the fuck?* expression on his face but then shrugged it off.

The orb in the sky beat down on us, and the waves of heat reverberated around the shade of the umbrella in mirage ripples. I wiped some sweat off my forehead with the back of my hand. "You bring any water?" I asked, hoping Frank would go get it.

"You don't want another beer?"

"Oh shit, we have beer left?"

"You should stick with water, pal."

"Oh man, this hangover is killing me."

"Guess it would, considering you never make it to that stage."

"Yeah, yeah. Little more hair of the dog?" I asked.

"God, you're a whiner. You know what's even better for a hangover? Hydrating."

"OK, *Dad*," I said, rolling my eyes. Frank chuckled and walked over to the back of his truck bed. He sat on the tailgate with a sharp creak of the springs. It was an old '70s Ford rust bucket that had seen better days but by sheer willpower and elbow grease had managed to cling to life under Frank's care for the last fifteen or so years. He dug in the cooler and pulled out two bottles of water, chucking one at the back of my head. The plastic crinkled against my neck as it made contact, leaving cool wet drips running down my back. "Ah, that's cold!"

Frank laughed, obviously impressed with the accuracy of his toss. I picked the sandy bottle off the ground and opened it, taking a swig. It was refreshing, this water stuff. "Maybe this is why the aliens are here," I said. "They want to learn the most harmful ways to store water." Frank scoffed and took a drink. We sat quietly for a few moments, taking in the heat.

"Gonna shoot today?"

I squinted at him. "Need me to show you how it's done, old man?"

"Put your money where your mouth is." I shook my head and walked over to the truck bed, grabbing three rounds from the box and dangling them in front of Frank's face. He waved me away. "Yeah, yeah."

I lay down, saddling up to the rifle—a Remington 700 Long Action— and loaded the three shells into the clip, sliding the bolt forward and chambering one. Looking through the scope, I aimed at the target that Frank had already punctured. I hesitated for a moment before smiling to myself and shifting my position slightly, adjusting my line. I took a deep breath. Frank lifted the spotter scope to his eye and looked down range. I exhaled slowly and squeezed the trigger.

BANG!

The shot rifled away, and I ejected the casing, launching the next round into the chamber with the forward drive of the bolt.

BANG!

The second shot hurtled down course. The shell flew out, and the last round chambered with a smooth ratcheting click.

BANG!

The last bullet cruised out with a burst. I pulled back the action and let the last shell flick out into the sand.

Frank slowly lowered his scope and stared at me. "Three perfect shots...through the eight-hundred-yard target. Son of a bitch."

"Darn. I *was* aiming for the five."

"Fuck you." Frank laughed, shaking his head. Just then a faint alarm chimed from Frank's phone inside the cab. "Hey, the broadcast is coming on." We climbed into the truck. He put the key in the ignition and turned on the radio. It crackled to life and with the strange ambiance of a time long gone, the broadcaster's voice sounded across the airwaves.

"Well, folks, the long-awaited moment is almost upon us. The leader of our visitors to the cosmic north will finally be shedding the silence in a tell-all broadcast live around the globe."

A second radio DJ's voice chimed in. "What do you think about this announcement that our new supreme overlord's name is *Arthur?*"

"Well, Phil, word on the street is that during that loooong period in orbit before making contact, our guests were absorbing every bit of information we had down here."

"At least buy us a drink first, huh, Ted?"

"You said it, Phil. Well news is, each of the 'Lumenarians,' as they're calling themselves, chose their own *Earth names* based on the research they had been conducting—or whatever word or name seemed to translate the best. I'm still a little hazy on it, to be honest."

"That makes two of us. And 'Lumenarians,' where's that coming from?" The DJs droned on as they traded their semi-scripted information back and forth. Frank and I settled into the truck's bench seat, waiting for the big moment and wishing the two idiots would shut up. I stepped out of the truck for a minute and poured some water on my head. Shit, it was hot. My sweat smelled like rancid beer.

"Hey, it's starting," Frank said.

I leaned in the window to listen.

"Alright, guys, we're patching in now to the Lumenarian address live in Cairo, Egypt."

The radio fizzled slightly as they plugged in the new feed. After a long pause of dead air, a deep, human-sounding voice rasped over the radio, only a slight tone of roboticness to it. "Thank you for allowing me to speak with you today." The cheers from the surrounding crowds made the speaker pause, waiting for the cue to continue. "My name is Arthur, and I come to you on behalf of all Lumenarians."

Frank and I glanced at each other, unable to hide our excited curiosity, then turned back to the radio, as if doing so would help us see him better.

"I wish our species could have met under different circumstances, but I come to you with a desperate plea." What could these interstellar beings possibly need from us? "The request is no small matter, and it carries with it a grave burden." There was a crackling pause before the alien continued, stretching out the elastic band of tension. I couldn't keep from leaning closer into the truck, hanging on every word. "We have come...for your help."

The speech continued for a few more minutes but was surprisingly short. Either way, the effect was potent. I climbed into the truck and sat in stunned silence next to Frank, staring out the windshield. War. They wanted us to help them fight a war.

The alien leader had briefly described the logistics of his request, the inherent dangers it posed, the travel timeframes, the fact that Lumen (their home world) was a hub to four other peaceful alien races (another bombshell), and finally stated that more information would be presented in the coming days—just enough to get the bug in people's heads to consider volunteering. He offered nothing in return for our service but instead had already begun the process of providing Earth with invaluable technological upgrades regardless of how many souls ventured with them into the abyss. The choice to join would be ours alone. A chance to venture across the stars and see things no human had imagined they'd ever see and to fight in a vicious war. He was right; it was no small ask of a young species that had barely marched past their own moon. Sounded like someone else's problem to me.

"Well...that was dramatic," Frank said, a look of shock on his face.

"And why the fuck, *Arthur?*"

The sun set lazily over the foothills as we drove back to town. Neither of us spoke. Frank stared straight ahead, focusing on the road, and I gazed out the window at the freshly twinkling stars, new questions rattling through my mind.

Sometime later, Frank pulled into the stall behind his bar and shut off the engine. We sat in silence, both of us unsure how we felt about what we had heard.

"Holy shit," Frank muttered.

"Yeah." I reached up and rubbed my forehead, suddenly realizing I'd been sitting with a wide-eyed expression on my face for the last hour and a bit. Another long quiet moment stretched between us, neither of us moving for the doors.

"What do you think?"

"What do you mean what do I think? It's all fucking crazy man," I said, staring at the dashboard and falling back into the incredulous wide-eyed look. "Six new alien races, and one wants to kill everything." I laughed. "I mean, Christ, what do they expect us to do? Just drop everything here and move to a new neighborhood light years away? Fight a war against a bunch of technological wizards?"

"Because we have so much here?" Frank asked softly. I went quiet and avoided his eyes, looking out the side window, every spirit dragged to the front of my mind, phantom echoes ringing in my ears.

"Hey, you remember that time J-Rock said he saw a UFO over Kabul?" I asked, trying to steer the conversation away from my dark thoughts. "Absolutely sure of it. Would not shut the fuck up about it. Maybe not so crazy after—"

"I'm going to join up," Frank said, glaring out the windshield.

I turned and stared at him. "What?"

"I'm going to apply—or go through that...that compatibility testing. Whatever he was talking about. I'm volunteering."

"Yeah, no. That's what I thought you said. Shut the fuck up, Frank."

"I'm serious."

"That's insane."

"This whole fucking thing's insane, Will. I sure as hell ain't denying that. But it's also insane thinking that the rest of life is me sitting behind that shitty bar pouring drinks."

I went to speak but then stopped myself, unsure what to say, anger boiling to the surface. "Well, what the fuck would you have done if they hadn't shown up?"

"Listen, I'm just saying I think this could be—"

"Are you fucking kidding me, Frank?" I growled, my teeth grinding. "You want to join another goddamn war? One hour! You hear about a new war one hour ago, and now you're jumping to start killing again? Run away from everything here?"

Frank lowered his head and rested it on the steering wheel. "Everything here," he said, shaking his head. The dry air was tense and still, an uncomfortable fizzle between us. Or maybe just inside me. "You know what my first thought was when that alien spoke today?" he asked. "Thank God, a way out." As I stared at Frank, I saw something I hadn't seen before—or maybe I had seen it and ignored it. Something more broken than I thought. Something painfully familiar. "Everything's gone, man," he continued. "Everyone. After my parents, it was just you and..." Frank's voice cracked slightly, and he cleared his throat.

"I'm still here, Frank," I said.

"Are you?" Frank lifted his head off the steering wheel and gave me a hard look. I fell silent and looked out the window. I knew what he meant, as much as I didn't want to admit it. Some feeling of fading away. A quiet whimpering out. I felt his glare, and then I felt it soften as he turned and looked out his window. His fists creaked the worn leather of the steering wheel as he squeezed out his frustration and pain.

I couldn't sit there any longer. "Fuck you, Frank."

He didn't respond, just stared out his window, clenching his jaw like he did so often when having to deal with a shitty situation—when having to deal with me.

I got out of the truck, slammed the door, and walked away into the tepid night air.

I wandered through the town's sleepy streets, figuring I'd head toward the only bus stop for miles. It all felt melodramatic as fuck, but realistically, I didn't have anywhere to go. I didn't just occasionally sleep in the back room of Frank's bar; I lived there, but I couldn't be near him at the moment.

The hot-as-hell day had cooled to something slightly more tolerable, and a gentle wind blew dust and sand through the empty avenues in random gusts. Through the windows I saw families gathered around television sets, watching updates on the news. The recent days had pushed the reality TV bullshit and other garbage programming to the peripheral. Every part of life revolved around the visitors. Even the devices, ever in the hands of the cellphone generation, flashed with bulletins and articles on the aliens—not to mention the build-an-alien and invasion games, alerts, and tracker apps.

At the edge of town, the last shop on the right blinked a bright neon "Open" sign in my face. I had been there more times than I'd like to admit. I knew every crack in the lopsided brown siding that hung from its walls, every water-stained spot along the trim of the windows and door, and every squeaky creak in the knob as it turned. I could close my eyes and hear the tinkling of the rusty bell above the entrance. I stared through the large, steel-grated glass window that looked into the flickering, fluorescently-lit rows of alcohol. *If ever there was a time for whisky, it's now,* I thought. Pretty much always.

To my right on the other side of a small laneway between the two buildings, I could still make out the faint trace of graffiti under a thin skin of grey paint. The cinder-block wall of Larry's hardware store was rough and weathered, and the new coating stuck out poorly. The crimson, spray-painted lettering bubbled out in a smooth contrast to its adhered surface, "We are the OnSpec" still clearly visible. Fucking assholes. I shook my head and then turned back, inevitably, to the liquor store.

By the time I reached the grimy and heavily graffitied bus bench, I was halfway through my paper-bagged bottle of whisky. My steps were increasingly crooked as I set my eyes on as smooth a landing as possible. I aimed and missed, shinning myself hard on the descent and collapsing onto my side on the bench. I grabbed my leg, groaning through gritted teeth and chuckling. Son of a bitch.

"Smooth, dumbass," I mumbled. I brought the bottle to my lips and let the smoky liquid scorch my throat, in a large eye-watering gulp. It got ahead of me, and I coughed hard, trying to purge it from my lungs. Slumping in the seat, I felt the weight of my body settle into the bench's uncomfortable concrete-cast form. Toward the horizon the spectral shimmer of the massive alien motherships flickered amongst the stars. I curled a gob of spit in my mouth and hucked it toward the pavement, a thin, straggling bead drooling down my chin and chest. I sloppily wiped it away.

"Couldn't've just come to say hi, huh? Want to take someone else from me?" I took another long swig and sat for several moments in silence. I raised my arm and pointed at the ships trying to think of something else to yell at them, but I stuttered, lost for words. I frowned and lowered my arm, a deep feeling of inadequacy settling in.

War. As simple and as complicated as that. I heard what Frank had said, and part of me agreed with him, but war. People lose everything in war, and we knew that better than most. But after a few words from some random fucking alien, Frank was ready to dive back into it, leaving me behind. The last person in my life wanted to disappear. Bitter thoughts swirled in my mind, mixed with and accentuated by the whisky.

Then, as with most moments of my loneliness, the pages flipped violently, and the phantom smiles leered at me from the deep recesses of memory, marching around the peripherals. Maria stood in front of me, a calm smile on her face. I couldn't bring myself to look into her eyes, but I knew what I'd see there. I blinked, and she was gone. In her place stood a Middle Eastern boy of fifteen, the genesis of facial hair just beginning to creep along his face. He had bright, unflinching eyes that seemed to glow out of his dark, deep-set sockets.

"Hey, Ali," I said, looking toward the ground again. He never smiled, never frowned, never reacted at all to me. Just stared relentlessly, and that was enough. The tears welled up in hot pools, dripping free with a whisky burn until the dark hold of night faded around my vision, and I tipped to sleep on the dirty bus bench.

The world shook and rumbled. Light flashed past my closed eyelids.

THUD!

I woke with a start as the truck lurched over a rough pothole, my head whacking the passenger window. I blinked the sleep out of my eyes and rubbed the bump on the corner of my forehead, squinting in the bright morning sunlight that shone through the windshield.

"Morning," Frank said in a stern but gentle way. "You OK?" I glanced over at him but stayed curled in the seat, my head throbbing from the knock and the hangover, the early heat of a new day adding to my nausea. Frank didn't look at me, just stared determinedly straight ahead.

"Yeah." The awkward silence between us seemed to stretch for ages. I didn't know what to say. Neither, it seemed, did Frank.

"Will, I—"

"I'm coming with you," I said, the decision leaping out of my mouth. Frank's lips tightened into a hard line. "Somebody's gotta watch your six," I added. Though he tried to hide his relief by staring straight ahead, a small smile fought its way across his face, and he nodded his acceptance.

CHAPTER IV

Fucking Budgers

We attended several of the information seminars set up at various locations across the southwest to learn as much as we could about the mission ahead. It was a requirement by the authorities involved (human and Lumenarian) to ensure everyone had a solid understanding of the commitment and the risks—the surprisingly little that was known about the mysterious enemy, the levels of biological engineering we'd be undergoing (mostly unchanged on the outside but essentially becoming part cyborg on the inside or some weird shit like that), and the time-dilation effects of interstellar travel, just to name a few. After receiving the pseudo certificates of completion and rubber stamps, like some fucking free-coffee punch card, we waited in long queues to complete the other mandatory assessments and tests needed to progress in the application process. Luckily, we were ex-military, which put us in a smaller preferables' pool.

It was a slow tedious routine over several weeks that saw us sitting for hours at a time in different doctors' offices, law firms, and testing facilities, all the while keen to meet the aliens we'd be living with for the foreseeable future. We had seen videos and images of them as well as amazing holographic projections in the lectures (gifts from our new allies) but so far nothing in person. Best way I could describe them would be humanoid (two arms, two legs, torso, head) dinosaurs. I guess the demands of preparing for the journey back to their world, transferring and retrofitting technology for Earth, and coordinating the next stage of the recruitment left few Lumenarians available for face-to-face meetings.

When the day finally arrived, the sheer number of volunteers was staggering to all parties involved as the recruitment camps around the world swelled with hordes of eager participants—or rats trying to get off a sinking ship. I always question motivations. Even if the Lumenarian tech would most likely save the planet while we were gone, grass is greener sort of thing. Either way, the lines stretched farther than any one person could see.

The three alien vessels could load around 1.5 million people between them: 600,000 or so on each of the two larger carrier ships, constructed almost solely for mass crew transport, and another 200,000 on the smaller flagship designed primarily for war. Though the third ship was smaller, every volunteer prayed they'd be assigned there. Something about going to war on an actual warship. Plus, rumor was it was brand new and cutting edge even for the aliens, commissioned just before their departure. It also just looked cooler from the footage we'd seen. The metallic teardrop shape was more streamlined and agile, less bulbous than its counterparts.

If they could've spared more ships, they definitely could've filled them, but apparently, the situation at home was dire, and the three for Earth were all that could be spared. Another nine ships had been sent to three other points along a stellar compass in search of more help. So, possibly, the universe would be getting even bigger soon. Either way, it was more than just a resource issue—at least that was the candid tale the alien leader had spun, including a warning of the controversy over them having come at all. Other Lumenarians believed the journey to Earth and beyond was an unnecessary risk for so many of their potential fighting forces and a direct contradiction to their general foreign policies regarding species deemed "instinctually violent" (something about not opening a can of worms—my words, not his).

The limitations on crew sizes further stirred the rushing masses to line up and proceed through the testing as quickly as possible. Everyone wanted an opportunity to travel the stars, or at least escape from the orbit of the nearest one.

Frank and I had been in line for the recruitment camp set up in the Los Angeles Coliseum for over six hours. We all marched, inches at a time, like zombies drawn to some distant promise of brains and blood. Thankfully, the sun had finally faded below the ocean and the horizon of buildings and thick smog. The path around was lit with flaming garbage bins—strangely apocalyptic lighting for a quest to reach the otherworldly glow of a galaxy far away. The cool desert breeze was a welcome change from the scorching furnace of the daylight hours, and I closed my eyes as a gentle gust flirted through the line. The world we'd made—heat waves and wildfires in late November.

"Fuuuck. I wish I wasn't sober for this."

"You'll survive," Frank said with a chuckle.

Some guy with a massive beer gut spun around to face us. "Man, I'm so excited," he said, practically vibrating. "I can't wait to see the Chargers' locker room!"

We stared at him with our eyebrows raised. "*That's* what you're excited about?" I said.

The camps had been established as pseudo embassies for the Lumenarians during their stay, so most of what was inside was under their purview while the line to the stadium and its outer rings were being handled by FEMA and other such governmental agencies. That explained the shoddy management of conditions outside. The last passing of water down the line by agency officials had been about three hours earlier. They were struggling to keep up with the demand of a dozen camps across the United States, and everyone was feeling the energy decay. More than a handful of people, just within our view, collapsed in line and were taken to nearby tents to lie down and recuperate—each vowing as they were dragged away to return the next day and rejoin the queue. I had a feeling that if they couldn't handle a long line, they couldn't handle a war. Despite the fatigue, there was an excited buzz in the air, everyone sharing their ideas about what was to come. The mission was drawing the daring and the desperate. The more candid ones explained in great detail why they needed to leave and where they were coming from. Still not sure what about my expression encouraged the sharing. Frank seemed entertained by my irritation though.

Luckily, we were getting close to entering the stadium, and we stamped our feet to keep the blood flowing in our stagnant legs.

"Thank Christ we're almost there," Frank grumbled, finally letting slip that he was getting anxious to move too.

"No kidding. I hope they have snacks in there."

Frank rolled his eyes but snorted a chuckle regardless. "Reminds me of that time in Baghdad when you kicked in that vending machine."

"I had low blood sugar!"

More than most in line, we had a better understanding of what we were signing up for. War is only ever fought one way for those on the ground—kill or be killed. This was potentially a one-way trip, most likely so, and even if we returned, there was no guarantee we would be whole. Both of us carried scars inside and out from the last war, so we took the opportunity to joke or be smartasses when we could (not that I needed an excuse). We weren't astronauts; we didn't think we'd be colonizers on Mars or digging up lunar rocks. Hell, give it a couple of decades, and we figured we'd be scavenging amidst the rubble of our climate-ravaged world, if we were lucky. We were soldiers, and war was what we knew best. A soldier can go back to school, learn a trade, bang like a rabbit, move to a beach, surf every day, love his family, or retire in a bar, but he'll always feel battle in his bones. It was not a decision made lightly, but the adventure and intrigue were cantilevers to our apprehensions, and we had nothing to lose. The more we thought about it, the more it seemed to fit us.

From just behind us, a commotion jostled the line into our backs.

"What the hell?" Standing nose to chest with a behemoth of a man was a little Hispanic bulldog, his fists clenched. The big guy's almost equally large buddy stood just behind him, ready for whatever came. They looked like skinhead Nazis, and if there's anything I hate more than Nazis it's…well, Nazis are pretty much at the top. It wasn't the first physical disagreement of the day, and it probably wouldn't be the last, but Frank and I stepped in closer to potentially play the peacemakers. Not my forte, but I'd been waiting in line too fucking long to blow it now caught up in someone else's brawl.

"Problem, fellas?" I asked.

Without turning, the small Latino held his ground. "These pendejos think they can walk through the line," he said. I glanced from him to the big lugs. No sign of a waver from the little guy—I liked him already.

"Come on, guys," Frank said, using his most diplomatic tone. "We're all tired, and we've all been waiting for hours. We're almost there, so just relax." Between the two of us, we probably could've taken the 'roid-monkeys (since I was goddamn sober), but it was almost guaranteed not to be fun. That's a lot of weight behind a punch.

"Mind your own fucking business," the lead brute grunted while maintaining his aggressive stare down. His accomplice crossed his arms and flexed.

"Well, if you budge past this guy here, we're next in line, which means you're eventually going to try and weasel past us. Which I can tell you right now is not a good idea."

"No es buena idea conmigo también," the Latino growled, taking a step closer, nearly able to bite the head beast's nipples.

"Well, I don't speak Spanish, but I'm pretty sure that was a double fuck off," I said. Frank and I took a step closer, covering the flanks of the little bulldog. We saw the meathead contemplating his options and weighing his confidence in his own abilities against what he suspected ours were.

"Listen here—" As the showdown was reaching the tension-breaking point of fight, fuck, or fuck off, the meathead glanced to his left as an agency official walked past, updating those in the line of the likely wait times and finally handing out more water.

"Oh, hall monitor is coming," I said.

The large fella slowly came to his senses and eased back from us. Most of the officials were cops or gov reps and had the power to boost people out of line or even arrest them if it came down to it. Last thing they needed were troublemakers starting a riot in front of our extraterrestrial visitors.

"You guys are lucky," he said, turning his back to us and muttering to his lap gorilla.

The feisty Latino turned to us and nodded. "Gracias. I am Miguel," he said, shaking our hands.

"Frank."

"Will. Don't worry. I would've started yelling 'Budger!' at the top of my lungs if he started shit."

Frank and Miguel laughed as we all turned and faced the front again. I could tell Miguel was one of those sturdy sons of bitches who probably didn't look for a fight but never backed down from one either. A lot like Frank in that way. He told us he had travelled up from a small town outside Tijuana. There were camps in Mexico, but the LA camp was the closest recruitment opportunity for him. Countries all over the world were offering temporary REC 1 visas or something similar to folks travelling across borders for the purpose of trying out, and Miguel had signed up for one. Apparently, even after discovering aliens from another galaxy, we still thought borders on Earth were important.

Really, he wasn't that short, only in contrast to the shrunken testes behind us, and he had a solid boxer's build. His hair was buzzed, and the back of his neck was dark brown from days working under the sun as a carpenter. He was quick to laugh and joke with us, his friendly demeanor disarming and genuine. It was almost difficult to see where the bulldog lived in him once he stepped away from the fray.

He hadn't been directly behind us in line at the beginning, but luckily for a us, a series of people giving up, having second thoughts, or collapsing had brought him into file. We chatted for the better part of an hour before it was our turn to step through the first gate.

Entering the outer rings of the stadium, we were led through the hustle and bustle of human representatives shuttling the various applicants through the stations. My chaperone guided me to a post a little ways from Frank and Miguel, and I nodded my temporary farewell to them. Cubicles were set up in a long row with agency officials sitting behind desks and computers. I waited for mine to usher me into the seat. A man of around sixty with white hair, chic square glasses, a stylishly trimmed beard, and a three-piece suit (minus the jacket, which hung on his chair) sat before me. Only in LA. Bet a billion bucks he had an anchor tattoo somewhere, or a sparrow, and he'd never sailed a ship. He finally looked up from his terminal and waved me in. I took the chair and stared across the desk as he pinned a couple of keys.

"Welcome. I understand it was quite the wait out there. Sorry about that. But you're here now. Do you have your identification? Driver's license, passport? Also, I'll need your sign-offs. Medical, psych, etcetera." Despite being a hipster, he seemed nice enough. I wondered if he was also a barber in his spare time.

I dug my wallet out of my back pocket and handed him my driver's license. Pulling an envelope out of my jacket pocket, I also handed him the various pre-test forms every applicant required. Basically, they just made sure we were mostly healthy and not completely fucking insane. It's a miracle I passed the latter. If only they knew the truth.

"Just a moment," he said, smiling as he took the documents. It suddenly dawned on me how archaic it seemed to physically hand over paper forms in light of what was ahead; there wasn't even a phone app. Yay government. Breezing over the paperwork, the man jotted down some notes and authorizing signatures and then placed it all in a folder, which he stacked onto a heaping pile on top of a filing cabinet bursting at the seams. He turned back to his computer and glanced back and forth from the screen to my license, typing in all my information and checking boxes.

"OK, great. Do you have your social?"

"Yeah." I recited it to him.

"Great, thank you." He typed in the number and examined the screen for several moments, occasionally scrolling with a stroke of the keys. "OK, so…William Adam Reach. Looks like you've got no assets—"

"Rub it in, why don't you."

"Oh, I'm sorry. I just meant—"

"I'm just kidding."

"Ah. Good one." He chuckled and went back to his checklist. "Liabilities are within the allowance range…" He scrolled a little farther down and froze, his face falling as he read the next few lines of information. He glanced at me before continuing down the page, swallowing hard. "No dependents. They…I'm sorry—"

"Is what it is," I said with an involuntary head twitch. His eyes sparkled behind his thick glasses as he stared at me for a moment. I avoided his eyes for as long as I could. Pity. I hated pity. "It's OK. Appreciate the condolences," I said in a conditioned-nicety response.

"I have to go through the checklist," he said. "I'm sorry." I nodded. He turned back to the computer to finish the report, clearing his throat. "University of California Riverside. Bachelor of Arts in history… incomplete. Military service…ten years…" The rest of the regurgitated information droned in my ears as the man completed his work.

Several minutes later, nodding occasionally to the buzz of dialogue, I looked up to a stamped form held out by Walter, as I now noticed on his nametag. "Take this form back there and to your right, and present it to one of the representatives wearing a blue armband," he said. I took the forms and stood. Walter rose creakily from his chair as well and held out his hand. He gave me a warm smile and looked me in the eye as we shook. My eyes flicked down, and just past his cuff I caught the edge of an anchor on his wrist. Ha! Called it. "You've still got to pass the compatibility testing, but the world thanks you for your service and sacrifice. Got a taste of service myself in the navy, but you get to do it for all humankind."

Ah. I'm an asshole.

"If I was young again…" His voice drifted off.

"Thanks, Walter." I smiled and then took my form and walked back into the fray.

I looked around for Frank, spotting him in a cubicle a ways down still chatting with the representative. I knew he'd be along shortly, so I proceeded down the thoroughfare in the direction Walter had pointed. Milling through the horde, I finally reached an agent wearing a blue armband. She was red faced and flustered, obviously having gotten the short straw as far as responsibilities for this gig. She took my form while trying to juggle giving directions to two other people who had lost their clearance paperwork and another person hassling her about a failed application.

After a few minutes of managing the others, she turned back to me and forced an exasperated smile. "OK, sorry about that. The days are just getting crazier." Glancing at my stamp of approval, she guided me to the next ring in the stadium, making sure I was in the right place. Then she shook my hand, took a deep breath, and returned to the previous hallway.

The next stage of the process was basically a hardcore TSA screening line that eventually led to the inner sanctum of the camp—the playing field and compatibility testing zone. Like an airport, the line also moved irritatingly slow. Add to that the heat of the thousands of bodies roaming around the stadium, and the mounting frustrations were raising the temperature to a sweaty stew.

The walk-through scanner was unlike anything we had seen before. People walked between two metallic posts that emitted a water-like wall between them. No one had to empty their pockets or take off their shoes; all they had to do was walk slowly through the device. Eventually, I reached the front of the queue and stood in front of a stern-faced, dead-eyed security guard.

"Step forward," he ordered. Walking up, I stopped on two outlines of feet in front of the scanner. The guard punched a few keys on a small touchpad next to the scanner before turning to me. "Walk through the field. Slowly."

"Given the circumstances, can I moonwalk through?" I asked as seriously as I could. The burly guard stared at me, and I stared back for a long awkward beat. "Cuz of...space and stuff—"

"No." Not even the glimmer of a smile. OK, didn't win a friend there. Maybe he was ineligible and jealous. I nodded sternly to the guard and stared ahead at the watery energy wall.

"Through the Stargate I go." I took a deep breath and then stepped through the scanner. As I passed through the field, it felt like every molecule of my body vibrated like a tuning fork. It wasn't painful, but it wasn't particularly comfortable either—unsettling would be a good way to put it. I expected to be wet coming out the other side but emerged dry and unscathed.

The guard on the other side looked at her touchpad and gestured for me to approach. "Hold up your right arm."

I obeyed, and she pulled a metallic bracelet made of hundreds of small hexagonal links out of a bin and strapped it around my wrist. A self-adjusting whir and click locked the device on skin tight. It was definitely some sort of alien metal, but it felt like neoprene. "This checks you through to the facility and monitors your vitals throughout the testing. You may proceed that way." She nodded to an adjacent hallway. "A moonwalk would have been funny," she muttered.

"Right?" I said as I marched out of the room, leaving the chuckling guard. Knew I could be a charming motherfucker sometimes.

The human factor of the camp was nearly at a close as I approached the players' tunnel that led to the field, Rams and Chargers logos along the walls. Two guards stopped me and raised a handheld scanner to check my wristband. The beep bought me passage, and I proceeded down the long, dim tunnel, the lights of the field shining ahead.

The Lumenarians had landed several temporary structures on the field to conduct the compatibility testing. Each building, like some sort of double-wide, futuristic, windowless shipping container, glowed in the moonlight shining down through the open dome. Temporary cribbed landing pads lined the seating levels to accommodate small shuttles and drones, which buzzed frequently around the stadium and occasionally rose out of the dome and disappeared. Bright lampposts spaced throughout the center of the field supplemented the glaring stadium lighting, as if any shadows thrown by the temporary structures couldn't be allowed.

I stepped onto the field and gazed around the opening in amazement. Human aides walked around conducting tasks while several large aliens helped them with the chores and guided them in what appeared to be research. I felt my mouth hanging open and then promptly shut it, trying to retain some semblance of cool.

Just then one of *them* approached, stopping several feet in front of me. She stood about seven feet tall, as they all did, and was made of pure sinew and muscle. Despite their wide, solid build, every motion seemed perfectly fluid and incredibly graceful, like a species that had mastered every twitch of muscle memory for every task they conducted, from the most basic to the most complex of movements. It was almost unsettling seeing the graceful flow ebb from their strong boxy frames, like the way an octopus's tentacles look natural yet chaotic at the same time—a hint at the lethality they could muster.

Her skin was a charcoal-slate color with a texture that resembled that of a dinosaur, only slightly smoother than what I'd seen in *Jurassic Park; because apparently, in reality dinosaurs are giant feathered chickens, which really shits all over my vision of dinosaurs to be honest—thanks, scientists.* Anyway, the Lumenarians' skin was varying shades of grey, from a pallid ash to deep, almost purplish basalt. Over the grey, streaks of deep navy-blue, black, and dark maroon ran jagged stripes across their bodies, patterns as diverse and individual as fingerprints. Leftover primal markings of the apex predators that had evolved into their planet's dominant species.

Two of her eyes were placed on her face similar to that of a human's, but they were quite a bit larger, and they smoothly transitioned from color to color depending on the lighting and the requirements of the situation. Starbursts of golds, reds, and greens sparkled in their depths. Slightly higher and set just back around the gentle corners of her face were a second set of smaller eyes, which allowed the Lumenarians to have a visual range closer to that of a spider or a chameleon. At any given moment at least one eye was open as they blinked independently of each other, and millennia of ingrained instinct kept constant vigil on the world around them (unless they purposely closed all of them). All her eyes were focused on me, but I knew they could move individually.

Their mouths were wide and upwardly curved, adorned with thin, scaly lips that barely traced an outline and gave them a perpetually tight-lipped appearance that barely hid an upper and lower row of small sharkish teeth. Chimeric beings.

Her legs extended down in a form similar to a horse's. Her hips rolled forward with the lower legs jutting ahead from the knees before ending in wide pad-like feet. Her inverted knees were thick, adjoining bulky quads and calves that hinted at an ability to run and jump with super-human ability.

She wore loose, slit robes over a padded synthetic base layer that supplemented her natural bulk with extra combat padding. Amongst her natural genetic striations, tattoos that looked like a simplified wiring schematic for an electrical circuit (lines and dots) ran along key areas of her body and then disappeared under her padded bodysuit. Each line occasionally possessed a faint and rippling emerald glow, like an aurora borealis.

Suddenly, but not quickly, she extended her large, four-fingered hand. I flinched, snapping out of my wonder. *Smooth, Will.* Trying to recover, I extended my hand, taking hers in a welcome shake.

"Not the first and won't be the last to jump like that," she said with an unfortunately naturally aggressive smile. "Wait until you see the other races on Lumen. Hello, William. My name is Sky. I'll be taking you to the compatibility testing."

Finding my voice somewhere deep in my throat again, I replied. "Sorry, just…uh…the…uh…" I couldn't even string together a simple sentence while looking at her. "Sky. Nice to meet you. Just Will by the way. How do you—"

"Know English?" she asked. I nodded. Sky pulled down the hood of her robe to reveal one of the glowing tattoos that traced from behind one of the boney protrusions that I inferred to be her ears and scored a line around the base of her skull to the other side of her head. "This biotechnology converts received auditory stimuli into my language in my head." She gestured to a small mechanical box attached to the base of her throat. "This projects back sound in the language required. A universal translator basically. Our natural voices aren't on a frequency humans can perceive without some discomfort." She smiled patiently, obviously having had to answer similar questions repeatedly.

"Wow. So that's what you were doing in orbit all that time."

"Among other things."

"Not ominous at all when you put it like that."

She chuckled, a slightly robotic-sounding laugh, the translator obviously still having some personalization kinks to work out. "You humans have certainly been creative when imagining first contacts. Don't worry; there are no probes during the test." She winked two of her four eyes at me, which was simultaneously charming and unsettling. She turned and gestured for me to follow her, walking toward one of the alien structures.

"You're definitely not what I was expecting," I said, falling in behind her.

"I think one of the major revelations your species has had since our arrival is the knowledge that an alien race can have personalities as unique and diverse as your own. A higher intellect and technological capability does not necessarily equate to mechanical consciousness. We all have different fears, loves, humors, and rages," she said.

"I guess we've always loved the idea that we're ultimately special in the universe," I said as we arrived at the building.

She stopped and turned to me. "You are. But so is all life, in different ways. Don't worry, you'll have plenty of time to learn more later." Sky waved her hand in front of the building door and stepped through the opening as it split in two and slid into the walls.

Inside, the building was one large, spartan room that looked like a high-tech firing range. An open forum ran perpendicular to eight partially divided twenty-yard shooting lanes. A metallic table to the right housed several alien instruments and a small crate of mercury-like orbs. The walls and ceiling were light grey with white ambient floor and lane lighting.

Standing next to the table were two other humans, obviously waiting for the room to fill up to begin their testing. Both turned to us as we entered. For a split second it seemed as if my mind had taken a snapshot and frozen the image in some sort of rosy amber to dog-ear the moment. One of them was a thin, jittery guy, who couldn't have been much more than twenty-one, but the other was a strikingly beautiful woman in her late twenties, maybe early thirties. Light seemed to radiate from her in a warm glow. My breath caught in my chest, and a warm flush spread up my neck. With absolutely nothing around my feet, I stumbled a half step as if I had forgotten how to fucking walk. She quickly set one of the metallic spheres back in the crate and smiled sheepishly.

"Sorry, couldn't help it," she said.

"Quite alright," Sky replied.

The two humans each smiled and nodded as we made eye contact. Looking closer, I would've guessed they might be related. They were both Asian; younger brother and his big sister. She was slightly above average height and athletic with dark hair that hung freely around her face, and a wild look shone from her bright, emerald eyes. The man's features resembled hers in the way families share noses and basic facial structure, but his skin was paler, and he lacked the aura of adventure that oozed from her. Instead he projected a nervous energy. Jesus, auras and energies, I'd been out of the service too long. Also, their body language suggested close familiarity. I almost felt bad for him in that moment, thinking he might be taking on something he didn't want in order to tag along with his idolized older sibling.

"Hi! I'm Sarah, and this is my little brother, Mikey," she said.

Called it. Family.

They came over and shook my hand. Mikey's slightly clammy and overly hard squeeze reinforced my belief that he was very uncomfortable. "Just Mike," he said.

I set my lips into a firm line, holding back a chuckle, and nodded. Sarah took my hand with a perfectly controlled grip that matched her confident and relaxed demeanor. I stared into her green eyes, which were speckled with auburn rays, and she held my gaze for as long as I gave it. Her stare seemed to go through me, and I excused myself by glancing around the room, as if I hadn't already clocked it all the second I walked in.

"Will." I smiled back, cut short again in my mind-mouth gap from the new visions and deep-rooted feelings of survivor's guilt that I often felt whenever I glimpsed the possibility of a connection with a new woman. Not that that happened often in Frank's bar, or ever.

I felt her trying to read me. "This is pretty crazy huh?" she said, smiling and maintaining a keen gaze.

"Yeah." Before I could continue, the door opened again, and another Lumenarian walked in with Frank, Miguel, two others, and to Miguel's obvious distaste, one of the meatheads from the line outside.

"They actually let you through?" Frank said when he saw me.

Everyone quickly introduced themselves except for the brute asshole, who parked against the back wall with his arms crossed and just grunted. Despite his standoffish mood, he had a sheen of sweat on his brow and looked nervous. Couldn't really blame him. None of us knew what was next.

The new alien's name was Herb. Remembering all our guests had been free to choose their own Earth names when they arrived, for some reason it seemed funny that this one had decided "Herb" was a good idea.

The differences between the males and females of their species were not substantial but could be described mostly as edges. The females' facial features were rounded, while the males possessed sharper ridges angled down between their eyes and another line of rigid bumps running from their forehead over the top of the skull and partway down their necks in a straight line. Nothing too drastic or pronounced. From a distance they'd be hard to tell apart.

Sky and Herb turned from the table and faced the group. Herb held the crate of mercurial spheres while Sky looked at a holographic projection emitted from a band on her forearm.

"Everyone please gather around, and we'll begin the test," Sky said. We marched over to the two aliens, the lug standing behind us. Sky picked one of the metallic orbs out of the box and held it up for us to see. It was about half the size of a golf ball and perfectly smooth. "This is a piece of biotechnology designed to integrate with the host in order to harness the natural energy created by your bodies. This is the esthetic result." Sky held up her arm and pointed to the circuit lines along her fingers, hand, and forearm, the faint emerald glow rippling through them. "The tech not only floods your system with highly advanced nanites but also harvests, stores, and amplifies kinetic, environmental, and bodily thermal and metabolic energy output. This is a tool and a weapon."

We all shifted uneasily as we stared at the small article of tech, except for Sarah, who wore a fascinated smile. "That's amazing," she muttered. I couldn't help but smile as I watched her eyes light up.

"We've learned that only a small percentage of humans are biologically compatible with our technology, and we rely heavily on it. Meaning if you have no reaction, we will have to deny your application, as much as we appreciate your efforts."

"What are the biological markers for compatibility?" Sarah asked.

Sky glanced at Herb, then back to us. "We actually don't know," she replied. There was a collective raising of eyebrows. That was surprising. Granted, if they already knew, I suppose the whole process would have been unnecessary. "We have found some correlations but nothing uniformly consistent among those who have accepted the tech. You will know almost immediately if it takes, however."

Everyone became tense, all of us presumedly praying we wouldn't be turned away. Sky passed each of us one of the silver spheres. "What do we do with it?" one of the other applicants asked. He was a fit man in his thirties whose name was…Ted, I think—forgot it pretty much the second he said it.

"Please take a position in one of the lanes, and I'll guide you through it," Sky said.

We all obeyed and claimed a lane, holding the tech out in our palms. Once we were all aligned, Sky fiddled with her forearm band, activating some sort of teal energy field between each of the lane dividers. The brute took a half step back, startled by the sudden technological flex.

"Cuàl es el problema gordo, scared?" Miguel said, glancing over at him.

"Fuck you," the beast replied, stepping back into place. The field didn't buzz per se, but it hummed against us with a low-frequency vibration like an ultrasound. On a ledge that extended in front of each lane, just inside of the energy field, sat a perfectly square, perfectly smooth onyx cube about the size of a small beer cooler.

"By you placing your hand in the activation field, the biotech will open and begin synergizing," Sky explained. "If it works, you'll feel a cool sensation followed by an admittedly uncomfortable sharp heat."

"Don't remember that in the brochure," I muttered to Frank.

"Don't be a pussy," he replied.

I chuckled, looking down at my hand.

"There's no judgment if you decide this isn't for you," Sky said. "This does become a permanent part of your body. Even if you choose not to join us later, the tech in your hand will be there, inactive." It was definitely a nerve-wracking threshold to cross, becoming fucking cyborgs and all.

One of the other men in the room suddenly stepped back from the line and held out the sphere to Herb. "I'm sorry. I can't do this," he said, avoiding eye contact. Sky and Herb smiled back at him and nodded, then guided him out of the building.

After she and Herb returned to their positions, Sky turned back to us. "If there's no one else, please proceed when you're ready."

Sarah and Frank were the first two to put their hands in the field, each without hesitation. I glanced at the ball in my hand and took a deep breath. Then I slowly pushed my hand through the blue-green semi-translucent energy. The sphere sat in the middle of my upturned palm as I waited for a reaction. For a moment, I was worried nothing would happen. Then the orb quivered and broke apart into several smaller perfectly smooth spheres. Each new pellet rolled around my hand and positioned itself at various points. It felt like small chips of ice melting on the warm surface of my body, their watery trails leaving cool imprints on my skin. I rotated my hand in the field, staring in amazement as the orbs took their places at the tips of my fingers, the center of my palm, and the backs of my first and second knuckles on each finger. They hung there for a long moment, trembling in place.

"That didn't seem too bad—" Before I could finish, the spheres flattened into discs. Frank and Sarah blurted out grunts of pain first. The discs flashed a bright hot red as they seared into my skin, diving through the layers into my body. My hand tensed up, but I couldn't pull it out or make a fist as my fingers stretched out, forced straight in bone-cracking agony. I gritted my teeth, trying not to yell despite the chaos of pain clawing into my brain. The circles on my skin glowed as they shot fibrous metal threads beneath my skin, tying all the points together in the familiar circuit-board design. For several excruciating seconds, the pain shot up my arm until suddenly it was over as quickly as it had begun.

I breathed several ragged breaths, letting my mind catch up with the relief, a thin bead of sweat rolling down my temple. I glanced to my left, catching Frank's eyes as he shook his head, glad it was over. Looking back at my hand, I saw the glowing red circles and lines that decorated my fingers and palm, like henna ink, shining a vibrant sapphire. Or maybe that was just an effect of the field.

"Uh…" I trailed off, glancing over at Sky.

"Yes, Will?"

I looked back down at my hand. The markings had faded to a black tattoo. "Never mind."

Sky tapped her forearm again, dismantling the energy field. I pulled my hand back, turning it in front of my eyes and taking a closer gander at what had happened. Everyone else did the same. Sarah and I shared a look as we both noticed each other, her smile glowing with excitement and fascination as she studied her own hand. Frank and Miguel energetically examined each other's hands, comparing the markings.

"I don't understand. Mine didn't work." We all glanced over at the man named Fred or Ted or whatever. He stepped back from the line holding the unscathed sphere in his hand, confused and frustrated.

Sky wore an expression that I took to be sympathetic. "I'm sorry, but you are not compatible. We appreciate you coming to—"

"No! Try it again," the man sputtered. "I just got a broken one."

Sky and Herb shared a look. "I'm sorry. There's nothing we can do," Sky said as compassionately as she could. "The device doesn't malfunction." Ted pleaded for another chance, but they didn't humor him. They'd seen tens, maybe hundreds of thousands of failed compatibility tests over the last few weeks, and this one was no different. After calming him down, they ushered him out of the room and then guided us toward the next trial.

"Now, in each lane you can see a small black box." Sky tapped her display again, and the boxes sprang to action, levitating a few inches off the ledge on which they were sitting. "The goal here is to place your hand on the box and transfer your energy through your hand and into the side of it, hopefully pushing it back slightly." She positioned herself in front of one of the boxes and placed her hand gently on the side of it. "Like this." The circuit lines on her hand glowed a bright emerald against her skin a split second before she released a powerful blast. There was a bright flash of green light as the percussion between her palm and the box sent the black cube shooting back down the twenty-yard lane. It stopped just short of hitting the back wall. We all stared in amazement as the die slowly floated back up the lane to its original position. "Now, we don't expect any of you to be able to do nearly that. The tech you have is incomplete, and this is your first time, after all, but any movement you can get is a great achievement." She gestured for us to take our positions.

Seemed simple enough. Surprisingly, the first to move his cube was Mike. Almost the instant his hand touched the box, it shot down the range a couple of feet and then returned to the starting position. He smiled triumphantly around the room.

Next was Sarah, who managed to send her target a solid ten feet, a small spark of blue light emitting from the shot. Celebrating, she hugged Mike, and then they stood back watching the rest of us attempt to muster and focus our energy into the cubes.

The black cube had a dull whir to it as my hand rested against its side, a warm pulse. Its surface was like dark glass, and I saw my reflection looking back at me from between my fingers. Staring hard, concentrating all my thoughts on moving the box, I took a deep breath and clenched my jaw for several seconds. Nothing happened. I pulled my hand back slightly and looked at the marks on my palm, seeing if there was some sort of obvious problem. Looked normal to me.

Just then Frank, Miguel, and the brute whooped their successes next to me. I was the only one left, and nothing was happening. I felt everyone's eyes on the back of my head, boring into me. I cracked my neck and took another deep breath, trying to forget the prying eyes.

As I placed my hand on the cube, Sky walked past behind me. "Don't think about trying to push the box back. Focus on a small point just between the surface of your hand and the middle of the box."

I felt the pressure and embarrassment mounting as I stared stupidly at the cube's dark mirrored sheen. "OK, yeah, sorry. Just a little performance anxiety. *Don't try to bend the spoon*," I said with a nervous chuckle. I heard Sarah laugh at the reference and saw Frank shake his head out of the corner of my eye.

"Don't think about it logically," Sky said. "Think about it emotionally. Anger and love are our strongest motivators. Focus on something that you would channel every part of yourself into protecting, and then think about your hand." A hot lead ball formed in my stomach and rose in a prickle along the back of my neck and into my cheeks. *Protecting*. I closed my eyes. Everything seemed to slow down as Sky's voice droned in the background.

The scrapbook pages flipped rapidly behind my eyes, leaflets in a tempest. I saw the long ponderosa pine tree needles falling through the air in lazy wisps. The blue sky was mostly clear, save for a handful of cotton-candy clouds. The faded white lines on the side of the highway had been reclaimed by time, the earth encroaching on the shoulder. It was like I was hovering inches above the ground, seeing every crack and crumble in the road, pulled forward by the inescapable draw of fate. Then faded, copper-colored sand, too fine and out of place for the area, littered the pavement, covering up the rainbow sheen of leaking gasoline but not the smell.

Farther along, I floated over bits of broken glass, tarry tire tracks, and random debris that haphazardly decorated the way. I looked up and saw the twisted metal form ahead of me. A car resembling a crumpled tin can pressed against the enveloping wall of boulders ahead. The destruction made it hard to tell how the vehicle was oriented because the back half was torqued three-quarters prone, and the front was resting unnaturally on its side. The rental company's logo was half obscured by the damage. The steady dolly forward revealed blood dripping from cracks in the windshield and the peeled-back edges of the door. A river of blood flowed down toward me. *No.*

My eyes snapped open, rejecting the final vision. I looked down just in time to see an eruption of cobalt-blue energy separate the cube from my fingers and ripple along the lines on my hand. The blast kicked my arm back as the box rifled down the range, smashed into the back wall of the building, and dropped to the floor.

Everyone stared in stunned silence, no one more than me, gawking down at my hand. The box limped back into the air and floated back toward me, clunking down on the ledge, a large dent in the front. Glancing over, I saw that even Sky and Herb sported surprised expressions. I looked down at my hand again and saw the lines fade from the glowing blue fire to dull tattoo black.

"Jesus, Will," Frank said, staring at me with a worried expression, no doubt wondering at the pain in my psyche that had caused such a violent outburst, though he knew. A similar sentiment was reflected in everyone else's eyes.

The brute in the back edged his way around the side of the room, close to Herb. I barely clocked him moving. With his extra range of peripheral vision, Herb turned to the lug and held out his hand. "Congratulations on passing the test—" With surprising speed, the thug sprang behind the alien, kicked out his knee to lower him to a manageable height, and grabbed him by the throat, putting Herb's bulky body between himself and the rest of us. His hand glowed light blue as he applied pressure with his recently upgraded appendage.

Sky rotated slowly to face him and to put herself between us and the threat, her hands balled into glowing green fists. The attacker shifted nervously, the way a bank robber jockeys around his human shield in a hostage situation, his eyes darting around the room but never straying far from Sky's aggressive form. Fucking budger.

"It's Theo, right? Let's just take a deep breath and—"

"Shut the fuck up, you alien scum!" he yelled, peering around Herb.

"What do you want?" Sky asked, turning herself slightly sideways into a subtle fighting-ready stance. She stretched out one hand in a diplomatic gesture of non-threatening calm while the other reached to her back hip and grasped a small cylinder of metallic tech, keeping it hidden but ready.

Theo took a deep breath and shook his free hand, liberating some sort of switch secreted away in his sleeve. Grasping the object firmly, he held it up for everyone to see as he placed his thumb on the red detonator button. How the fuck had he gotten that past the scanners?

He locked eyes with Sky and sneered. "We are the OnSpec." Everything slowed as his thumb pressed the button, and a faint click echoed through the room.

BOOM!

The explosion ripped from Theo's body, tearing him apart and liquifying Herb along with him. The last fleeting glimpse any of us caught before surrendering to the dark realm of concussive unconsciousness was Sky raising the silver cylinder in front of her and releasing a wave of green energy to meet the bright orange-and-yellow wall of fire.

CHAPTER V

Terra Farewella

I woke with a start and glanced around the space. I was on a cot in a makeshift medical triage room somewhere in the stadium—at least judging from the Chargers and Rams logos. I looked down at a burn on my forearm that was coated in some sort of medical gel. Didn't hurt. Sitting up, I hazily scanned the room for Frank and the others. On the other side of the room, Frank was sitting up and stretching his neck, ashy residue on his face and clothing and a small lead-looking patch on his forehead that glowed light blue, but otherwise he looked mostly unharmed. We made eye contact, and he nodded, acknowledging our shared relief that we were both OK.

Miguel was in a heated debate at the door with some government officials, alternating between agitated Spanish and broken English. Sarah and Mike remained unconscious (but seemed to be OK) on cots next to me. I reached up, wincing, and felt a large bump forming on the back of my head. When I pulled my hand away, gooey half-clotted blood painted my fingertips. Everything felt painfully stiff, and I rotated my shoulders slowly and stretched my back trying to loosen up the discomfort. I didn't know how long I had been out, but apparently, it was long enough for all the injuries to settle in.

The room was fairly muted, save for Miguel's argument to be released and the official's reasoning for keeping us all at bay. Every time the door opened to allow a new representative or medical staff member in, the cacophony of urgent and angry chaos in the hallway flooded in with them.

Frank limped over, obviously having messed up an old injury in his knee that he'd received in the Gulf. He sat on the cot next to me. "Holy shit, huh?"

"Yeah," I replied, replaying the attack in my head. "Your knee OK?"

"Yeah, should be fine...all things considered." We sat there in silence for several moments. "I don't understand how we're even talking right now," Frank said, shaking his head.

Just then Mike and Sarah regained consciousness and sat up on the edge of their respective cots, rapidly checking their bodies for injuries. They turned to us and shared in the relief that we were all OK, for the most part. We sat for some time discussing the last seconds we could recall before the explosion. By whatever technological miracle, we all agreed Sky's quick reaction had saved our lives.

As if on cue, the door opened, and Sky hobbled into the room, ducking to pass through the doorway. Everyone fell silent and stared as she entered. She stopped just inside the entrance and bowed her head in solemn apology. Her robes were dirty with ash and dark splatters of blood (Probably from Herb and the OnSpec fuckhead), and she sported what I assumed were the early signs of bruises on her face. Her right hand was also wrapped in a metallic bandage, and faint trails of black blood ran down the side of her head and had dripped onto the shoulder of her robe.

"I'm sorry this happened to all of you," she said quietly. "We are currently investigating how the terrorist was able to circumnavigate our combined agencies' security." She threw a thinly veiled, angry glance at the human representatives, obviously believing it must have been an inside job or the fault of Earth's side of the security. Seeing their technology, I was inclined to agree. However, as quickly as her frustration flashed through her calm demeanor, it was replaced with an expression of deep, heavy sadness. I understood her pain more than she knew. Not the first time Frank and I had experienced a suicide bomber, though it was our first time being that close. "I'm glad to see you are all alright. Please allow the medical personnel to fully assess you before you leave.

They'll take good care of you." She nodded to us and then turned to leave the room.

Sarah stood up and faced her. "I'm sorry about your friend, Herb," she said.

Sky paused and turned toward us. "Thank you. He will be missed." For a moment her biotech lines glowed a faint emerald across her body—possibly an involuntary emotional response. She took a deep breath and exhaled slowly, the tattoos returning to their black hue. "I hope you all decide to continue on this path. Please be well." With that she bowed her head and exited the room. The door closed behind her, leaving us in silence.

The OnSpec attack at the stadium left twenty-two dead (mostly human) and dozens of others injured, including members of our group. Theo and Herb were gone, and two passersby outside the building had caught the full brunt of the debris field blown out the side of the wall. The device Sky activated had created just enough of a pillow to curb the most lethal effects of the explosion but had sent all of us crashing into the far wall. Back in the TSA screening room, a second suicide bomb had been detonated by Theo's accomplice after he heard the first one explode, killing eighteen people there.

Compatibility testing went on for another two weeks until the quota was filled for the three alien carriers. Our group was an anomaly for the number of passed tests. All over the world, people's dreams were dashed or renewed as they stood in front of those black metal cubes with the searing spheres in their outstretched palms. Now that the ranks were swollen with fresh recruits, we were given a rapidly approaching departure date, and everyone took the last week on Earth to prepare for the long journey to WOH S140 in the Dorado constellation—nearly 170,000 light years from our sun.

The exoplanet we had suspected in the system and creatively titled WOH S140 - C was the home world of our friends, a place they named Lumen from the Latin for "light" or the process of light shining out from a single source, like a candle in the dark void of space. Though the Lumenarians had colonized over a dozen planets, Lumen was the core planet and their source of origin, the brightest gem in the helm of their empire. Lumen would be our staging location from which to launch the new campaign. But we had to get there first, and the journey would take us roughly eighteen months traveling at several times the speed of light—sort of. We wouldn't actually be travelling past the speed of light, but we would be covering the distance as if we were. Something about wormholes. I didn't have any understanding of it outside of science-fiction shows.

Maximizing the use of our time, the journey's duration would be filled with training in such disciplines as advanced combat and weaponry, science and technology, field medical, intergalactic history and culture, engineering, and multi-planetary survival, including education on flora and fauna. The travel wouldn't be a cruise; it would be an intensive assault on our senses as we expanded our minds and pushed our bodies to new limits preparing for the conflict ahead—military boot on space 'roids.

Neither Frank nor I needed to do much to prepare for the mission. Having only each other made it easy that way. Frank had sold the bar in the days after our acceptance into the program. Banks were greedily buying up properties and assets from all those departing for the new world. They offered long-term trusts in the names of the volunteers, knowing there was a real possibility that none of us would return or that, if we did, the managers in charge would no longer be walking the earth. For that matter, the banks themselves could be dust. In the meantime, no doubt they'd make a killing on their new bounties.

Time dilation is a bit of a bitch as it turns out, one of the main sources of hesitation for anyone tagging along. Even if all we did was fly there, turn around, and fly back, the three years of our perception would span decades on Earth, and there was no telling how long the complete journey would take. Sure, once we arrived relativistic time would return to linear time, but apparently trips between the Lumenarian worlds our campaign might take us to would range from weeks to months, accumulating time discrepancies for us and observers on Earth, or so it was explained during a brief conversation that Frank and I had had with Sarah. Little above my intellectual paygrade. I'm sure it was mentioned during the information seminars too, but I was mostly drunk for those, and I found it a lot easier to listen to Sarah.

So, we took the time to compress our lives into the one duffle bag we were allowed to bring with us. Once embarked, all our equipment and clothing needs would be cared for, so people loaded up their most valued and sentimental trinkets to carry the memory of Earth and our lives into the cosmos. I packed some casual clothes, including my favorite Hawaiian shirt, some photos (the few I had), an old flask, my dog tags, pocketknife, the punched bullet, and as many bottles of whisky as I could fit in the remaining space.

The last week of waiting was filled with everything we feared we'd miss most about our home. We were told that the food processors on the ships could replicate just about any dish—not in appearance but in flavor—but that there might be some slight variances due in part to different textures and imperfect simulation or our minds not quite satisfying the gap between visual and taste receptors (experiential programming is hard to break). On the plus side, the thousands of recipes accumulated and analyzed by the processors were from world-renowned chefs from around the world. I guess that meant Grandma's meatballs wouldn't make the cut. So, Frank and I went out and tried all the foods we thought we'd miss most and others we'd never tried before, collecting a mental sensory bank that we could carry into the void. Damn, I was going to miss proper lobster rolls.

As well as satiating our appetites, we played pool, went bowling, toured museums and art galleries, and even took a day trip to a hidden waterfall. Really nice man dates, actually. Also pretty sad. It was a stark illustration of how boring our everyday lives were—how little we'd experienced or sought out. Our greatest adventures had involved travelling the world to kill people, and look how we fucking ended up. Something we had started with such idealism had twisted into the ultimate cynicism of country and purpose. Maybe we were just repeating a cycle, or maybe we could finally make a difference. That's what I thought drew Frank to it anyway.

On the last night before we were to rendezvous with our pickup shuttle, I splurged on a $1,500 bottle of scotch, a rare twenty-five-year-old bottle of Lagavulin from the western isles of Scotland. Frank and I made the oddly quiet drive from the dive hotel in Los Angeles to Joshua Tree National Park. The normally congested and slow drive cruised by in a little over two hours as people all over the world spent their last night before departure with family and friends—those who had them, that is. The desert air was cooling with the descent of day, and we drove with the windows down and the wind whistling through our hair. The sun set behind us over the ocean in streaking rays of pink, purple, and gold. A perfect send-off for our last evening on Earth.

By the time we pulled into Joshua Tree, the golden orb had dropped beneath the horizon, and the stars shone brightly overhead. A full moon provided natural ambient light for us to toast away the world. Popping the trunk of our pussy-ass rental sedan (Frank had to pay someone to take his truck), I pulled out the beautiful bottle of scotch. "Uh…Frank? Where are the glasses?"

"I thought you grabbed them." I stared at Frank and then back down at the bottle in my hand. Son of a bitch. We both laughed at our mistake, but it did hurt.

Half an hour later, we found a large boulder to set up on for the night. I lifted the bottle to my eyes and studied the majestic scrawling of the storied label. "Islay Single Malt Scotch Whisky" peered out from between the bold Lagavulin lettering and the twenty-five-year-old moniker. I stared at the label for a long moment. It hadn't even occurred to me when I bought it that the last time I had drunk the sixteen-year-old version was when a bottle had been shared during an after-action debrief in Iraq. We had lost four good people during a mission. Friends. I saw them walk beneath the boulder, stare up, and glow in the moonlight.

Peeling the tinfoil cover off the cap, I cleared my throat and shook off the memories. I pulled the cork stopper out of the bottle and put my nose to the opening. Earth and fire rose into my sinuses, causing a slight watering in my eyes. Doesn't matter how much you drink; that shit burns your nose when you dig too deep. Sea salt, dark chocolate, and tobacco danced with the potent aroma of boggy peat as I took another whiff.

Frank pulled the two In-N-Out soft-drink cups from his jacket pocket and passed them to me. The juxtaposition of the scotch and the cups couldn't have been further apart, but short of straight swigging, it was our best option. At least we had had some water to rinse them out.

"Shouldn't you be pouring these?" I said with a grin as I poured healthy slugs into both cups, setting the bottle down on the boulder and handing one cup to Frank.

"Ah, fuck you." We saluted the cups and took a slow drink of the tawny liquid, savoring every drop.

"Cheers."

The scotch had the kind of smooth refinement that only comes from decades in a perfectly charred oak cask. The charcoal and wood bled their quality into the liquid over time and drew the harsh imperfections of freshly distilled spirits through the barrier and out into the world. I closed my eyes, allowing my focus to remain intent on the experience and away from darker wanderings.

"Well, that's scotch," Frank said with the inexperienced passivity of a non-scotch drinker—he had always been more of a mezcal man. My mouth fell open as I stared at him, at a loss for words. Rather than bashing my indignation against a brick wall of indifference, I simply chuckled and shook my head.

"You're a piece of work, Frank." He smiled and shot back his drink before lying down on the boulder and staring at the stars. I finished my scotch in a long swig and poured another solid portion into my cup. "Hey, check this out." I held the bottle in my tech-enhanced hand. The wristbands they gave us during compatibility testing had been locked on, some sort of tech-dampener until we departed, so we wouldn't hurt ourselves or others accidently or get into any trouble, like the anklet of a prisoner under house arrest. That was a good thing because we definitely would have fucked with them. The most I could muster was a light-blue glow from the tech lines when I really concentrated (Frank couldn't get anything). Nothing as exciting as blasting away a levitating cube. I focused as hard as I could, and the bottle lit up like a sapphire lantern, the liquid reflecting kaleidoscope prisms along the rock and into the dark night.

"Nice," Frank said, leaning on his forearm.

Suddenly, the bottle exploded in my hand and showered Frank and me with glass and scotch. We both stared wide eyed at the place where the bottle had been. A moment later, the cap landed between us. Then Frank burst out laughing, practically rolling around on the boulder in hysterics.

"Son of a bitch!"

The scorching sun was high in the sky as we waited for our ride up to the Lumenarian ships. The southwest launch site was designated as an area on the edge of the desert outside Slab City, only a few hours south of Joshua Tree. The military had cordoned off a large space with high chain-link fences for the comings and goings of the transport shuttles. Outside the fence, thousands of people gathered to stare in awe at the vessels' rise and fall and to cheer their support for Earth's "heroes." Inside the fence, thousands more of us waited for our lift. In the horde, Frank and I had linked up with Miguel, Sarah, Mike, and an African-American woman named Megan.

Megan was a tomboy in her early thirties who looked exactly how you'd imagine the daughter of a mechanic with no sons would look. She wore her hair tied back in a messy knot, and her hands had the permanent grit and roughness of someone who worked in grease all day and scrubbed it clean with heavy-duty, orange-scented, pumice soap. Her tight ripped jeans were earned, not fashioned that way, and were decorated with spots of oil. She was her father's girl, and she had idolized the man right up until his death two years earlier. She was also a quick sharer. However, she was blunt and rough around the edges, which I respected.

Many of the volunteers were orphans in some way. Those with few to no blood ties left, whether by the unfortunate clippings of fate or the distant coldness that forms between people from trauma and pain. We all knew the time commitment of the journey ahead, and few with healthy living relationships would sacrifice them for a war light years away. Fair enough. There was also a stipulation in the application process that ensured no one was running away from important family commitments. People could appeal failed attempts, but they had to present their case in front of a human tribunal that rarely sided with anyone attempting to ditch important spousal or dependent responsibilities. So, we were mostly a band of leftover souls who had nothing to lose except each other. Of course, not everyone came from rough or dysfunctional backgrounds, but the ones closest to me seemed to, kindred spirits gravitating inevitably near.

"Holy fuck. I hope we're getting lifted soon. It's hot as hell out here," Megan said, lying back on her luggage and wiping sweat from her brow. I squinted through my sunglasses as I looked up into the sky, searching for another shuttle. Frank and I were sitting on our duffels playing a game of Go Fish.

"Maybe last real, uh...*sol* we get for the next while, eh?" Miguel said, also lying back on his bag. Huh. Hadn't considered that. All the same, the heat was oppressive in the vast desert expanse. Clouds of dust occasionally blew past, forcing us to shield our faces.

We killed the time playing more card games, reading, chatting, and listening to music. A few peppy groups made the rounds introducing themselves with irritating eagerness. They came and went. Our cluster shared the standard conversations spoken between strangers considering their company as potential friends. *Where are you from? What did you do before this? Why'd you join up?* Small talk bugged the shit out of me for the most part, but I liked our budding squad and appreciated it as a first step toward something more. That, and Frank always harped on me for being anti-social. "Talk's only as small as you let it be," he'd say. Real social fucking butterfly he was. I learned that keen intelligent look behind Sarah's eyes wasn't just a worldly gaze but that she was a graduate of MIT and Berkeley. Mostly a brag by Mike about his big sister. Sarah held her cards pretty close to her chest. She was probably the smartest human in the field, as it turns out. I wouldn't have said anything about smart Asian stereotypes out loud, but Megan had no problem joking about it.

After what felt like hours, a large shadow passed over our group. We looked up to see Sky standing over us carrying a small case. We got to our feet and shook her hand in turn.

"Hola Cielo. Como estas?"

"Hola Miguel. Bueno, Gracias. Usted?"

"Bueno, Gracias."

"It's nice to see you all."

"Nice to see you too," Sarah said. "Oh, this is Megan—"

"Megan Daniels. Yes. I didn't perform your intake, but I have your information. Nice to meet you." Sky smiled warmly at Megan, who returned it and nodded. We were all still getting used to the aliens and occasionally found ourselves lost for words.

"Ready to leave all this behind?" Frank asked. Sky held his eye contact, took a deep breath, and nodded, an acknowledgment of our brief and turbulent shared history and the deeper meaning of the question. She didn't need to address it directly; we could see it on her face.

"I'm excited that the day has finally come to return home. Though I imagine you're all a little apprehensive," she said, glancing between us.

"A little nervous, but it's an amazing opportunity and adventure," Sarah replied, smiling that brilliant smile.

"I understand. Well, I've come to deliver one more small piece of tech before you board the ships." She pointed to the voice-projection device at the base of her throat. "These were improvised for those of us planet side to communicate. Once aboard we won't have these, so you'll need your own translators." She drew several more of the small metallic spheres from the case. We all grimaced slightly at the sight of them, remembering the searing pain as the previous spheres bored into our skin. "I know, I know. They're not very comfortable, but it'll be over quickly." She handed each us a sphere and then showed us where to attach them. "It's different from most of the other tech, which is fairly simple in comparison, essentially synergizing with and enhancing your entire nervous system."

"Fuck me, that sounds fun," I muttered to Frank.

"This feeds right into your auditory receptors and Broca's area, angular gyrus, insular cortex, and Wernicke's areas of the human brain," Sky continued.

"And double fuck me." Some small comfort (maybe?) was Sky didn't seem very concerned with any of this, since she filled us in as if we were going for a routine oil change. Guess I'd have to take her word for it that this wasn't gonna nuke my brain.

After passing the gumball-size orbs out to us and a few others nearby, Sky pulled out a small taser-looking device that clicked open as she pulsed some of her bioenergy into it. "It's perfectly safe," she added. The device's end split apart with a ratcheting sound and unfurled like a flower or a parabolic microphone. "Who's first?"

I stepped forward, eager to get the feeling over with. "We better not find out in a year that all these energy fields gave us cancer," I muttered.

"You're part of the Union now," Sky said with a smile. "Cancer is a thing of the past."

I turned my back to her and held the small metallic ball just behind my left ear. She held up the device and triggered an activation field that made the back of my neck and head feel warm and fuzzy. What a tease. The sphere trembled to life and divided in two, one orb staying where it began and the other rolling around the back of my neck to a symmetrical location behind my right ear. I had to fight the urge to giggle from the ticklish feeling. After a slight whirring, they flattened against my skin, glowing the familiar molten red and searing into my neck. I clenched my jaw and grunted in pain as the sharp, hot threads shot sub-dermally across to each other and into my fucking brain. I remembered hearing in a movie that the brain couldn't actually feel anything. That didn't seem like the case. It felt like a hot laser was bouncing around inside my skull and burning into the backs of my eyes. I realized I was paralyzed as this was happening. The others winced as they watched the process. A few moments later, the pain was gone, and the circuit markings faded to the standard black tattoo. I wish it only hurt as much as a tattoo.

"Oh yeah, that's a super-fun feeling. Enjoy, whoever's next," I said, gingerly rubbing the back of my neck and feeling the slightly raised skin around the tech. Sky smiled sympathetically and gestured for the others to step forward. Looking around, I saw pockets of people gathered around other Lumenarians as they worked through the crowd, doling out the upgrades.

As Sky finished installing the last piece of tech on the back of Sarah's neck, she tucked the activator device into her robes.

"How many languages can this translate?" Sarah asked, rubbing her hand along the base of her head.

"Around fifteen thousand," Sky replied. Everyone's eyebrows arched up. Whoa. "About seven thousand of those are human, and the rest belong to the other races."

"So, there's only eight thousand other languages between five other races?" Sarah asked.

"Two of those races don't communicate verbally, and because of your species' youth, humans have fairly inefficient means of communication. In time many of your languages will be lost to cultural melding and attrition. Fewer than one hundred Lumenarian dialects remain."

"I feel like that was bragging. Was that bragging?" I asked Sarah.

Sarah shot me a smile and chuckled. "How come the other races don't have names yet?" she asked, turning back to Sky.

"Because *you* haven't named them."

"*We* get to name them?" Frank asked.

Sky nodded. "In time, after you learn more about them. Arthur felt it was a privilege that should be reserved for the volunteer crews. Whatever you decide, they and we will hear the names the way we know them regardless, but you will name them for humanity."

"How come none of them came—"

"I'm sorry. I would enjoy answering more questions, but I really need to continue administering the tech. You will have plenty of time to learn more aboard the ships," Sky said. Sarah looked like someone had cancelled Christmas but nodded her understanding. Sky smiled and bowed her head. "I will see you all again soon." She turned to approach another group of eager recruits and then paused. "I almost forgot. You all will be departing on the next shuttle destined for your assignments on the *Albatross*."

"Fuck yes!" Megan blurted. Everyone looked over at her. "Sorry."

A few days earlier, it had been announced to the world that each of the three ships in orbit had been given names. The larger twin vessels were the *Pelican* and the *Osprey*. The third, smaller, craft was the *Albatross*.

"They're all incredible ships, but it'll be nice to have you all there."

"You're aboard the *Albatross* too?" Frank asked Sky.

"Yes. I'm the chief medical officer. See you aboard." She smiled and turned away, walking over to another expectant group.

"The *Albatross*! That's awesome!" Megan said. "You see the footage of it? It looks wicked cool. Can't wait to see what's under the hood." She stared up into the sky. We all looked up with wonder, excited that we had received the most sought-after post. Really, nothing would be very different training or living-wise aboard the other ships, but a certain prestige came with being assigned to the flagship of the small fleet—the ship that the alien leader, Arthur, commanded.

"Hey, you guys hear a couple of Lumenarians are staying behind on Earth?" Sarah asked.

"No kidding? They might never see home again," Miguel said.

"I know. Guess it's not anything we aren't potentially signing up for though. Apparently, they want to learn more about us and teach what they can. Be the ambassadors for Lumen. Building an embassy and everything."

"Here in the States?"

She shook her head. "Reykjavik, in Iceland I heard."

"Huh. Seen pictures. Nice spot, I guess," Miguel said. "Little cold for my tastes."

"Man, your English sounds way better all of a sudden," I said. "No offense."

"I was speaking Spanish. Thought you guys were too."

"You know I don't speak Spanish—Ooooh." We all instinctively reached up and touched our new translator tech lines. "Cool." It wasn't just for the Lumenarians; it was for everyone. Everything we heard and replied to was in our native tongue, and the same went for everyone else. What sounded like English to us was actually Miguel jabbering away in Spanish and vice versa. The translator was seamless, and whether by a trick of the eye or a quirk of the gear, the person speaking didn't look like a character in a poorly dubbed movie, or at least it minimized it. It translated so quickly that there wasn't even a lag between what we thought, the formation of words, and the actual projection of them. The same went for how we heard it.

"Hey, isn't an albatross basically just a big seagull?" Mike asked out of left field.

One more hour ticked by as we waited for the next shuttle. When it eventually came, almost every one of the thousands awaiting their rides rose expectantly. We groaned and stretched as we shook the stiffness out of our bodies. The shuttle landed a little ways from the main group of people, but because of the minimal downdraft generated by the vessel's propulsion systems—no more than the rotor wash of a small helo despite being several times bigger than a Sikorsky—it wasn't too far. After the minor dust cloud settled, the rear of the ship opened, and a wide ramp descended to ground level. Each load could carry close to a thousand people, and they had been operating transports from the surface to space over the last five days twenty-four hours a day. Luckily, or unluckily, we were slotted to go up on the last day on one of the last shuttles to depart Earth.

A sudden buzz and beep came from our wristbands. Looking down, we saw our devices pulse with a bright green light.

"Guess that's our cue," I said as I picked up my bag and slung it over my shoulder. Everyone with the green light did the same and worked their way through the crowd toward the shuttle. The cheers from the observing mob roared in the distance.

The shuttle was smooth and oval, like a slightly elongated and flattened egg, more bulbous in the rear and narrowing toward the nose. I wouldn't call them wings in the traditional sense, but rounded protrusions bubbled out from the sides and ran almost the entire length of the craft, coming to a point at the front of the fuselage. It was windowless and so flawless that it seemed like the hull was a solid sheet of the material curled tightly around inner ribs, like it had been dipped in a coating of hot latex. Where the cargo doors opened, the support struts seemed to stretch rather than unlock in a series of hydraulic or mechanical parts, some kind of flexible smart metal.

Several Lumenarians stood at the base of the ramp and ushered us to our seats. Inside, the door gave way to such a clean, expansive opening that it made me question the thickness of the hull that would protect us from the unforgiving vacuum of space. Bench seats lined the outside of the galley, and several rows ran up the middle. Thin seams traced along the floor in front of the benches, outlining panels that I assumed were hatches for the ship's drop-troop capabilities that we'd all heard of. No more rappelling, which was nice. Never liked that aspect of the job.

It was funny observing those already seated. The benches had obviously been designed to accommodate the significantly larger forms of the Lumenarians and made each passenger look somewhat childlike, their feet dangling above the floor.

Out of nowhere a man of around sixty squeezed into a space between us, pushed forward with the throng of people. He was fairly round and sported a thin white mustache and circular glasses that seemed to be constantly sliding down his nose. He wore a simple business suit and tie that, along with his age, caught us off guard. Since we were all recruited to be soldiers, few of those tagging along pushed much past their late thirties or forties, and most were younger. Hell, I felt like an old man in the group. His face was red, and he dabbed his sweaty forehead with an embroidered handkerchief.

"Hello!" he said energetically, glancing between us.

"Uh, hi…" Megan replied. "Aren't you kinda old?" she asked, causing us all to stare at her.

"Oh, you speak German?"

"No, English."

"You're speaking English right now?"

Sarah nodded. "Yeah."

He suddenly clicked that it was the universal translator working its techno magic. "Incredible. Just incredible. I'm speaking German!"

We all chuckled and stared at him. "Are you going to be…fighting?" Sarah asked.

The old man flashed an alarmed but cheerful smile. "Oh, heavens no. No, no. I'm one of the ambassadors for Earth, Frederik Lyons, at your service."

We all stared at him, wide eyed. "An ambassador for Earth?" Frank repeated.

"That's right!" Frederik replied, glancing distractedly around the shuttle.

We all shared a look that said, *This guy's fucking senile.*

"But you won't be able to contact Earth while we're gone. Or at least not for decades," said Frank.

"Yes, it's going to make my job very interesting. Think of me more as a liaison, if that's easier. Oh, I need to check in. Be right back." The old man turned and darted off through the crowd toward one of the Lumenarian overseers. We all stared after him, dumbfounded. A new person took his spot.

"How did that old guy even get on the shuttle?" I asked.

"Maybe he really is the ambassador for Earth," Megan replied. We all stared for a moment, then burst out laughing.

Despite the quantity of recruits boarding the shuttle, it only took about half an hour to get everyone situated. Before long the large ramp folded up, merging seamlessly with the hull. The craft vibrated to life and lifted off from the ground. It was incredible how smooth the launch was. We barely noticed until the panels on the inside of the hold lit up, displaying a 360-degree view of the outside and the ground rapidly disappearing below. The panels were so clear and vivid that none of us were sure whether massive windows and skylights had opened or if they were simply projections.

Thin wisps of grey-and-white clouds streaked past as we rose through the ever-darkening blue sky of our home world. As the color outside faded to black, jets of a substance that resembled water shot out from several ports around the ship. Somehow the fluid kept pace with us, though it never touched the hull, and it flowed around in an enveloping cocoon of protection. The hydro shield buttoned together around the ship and shimmered like the surface of a calm pond.

As the shuttle rose higher, the sun came into view, shining brightly and magnified against the sheet of liquid around us. Realizing how high we must be, I wondered when we would start to feel the atmospheric punch as we broke into space. But it never came. For a few seconds the aquatic forcefield around us vibrated more forcibly, like a handful of gravel being tossed into a lake, and we felt a slight increase of pressure on us, but after a few moments it calmed, and we were left with the peaceful reflection of stars through the panel's view. Once we cleared the atmosphere, the water collapsed toward the hull and streamed back into the ports from which it had been released.

The artificial gravity must have kicked in without anyone noticing, and we all missed out on the expected weightlessness that we imagined being synonymous with space travel. For some of us that might have been a relief because even with the gentle rise, many people were looking worse for wear the farther we got from terra firma. One of those people was Frank, who was turning a bit green around the gills.

"I swear to God, if you throw up on me, Frank…" I warned with a raised backhand and a smile. Frank chuckled but then closed his eyes, trying to muster his stomach into cooperation.

When we arrived at the three massive carriers, every soul aboard leaned forward and gazed out the translucent panels, several standing to get a better view. Possibly sensing our curiosity, the entire inside of the shuttle became translucent, as if we were sitting on a platform in the middle of space. Then Frank threw up.

The size of the ships was incredible, and I couldn't help but stare, my mouth agape. The *Osprey* and the *Pelican* were so massive they seemed to dwarf the moon from our perspective. A steady stream of shuttles caravanned into the loading bays of each leviathan, and a cloud of drones zipped around the outside of the hulls, conducting tasks and transporting resources. As we approached, the smaller command vessel came into view, tucked between the two giants.

Our shuttle took us on a scenic, looping ride around the majestic ship, weaving between other shuttles and supply boats. The smooth teardrop or apple-seed shapes of the main body and pseudo-wings loomed beneath us as we floated above the flawless form, more streamlined and aggressively molded than the shuttles' egg-like design. However, like the shuttles, it had no visible windows, and the only openings were the cargo bays that would apparently fold shut during transit. She was beautiful. A menacing beauty. Unassuming and deadly. A naval destroyer or aerial gunship look like things made to kill. This looked like something made of stardust and magic, an elegant, cosmic yacht that could wipe the floor with Earth's military. I wanted to see what kind of weapons she had hidden away.

Passing along the ship's port side, we saw several unmanned drones laser-etching lettering into the otherwise perfect surface. *Albatross* was carved in slanted bold type against the bright metallic hull. The name was repeated in several different languages along the side, even in an odd scrawling of Lumenarian that resembled cuneiform and the line of an EKG heart monitor jumbled together.

"Wow," I whispered without meaning to.

"Yeah," Sarah quietly affirmed. We glanced at each other in that shared moment of wonder. I searched behind her sparkling jade eyes for the reason she had joined the mission, for why I found it so difficult to take my eyes off her, beyond her natural beauty, for who she really was beneath the fierce intelligence. Maybe sensing this, Sarah smiled shyly and broke eye contact, turning back to the view outside the walls.

The shuttle keeled and dropped around the side of the *Albatross* like a helo in an evasive bank and fell in line for the approach to a loading bay on the ship's starboard side. Another watery energy field covered the entrance to the mother ship, and our shuttle dipped through its sheen with a ripple, entering the gigantic cargo bay. Then Frank threw up again, right on my shoes.

Thousands of Lumenarian crew members and human recruits milled about the busy, cavernous room. Crates of supplies and equipment were stacked throughout, and drones transported gear to its intended destinations. Along the edges of the space stacked in rows on heavy-duty shelves sat relatively small fighter ships, hundreds of them like comparatively miniature models of the shuttle we were on, only more pointed at the nose. The walls and ceiling were sterile tones of grey and white with dark obsidian-colored flooring throughout. More autonomous bots buzzed along the ground reorganizing materials and transporting goods from the backs of recently arrived shuttles to their new homes. The bots were smooth, rounded-edge prisms with four glowing emerald "eyes" that looked off in each direction as they levitated several inches off the floor.

A long, semi-organized line of people stood in front of a group of Lumenarians, who were giving directions and trying to wrangle the easily distracted humans. In the distance I vaguely made out a holographically projected form that looked like a seven-foot-tall stick figure made of blue lightning. The image led a group of recruits toward a hallway off the main bay.

The windows of our shuttle returned to their original opacity, and the loading door cracked open and lowered with the same bizarre stretching metal we had seen before, like sinuous mercury. We descended the ramp amongst the crowd and took our first steps onto the deck of the *Albatross*.

CHAPTER VI

The Albatross

After the slow process of being sorted through intake at the shuttle bay, each person was assigned to one of five housing complexes within the ship, nicknamed "aviaries." Fortunately, our little group had been stuck together and we were all assigned to Charlie aviary.

Once we received our housing designation, one of the Lumenarians set us up with our own personal guide; a holographic iteration of the *Albatross's* artificial intelligence named Code-CC or just "Codec," as we came to call him—it. Codec was the sapphire electric stick figure we had seen from our shuttle when we first landed. He could be called upon or dismissed in a flash and helped with just about anything, whether it was directions through the massive maze-like structures of the *Albatross* or answers to any questions we might have. Codec's features were flexible and possibly altered after the fact when humans became passengers aboard the ship. His torso and limbs resembled a display you might see at a Body Worlds exhibit, where scientists and artists had dissected the body and left only the blood vessels and nervous system intact. Each twisting internal structure was a cord of arcing, blue electric sparks. On top of the charged body was a face that seemed to be in constant flux between a human face and that of the Lumenarians, like a radio tuner that couldn't quite settle on a station. All that aside, my favorite part about Codec was that he was a smartass. Some intuitive algorithm or quirk in his programming, or maybe just what happened when he was allowed to glimpse humanity and all its shit.

The hallways of the *Albatross* were all at least ten feet high and twice as wide with the same grey-white paneled walls and dark floors as the shuttle bay. The bright but never harsh lighting that flooded every chamber and passage seemed to radiate from the whites of the walls and ceiling rather than traditional bulbs or light fixtures. It was all automatic and efficient, the lighting naturally dimming a section or two in front of and behind any areas not occupied.

As we marched through the corridors among the flood of people in line behind Codec's flowing spectral form, we buzzed excitedly. I felt waves of that strange feeling I got when I entered a foreign room, and there seemed like too much new information to take in, sensory overload washing over me like an intense déjà vu. I reached out and ran my hand along the smooth wall panels. They had a tender warmth to them and seemed to pulse slightly. It was barely noticeable, but there, a gentle throb like a heartbeat.

The journey to the aviary took over half an hour at a brisk pace, and apparently, we had only traversed less than a third of the ship's total width. Multi-directional transport elevators darted around the ship for ease of travel, but the tour was a good way to start orienting ourselves within the titanic structure.

When we finally arrived at the aviary, it took my breath away. Everything on the *Albatross* made us feel small in comparison but nothing more so than the superstructure that made up the housing complex. The hallway opened into a massive atrium so large that we could barely see across it. It had to be a quarter-mile to the far side. From the tunnel we walked onto a grand arched causeway that ran toward a large central spire. The helical column rose to the ceiling with bridges at various levels shooting out toward more apartment units that spanned up and down the walls of the oval room. It resembled the bonds that held together strands of DNA or the spokes of a wheel.

The ceiling was translucent all the way around, and the night sky of space and stars twinkled down from above. Codec informed us that the surface would also simulate a variety of daylight scenarios at timed intervals similar to Earth's day cycles. Much later it would simulate the cycles of campaign worlds during our Lumen local transits, something to aid in balancing our circadian rhythms even in the depths of space.

The first level was lush with foliage harvested from Earth; large grass lawns and stone and bark mulch walking paths lined with different trees—maple, spruce, fir, and a few particularly large oaks. It looked completely natural, like we were walking through a real park rather than an artificially manicured biodome. To add to the effect, birds whistled past us, dancing through the air and weaving over and under the entrance causeway before settling in the branches of some nearby trees. Two ponds ran along each side of the open space, alive with a multi-colored variety of koi and…other fish. Never was much of a fisherman. Frank said I was too loud and impatient. That and the last time we tried I got drunk and tipped our tinner over. The only thing that hinted slightly toward its oddity was the lack of insects, and that we were on a spaceship. Everything was managed with horticultural drones that buzzed around trimming the vegetation and discarding the clippings as well as feeding the birds and fish.

"Are the fish here for food, Codec?" Mike asked as we crossed the bridge.

Several people nearby chuckled, overhearing the question.

"Technically, you could eat them, Michael," Codec replied. "But we'd prefer it if you didn't. There's plenty of sustenance aboard the *Albatross* without having to resort to your hunter-gatherer tendencies."

Smartass. Mike averted his eyes, regretting the question. Sarah and I smiled to each other, stifling our laughter for his sake.

The people who had arrived in the hours or days earlier wandered around the park chatting with each other and pointing out new discoveries. Others leaned on the railings high above watching the new arrivals filter in. A group of men and women kicked a soccer ball around one of the smaller fields, and a holographic net flashed green as the ball passed through it. Some sat in café-like chairs around small round tables that lined the base of the giant central spire and sipped drinks, read books, or watched clips on flexible glass displays that could be folded up to fit in a pocket. The area was tamped down with paving-stone type flooring and spun a wide circle around the tower; a place for eating, drinking, and bonding over the adventure ahead. Several dining halls or messes were spread throughout the *Albatross*, but for the days off or later evenings, I assumed most of our meals would be taken in the atrium and in small alcoves inset along the levels that rose up its sides. Despite the aviary's sterile, grey-white walls and otherworldly design, it was an incredibly warm, welcoming space, like some futuristic concept of what home *could* be one day, no doubt to alleviate the doldrum-like time spent travelling the stars when nothing seemed to be moving. Any fears that we'd be spending the next year and a half crammed into something like a submarine or those little hotel cubbies infamous in Asian metropolises were quickly discarded.

As we approached the base of the central spire, we looked up and saw the first taste of humans customizing our new home. A large flag unfurled off one of the railings about halfway up the giant structure, and the two people holding each end walked out in different directions, stretching it out proudly and tying it off. The banner was the blue-and-white international flag of Earth. The seven interlocked, overlapping, white rings formed a flower (symbolizing life), set centrally over the blue backdrop representative of the world's oceans. A wave of cheers echoed through the aviary as people noticed the addition to the room's decor.

Frank and I had been assigned neighboring rooms on a level about two-thirds of the way up on the starboard side of the complex's walls. Even only partway up, the height was dizzying—about forty stories. Sarah and Mike were also on our floor several units down, while Miguel and Megan were placed into apartments on the central spire just across the nearby bridge. All of us were within a stone's throw of each other.

Standing in front of my new front door, I stared at a smooth sheet of metal. My name, William A. Reach, and the code AC-4060 were laser-etched in dark, slanted lettering on my door, like the lettering of "*Albatross*" on the outside of the ship. I smiled at the sight of my new home and stepped forward—right into the closed door. That was stupid. I'd just assumed it would open automatically. I cleared my throat and glanced around as inconspicuously as I could, checking to see if anyone had caught that. I turned back and stared for a moment, expecting it to open, but it didn't. There was no handle either.

"Door open," I said. Nothing happened. I tried again. "Will Reach." *How the hell do I get in here?* "Open fucking sesame." I leaned back and glanced down the line of units again. Someone a few doors down placed his hand on a barely perceptible panel next to the door and pulsed a small amount of energy into it. I did the same, and the door opened with a pneumatic whoosh.

Codec's voice automatically sounded from somewhere around me. "Bio-sync complete. William Adam Reach."

I stepped over the threshold and stood inside what would be my new home for the next eighteen months, possibly much longer. The lighting faded up to reveal a simple, spartan space about ten feet wide by twelve feet deep. I lowered my duffle bag to the floor, the clink of bottles settling gently, and paced around the room, running my fingers across the various surfaces. I pulled the flask out of my jacket breast pocket and took a swig of whiskey. A single bed (Lumenarian single, closer to a human double) was tucked along the left side of the room set upon a row of metallic drawers that pulled out for storage.

In the back-right corner was a decent-sized, glass-paneled shower with a metal toilet and a small sink next to it. The toilet was surprisingly normal looking, and I assumed it was a recent retrofit for us. I had had brief moments of worry that the Lumenarian waste-disposal systems would need a stepladder and pose a real risk of drowning or that they would require some sort of attached suction apparatus, so I was happy to see they had adapted them for us. I still didn't know how our new allies actually did their business; that'd be an interesting conversation. I walked over and investigated the toilet—important equipment, after all. The lid opened automatically as I approached.

"Aaah, Japanese style, nice," I said. "What the hell do I wipe with—" Suddenly, a jet of water shot out and splashed near my bed. "Jesus Christ. That's gonna take some getting used to. Also hope that pressure is adjustable."

To the immediate right of the door was a sleek metal desk that supported a large, paper-thin glass monitor and levitating chair. To the left there was a wardrobe that held several changes of the same three articles of clothing; a sleek, charcoal-grey bodysuit—similar to the one Sky had been wearing when we first met her—a loose-fitting robe with slits up the side, and lastly, a navy-and-maroon two-piece suit that I equated to a military dress uniform.

I sat on the firm but comfortable bed and slowly exhaled, taking in my surroundings. Sure wasn't a grunt barracks or bunkhouse or shoddy desert ranger tent. It looked like everyone was getting the officer treatment.

Suddenly, Codec's energetic voice sounded throughout the space. "Welcome to your new habitation unit, William Reach. Your room is voice controlled and biologically locked to your signature alone, unless you designate access to others. Is there anything I can do for you?"

"Uh, hi. It's just Will, actually."

"Hello, just Will," Codec replied.

I chuckled and shook my head. "Didn't realize you came with a dad-joke feature." Jokes I had made at one point. "Uh, what can you do in here?"

"Well, Will, I conduct the basic functions of your room, such as lights, temperature controls, bed settings, activating the shower, and automatically flushing your toilet. Your room can also play music." Suddenly, "Brother" by Jorge Ben started playing.

"Oh, shit. Great song. How'd you know I'd like it?" I asked, swaying my head to the music.

"It was on your cell phone—Fresh Jams Playlist. Which is now obsolete, by the way." I reached into my pocket and pulled out the iPhone that was habitually with me, even though I only ever talked to Frank.

I set it on the shelf above the bed. Wouldn't need that ever again. The music faded out as Codec continued. "The complete library of human music is now available upon request."

"Cool."

"I can also alter your room's display to show just about anything you want. Sifting through the digital mountains of pornography, some of the popular ones from the crew who have embarked so far are—"

"I'm gonna ignore the porn comment for now, but—"

Suddenly, all four walls, the floor, and the ceiling displayed a perfectly vivid moving image of a desert on Earth. The clear, cloudless blue sky hung above endless golden sand dunes, that stretched as far as I could see. Light wisps of sand blew off the tops from a gentle breeze. I stood and slowly spun 360 degrees, taking in the view.

"Holy shit," I said through a gaping mouth as the sand faded to a serene forest landscape. Tall trees swayed and creaked in the wind, green moss growing up the northside of their stems and along the rich dark ground. The faint sound of a nearby creek trickled throughout the room. As I walked over to the wall to investigate the image more closely, the forest melted away to reveal the dark void of space. Stars shone in the empty black, and on the adjacent wall a massive blue dwarf star rotated slowly on its axis. The star's surface was a constant flowing explosion of blue fire that licked out at the edges of space. I couldn't look away as it floated around the walls of my room. As I absentmindedly reached out toward it, the display faded away, returning to the normal style of the room.

"I can also display the porn if you'd prefer."

I chuckled but then shook my head. "Not now..."

"As you wish. Command would like all new arrivals to change into their flight suits as soon as they're squared away."

"Roger that," I said as I took off my jacket. I glanced into the wardrobe. "I know there's only three things in there, but just so we're clear, the flight suit is—"

"The tight one."

"Thanks." I heard a faint chime as he signed off, leaving me to my own devices. I pulled out one of the charcoal bodysuits and examined it. It did look very tight.

"Hey, Codec?" I prompted, instinctively looking up at the ceiling.

"Yes, Will?"

"Are we gonna get to meet this Arthur guy at any point?"

"Arthur will be addressing the crew once we have activated the thread drive and are on our way. As far as meetings in person go, Arthur is a teacher, among other things, and likes sitting in on lessons from time to time, but your interactions will most likely be very limited."

"Yeah, fair enough. Thanks, Codec." Once again, his chime signaled his departure.

I knew the burdens and time commitments of leadership, and this was so far beyond anything I could comprehend I wasn't surprised with his answer, but part of me was disappointed. I was immensely curious about the figure and wondered how much of what we had heard was fact. The original news broadcasts had given us glimpses of Arthur, but after his initial addresses, the Lumenarian leader had remained mostly behind the scenes. Soldiers bonded with the men and women next to them on the firing lines and forged their opinions with blood, sweat, and tears, but often they idolized or vilified the commanders from a distance—their merits or failures transferred by a cruel or flattering game of telephone. I wanted to make up my own mind.

A little while later, after I had unpacked my duffle bag and changed into the flight suit, I walked out of my unit and over to the railing overlooking the massive atrium. Frank, Megan, and Miguel joined me, approaching from a little ways to my left.

Frank tugged on the groin of his suit, trying to create some space. "These are definitely going to take some getting used to," he said, finally leaving himself alone. I reached over and lifted his forearm, showing him the built-in display. "What are you doing?" he asked as I scrolled through a few options on the panel and then selected one that read "Casual." Frank's suit suddenly loosened slightly all around. It was still a slim fit, but at least there was some breathing room in the areas that mattered most. "Oh, man, thank you. That is so much better," he said, sighing with relief.

I shook my head and looked at the others. "You should see this guy struggle with a TV remote." Frank rolled his eyes. "But in all fairness, had to get Codec to give me a rundown. Figured there was no way they'd expect us to be in these all the time if they were that fucking uncomfortable. Check this out though." I held up my forearm band. "Combat." My suit rapidly tightened against my body, but several sections of it hardened into flexible plates protecting my torso and back and padded my joints. The flight suit doubled as light combat gear, which would also be worn under whatever our tactical field equipment was. In fact, the more we learned about the suits, the more we realized how diverse and adaptable their capabilities were—having the ability to shorten or lengthen on command, thermo-regulate for hot or cold climates, ballistic shielding, holographic map display, and more.

"Now that's cool," Megan said as she fiddled with her own forearm display.

"Right? Casual," I said into the device, my suit returning to the comfortable fit.

"It's a type of nanotechnology, and it's lined with the same material that makes up the *Albatross*'s hull," Sarah said as she approached, Mike in tow. The suit hugged her body, and I had to make a substantial effort not to gawk at how perfect she was. "An alloy mined on one of the Lumenarians' colony worlds," she continued. "It's powered by our body heat, kinetic movement, and our biotech." She smiled that beautiful smile as she made eye contact with me, making me feel like I was the only one there. "Did you guys notice the way the door struts on the shuttle seemed to stretch when they opened? The entire shuttle can do that. It's a flexible self-healing metal. Same stuff in here. They call it 'lumenium.' Can't even find the element in our solar system, far as we know. It's incredible. I haven't been able to stop asking Codec questions since we got to our rooms," she said while studying her own suit. None of us could keep from smiling as we listened to how much she had already learned in such a short time.

Just then Codec appeared next to our group, and we saw dozens of other copies of him appear throughout the complex. "The last of the shuttles has arrived, and we're preparing for the jump. Should be within the hour. If you'd like I can guide you to the nearest observation deck for a last glimpse of Earth." The message echoed through the space as he said the same thing to everyone. We nodded and followed as he led the way out of the aviary.

The *Albatross* was divided into six major sections, each broken down into multiple subsections that contained all the elements we needed to live aboard the ship and complete our training. It had two aft sections toward the stern, two midship sections, and two fore sections toward the bow, all divided down a central line that overlapped the main channel of the thread drive that ran from nose to tail. Each of the six aviary housing complexes encircled the main reactor located in the middle of the ship, the place where the forward locator beam emanated from and drew in exotic particles and where it was converted into the rear drive engine—Sarah's layman's description, still beyond me. Mess halls, armories, brigs, engineering facilities, observation decks, med bays, ready rooms, and the like were spread through each section, meaning we were rarely required to venture out of our zone except to explore.

Bravo through Foxtrot aviaries had human tenants while Alpha was the Lumenarians' home and had been since they departed Lumen. The only departments not evenly distributed throughout the ship were the cargo and shuttle bays located on the port and starboard sides and to the rear at lower levels and the command deck or bridge located about two-thirds back along the center line at the top of the ship. Everything else was designed to make each area self-sufficient and streamlined to house crews for potential extended deployments.

To reach the observation deck, we took one of the many transport elevators, large rectangular boxes that moved around the ship in all directions. It was almost disorienting how smooth they were. Inertial dampeners within the crates made it impossible to tell what way we were travelling or how fast. The result gave the impression of teleportation when the doors closed on one location and opened seamlessly on another a few minutes later.

We stepped out of the elevators into the wide observation deck, a mostly empty room save for a few rows of benches that faced a massive floor-to-ceiling translucent panel. It was another projection since the *Albatross* didn't actually have any windows, but we somehow felt closer to the view—to the world. The room was crowded, so we squeezed in, trying to jockey for a good look. Outside the window we saw the hulking form of the *Osprey* just off our starboard stern and in the gap between us, Earth. The bright marble shone as the sun's light glanced off the atmosphere. Its deep blues, dry browns, and lush greens turned slowly beneath lethargic cotton-bloom clouds.

As I looked down at our home, I was gripped with a powerful emotion. I hadn't been feeling much of anything only a second before, but the sight rocked me—the scrapbook of faces flipping before my eyes, lashing against the inside of my skull. I turned away from the view, closing my eyes to gather myself. So many goddamn memories. So many bad ones. When I opened my eyes, I noticed a bunch of others in the room also struggling to contain their painful and happy nostalgia. Some surrendered, allowing their tears to flow freely, while others, like me, tensed up with the societal conditioning that told us tears were weak. It's funny. In others I rarely ever considered crying a form of weakness; more of a strong liberation. I never felt that freedom myself. It felt more like drowning.

Frank put his hand on my shoulder and squeezed. When I locked eyes with him, I saw he was fighting the same war. He nodded to me, and I nodded back. Then we turned and looked out the window again, just in time to see the metallic apple-seed wing of the *Albatross* start to compress beneath us.

Across the way, the *Osprey* followed suit, giving us a better view of what was happening. Each of the stubby, rounded wings melted in toward the main teardrop dimension of the body, creating a single streamlined form with slight pushouts along the sides where the appendages had been. The mercurial lumenium alloy folded over the shuttle bays and sealed off the light emitting out; one flawless droplet of metal. Then, just as it was finishing its compression, a line split straight down the middle from bow to stern, and the two lengthwise halves of the ship began to pull apart. Exposed in the middle were the rotating spheres of fusion energy that formed the main reactor. Sealed corridors and struts connected the two sides around the thread-drive channel and at the nose and tail, but it seemed like any stray cosmic branch down the pipe could break us in two.

"It's incredible," Sarah whispered, her eyes glued to the *Osprey*.

Once the ships had achieved their final travelling form, they turned in space, pointing their noses toward our destination. As we watched, an iris opened in the front of the ship at the conical unsplit nose, emerald light spooling within its center like some sort of focusing lens. Another massive port several times the size of the forward one opened in the rear. The components of the thread drive engaged. The fusion cores of the reactor spun faster and faster within the central orb until they seemed to blur into one massive, alien-made star. Everything seemed to freeze as we stared out in curious amazement. Then, like a cosmic spider's filament, a brilliant light shot out of the *Osprey's* bow deep into the recesses of space. Moments later, another beam erupted out of the stern. With the blink of an eye, the *Osprey* was gone like the shuttlecock of a loom along its thread, leaving only a spectral jade trail in its wake.

For the first time since we'd arrived, we felt the *Albatross* give signs that it was powered by something other than magic as our own thread-drive ports opened to a low vibrating hum, like landing gear retracting during a flight. We all held our breath waiting for the plunge. Then, just when the tension seemed like too much to bear, the emerald beam shot out in front of us, and Earth disappeared in a flash.

PART II

(SARAH)

And now the STORM-BLAST came, and he
Was tyrannous and strong:
He struck with his o'ertaking wings,
And chased us south along.

—"The Rime of the Ancient Mariner"
by Samuel Taylor Coleridge

PROLOGUE

The Beginning is The End

An ocean of debris floated haphazardly past the command deck display in the zero gravity of space—the shrapnel occasionally glancing off the hydro shield with small flashes and buzzes like a Louisiana bug zapper, sending tiny ripples across its surface. From orbit, land masses on the planet were hard to make out through the thick haze of black smoke. In fact, it was hard to tell any of the features, water or otherwise, through the dark cloud. Sinister orange-and-red glows pierced the veil in sporadic bursts over the entire circumference.

I stood from my seat behind the holographic command console that twinkled its warnings and updates in blue, red, and green. Walking forward, I stood at the edge of the room and placed my hand against the display panel that showed the hellscape scene. I exhaled loudly, suddenly realizing I had been holding my breath. I glanced to my left, tracing the path of an object floating across my view. The corpse was unmistakable and drifted eerily past, weightless but stiff from the cold vacuum of space. Skin taut and cracked, eyes bulging and bloody. Ice crusted around his features and a dusting of frost froze his clothing in a rigid billow around his form. I watched with morbid curiosity as he faded from sight.

I refocused on the planet, wishing beyond anything that I had a better idea of conditions on the ground. The images in my head were swirling with horrific scenes of death and chaos amongst the raging fires. Survivors, if there were any, scuttling from one rubble pile to another, scavenging resources and attempting to stay hidden, the animals all but gone save for the ones hidden deep in the rocks and ruin. Maybe I had seen too many post-apocalyptic movies, but no matter how optimistically or logically I thought about it, things would not be good down there.

I chewed on my lower lip, mulling over my fears and next steps. I wasn't alone; the terror, grief, and uncertainty were palpable on the bridge as others stood near the panel next to me, staring down. Just then I felt a cold metallic hand slide into my own with a gentle squeeze. I didn't need to look over to know who it was, but the icy metal sent a small shiver down my back.

"Sorry," Miguel said as he walked to the other side of me, his cybernetic leg clicking as he stepped and held my other hand with his warm human one. "Forget sometimes." His hazel-brown eyes stared into mine for a moment, sharing the torment, before breaking off and looking through the panel. He nodded slowly. "It's going to be OK. *They're* going to be OK." I tried to force a smile, but the tension in my face wouldn't allow anything but a tight-lipped grimace.

Suddenly, I felt a sturdy kick, followed rapidly by another one. I looked down and placed my hand on my belly as a sharp pain pierced my stomach, and water ran down my legs. I doubled over, holding my middle. The baby was coming. Now.

CHAPTER VII

Full-Techno Jacket

Light speed, or what we were calling light speed, didn't look like it appeared in science-fiction movies. Most people expected the tunnel stretch of a trillion stars ripping past us, but I knew better. What we saw was a bright, greyish-white, vibrating blur that resembled a wall of fog just before we drove into it. A doppler blueshift effect where we essentially became unable to register the light emitted by stars, but the visible spectrum of background Big-Bang-sourced cosmic radiation showed up. Technically, the *Albatross* wasn't going light speed itself—some very high percentage of it but shy nonetheless. It was, however, covering light years in a timeframe equal to several times the speed of light.

In the most rudimentary of explanations, the Lumenarian ships achieved this by an engine they called the "thread drive," a traversable wormhole-creating technology. The hurdle was size. It required an immense amount of energy to open and maintain a wormhole, especially if the distance was substantial. So, rather than one massive fold in spacetime from point A to B, the Lumenarian drive created hundreds (or thousands) of smaller portals linked together in progression, more like a needle and thread completing a straight tack stitch—the ships constantly dipping in and out of folded space and static space. The forward beam opened the bridges and siphoned the incredible amounts of exotic matter into the main reactor, located midship. There it created negative mass to cocoon the craft in a protective field, which countered increased pressure from X-rays and other forms of harmful radiation. This field also pushed outward to maintain the integrity of the tunnel that was constantly trying to collapse on itself. The rear propulsion beam further harnessed that energy and focused it into a powerful jet that propelled the craft at incredible speeds. We were slackliners on a cable of light that stretched fifty kiloparsecs across the Milky Way and into the Large Magellanic Cloud. It was fascinating, and I wanted to learn it all.

When everyone finally realized they'd have plenty of opportunity to stare out at the ebbing, chalky-grey waves of interstellar travel, the observation deck slowly cleared out. I hung back, taking in the room with a handful of others.

"Little anticlimactic but still pretty incredible, huh?"

I turned to see Will's tall, strong figure staring out the window. He glanced sideways at me with a smile. His old friend, Frank, was chatting a few steps behind him with Megan, Miguel, and my brother, Mikey. Will was an interesting character. He carried himself with confidence and a witty sarcasm that sometimes came off as cocky, but in the short time I'd known him, he seemed honest. He was quick to smile and laugh, but the unmistakable glint of pain hid just behind his eyes—some dark shadow there. Still, I found myself drawn to him in the inexplicable way we love underdogs and rogues, though I had a feeling the only thing that made him either one was his own mind. What had happened to him? It was a puzzle I wanted to solve. The type of curiosity that people feel bad about when they believe they should be having a purely empathetic response instead.

"Yeah. I mean, I actually had a pretty good idea it'd look like that, but it would've been cool to see the *Star Wars*-ian light-speed stretch. Cool to see the real hypothesis confirmed too, though."

Will raised an eyebrow and chuckled.

"Wanted to become an astronaut," I replied with a shrug.

"Ah. Like, as a kid or in the real world?" he asked with a charming grin. Not the first time I'd been asked that question.

"I was working my way through the program."

"No kidding? Go through the service?"

"Air force."

"Well, I'll try not to hold that against you." He winked and looked back at the panel.

"Ahhh. Must be…marines?" I asked, trying to size him up.

He held that same unwavering, secretive smile and glanced at me from the corner of his steel blue-grey eyes. "Something like that." Must have been Special Forces of some kind. Old habits. Frank and he certainly had the feel. He was handsome in a rugged way—rough around the edges. The beginnings of crow's feet made him look slightly older than I took him to be. Since I'd known him, he'd maintained a three-to-five-day scruff that looked good on him but also sported the odd ashy hair within its sandy cover, further shadowing his years. Either way, I put him only a few years older than me—maybe thirty-five.

"Should we head back?" he asked after staring out the window for a few moments.

I wanted to spend more time staring at the space outside, but there'd be time later, and I wanted to learn more about the people I'd be sharing my life with for the next eighteen months and beyond. I took one last glance out the display before nodding back.

Back in the aviary, Mikey and I leaned against the high railing of our forty-story level in the complex and gazed down at the multitude of people milling around below. The indistinct murmur of new introductions between people from all over the world created an excited buzz that echoed throughout the space. Mikey fidgeted with his hands next to me, occasionally chewing his fingernails with an obsessive unawareness.

"Stop biting your nails," I said. He glanced over at me and rolled his eyes. I knew he was thinking I was ever the big sis. I smiled knowing that, mothering or not, I was right. It was a terrible habit. He looked nervous at the best of times, like he was living his life and judging it simultaneously, but he usually managed to cover it with an energetic contentment and agreeability. Rarely did anyone, beyond me, see the more sullen side of his insecurities. Now that we had reached the point of no return, I feared he was desperately regretting his decision.

When the Lumenarian ships had first appeared in our skies, Mikey had moved to Cambridge from California to be close to me in case things didn't go well—boys and their protector complexes, I guess, even though I was always the one taking care of him. I was completing my doctorate in astronautics at MIT and rounding out my applications to NASA, SpaceX, and various engineering companies when everything came to a standstill. What had begun as my little brother crashing on my couch until the news broke turned into my den being converted into a second bedroom as the days turned to weeks and the weeks to months.

A few days after Arthur's global address, Mikey sat me down in his room/my den and notified me that he was joining the mission, whether I agreed with him or not. He was barely twenty-one; the minimum age. The thought had crossed my mind, but I was also juggling an offer from a former professor to work with one of the many teams adapting the new technology being offered by the Lumenarians. It was a chance to be on the front lines of progressing humans to colonies in space, to make the world a better place and turn back the clock on the ravages we had inflicted on our planet. That and I had already put so much time and effort into my goal of reaching space that it almost seemed like cheating to sign up. But I also didn't want to say goodbye to my only remaining family member, a sentiment that ultimately won out when I couldn't convince him to stay—and I tried. So, I sold or gave away all my possessions (that weren't sentimental), and we headed back to California to settle up Mikey's old place and go through the enlistment process.

"Everyone here could die," Mikey said suddenly.

I looked over at him. "What?"

He went quiet and stared down into the atrium.

I watched him, knowing he'd shrug off any attempt to allay his fears. He was stubbornly pessimistic that way. "There's a chance, yeah," I said, glancing out into the aviary again. "But I mean, statistically, for the next eighteen months anyway, more will probably survive here than home.

Car accidents, fires, natural disasters, viruses, etcetera." Mikey clenched his jaw, breathing through his nose. "Mikey…" I looked over and saw his eyes straining wide in fear, his breathing increasing to a steady rasp as he clutched his chest. "Mikey!" I quickly ushered him into his room.

Inside, I forced him to sit on the bed, crouching beside him. "Hey, just breathe, OK? You're alright. Just focus on me."

He stared into my eyes, straining against the ragged breaths.

Just then Codec materialized in the room. "Is everything alright? I've detected a spike in heartrate and labored breathing—"

"He's fine, Codec. Nothing to worry about." I wasn't sure how a panic attack would be received by the *Albatross's* medical crew.

Codec hunched over to face Mikey, his blue glow reflecting on our skin. "You're not having a heart attack. Panic attacks are perfectly understandable given the flood of new stimuli and the gravity of the task at hand. It's a monumental undertaking—"

"Thanks, Codec," I said. "Probably not helping."

Codec nodded and stood upright again. "Just breathe, Michael. Everything will be alright. It seems you have everything in hand. I'm just a word away." With that Codec evaporated into the ether again.

I put my hand on Mikey's chest to calm him, forcing him to maintain eye contact. The fear in his eyes slowly subsided, and his breathing returned to normal. We sat there quietly for several minutes.

"I'm sorry," he said finally.

"Nothing to be sorry about, Ninja Turtle."

He gave me the old disdainful look that only younger siblings can give their elders. "I'm not a kid anymore, Salamander."

"Oh, that was never my nickname."

"Oh, yes it was."

"Jerk," I said, laughing and shoving him over.

Codec had informed me about the various alarm settings for the morning wakeup, everything from automatically blaring metal music to spiking the temperature to tilting my bed. I chose the gentler nudge of gradually brightening lights. The panels of my walls faded up to a harsh white glow until I finally signaled I was awake and ready to get up.

I showered and got changed into my gear for the day; my multi-functional charcoal bodysuit and looser-fitting robe over top, our basic uniform for the trip. The robe, I assumed, was mostly for modesty since the base layer was so tight—a respectful acknowledgement of our societal conditioning. I had noticed several straying eyes the other day when I was wearing only the suit. "My eyes are up here, buddy." Will did a good job of keeping his gaze level though.

When I entered the hallway, I was greeted by Will, Frank, Megan, and a Middle Eastern woman wearing a hijab, whom I hadn't met yet. They all smiled their hellos. Will looked tired, obviously not a morning person. I wasn't positive, but I thought I caught a whiff of alcohol on his breath as well.

"Sarah, this is Seyyal. She's just a couple of units down," Frank said. Seyyal smiled and shook my hand. She was in her early thirties and pretty with almond-brown skin and auburn eyes rimmed in dark shadow that brought out the amber. She had an intense stare but a wide, warm toothy smile.

"Pleasure to meet you. Looks like we're all going through this together today," she said.

"What do you mean?" Frank asked.

"We're receiving the rest of our biotech now. They want to give us as much time as possible to get used to it, according to Codec." Everyone grimaced, remembering the discomfort of the first two installments on our hands and neck. This time was going to be much worse.

"Ah. Didn't realize *that's* what *integration* meant," Frank said with a glare at Will, who stifled a laugh.

"I told him it was just a long safety briefing and orientation," Will said as he chuckled and jostled Frank.

"Anyone know if Mikey's up yet?" I asked.

"Yeah, he went to grab some breakfast with Miguel and Travis— uh, another new neighbor. Their time slot isn't until a bit later," Will answered, holding my eyes in his.

"Oh. Thought maybe they'd keep us together."

"Aw, miss your little bro already?" Megan jabbed.

"Yeah, yeah," I said, glancing at Will, who smiled back.

"We should get going if we want to walk," Seyyal said. "Nearest medical bay is still a decent journey." We all nodded, keen to explore, and left the aviary.

The closest med bay took us about twenty minutes to reach, though we stopped a few times to investigate different rooms along the way. The halls were busy with Lumenarians marching between their posts, conducting the many routine tasks that filled a day aboard a starship. Humans also wandered around taking in the sights, some going to their integration appointments and some coming back from them and looking quite a bit worse for wear with their new circuit tattoos adorning their bodies. A sense of anticipatory dread took hold of us the closer we got to our destination.

When we finally arrived at the infirmary, it was dazzling. Unlike the mostly grey walls and dark floors of the passages, the room was brilliant white. Light seemed to radiate from every surface. Dozens of recovery platforms lined each wall of the long space. Each unit was furnished with high-tech monitoring equipment and smooth mechanical arms that looked like tentacles. They assumed most of the responsibilities for non-critical cases. Dividing the front half of the space from the back, two hallways split off and ran perpendicular—one side filtering into a series of adjoining rooms designated for medical research laboratories and the other side leading to several autonomic surgical wards and intensive-care units. I wondered what was left of traditional medical training in Lumen society or whether all the crew were mostly engineers, monitoring and occasionally servicing equipment.

As we entered, Sky looked up from her display and greeted us with a smile, her assistant standing off to her side.

"Who's ready to get naked?" her assistant asked, clapping his four-fingered hands.

We all stared, a little dumbfounded.

Sky turned and glared at him through two of her eyes. "Hector is very blunt, and he thinks he's funny. I'm sorry about that," she said. Hector shrugged and grinned. "You *will* need to disrobe in an adjacent room for the procedure, though."

We all glanced at each other. Then we followed Sky and Hector to the far end of the room with another group of twenty or so people. At the back was another chamber that spanned the entire width of the previous bay. Inside was a long row of translucent cylindrical tubes, big enough for us to step inside, but with not much room to spare. In front of each one was a small table with a metallic biotech sphere on it, this time about the size of a large softball. We all filtered into the room and looked around, Sky and Hector folding in behind us.

"There's no anesthetic for this?" one of the others asked.

"Unfortunately, no. For the technology to synthesize fully with your bodies, your nerves and their pathways to your brain must be completely unencumbered. Any chemical interference can result in a rejection and the procedure having to be re-administered. So, if anyone is on medication or the like, please come see me," Sky said. I looked over and saw Will flinch slightly. "As you can see, the cylinders are relatively tight," Sky continued, "so I recommend taking most of your clothing off out here. Once you enter, the glass will become opaque, and you can remove the rest inside."

Everyone glanced around shyly, hesitant to strip down to their under-wear in front of each other. Seyyal looked the most uncomfortable, which was understandable. The Lumenarians might have been somewhat sensitive to our gender differences, but they had overlooked some of the cultural ones. Guess no one is perfect.

I went to say something. "Seyyal—"

"It's alright," she said, forcing a smile. "Everyone else has to. I'll just keep my hijab on until I'm inside. It's fine. Thank you, Sarah." I nodded to her. Slowly, one by one, we overcame the discomfort and began taking off our robes and bodysuits. I was glad I had put on underwear and a sports bra beneath the suit, though I had considered not doing so and probably wouldn't in the future. They chafed.

I glanced over and saw Will snag Sky as she walked by, avoiding her eyes. He looked embarrassed. The only word I could make out was "alcohol." Sky listened to him with an expression that seemed mixed with sympathy and consternation. She reached into a compartment behind her and pulled out an injector with a milky solution inside, holding it up to Will's arm, which he presented. I tried not to eavesdrop again as I continued taking my clothes off, but my curiosity got the better of me.

"Not the first one. This will neutralize the compounds. It will be uncomfortable."

"Fair enough," Will muttered. She injected the formula with a pneumatic whoosh. There was no immediate reaction as Will stood waiting. Then his whole body tensed as the cocktail took hold. A few others glanced over as Will stifled a grunt. I saw Frank watching as well, shaking his head slightly as he seemed to understand. After a few moments, Will exhaled slowly and unclenched his fists. Sky nodded to him, and he marched over to his designated tube to begin undressing.

"Well, this is gonna suck," he said, keeping his eyes down.

After a minute or two, we all stood in our underwear in front of our glass compartments. I couldn't help but shoot a quick sideways glance to make sure I wasn't the only one feeling self-conscious and vulnerable in just my delicates. I wasn't. Everyone shuffled in place awkwardly. I cleared my throat and quickly looked forward when I noticed Megan had decided not to wear underwear beneath her suit. She didn't seem to care at all that she was the only one fully naked. I'm pretty sure I even caught her staring curiously around the room and checking everyone out, mostly the other women.

In my brief stolen look, I couldn't help but notice Will, who was positioned in the pod right next to mine. His body was firm and muscled save for a small paunch that I attributed to what must be a drinking problem. Across the shoulder and arm nearest to me were a series of scars that seemed to originate in the front and streak around toward his back—some sort of shrapnel souvenir. I snapped forward again when I caught him also steal a look over, possibly feeling my eyes prying.

"Please take the sphere in front of you and enter the chamber," Sky said. We all obeyed and entered the tubes with our tech. Behind us, they sealed seamlessly, and the glass faded to a frosted opaque, which was a relief. I relaxed slightly, then took off my bra and panties, balling them up. A small hole opened in the glass, and I tossed them out.

Via an intercom, Sky's voice echoed through. "I'm activating it now. It will be over shortly, and you'll never have to do this again." The foreboding announcement made my stomach lurch as I prepared for the pain to come.

I heard a slight hum as the device activated. Suddenly, the familiar teal energy field filled the space, and everything became light and warm. For the first time in my life I experienced the feeling of zero gravity as I floated into the air, my body suspended in the sea of energy. It was something I had always dreamed of, part of what I had been working toward my whole life, and it didn't disappoint. If the thought of what was coming next hadn't been looming, I might have cried from happiness. If only there were more space in the tube to swim around. I released the orb, and it hovered in front of my face.

I felt a sudden pulse as the second stage of the process began. The ball disintegrated into hundreds of smaller spheres, all slowly twirling around my body like a tornado and then taking their positions. They formed around my other hand, partway up my forearms, across my shoulders, on each point of my vertebrae down my neck and back, along the sides of my torso, the underside edge of my jaw, down my legs, and even on the bottom of my feet. This was going to be veeery unpleasant.

As if on cue with the thought, every point ignited into a scalding red spot, burning into my skin. For several moments my body contorted violently with the pain and flailed through the gravity-free tube, every nerve screaming for it to stop until everything went into a rigor and I was held in a Da Vinci's *Vitruvian Man* position, though more cramped. I screamed for it to stop. Even through the glass I could hear the others' torment. The acidic threads dove through our skin and joined everything together. It was pain like I couldn't have imagined, steel splinters burrowing through my flesh, seemingly hitting every pain receptor in my body. Just when I thought I'd pass out from the hell, it stopped, the scarlet lines gently cooling across my body.

I breathed hard, trying to erase the pain from my sensory memory by thinking of nicer things; coffee, zero gravity, sex, a back massage, anything but what had just happened. Then I floated down in the tube, my feet contacting the floor again. I fell to my knees, catching myself with my hands. The dark markings of the tech were now etched across my body. The energy field dissipated, and the glass turned translucent once more.

This time nobody seemed too worried about being naked as we stumbled and crawled out of the chambers, disoriented. A few people threw up. I felt severely nauseous, and sweat glistened on me from head to toe. The worst full-body hangover ever.

"It's OK, everyone. You're OK. It's over," I heard Sky say as she and Hector walked down the line, helping us gather our clothing. Through heavy panting breaths, I glanced over at Will, both of us clutching our bodysuits in front of us. We made eye contact, each acknowledging the experience and immensely thankful it was over. He forced a weak smile, which I tried to return.

As we looked at each other, I noticed that Will's new circuit tattoos were rippling with pulses of glowing sapphire energy, a dim wave like a mirage ebbing off him. Everyone else's had faded to solid black. Sky noticed as well, pausing in front of Will. He broke eye contact and stared at his hands and arms. He made a fist with his right hand, and the circular markings along his fingers connected, crisscrossed, and struck blue arcs like a taser or like he was wearing electrified brass knuckles.

"Whoa," he said looking up at me again. For a moment the whites of his eyes flickered cobalt around the blue part of his eyes. He looked worried. "Is it rejecting?" he asked, turning to Sky.

Sky looked down at her forearm band, then shook her head. "No. It should settle in a moment." We both watched as he looked down at his tech, the blue energy slowly subsiding and his tattoos fading like the rest of ours. "There we go," Sky said, glancing down at her band again, a curious expression on her face.

As we all left the medical bay, fully dressed, Will turned to the rest of us, still wide eyed and looking fairly traumatized. "Who wants to go again?"

CHAPTER VIII

Class in Session

By the end of the third week, everyone was starting to get somewhat used to their newly enhanced bodies—or at least the obsession over the tech was waning. For the first few days, I don't think anyone got much learning accomplished outside of fiddling with their electric sparks to create light shows and shock each other. Regardless, I still did some actual research. I learned the blue hue of our biotech arose from an interaction between copper and electrolytes in our blood—copper mostly absent in the Lumenarians. Their bodies still created action potentials by the exchange of sodium and potassium ions passing through gated ion channels in neuron axons (as did ours), but naturally high levels of boric acid in their bodies produced the emerald color we saw. For us, when the tech was focused and engaged, excess stored positively charged sodium in the cybernetic fibers (an unpleasant nutrient build on day one of integration with subsequent "stockpiling" in the form of enriched gel pouches) was channeled and magnified through synthetic, hyper-dense axon bundles (our synapse biotech lines) to create the charge—trace copper and chloride ions in the bloodstream were drawn and purged through the pores from the reaction and thermally reacted to the arc.

The reaction varied from person to person. I was somewhere just north of average, whereas Will was an anomaly with no equal in sight. Most of us were lucky when we produced any blue glow during sparring, besides quick flashes. Will not only shone brightly but almost never physically made contact with anyone—the electric and thermal energy creating a barrier between whatever striking surface he was using and the points of contact. Luckily for him (and maybe for all of us if our tolerances ever built up to that level), the nanites in our blood also rushed to supercool areas of use, preventing us from burning our own skin away. Either way, being near Will during combat training was like having an oven door repeatedly opened and closed whenever he struck something.

Less visibly, the nanites were also conducting other tasks inside us. Three distinct types wove through our bodies: combat nanites programmed and reserved solely for managing the weaponized implants (repair and the aforementioned cooling); medical nanites, which chaperoned different elements (white blood cells, platelets, fibrin, enzymes, etc.) to sites of infection or illness and to help rapidly clot wounds when needed; and lastly, enhancement nanites. These worked more slowly over time to funnel excess calcium to our bones, form a protective mesh around our hearts, embed in our lungs to syphon, compress, and store emergency oxygen and nitrogen (among other elements) for balancing varied alien atmospheres, and increasing the conductivity of our original organic nervous system (essentially improving our muscle memory and reflexes).

Apart from the new biological changes, everyone started to fall into the routine being set aboard the *Albatross*. Those underestimating the military-esque programming of it were rudely awakened to the change in their usual schedules. Early risings, breakfast, morning PT, lectures, lunch, combat and equipment training, dinner, free time, study, and then bed. Rest and reset for the next day. Realistically though, the training wasn't that strenuous compared to the armed forces back home, at least not so far. I would've classed it closer to a full university class load rather than military. The schedule was demanding, but there were no unexpected deviances from it, like 3:00 a.m. surprise wakeups for drill or forced marches and no real disciplinary enforcement of bunk, grooming, or dress (besides our basic training uniform), and the Lumenarians also seemed gentler than human military leaders.

The Lumenarians were smart enough to know that although they needed to cram in as much information and conditioning as possible to prepare us for the conflict to come, the isolation and confinement of space made bad bedfellows for the worlds inside all our minds—probably as much for them as for us. They had been out to cosmic sea for a lot longer than us, after all. They couldn't break us down and indoctrinate us in quite the same way the forces could back home. It wasn't like anyone had weekends of leave or anything either.

I sat at a table in the nearest dining alcove with my brother, Frank, Seyyal, and one of our classmates, a Japanese man named Jiro. He was lean, fit, and made of sharp edges all over. Deep-set dark eyes glinted out from their sockets with a keen intelligence that bordered on cold calculation. He was an avid student whose focus never wandered. Most of the time, he was overly serious. He didn't speak often (maybe just because he wasn't fully comfortable with us yet), but when he did, he chose his words carefully, a trait learned from a successful career in business with a multi-million-dollar company back in Tokyo. He had given it all up overnight for a journey across the stars.

"Morning, Li," Jiro said with a nod.

"Morning, Jiro, everyone," I replied.

We all stared hesitantly at our plates of food. It still took some getting used to. Our metal trays were divided into several sections that each housed identical-looking gelatinous grey blocks.

"Yay, forced veganism," Frank said with an unenthusiastic fork prod.

Each slab was a processed combination of proteins, fats, carbohydrates, and nutrients that made up a balanced diet. It was a superiorly clean process that didn't resemble any of the sugary or preservative-laced foods we would be wary of back home, or so the science said—vetted by experts on Earth before the mission began. Each chunk actually tasted remarkably like the foods it was supposed to simulate. That day's breakfast of eggs, hash browns, oatmeal, pancakes, bacon—anything we wanted really—tasted just like the real thing. The only hitch was the look and the consistency. The slate appearance and rubbery texture made it difficult for our minds to complete the sensory experience. At least the coffee was black and aromatic.

"People would love this in Japan if they added a bunch of colors to it," Jiro commented with a light chuckle.

"And stamped it in the form of Hello Kitty," Mikey added, also laughing. Jiro went dead still and glared at him, causing my brother to cut off his laughter abruptly and clear his throat.

After a tense moment, Jiro broke out laughing and jostled Mikey. "Good business idea when we get home!" he said with no sign of sarcasm. He was more optimistic than I would have thought.

I glanced over at the dispensary queue where Will was just passing through the line. He had been fairly discreet with his drinking since the integration procedure, but I saw him glance around surreptitiously and then slip a small flask out of his robe and pour some liquid into his coffee cup. I wondered how much alcohol he had managed to smuggle on board. Tucking away the flask, he picked up his tray and joined us at our table. He looked tired, or rather, hungover.

"Mmmm…grey eggs and ham, huh?" he said as he sat down.

"One day we're going to forget what real food looks like," Seyyal said.

"Still beats MREs. I like to close my eyes and just imagine what it's supposed to look like," Frank said, closing his eyes and taking a forkful of the sustenance.

"You're doing it, Peter, you're doing it!" Will quoted.

"I thought your name was Frank," Jiro said.

"Quote from a movie about Peter Pan called *Hook*," I informed him, chuckling.

Will smiled at me, impressed that I had recognized the reference. Then we all took the plunge and ate our breakfasts with no shortage of sarcastic comments and comparisons.

After the meal we beelined it for the elevators to get to PT on time. The morning physical training sessions ran for two hours and consisted of an equal blend of aerobic fitness (high-grav runs could go to hell) and strength training. The fitness leader for our group was a Lumenarian named Tracker, who catered the training regimes to each person individually based on in-depth biological scans that would optimize our progress based on body type. Understanding that not everyone came from a military background, Tracker didn't conduct himself like a drill sergeant, but that didn't mean he let anyone off the hook. His firm command enforced the necessity of the training as not only a way to stave off the psychological effects of space travel but also to sharpen us into efficient weapons and maximize our energy potential, which was now tied to our tech capabilities. This truth alone was supposed to drive everyone to excel. I thought that was a strange approach, considering few who entered the service back home were soldiers to start; however, the fear of burning people out was a constant concern. I got the feeling that our hosts might be underestimating us or overestimating our fragility. That being said, no one fully knew how our minds and bodies would handle the stresses of a long-term interstellar journey.

The strength-training facility was almost comical as strong men and women strained under high-tech cylindrical "grav bars." Each metal rod fit in the hand like a normal dumbbell or barbell handle but didn't have any weights attached to the ends. Instead, several platforms and benches lined the room with touchpads that selected the various exercises. Once we made a choice, the energy field would activate, loading weight onto the units by gravitational magnetic sensors around the room. The result was fit men and women grunting under empty bars that looked like they should weigh about five pounds.

I labored under the two grav bars in my hands, pushing upward in an incline dumbbell press. Just as I felt like I was getting stuck at the bottom of my repetition, Will stepped in and spotted me. I got to the top of the repetition and released the bars, leaving them to levitate in midair. "Sorry, thought you might've been stuck," Will said.

"Thanks," I replied, a little irritated at the help. "Sensors in the suit and bars actually kick in restrictors when you reach your limit, though."

"Ah, right," he said. "Well, you have everything in hand then…literally." He turned to go back to his platform.

"Hey," I said, stopping him, "if *you* need a spot, just let me know." I flashed a pistol finger and then immediately regretted that decision. Nerd. Well, I guess we both had floundered. Will grinned and nodded, going back to his platform and beginning a new exercise.

I knew we had different reasons for being awkward around each other, despite an attraction I was fairly certain was reciprocal. By and large my life had been a tireless pursuit of my career. I had had the odd fling here and there when the situation arose and I had the time but nothing substantial for years. I'd mostly raised my brother until he could be self-sufficient, then I'd committed to the military for a term, and then school had me consistently on the move and with little room for much else. Any port in a storm sort of thing, and some ports were pretty fun. It was something that I had come to terms with and could find enjoyable some of the time, but strangely enough, now that we were aboard the *Albatross*, my life felt like it had a particular concrete certainty that was making room in me for something more.

Will, on the other hand, was an enigma. Since I had met him, he had seemed at times outwardly confident and flirtatious, punctuated by periods of quiet awkwardness or stoicism. It seemed something frequently drew him back into himself whenever he flew too close to the sun of happiness. A guilty hesitance that made me guess toward loss, but I didn't want to press the subject, and I didn't want to ask Frank behind his back. But something was there; I was sure of it. A lot could hide behind the eyes and a smile, but a lot could not.

After our workouts we had a quick break to use the coed showers adjacent to the fitness facility. In Lumenarian culture, the differences between the sexes were so minor physically and even less so with how they viewed each other societally that nudity wasn't an issue. The small allowances they made for privacy in certain places were just for us, but they couldn't change the entire ship for our comfort. For the most part men and women naturally segregated in the area, and the few creepy guys who tried to skirt the line for a peep were policed by Will, Frank, Miguel, and others in our group who weren't children.

I still got uncomfortable prickles on the back of my neck being naked in public, but I was more self-conscious of the smells and sticky sweat we all worked up during the exercise. Our schedules rarely allowed time to make it back to our housing units during the day, so it was either be uncomfortable all day or for a five-minute shower. The showers were also a good refresher for the next few hours of lectures we had to sit through. On the plus side, I got a few accidental glimpses of Will, and I was…impressed.

The *Albatross* had not been designed to be a flying school, but it had several immensely large ready rooms throughout the ship, places where crews would brief and debrief an action. Unlike the often cramped, low-ceilinged spaces on a naval carrier, the *Albatross's* ready rooms were amphitheater-style chambers that could hold a couple hundred people and doubled as classrooms for the purpose of our journey. Due to the quantity of human personnel on the ship, classes were meticulously scheduled, so everyone had time in all the fields required.

We had been on day-shift training for the last week and would be for another before switching to night shift, doing two-week rotations back and forth for the foreseeable future.

The Lumenarian instructor at the front of the room was a male named River who had been with us for the last several days, rotating in for his topic of expertise. In this case, alien flora and fauna that we'd be encountering on Lumen and the other colony planets to which our future campaigns might take us.

River paced around a large holographic image of a glowing yellow-and-red flower projected in perfect detail while I brought up the plant's description on my seat's personal display. The flower had broad leaves extending from a stocky, sinuous base that branched off into three to five main pedestals, each reaching above the waist. The petals were jagged, elongated spades about two to three feet long with golden hues streaked with bright-crimson veins. The stalk was a deep navy color with a texture like a frayed rope.

"Beautiful isn't it?" River said as he stared at the hologram. "Abundant on the city outskirts of the planet we call Ashwood, which you'll learn more about later due to its importance for the extraction and refinement of fostrogen. The star-flare flower, though pleasing to look at, is highly acidic and toxic unless harvested properly. Contact with the leaves disturbs spores that cause symptoms of vertigo and eventually paralysis. Direct contact with the flower's blood will also cause severe burns. Something to take note of should fighting ever occur in their proximity." He paced around, pointing at the various parts of the pretty but treacherous plant.

Obviously, the importance of learning about non-dangerous plants and animals was not a priority (unless for survival sustenance or medical properties), but the more we sat in those classes, the more we all realized how many things in these new worlds wanted to kill us, specifically as humans. It was critical knowledge but did little to allay the fears shared about the mission, though I guess that wasn't the point. The point was to be as prepared as possible for what was coming and to learn how each difficulty could be flipped into something useful. I pulsed a small amount of energy into my armrest, illuminating my seat's light to signify I had a question. Will had tried this on the first day of class and overloaded his chair, which he still got razzed about—and was why he still raised his hand and called out on the rare occasions he asked questions.

"In extreme cases, could the sun-flare's blood be used to cauterize wounds?" I asked. "Or would the caustic elements pose a greater risk of exacerbating the trauma?" Several people turned to stare at me.

River smiled at my question. "Very good, Ms. Li. Turning a disadvantage into an advantage, which is always the goal. The paralytic agents in the spores are not present in the blood, and though it would be immensely painful, the corrosive elements could work as a last-ditch effort to stem a bleed without poisonous side effects. Next we'll illustrate the safest technique for extracting the blood and utilizing its potential." I couldn't help but blush slightly at the praise and the uncomfortable stares in my direction—flashback from university.

Frank leaned over and gave me a wry smile. "Sure you were in the air force and not the marines?"

"Shut up, Frank," I replied with a grin.

The rest of the lesson covered another fifty or so different plants native to Ashwood before we were dismissed. River was one of those natural, passionate teachers who often needed to be reminded that class was over; otherwise he could have rattled off information for hours more. It was an unexpected trait judging from his appearance. Like many others in the Lumenarian crew, he bore scars of a war that had been fought since before our great-great-grandparents were born. He had two prominent battle scars; a black-grey, jagged line down his right forearm from the elbow to the hand and a faint emerald glow from the prosthetic that was his left leg. Regardless, his eyes shone with a passionate intensity for sharing knowledge. A true warrior scholar.

When he finally released us, we hoofed it to the mess between the ready room and our next assignment to load up on our grey sustenance bricks. The afternoon sessions were almost always more intensive and usually involved more hands-on training. That day was no exception.

Arriving at the sim field was always exciting and usually a bit nerve wracking. The several hours blocked out for the training there were never specified because they wanted us on our toes. It could be anything from hand-to-hand combat, obstacle courses, and weapons and equipment training, to squad drills or biotech manipulation. Technically, all our weapons integrated with our biological enhancements in some way, but biotech manipulation was teaching us amazing new ways to control and build the energy in our bodies that could be harnessed through our implants. One class was just about breathing. The operational complexity revolved around multi-tasking; teaching ourselves to focus on precise applications and locations of where we distributed our energy while also taking in what was happening around us. Any slip of concentration could result in striking with an uncharged hand or, when it came to weapons, not being able to shoot and move at the same time. We were all essentially learning to pat our heads and rub our bellies at the same time. We wouldn't get to use live-fire weapons for a while, but the promise of it kept us excited—some more than others.

During actual deployments, the sim field would be used primarily to run glass-house scenarios for special operations and to keep recurrent field drills fresh. Glass-house scenarios were practiced on Earth as a way for teams to rehearse breaching and clearing buildings—skeletal re-creations of architectural drawings and intel. Such exercises on the *Albatross* were no different, except the room used advanced nanotechnology (trillions of particles) to recreate environments down to minute details. A slight step up from scabbed-together two-by-fours and rough-cut plywood used back home. And it wasn't just a light show; we could fully interact with whatever setting was programmed with near-perfect physics.

On that day the room was a giant black shell (setting not yet programmed), dimly lit with hovering orbs of light that gave the strange appearance of an abandoned warehouse. I glanced around the room, caught off guard by the emptiness of it. The setting always had some purpose, sometimes even if only to be dramatic, but I was anxious to discover what was going on. We all huddled together in groups under the lights and chatted, waiting for Flak to enter and initiate the lesson.

Flak was the *Albatross's* quartermaster and a soldier through and through. He was an imposing figure, larger than average, and his pale, soot-colored skin was streaked with dark scars, like an old birch tree with sap-sealed wounds. One eye was synthetic and glowed with a dim green glare, and two of his fingers on his left hand were mechanical silver prosthetics, the cybernetic add-ons as good or better than the real thing, apparently. He also wasn't the kind of instructor who yelled directions with his hands on his hips but instead demonstrated everything himself with violent precision and force, usually leaving several mouths hanging open in awe (impressive for someone who was around 220 years old). When we first met him, he detailed his extensive combat resume, which involved almost a hundred years of war and several years as a leading member of LUMSET (Lumen Special Equipment and Tactics), the cream of the crop in the Lumenarian military. They made navy SEALs look like untrained puppies, or so he boasted.

We all turned to the sound of the chamber doors opening. Flak marched in, surprisingly with Arthur in tow. We all murmured amongst ourselves as we watched the pair take their place in the middle of the room.

Arthur moved gracefully, his hands folded behind his back, shielded from my view in an at-ease posture, but I knew one of his hands was a half-cybernetic prosthetic like Flak's, a shiny reminder of a battle long ago. He always seemed to keep his head somewhat tilted down and to the side, like every glance was to study us and keep himself secret. His eyes reinforced the feeling as they stared out, blinking in slow, measured beats between readings. His skin was a dark walnut that seemed even darker next to Flak's paler tones. One noticeable effect of his darker skin was the camouflage it provided for his battle scars. Only upon close inspection could I make out the shiny gloss of their trails on his body—burns running down his neck and disappearing beneath his bodysuit.

"Can it, humes," Flak growled. "Humes" was a term that some of the Lumenarians had been using throughout the ship. It wasn't directly offensive, but we all had the feeling that at times it was uttered as something meaning "less than." On the other side, we had already come up with a plethora of nicknames for our hosts as well. "Lizzies," in reference to their reptilian characteristics, was the dominant one circling around.

"Flak," Arthur said in a calm reprimanding tone. His voice was deep and unwavering and carried a quiet power.

Flak bowed his head. "Sorry, Arthur." Everyone was taken aback to hear Flak apologize. "As you all know, this is Arthur, commander of the *Albatross*. Today he'll be sitting in on the beginning of the lesson." He looked somewhat annoyed that his plan for the day had been disrupted.

"Thank you, Flak. The main reason I am here today is to properly introduce you to the Forsaken." Arthur and Flak seemed somewhat rattled even speaking the name, but they hid it well—only small tics any time the word was spoken, like whenever someone on Earth talked about Nazis. Arthur continued in a steady, deliberate pace that seemed to be trying to soften the blow. "You all should have been briefed during the information sessions on Earth about the history of our war and the enemy we face. But today we are going to show you a more detailed rendering of them. It is important that you fully understand what we are up against and how to exploit their weaknesses." Everyone listened intently, not wanting to miss a word, apprehensive about the coming revelations. To the side of me I overheard Travis and his friend Tariq chatting.

"Oh yeah, they gonna give all the details now we locked inna the journey and can't go back—"

"What was that, recruit?" Flak snapped from the center of the room. Travis flinched and glanced around the room, then lowered his eyes. "Didn't catch what you said," Flak prodded again, not letting up.

"Sir, it just…Shouldn't e'ery detail have been made available ta us 'fore we left Earth? Now you tellin' us these Forsaken are worse than we already believed. Seems kinda fubar, sir," Travis said in his thick southern lilt. There was a stunned awkward silence in the room, all of us surprised he would challenge Flak and Arthur so openly. Flak glared at Travis, but just as he was about to speak, Arthur silenced him with a wave.

"You are right," Arthur said. "The truth is, what we know of our enemy is devastatingly incomplete. In the one hundred and fifty years of our conflict, not one has been captured. None of our considerable scanning capabilities has been able to penetrate their armor or their ships. An enzyme in their suits releases upon their deaths and destroys any organic material within. They are enigmas. Shadows. We gave you enough information to know it was incredibly dangerous, just not the complete specifics of that danger." We all shifted uneasily upon hearing this. No one knew how to respond. "I am sorry if you feel deceived," Arthur said with a solemn bow. As I looked at him, I didn't see cold manipulation. I saw someone who carried every painful memory and every weight of guilt upon his shoulders, the sin eater for his entire species.

"Yeah, well—"

"Doesn't change anything," someone behind me said cutting off Travis. I turned to see Will standing with his arms crossed. "We all knew the risks. We all knew our allies were far more advanced and losing a war, but we all decided to say fuck it and join anyway. If you thought we were gonna be given magic weapons and this was gonna be easy, you're an idiot. Excuse me, sir."

Arthur nodded to him, allowing his interjection and seemingly curious about the man himself. I stared at Will, unsure whether his stoic glare came from courage or a darker place that spoke of reckless abandon and self-destruction. A fire that said, If I'm going down, I'm taking every son of a bitch with me I can. It was the first time I'd ever seen him switch so absolutely into a soldier. Arthur saw it too and barely covered what I thought was the corner of a smile.

"What are their weaknesses, and how do we exploit them?" Will asked.

Arthur nodded to Flak, who brought up his forearm display, tapping on the feed. They stepped back slightly to allow the simulation to fill the center of the room. As they did, one of the Forsaken appeared in the middle of our group. Several people gasped, and more than a few stepped back instinctively.

The enemy soldier heaved with simulated breath as it floated in the air before us, rotating so everyone could get a good look. They were large, brutish forms that rose taller than the average Lumenarian by six inches to a foot and were significantly bulkier. As far as I could tell, they didn't just wear armor. It was a head-to-toe mechanical suit with thick, jet-black plating and glowing red lines streaking down its sides and over its shoulders. Like both species aboard the *Albatross*, they were bipedal, had two arms, and a head. Whether that directly corresponded to their biological components inside, I didn't know, but that was the form of their exo-build. The helmet was squarish, narrowing toward the front, with three crimson dots shining out of a triangular visor. They were broadest in the back where the suit jutted out around a built-in rectangular box. Maybe an air supply or a power unit? The forearms were bulky with razor-like runs along the outside edge up to the elbow. Above the wrists were glowing energy ports that extended out from the fist, presumably some sort of built-in cannon.

"As you can see, they're like one of your tanks," Flak noted as he paced around the figure. "Heavily armored and powerfully weaponized, but unlike a tank, surprising agile. Over the coming months, you'll learn every tactic in the book to take these bastards down and keep moving to the next." Flak nodded to Arthur, who stepped forward.

"This enemy is like nothing our system has ever seen," Arthur said. "I know it is an astronomical thing we have asked of you, but we are counting on you to help us turn the tide in this conflict. I truly believe in your potential." Arthur glanced between us all but lingered on Will, who gave a nearly imperceptible nod.

It wasn't just our small group of friends who knew Will was special. Word had obviously reached the upper echelons of the Lumenarian leadership. The short speech was probably something Arthur had had to pitch to every group before us and every group that would follow, but looking around, it didn't matter. The simple words of hope and trust caused nearly everyone in the audience to swell slightly as they took them in. Each day closer to Lumen meant another day closer to death, but the more we gave ourselves over to the cause and the training, the better chance we had to delay the end. It was all still quite vague, but I suppose we had lots of time to fill in the gaps. For the moment, hope would do.

"I will leave you in Flak's capable hands to continue your session." With that Arthur nodded and walked through the parting crowd to exit the room.

When he was gone, Flak turned back to us. "OK, humes, sideshow's over. Everyone pair up for hand-to-hand combat training."

Training in hand-to-hand combat on the *Albatross* was like doing a combination of Wing Chun, street fighting, and Krav Maga while on some sort of energizing narcotic. It was a culmination of forms from Earth and Lumen to create what was determined to be maximized lethality and energy conservation. If we had one physical advantage on the Lumenarians it was that all of our force could be easily directed forward from all of our limbs. Our comrades' inverted legs meant kicking was almost solely a backwards action, like horses, hence our techniques were slightly different. The systems we learned were fast, fluid, and violent, meant to neutralize our opponents with brutal efficiency. To add to that, each blow was accentuated by the biotech that ran through our bodies. Each contact was a concussive burst of energy that could rattle even the most solid training partners (I was curious whether any of it would be useful against the Forsaken, though). I often paired up with Megan or Miguel during these sessions because they were close to my level but still challenged me, trading advantages each day.

It was hard for people not to pause occasionally and watch Will, something I was guilty of from time to time (for a few reasons). Frank was one of the only people who would willingly partner with him because of Will's skill and power. Occasionally, Travis would tag in to compete, but I think Frank knew that Will would always pull punches with him a little bit and that Will might accidently hurt Travis. So, he tried to lock Will down quickly at the beginning of sessions, unless Flak stepped in to re-pair the matches. However, even he saw that Frank was one of the only people who could actually get inside Will's defenses from time to time. Two titans, forged over years of conflict learning the ins and outs of each other's forms, had been given impressive new abilities.

The electric-blue blasts of each combatant hitting his mark flashed in our eyes during the fights. Will was completely at ease in this world—a world of war. He took the training seriously for the most part, but it also seemed like he was playing. The ease with which the old muscle memory returned was clear in every graceful slip and jab while he and Frank flashed cocky smirks at each other whenever a new tactic landed or was parried. What made Will tough to spar against was his style. He floated between the instructed forms and a brawler fluidity, improvising as easily as breathing.

I ducked just in time to avoid a haymaker from Megan and shoved her back to create some space. "Oooh, thought I was gonna get you on that one," Megan goaded as she bounced around me in a boxer's stance. I put my hands back up, ready to go again. "What were you staring at, Sare?" she asked with a knowing smile.

I shot left and low, swinging in with a hook to Megan's side that crumpled her. Switching high, she parried my headshot and counter jabbed, forcing my other hand to deflect the strike. She chased a flurry of jabs and crosses to keep the pressure up, which I blocked and barely avoided. On the last cross, I trapped her arm over my shoulder and fed her ribs with two hard punches. Megan ripped her arm back and threw a wild cross with the other. I dropped beneath it and weaved in a solid palm to her chest, the cobalt impact sending her onto her back. Megan rolled around on the floor, reeling from the blow as I stood up straight and caught my breath.

"I don't know what you're talking about," I said as I lowered my hand to help her up.

She took the offer and rose to her feet, rubbing her chest. She glared at me for a moment but then broke into laughter. "Damn, girl. You hit like a fucking mule." Still recovering, she chuckled.

Then there was a flash and a whoosh of air, like standing too close to a campfire being lit with gasoline. Frank launched past us, landing on his side and grunting in pain. He must've flown about ten feet before touching down on the floor.

Will rushed over to him. "Shit, man, I am so sorry!" He crouched next to Frank and tried to help him up. Frank batted away his offer of assistance and hobbled to his feet. "Frank, I didn't mean to. I just don't know my own—"

"You're an asshole, Will," Frank growled. They stood there awkwardly for a moment, several onlookers watching them. Finally, Frank shook his head, unable to hold back a grin. "I'm gonna make you pay for that one."

"Oh yeah? Let's see it, old man." Will danced backwards, bobbing on his feet and shadow boxing some playful jabs. Frank lunged, and they wrestled like brothers while everyone else returned to their matches.

"Reach! Farr! Quit flopping around and fight!" Flak yelled.

"Why do you think Will is so powerful?" Megan asked as we stepped to the side and drank some water, watching the bouts around us. I stared for several moments as Will and Frank flowed smoothly around each other, Will's tattoos glowing a faint sapphire color. I thought about the confused look on Sky's face after integration and about the look Arthur had given him—that momentary stare of fascination. I didn't know if it was curiosity or a clue that he had some idea what was special about Will.

"I honestly have no idea," I said. It was such a significant variance from the rest of us that it couldn't be something obvious like increased metabolism or neural activity. It had to be some overlooked genetic mutation or something. A trait so benign and unassuming that it escaped even our hosts but made all the difference.

Megan took another sloppy gulp of water from her canteen and wiped her mouth. "Anyway, pretty hot, right? Well, if I was into dudes," she said with a wink and smile, jostling me. I smiled shyly and glanced up at Will, who dropped Frank to the ground in a controlled roll. He looked up at me, breathing hard. The whites of his eyes flashed blue lightning like the arc of electricity between two wires.

"Li! Daniels! Get off your asses!" Flak barked.

CHAPTER IX

White Bird And Rock Bottom

Over the last couple of months, Will and I had fallen into a routine of meeting early for breakfast almost every day. In the extra fifteen to thirty minutes we shared before the others joined us, we talked about everything. Or at least *I* talked. Will listened intently and asked questions, and though he made jokes, told stories, and relived old memories, he rarely shared anything too deep, always deflecting from that dark something. I had gleaned from bits of conversation between Frank and Will that the connection was between them—a history shared, perhaps even the reason they were now like family—but for some reason, he couldn't say it out loud, couldn't give it a voice, at least not to me yet.

"I can't believe you don't like 'Jellians.' It's the perfect name. They look exactly like giant jellyfish on stilts," Will said. He was referring to alien race number four that we'd been learning about. Despite the fact that they did, in fact, look like large semi-translucent jellyfish sitting upon mechanical quadrupedal legs (apparently relying on evolution out of water wasn't fast enough for them), the recently voted and accepted name constantly brought an old shoe-insole advertising jingle to mind for me. Besides it wasn't very etymologically scientific.

Interstellar culture classes had been introducing us to the four other races that frequented Lumenarian space almost solely for trade, and we were finally nominating and permanently deciding upon names for them in the language banks. Unfortunately for our current alien shipmates, each of the other races were pacifists and not biologically capable of fighting. That had been great for Lumen in the pre-war days in terms of technological and resource commerce but was not so beneficial when the need arose for soldiers on the ground. In fact, their peacefulness was why the Lumenarians had brought them (and several other races) into the fold millennia ago and avoided races like humans. But now, out of necessity, their views had shifted. I guess we were strangely fortunate in that sense.

"It's a name that's being decided for all humanity to recognize—wait… how…stop changing the subject!" I said.

"I don't know what you're talking about."

"What's he like?"

"Who?"

"Don't give me that. You know who. Everyone knows you're meeting with him weekly now."

"Jealous?" Will flashed a sly smile.

"No." I shrugged. "I mean, maybe a little."

"Well, Arthur is a bit of a mystery," he said. I couldn't contain a small scoff and an eye raise. Pot calling the kettle black. Will's face twitched slightly, but he held the smile. "*Very* smart. Maybe even smarter than you. *Maybe*," he said with a wink.

"Well, he is from an advanced alien race. Kind of cheating."

"True. I don't know. Can't figure out exactly what he wants yet. Whether it's just an academic curiosity or something else. Grooming maybe. He's quiet and controlled. Compassionate…" Will drifted off for a moment. "Packs a hell of a punch though."

"You're sparring with him?"

"Among other things. He's helping me to try and control this," Will said, his biotech lines flaring up in a glowing blue.

"Is it working? How's he helping?" I asked. I saw Will's tongue play with the tip of his right canine tooth. Something I'd observed him do frequently when he was considering things.

"So, you wouldn't have joined if Mike hadn't guilted you into it?" Will asked, taking a sip from his coffee and roughly segueing. There was no point chasing a conversation he didn't want to have. He'd just stubbornly retreat more and make sarcastic jokes. I puffed my cheeks out and exhaled, rolling my eyes. It was maybe a little passive-aggressive, but I figured it might program a Pavlovian conditioning into him to stop switching so easily out of uncomfortable topics. I, and others, would only accept deflection for so long.

"No, no. Mikey was just the tipping point. I was torn between the two options. If anything, he was the excuse that freed up my conscience," I said.

"Well, at least you can blame him if things go sideways."

"I would never do that."

"I meant just to fuck with him, obviously. I'm definitely doing that to Frank if shit hits the fan. 'I can't believe you dragged me into this!'"

"Oh, you're an asshole," I said as we both chuckled.

"Meh. He knows I'm a big boy." Will shrugged with a grin and took another sip of coffee. This time I could smell the alcohol waft out of his cup. I was sure he couldn't have any left from Earth, unless he had smuggled way more than I thought, so I wondered where he got it. I had heard rumors that some other humans had found a way to ferment the foodstuffs into a type of beer. I guess it wasn't too much of a stretch to believe distillation had followed. Intergalactic moonshiners. I imagined it would be extremely harsh, though. It wasn't like there was an abundance of oak barrels around. We sat in silence for a few moments, eating.

"So, did Frank guilt you into the marines too?" I asked.

"No. We actually met in basic."

"Love at first sight?"

Will laughed. "Hated each other, actually."

"No way."

"Way. He hadn't figured out yet that I was the better soldier."

"Ah. So, you were both *those guys*."

"What do you mean *those guys*?" he asked, still smiling and holding his intense blue stare.

"Every training group had them. The cocky ones who figured the only real competition for squad leader was between them. Even if there were a dozen other good candidates, some just locked on to each other," I said, returning his sly grin. "Stubborn bastards."

"I am not stubborn," he said, feigning indignation. "So, who was your Frank?"

"Oh, I didn't have a Frank. I rose above it all."

"Mhmm..." He smiled and took another drink from his boozy coffee, then glanced around the mess.

"Hey, how come Frank's sister didn't join?"

"What?" Will's eyes snapped back to me, the whites flickering blue. The air suddenly had a tense crackle between us.

I stuttered for a moment, realizing immediately that it might have been a bad topic to broach. "I...I was just wondering what the story with Frank's sister was. I heard him mention her a while back. Wasn't sure if they had a falling out or something."

"No."

"Were they just not close—"

"She's dead."

An icy pit formed in my stomach. Will looked like a man about to explode. I saw him struggling to control it all. His mouth twitched between pursed lips in a half smile and bared teeth, like he was struggling to shake it off but couldn't. The tattoos on his body glowed their deep electric cobalt. I wanted to reach out and touch his arm but thought better of it.

"Will, I'm sor—"

Just then Frank appeared at the table with his tray of food. "Hey, what's going on?" he asked, glancing between Will and me, then settling on Will. "Will, you OK?"

Avoiding eye contact, Will rose from his seat. "Yeah. I'll see you guys later."

"Will, wait. What—" Frank cut himself off as Will marched out of the mess hall. He turned back to me, dropping his tray on the table and leaning forward on his hands. "What the hell was that about?" I was hesitant to bring up the conversation, and he saw it. "Sarah, spill it."

"I just...I asked him about your sister."

Frank's expression softened, and he sank into his seat. "Ah..." He put his elbows on the table and leaned his chin on his hands.

"I'm so sorry, Frank. I had no idea."

"Well, Sarah, I think you're smarter than that," he said, locking eyes with me.

"Excuse me?"

"I think you had an idea. You might have misjudged how deep the wound was, but you knew one was there." I went to argue, but Frank raised his hands to quiet me. "It's OK. I get it. You want to get to know Will better, and you knew something was off."

I broke eye contact and stared down at the table, ashamed that Frank had seen through my prying. "I'm sorry."

Frank stared at me for a long moment. "How much did Will tell you?"

"Nothing. He just said she had passed away. Then he shut down."

"Yeah, he'll do that." Frank glanced around the mess hall. He seemed to be trying to decide how much to tell me. "My sister's name was Maria." He looked much older and more tired suddenly, like this information was a secret he'd been carrying for years. "And her and Will's daughter's name was Evelyn." Frank smiled, a sad expression that faded painfully in his eyes.

Shit. "Why'd you tell me?" I asked.

Frank shrugged. "It's hard to talk about, but it's also nice to remember them out loud. And honestly, Will may never talk to you about it. Hell, he doesn't talk to me about it," he said, stoically maintaining eye contact.

Just then Megan, Seyyal, Miguel, Jiro, and Mikey pulled up to the table. Great timing. "What's going on, guys? Looks like some heavy shit," Miguel said, eyeing us up.

Frank broke from me and smiled at the others. "Staring contest." They all smirked at us, knowing that was bullshit, but they didn't press it and took their seats. I wasn't hungry anymore, but everyone else dug in, either having mustered the control to visualize something else or having passed the point of caring. I stole a glance at Frank, who nodded silently.

"Hey, you guys hear about this new hooch the guys in Delta housing have been making?" Megan asked. "They're calling it 'White Bird.' Like White Dog but bird because of the *Albatross*. Moonshine, baby!"

I glanced around the ready room looking for Will. Seats weren't assigned, but our small tight-knit group generally sat together, and he was missing. He had already skipped the morning PT, which was unusual as well. I turned to Seyyal. "Hey, have you seen Will?" I whispered.

She popped her head up and glanced around, reaffirming his absence. "I haven't seen him. Maybe he's just running late or isn't well."

"Whoa. We can take sick days?" Miguel asked, chuckling. No one ever got sick on the ships thanks to multi-spectrum immunizations and the nanites that coursed through our blood. "I'm sure he's fine. Probably just needed to see a man about a dog," he added with a wink.

Just then Dane walked in and headed to the front of the chamber. I took one last look around and then turned my focus to him. Dane was our Lumenarian teacher responsible for basic flight theory instruction—something that would be followed up with more practical training later in the shuttle bays and eventually in the space above Lumen if we had time before being deployed.

The class was incredibly interesting and directly in what my field would have been had I remained on Earth, but my worry about Will was distracting. He hadn't turned up, and I couldn't help but feel it was my fault. I was eager to get out and ask around.

After class I took Frank aside and brought it up with him. He assured me that Will did this from time to time back home and that there wasn't much cause for worry; he just needed space. He did agree to help me look for him if he didn't turn up for Flak's session though. I was reluctant to wait but also trusted that Frank knew Will much better than I did.

In the most recent sessions, Flak had been accelerating our hand-to-hand training to include team fighting, solo combat against multiple opponents, and work with dummy drill weapons. He had also lowered the levels on inertial dampening fields around the sim field that prevented impacts from becoming too severe. They created a sort of invisible energy pillow against the walls and floor that softened major blows and falls, as if the air within the ship was a non-Newtonian fluid with an adjustable shear rate rather than a gas. With the fields minimized, we felt every hard tumble. There was still no sign of Will as we paired up and then matched with a group of others to test our new skills.

"Alright, humes, get in your groups, and get to it. I want to see some violence," Flak ordered.

Miguel and I squared up against three others, two men and a woman who were near our skill level named Cory, Dave, and Janet. Miguel and I stood back to back as the others assumed their ready stances around us. Miguel and I primed the tech in our hands, ready for the fight. However, just as we were about to lunge in, Will stumbled into the room, causing a commotion. He had obviously been drinking and was swaying from side to side. Flak was on the other side of the room instructing, but I saw him glance across, curious about the scene.

"Whoa, shit. Sorry," Will blurted as he bumped into Travis.

Travis turned and steadied Will, looking him over. "Dude, you fuckin' drunk?" he asked as Will tried to regain his balance. Frank rushed over to help Will, taking him by the arm.

Will pulled away. "I'm fine. I'm fine, Frank! Fuck off!" He held his hands up to maintain the space.

Frank stayed close but eased off. "Will—"

"And you, I find that offensive," Will said, pointing at Travis.

"You find wha' offensive? You tha fuckin' alcoholic. Get your shit together, Willy," Travis said, poking Will in the chest. Will went surprisingly still and glared at Travis, the whites of his eyes flickering blue.

Travis pursed his lips slightly, worried. Will held the fierce eye contact without flinching.

Suddenly, he burst into laughter and patted Travis on the shoulder. "'Get your shit together,'" Will mimicked in a southern accent while wagging a finger. "And don't fucking call me Willy," he said going dead serious, glaring for a moment, and then cracking up again. Frank came in and put his arm around Will's shoulders, ushering him toward the door.

Travis looked relieved that there wasn't going to be a fight, but he still felt the need to mutter the last word. "Yeah, sleep it off, asshole."

Will froze in his tracks, sturdy and unmoving against Frank. He shook off Frank's arm and stepped around him. When Frank tried to insist, Will gave him a blow to the stomach that hunched Frank over, sucking air. Miguel and I rushed over to help Frank up, and Will stepped past us like he barely noticed. The dark side of Will's drunkenness was in full swing. At that point most of the groups had stopped sparring and were staring instead.

"Grab your partner, Travvy. Hell, grab two. Fuck it, make it three. I'll take this whole goddamn room," Will said as he strode over to him.

"Lis'en Will, just take 'er easy," Travis said, trying to reason with him, even though he was quite a bit bigger than Will. Tariq and Karen stepped up behind Travis, flanking him. I guessed a third person couldn't be found who wanted to test Will's anger.

Will raised his arms, gesturing to them. "See? Now we got a party. You're probably gonna want to start by circling me. Hit all the angles, ya know?" he said with a malicious leer. Tariq and Karen took a few steps out to the side, and Will stomped his foot in a fake rush forward. They both flinched and stopped their progress. Will's smile didn't waver.

At that point Flak took full notice of the conflict and walked over. At first it looked like he might intervene, but I think his curiosity got the better of him, and he stood back a ways to observe. Travis didn't look very confident, but at least he had backup.

"Waiting on you, *Tiny*," Will said with a nod and a slight stagger.

Travis lunged. The fight was brutal and quick. Will sidestepped the first swing with ease and floored Travis with one energy-laced punch. The moment Travis made his move, Karen and Tariq zigged and zagged to the sides to time their attack. Will rolled forward to avoid a haymaker from Tariq while getting to his feet and dodging a front kick from Karen. The next strike just missed his face as he locked the arm and gave two quick jabs to Tariq's middle. Karen lunged in to try and divert Will's attention but only managed to land a glancing straight across his cheek. The return side kick from Will sent her back several feet in a rolling tumble. With only Tariq left, Will fed him two more rapid jabs before leveling him with a devastating hook. Tariq made a loud WHOOMPF as he hit the floor. While this quick exchange was going on, every line on Will's body was glowing a brighter and brighter blue, electricity arcing between the synapse points.

Having partially recovered, Frank circled around during the fray to find a gap to step in and break it up. As Will hovered over his victims, panting through clenched teeth, Frank jumped in and grabbed him from behind. "Will—"

Will tightened up and then, without warning, a shockwave emitted from his body that made everyone take a half step back and caused Frank to release his grip. In the split second the hold was broken, Will spun and drove his fist into Frank's chest with a sickening CRACK. Frank soared across the room toward the wall just as Flak stepped in and tapped his forearm display, re-engaging the dampeners. Frank slowed just before making contact and gently lowered to the ground, but he was in serious pain. He clutched his chest, his face twisted in agony, most likely with several broken ribs. Everyone stared between Frank, the three writhing trainees on the floor, and Will. Miguel, Megan, Seyyal, and I rushed over to Frank while Flak stepped between.

"What the fuck, Will?" I said as I marched past, forgetting any sense of pity I had felt for him earlier. I saw the rage in his eyes dissipate immediately as the blue energy ebbed away. He looked lost. I was furious with what he had done, but the fear I saw in his eyes chipped away at my anger.

He stepped toward us, several onlookers shying away. "Frank, I—" he stopped. He seemed to be losing control of his emotions and was fighting desperately to keep them in.

"Reach, that's enough for you today. Go back to rack," Flak said. Will didn't try to argue. He took one last glance at Frank and at us, trying to apologize with his eyes, then turned and hurried out of the chamber, slanting slightly. Everyone watched as he went. I saw Flak stare after him, the soldier in him impressed, the teacher worried he had let things go too far. Frank wheezed as we lifted him to his feet and supported him. "Li, Reyes, get him to Medical, and get him checked out," Flak said. We nodded and hobbled Frank out of the sim field. Flak clapped his hands. "Back to it, humes. Until you can do that, nobody gets a day off!" he said as he paced the room again.

"Will didn't mean to," Frank muttered through labored breaths as we were leaving.

"It's no excuse," I said. "He could've killed you."

"But he didn't, and I'll smack him for this later. But there's only one thing that sets him off like this, Sarah," he said, wincing and glancing sideways at me.

"Travis?" Miguel asked with a sarcastic grin.

I don't think Frank blamed me for Will's outburst, but he did want me to understand—to remind me Will was human. Everyone has their own personal kryptonite or Achilles heel. Will was no different. I was still pissed as we walked Frank out, but the small truths and moments of pause worked their way through my head.

After we dropped Frank off at the medical bay, Miguel and I wandered back to the aviary. We were quiet for a long time before Miguel broke in. "That was insane," he said, staring off and remembering the fight.

"Yeah."

"Did you get the feeling that Will was barely breaking a sweat?" he asked, glancing at me. He looked somewhere between astounded and afraid. I had thought the same thing. Even while drunk Will had made the fight look like a mild inconvenience for him. A quick, easy way to vent some anger through his alcohol-induced haze.

"Yeah, I got that feeling."

"Fucking glad he's on our team."

Miguel and I wandered back to the housing complex and parted ways. He had been seeing a woman in Bravo complex who had an alternate schedule from ours and mentioned that he was going to make his way over there.

Twenty-four-seven confinement with the same people had the effect of evoking either hate or love, but I liked to think more often we leaned toward love. We saw people when they were at their best and their worst, their most tired, depressed, anxious, heartbroken, afraid, excited… drunk. There was no hiding in the hallways and training rooms of the *Albatross*. The closeness forced us to "hold a mirror up to nature" and observe the roots behind a flash of anger and the falter in a smile. It was hard to judge or dislike even our most irritating neighbors for too long, each recognizing the common sacrifices and fears. The sheer volume of information and training meant we were too tired to be stubborn in that regard.

I knew I was being stubborn holding onto my anger with Will, and I knew it was because he had made me feel guilty more than anything, but I continued to stew throughout the afternoon. With the free time I decided to distract myself and read up on some advanced engineering specs that one of our other Lumenarian teachers, Thatch, had passed on to me; the dizzying science behind the mercurial water shield that surrounded the shuttles and the *Albatross* itself.

I stretched out on the lawn of the atrium, feeling the soft grass beneath me and soaking up the artificial sunshine that shone down in the late-afternoon hours of the simulated day. The park was grounding. It smelled like home, and everything that grew there was real. It was supported by the *Albatross's* horticultural bots and gadgets but was nonetheless a part of Earth in the void of space. I took a minute to close my eyes and forget the metal walls surrounding me, taking deep, slow breaths.

It worked for a few moments until a drone zipped past to conduct a mundane task. The drones were mostly silent save for a faint hum and vibration that faded into white noise during the general busy, ambient sounds of life aboard the ship, but the aviary was comparatively quiet just then because most people were still out on training or sleeping.

I pulled out the holo tablet I'd brought down from my room, unfolded the flexible nano-glass, and thumbed through the supplied material. Technically, all this information was available at any point, but few swam in the engineering depths I did, so Thatch had highlighted some good reads.

"Codec?" I asked the air. The AI materialized next to me.

"Hi, Sarah. What can I help with?"

"Hey, Codec, I'm just curious about the hydro shield." I flipped through the notes. I was sure the answer was somewhere there, but I was feeling a bit lazy and distracted with everything going on. "I can see it uses a water and fostrogen solution—fostrogen is a new one, by the way—to make the actual shield. Then it diamagnetically repels to create the gap between the hull and its surface, but what stops the… bubble from floating off into space? I can't account for what holds it around the ship and prevents it from freezing or boiling off."

Codec simulated an impressed response—something I was pretty sure was a bit of programming to make people feel more confident asking the seemingly omnipotent AI questions, though it often came off as patronizing. "The answer comes from a combination of fostrogen itself and infused femto particles." Codec waved his hand, and a holographic diagram of the shield appeared. It zoomed in to a molecular level showing the interaction of the various substances. Femto particles were several times smaller than the nanoparticles used in the sim fields and required manipulation on the nuclear level (only hypothetical applications on Earth). "Fostrogen is ferromagnetic and binds with the water molecules. That, combined with the immense amounts of radiation the embedded femto-particles absorb, creates a stable field of opposing forces. The magnetic fields push away from the hull, but the particle bombardment and artificial gravity from the ship hold it close. Though the *Albatross* can send signals boosting the energy potential, the shield is self-sufficient for a time, powered by the background cosmic radiation. This reaction also causes the particles to vibrate at a harmonic frequency that resists the pressure and temperature absences of space."

"Almost like creating its own atmosphere," I said.

"Good way to put it! Physical projectiles or debris vaporize on the highly energized and radioactive surface while energy weapons will eventually overcharge the system, allowing the H_2O to gradually evaporate."

"If the particles create a harmonic frequency, couldn't it be interrupted or even negated with another frequency?" I asked, fascinated but naturally playing the devil's advocate.

"Good question. Frequency manipulation is actually what lets our shuttles pass through to dock with or exit the ship," Codec added cheerfully.

"But couldn't someone else hypothetically hack the signal and shut it down?"

"Impossible. The signal doesn't emit past the threshold, and the particle frequency operates in a state of quantum flux that's like a fingerprint originating from inside and unique to the *Albatross* and other Union vessels. Only ships with the *Albatross's* signature can pass through the shield. Any others need a physical opening in the 'bubble,' as you put it. Do you need anything else, Sarah?"

I tried to think of any other possible vulnerabilities, but nothing came to mind. "No, I think I'm good, Codec. Thanks. Just going to read up on it a bit more myself." The hologram gave a quick salute and then vanished.

Everything about space was natural, and yet nothing was, from the perspective of living there. These little marbles of life scattered across the cosmos surrounded by empty, black death. In our arrogance we strove to link the marbles together with ferryboats of metal and magic. Humans had only ever observed exposed water in space as a conflicting battle between boiling and freezing, the drop in pressure causing the molecules to shift rapidly into their gaseous state while then freeing up the surface area of said molecules to rapid cooling within the mean space temperature of 2.7 Kelvin. The Lumenarians had completely ignored what we thought to be an irrefutable truth and achieved a bit of technology that not only safeguarded their interstellar vessels from random passing debris but also made it a nearly impenetrable fortress in battle, or so we were told.

As I spent the next several hours poring over the science and equations in the complex field, I started to drift off. When I caught my head bobbing, I decided to make my way up to the mess hall. Everyone else would have finished the afternoon training and would be making their way there shortly, if not there already.

When I got to the entrance of the dining room, I looked around trying to find my brother and friends. Spotting them, I made my way over before stopping suddenly. Mikey was laughing and gesturing animatedly to Seyyal, Megan, and Jiro. I couldn't hear them, but I knew Mikey was replaying the action with Will. He mimed the haymakers and jabs and made an energy blast sound effect, really trying to sell the impacts. I wanted to go over and tell him to smarten up and take it seriously, to stop acting like a child. It might have been an impressive show of power, but it was a humiliating loss of control—not something to idolize. But then the impulse passed, and I was left with the tired feeling of my original guilt and anger. I had had a few hours of peace from the feelings and didn't want to dive back in just yet. Rather than joining the others for dinner, I snuck a quick snack by myself from another mess a few levels down.

After my meal I went for a run to clear my head and to avoid the group as much as possible. There was a meditative quality to the conversation in my mind when doing something I hated. I wasn't one of those people who enjoyed running; I did it for the fitness and the solitude. The conversation upstairs went back and forth like a tennis match between a voice that represented how my body felt and another voice that told me to stop being weak. Either way, it helped keep my mind off Will and the drama of the day. I also loved the ship. Feeling the pulse in its walls and exploring its corridors and seeing the wonders behind the many doors was meditative on its own. If I wasn't running, I was wandering after hours to take it all in.

The opal and brushed-metal panels whipped past as I ran down one of the many starboard corridors on the *Albatross*, my feet smacking the firm, basalt-like floor tiles. I felt my suit flexing with my body and radiating a faint cooling sensation like a freon breeze from an open freezer to help control my temperature. I passed a few ready rooms, the doors to the agricultural algae processors, a water-treatment junction, and a med bay. I thought about poking my head in to check on Frank but decided against it in case he was sleeping or wanted an extended talk. I ran past groups of people heading back to their beds and other groups just getting up for the night shift of training. Everyone seemed tired, either by the break of sleep or the day's demands, and nobody paid me much notice.

Then, as if it was orchestrated, the halls cleared—the purgatorial period between coming and going. I entered a peaceful dead zone of activity where my footsteps echoed strangely in the halls. The lights of the hallway illuminated around me but darkened in my wake.

I rounded a corner that led to a straight stretch of hall between the level-five armory and starboard-reactor engineering access. A gap of darkness lay between my lit section and one at the far end of the passage. As the lights faded on around me and I got closer to the distant glow, I saw someone slouched against the wall. I slowed down as I approached. The person's head was slumped down, his chin resting against his chest.

I recognized Will's shape even before I saw his face or the bottle roll out from beside him. I stopped, breathing hard, and glanced back and forth down the vacant hallway, surprised no one had found him like this. Or maybe they had and decided he looked like too much of a mess to deal with. I turned back to Will, who grunted and stirred against the wall.

"Jesus, Will," I whispered. I wanted to be irritated with him, to hold onto the anger that had sprang up from his violent, child-like behavior earlier, but as I crouched next to him and looked into his downturned face, it all washed away. Even in a drunken sleep his brow was furrowed, and his eyes darted beneath the lids. Slight twitches creased the corners as if something was playing painfully in the darkness of his mind. I realized in that moment that almost every room-brightening smile that we had seen from him was a battle, a fight against the demons inside. I put my hand on his shoulder, gently shaking him. "Will...Will." He finally stirred awake and looked around blankly, instinctively wiping drool from the corners of his mouth and chin.

"Mhmm. Yeah, I'm awake. Hmm." He seemed lost, like he was somewhere else, distant. When his eyes finally settled on me, there was a moment of confusion and then startled recognition. He dropped his gaze, looking down at the floor. "Hey, Sarah."

"You OK?" I asked softly. Will's lower lip trembled as he forced his mouth into a tight line, trying to bypass the emotion with tension. He involuntarily raised and lowered his chin as if holding his head high could out-bravado the torment. I saw tears pooling at the edges, trying desperately to get free. "Will..." When he finally looked up at me, I could barely hold his stare. He was so broken, and that brokenness passed through me like a knife.

"I'm sorry," he choked. "I'm so sorry."

I couldn't muster the words to reply, but I placed my hand gently against his cheek.

He closed his eyes and took in the touch. In a moment of clarity, his voice came out clear but soft. "Is Frank OK?"

I cleared my throat to respond. "Yeah, uh…he's fine. Little bruised but he's OK." Will let out a slow breath of relief. "Why don't we get you back to Charlie?" I asked.

Will nodded, and I helped him to his feet. He stood unsteadily and leaned against the wall.

I went to put his arm over my shoulder when I noticed the picture on the floor next to where he had been sitting. A picture of a woman laughing and holding a little girl on a beach. I picked it up and stared at it. They were beautiful with their coffee-colored skin and wide toothy smiles. The little girl had Will's eyes. Will didn't seem to notice he had misplaced it. I was worried that showing it to him might set him off again, but I couldn't keep it from him, and I also worried if he realized it was gone, it might make things worse. So, I hesitantly held it out for him. "You dropped this." He stared for a long moment and then took it from my hand and put it in his pocket. His legs buckled, and he slid down the wall, but I rushed in to catch him, throwing his arm over my shoulder and starting the lopsided walk back to the aviary.

CHAPTER X

New Toys

I woke at my usual early time and swung my legs over the side of my bed. At that point I was used to the morning routine and generally moved promptly to get my day started. I would habitually take a five-minute shower to fully wake up, get dressed in my bodysuit and robe, make my bed the way I was taught in the service, and then read for twenty minutes. Discipline kept more than just the body sharp; it kept the mind sharp too. Today was different. I sat on the edge of my bed and gazed around my room. I hadn't done anything wrong. I hadn't lost my cool and hurt people. But still, a moment of self-reflection came from seeing someone at their lowest—a soul searching that peered back through time and tried to remember the kindred moments.

I thought about my parents; what they looked like and how I had felt with them—safe more than anything. Mikey and I had lived without them for a lot longer than with them, but I still felt their loss occasionally in conflicting reflections of abandonment and love. Of course, they didn't plan to die; it just happened, but it didn't stop a young mind from spinning destructive *what ifs*. With time the control it held over me waned, and the main lingering thought was some half-guilty feeling that I wouldn't be who I was without losing them…and I liked who I was now.

Will and I both had trauma—different but deep. However, I had been dealing with mine for almost two decades, and not just for myself but for Mikey too. He was the one who'd had his rebellions and drunk-tank stays, his fistfights and breakdowns. When I had time to feel it all, I felt it quietly and privately. My demons stayed mostly in the unfocused dark, but Will's lived right behind his eyes. Some of us deal with the bad well, and some of us don't.

I fully expected to have the early part of my breakfast alone, so I was surprised when Will dropped his tray on the table and sat across from me, smiling.

"Morning!" he said, before taking a drink of his coffee and starting on breakfast.

I stared at him, my mouth agape. "Um, hi…"

He smiled at me and then continued eating. "Oh, hey, how awesome is it we finally get to start shooting stuff?" he asked as if he had just remembered.

"Uh, yeah…pretty awesome." I couldn't believe he wasn't going to acknowledge what happened the day before. I also couldn't believe how chipper he was considering the significant amount of alcohol he had consumed.

"You know what else is awesome?"

"What's that, Will?" I asked, glaring down at my food.

"How I could be such a complete piece of shit."

I glanced up at him, his blue eyes piercing mine. He wore a tight smile that didn't reach his eyes, and his stare didn't try to hide his shame. What looked back at me was a combination of guilt and gratitude.

"I'm sorry, Sarah," he whispered.

When I couldn't hold his intense stare any longer, I nodded and focused on my food. We sat in silence, eating for several moments. Out of the corner of my eye I saw Will take another big sip from his coffee, and I didn't smell the usual potent aroma of alcohol.

Just as I was about to break the silence, Miguel burst onto the scene. "Holy shit! If it isn't the big bully. Surprised you can even move right now, man," Miguel said, smacking Will on the shoulder and sitting down.

Will glanced over at me and then smiled his big smile, rolling with the punches. The worst thing he could do after screwing up was deny he had.

"Gotta love the nanites in our blood," he said. "Sure beats Gatorade and a banana."

"Man, how the hell did you do that?" Miguel asked, staring at him. Will shifted uncomfortably in his chair, avoiding our eyes. "Seriously, man," Miguel continued. "You got access to some sort of space 'roids or something?"

"Sounds like some sort of interstellar ass problem," Will deflected with a chuckle.

Miguel and I laughed with him, but Miguel didn't give up that easily. "What's the secret?"

Will shook his head. "I honestly don't know, buddy. Weapons training starts today, huh?" He turned to his food. He looked as unsure as any of us about the source of his power. While most of us were just curious, I saw how it scared him. His face spoke volumes.

"Hey, you guys ever wonder, like, why biotech? Why not just batteries?" Miguel asked through a mouthful of grey mulch.

The rest of the morning passed by with the standard fitness followed by lectures. Everyone was keen to see what sort of technology we'd be introduced to in the afternoon, and the anticipation made the beginning of the day crawl by. It didn't matter how interesting the talks were; everyone fidgeted in their seats, tapping their feet and trying to will the seconds to tick faster. When we were finally released from class, we all hustled to lunch and put it back quickly, arriving significantly early to Flak's training.

The sim field was already set up as an open shooting range. A long, thin table ran across the room dividing the firing position from the down-course targets. The targets were fairly generic metal torsos with heads, except they hovered in various distances throughout the field without support. The room had the odd look of an outdoor gravel pit within a factory warehouse, a large mound of nano-dirt behind the levitating targets.

We gathered in our habitual pre-class cliques and shared our excitement for the session. We had seen some of the weaponry we might be using carried by Lumenarian security near the brig and reactor entrances but hadn't seen them in action. I hadn't fired a weapon since basic training but hoped it would come back naturally. I believed a gun was a gun and that the alien weapons must operate in a similar fashion.

As we waited, Frank hobbled into the room and approached the group, several people turning and watching to see how the showdown with Will would go. When Will saw him coming, he stepped away from the group and faced him, holding his hands out to his sides in a peaceful gesture. "Give me a shot man," he offered. Without hesitation Frank clocked him across the jaw, dropping Will to one knee. Frank grunted and folded his arms around his torso; the swing couldn't have felt good for him. A few people stepped closer to break up the fight. I grimaced seeing the impact of Frank's punch, but Will did have it coming. He stood and rubbed his face. "Ow! I can't believe you actually took the shot!"

"Of course I took it, you dick. You broke four of my ribs!"

They glared at each other for a tense moment before Will broke in. "You good?"

"Yeah, you?"

"Yeah." They quickly hugged and then separated, Frank wincing slightly. "Sorry."

"Can't believe you didn't visit me in Medical."

"Didn't want to see you crying."

"God, you're an asshole." Frank exhaled slowly, shaking his head.

Megan leaned in to me. "Fucking guys. If you had done that to me, I would have at least punched you in the box," she said with a smile and wink.

"Jesus, Megan," I replied, chuckling. Frank and Will stepped back into the group, and everyone welcomed Frank back.

I wondered if there was a bond tighter than the type those two had formed. It may have been forged in the turbulent fires of war and loss, but it was love to the bone. I loved Mikey, of course, and I'd do anything for him, but it was different. It was a thing of dependence and persistence. It didn't make it wrong or necessarily less, but without the confines of family, I'm not sure we would've ever grown to be friends. I thought that, and I saw it in Mikey's eyes when he watched Frank and Will. A desire to belong to a brotherhood that a sometimes-overbearing big sister couldn't fulfil. Granted, I think most people who observed the pair from afar felt that way. As I watched Will, I realized how much I wanted him to think I was special. A thought that felt strange and adolescent but nonetheless…desirable.

A few minutes later Flak paraded into the room leading a small convoy of levitating crates. Everyone gathered around to get a glimpse of the gear, murmuring excitedly to one another.

"Settle down!" he barked. "Your hand-to-hand combat training will continue." A confused and disappointed ripple spread through the group. Flak held up his hand. "But from now on we'll be working in real weapons training," he added with a lopsided grin. Flak walked over to the first of the five cargo boxes and entered a code on his forearm display causing the lid to open. Several people nearby leaned in to see what was inside.

"For the appetizers," he said. He reached into the bin and pulled out a metallic hexagonal prism a little bigger than a hockey puck. He placed it on his chest and emitted a small flash of green energy with his palm. The piece of tech separated rapidly with a series of clicks. It was made of dozens of paper-thin hexagons stacked on top of each other. They linked at the edges and spread across his chest, over his shoulders, and partway down his arms, then around to his back, creating a sort of brushed-steel T-shirt. "Body armor," Flak said. We all stared at the impressive, super-thin armor in amazement. He took out a second prism and placed it on his hip. It whipped around his waist and down his legs to just above his ankles, essentially forming a matching plate-linked pair of metal pants and utility belt. "We call this Steel-Hyde. Of course, it's significantly stronger than your Earth steel, but gotta make sure you humes can relate. Obviously, it custom fits, is flexible, and it'll suck up the majority of level-four impacts without a scratch to the wearer." He rotated 360 degrees to show off the armor. As he turned, we saw his biotech lines glow a vibrant jade along the metal in correlation to where they would be on his body and then fade down to a charcoal mark. The already hulking figure now looked like a tank—an unstoppable wall of muscle and space-age lumenium.

He threw two of the armor pucks to Frank, who caught them, surprised. "You should probably toss those on in case Reach loses his shit again," Flak said. Everyone laughed as Frank and Will lowered their heads, trying to smile gracefully through the embarrassment. I restrained a laugh as Will glanced at me. He rolled his eyes and shrugged, accepting it. "Alright, come get your gear."

The armor discs initially felt cold running over my body, like my bodysuit was soaking through with chilled mercury. When it hardened into the shell of its final form, it gently squeezed around my stomach and breasts, tight but not uncomfortable. I realized I hadn't moved while it activated, as if stillness was the key to a perfect fit. Looking down at the legionnaire-like torso plating, I thought it'd be stiff and awkward, but as I moved my arms and hunched my middle to get a feel for it, it moved like a second skin and weighed next to nothing, like a fictional Tolkien-esque garment.

I was glad to see I wasn't the only one staring in amazement at myself when I looked around the room. No matter how incredible the technology was, we also looked really cool. I glanced over at Will as he turned around to check out Frank's armor. His back glowed with the blue striations of the biotech that ran down his spine, pulsing faintly.

"OK, now that you've all got your armor on, we'll move on. If it feels unnatural, toughen up. You'll get used to it. It takes no skill to wear, which many of you should be thankful for at this point," Flak said with his hands on his hips. "Now for the real reason you humes were all perky when I got here." He reached into one of the other crates and pulled out a pistol, holding it up for everyone to see. "This little beauty we're calling the Alpha 2-8 assault pistol or Warthog." The firearm resembled a pistol from home, something like a Beretta Px4 Storm except larger, heavier, and blockier. The frame below the barrel was thicker and extended from the tip of the barrel to the grip with a hole cut out for the trigger and enough space for our three remaining fingers below it. From the bottom of the grip a bar came straight out several inches and then angled up at around a forty-five-degree angle to the tip, creating something like a simple knuckle or bow guard of a rapier sword.

Flak wrapped his hand around the grip and held the gun in a sul-ready position against his chest, angled down with his finger off the trigger but ready to bring up and shoot at a moment's notice. His hand flared green, which lit up a strip of light along the sides of the pistol, seemingly activating it. He reached into the crate again and pulled out a small silver cylinder with a glass slit on the side. He held it up for us to see and rattled it slightly. It was filled with hundreds of small obsidian BBs.

"Might not look like much, but this is what you'll be shooting. And I assure you, they'll get the job done." Rather than in the base of the grip, he loaded the magazine into the back of the gun, where there would usually be a hammer, and opened fire on one of the targets down range. Most of us flinched as he blasted the hell out of the levitating metal mannequin. Each small round rifled down range in a ball of emerald energy, as if the metal BBs were just the carriers for his bioenergy. The shots left the barrel with a muted PHHT like from a silenced pistol, but they connected with the mark in an aggressive demonic howl. The metal target had practically melted by the time he stopped shooting. As quickly as he had raised the gun, he dropped it to his side and let it go. The Warthog snapped magnetically to the side of his leg just below his hip.

Everyone applauded and stared in awe at the devasting technology. "I was taking it easy on the target. Each of these weapons is only as good as their user." He quick-drew the pistol again, surprising us all, but this time he only shot once. The shot, however, had probably ten times the power of the previous ones, incinerating the mark. He lowered the pistol but kept it in his hand and turned back to us. "By the end of training, I expect all of you to be able to do that." He pulled a secondary cylinder out of the bottom of the grip and held it up. "Don't forget this. Highly compressed xenon. This will rarely need to be reloaded, but you'll carry extra mags regardless." So, it was essentially a plasma gun. The atoms in the gas were ionized by our biotech and carried by the pellets.

"Earlier you said our armor could withstand level-four impacts," Megan said. "How would that rate?"

"The first shots would have rated level one or two impacts, whereas the last one would class in at level five. You won't see much of the first level dropping things on the battlefield. That's suppressive fire and energy conservation. Good as a distraction or sustained salvo but lethal only if you hit precise marks; a joint, neck, directly in the helmet slot. Shooting at a level five and higher for too long will be hard to maintain for most of you. You need to control yourselves. Those are the kill shots and the make-a-fucking-hole shots," Flak said, glancing at Will. "The Warthog is fully automatic, powerful, and accurate. In tight spaces it also has this fun little feature." Flak flared up his fist again, and the knuckle guard bar lit up with sizzling green energy. It seared through the air as he swung it in a slashing motion. "This won't cut through armor unless you really give it some juice, but it'll cut through flesh like its foodstuffs." He stuck it back to his hip.

"Great. The Forsaken are pure armor," Miguel muttered next to me.

"They're basically giving us mini lightsabers, and you're complaining?" Will asked.

"Well, I mean, a *knife* can cut through flesh. I don't see the point of—"

"Jesus, you're picky."

"Shut up. You're picky—"

"But again, it's about control," Flak said, raising his voice to drown out Will and Miguel. "Any moron can shoot or slice with one of these. Whether you can last a whole fight is another thing." Flak glared around the room for a moment before settling on Will again. "Reach." Everyone turned and stared at Will, who immediately became uncomfortable.

"Yes, sir."

"I think we're all curious to see how you handle the Warthog. Step forward."

Will walked through the crowd of parting people. Flak reached into the crate and pulled out another pistol. "As you all can see, we've made your firearms smaller to fit in your little hume hands. But don't worry; they pack the same punch." He handed the pistol to Will, who held it naturally and safely in the same sul posture that Flak had sported. Will loaded the magazine like he'd done it a thousand times before and squared up to the target, all business. That same cold, detached gaze appeared, one I'd seen a handful of times during combat training; the serious soldier taking over.

"What level do you want me to shoot at?" Will asked.

Flak and several others chuckled, thinking Will was being cocky. I thought it was a legitimate question.

"Give it as much as you got," Flak said with a patronizing bow. Will nodded and looked toward his mark. Without hesitating, his hands pushed straight forward from his chest and flashed blue, lighting up the side strip. Will let three shots go in quick succession—and with deadly accuracy. The blasts tore three of the targets apart with only fragments remaining. They were as strong or stronger than the level-five shot Flak had fired. Everyone stared, surprised and impressed.

Flak looked frustrated that Will had done so well so quickly but covered it with an enthusiastic challenge. "Alright, let's try something else." He tapped his forearm band a few times, and a new target came up. It was a hostage taker standing behind his victim. "Take out the hostage taker." Will eyed the target and let out a slow breath. The shot was as powerful as his first ones and may have hit only the bad guy, but it also destroyed the victim.

"Shit," Will muttered.

Flak sneered. "As I said. Control. In case you all haven't figured it out yet, all our tech relies on that the most."

Will clenched his jaw and looked down at the floor. I knew one of the things Arthur was working on with him in their weekly meetings was control, but apparently, he still had a ways to go.

"OK everyone, come get your personal firearms. You'll notice your name etched on the side. You've all gotten the theory and safe practice techniques with the dummy weapons. Do not fuck around. These are not toys. I see you not giving it the respect it deserves, and you'll be paired with me in the next hand-to-hand session. Understood?" Flak glared around the room. There was a collective nod and murmur that we all got the message.

When I got my sidearm, it felt heavier than I thought it would. For some reason I figured it'd be like the high-tech armor we wore, nearly weightless. That wasn't the case—it wasn't unwieldly, but it was not light. I guess it was something we'd have to get used to. Along the front and back of the grip were smooth, charcoal-colored pads that I assumed were the receptors for our bioenergy and the way we controlled the output of our firing solutions. As complicated as I was sure the technology was, the gun itself looked simple on the outside. There was no ejection port because the rounds didn't have casings. There was no safety or slide release, and the muzzle was buried inside the frame. It was boxy, but it was also streamlined. No extraneous or showy parts, just a simple, alien death machine. I ran my finger along the etched lettering of my name on the side of the frame: "S. LI." I squeezed the grip and focused my energy into the gun. As soon as I did, the strip along the slide lit up blue.

"In the unlikely event of a jam or failed magazine ejection, you can check it like this." Flak held up the Warthog, placed his hand along the top of where the slide would be, and twisted. The top half of the gun pivoted sideways off a central pin and formed an X above the grip and frame. He removed the clip and then put it back in, snapping the gun back together. "Just like that. Go ahead and line up behind the bench.

Start getting a feel for the weapon and the different outputs it's capable of." We lined up behind the open slots and took turns shooting.

Firing the Warthog resulted in minimal kick, even at the higher levels, but I felt it in my body, each shot a small purge of my energy. We had been getting stronger and building up higher thresholds, but the weapons still drained us quickly. At the end of an hour, after everyone had gotten a fair shake on the range, we all stood sweating and breathing hard. Everyone except Will, who looked fairly unfazed.

Flak grinned as he looked around at us all. "Good. You're starting to feel it. You'll be able to last longer eventually, but you're going to need a boost if you want to finish the lesson." Flak tossed me a palm-sized metallic cylinder that looked like an EpiPen. I caught it and examined it closer. A thin band of glowing gold energy streamed down the side. "There's a port on your weak-hand thigh," he said, pointing down. I was right-handed, so I looked down at my left leg. I hadn't noticed it before, but amidst the hexagonal armor plates was a small round protrusion of raised metal located midway down my quadricep. "Touch the end to the port," Flak ordered. I hesitated for a moment, not sure what it would do. I glanced up at him as he nodded to go on. I pressed the end of the cylinder to the port. Like an EpiPen or a pneumatic injector, a thick needle shot out and drove the gold substance into my leg.

"Ow, shit!" Suddenly, my entire body felt like it had been zapped by a bolt of lightning, every cell reenergizing and every biotech line flashing a bright sapphire. My muscles tensed for an uncomfortable few seconds, like a bad calf spasm, and then released as the initial shock subsided. I wasn't sure if that was a shot of straight speed or what, but I felt brand new. As if the last hour on the range hadn't even happened. "Jesus. I feel like I just had a dozen cups of coffee."

"We call those jolt shots. If you're ever pinned down or engaged in a sustained action for a long period of time, these are better than three squares and eight hours of rack. They'll instantly replenish your energy and get you back in the fight," Flak said with a nod to me. "Be warned though; more than two of these in an hour, and you're liable to have a cardiac arrest."

OK, that was good to know. I'd have to look up what was in it later.

After we had all taken one of the jolt shots and felt recovered, Flak turned to the last crate. He couldn't hide his excitement. Whatever was in there, he was anxious to share it. Maybe aware of his giddy grin, he cleared his throat and put on a stern glare. "OK. Your last piece of equipment for the day. It might seem like a lot to give you all at once, but harden the fuck up. You'll have time to master them later."

He reached into the crate and pulled out another weapon. "The Delta 6-4 primary assault rifle. Call this one the Tempest." He aimed down the sight for the sheer pleasure of it and then lowered it and held it up for all to see. The rifle was another block of dark metal that extended forward from a standard pistol grip and square butt. It looked like a larger, longer version of the Warthog minus the electric knuckle guard. The front of the rifle had two barrels. One muzzle protruded about an inch while the other was a large hole flush with the casing. It also had two triggers divided by a break in the frame; the primary firing trigger and a smaller one in front of it.

"This beautiful death dealer has three main settings and several sub-settings. The first main setting is your standard assault loadout." Flak aimed at the targets and shredded several with quick, precise, three-round bursts, followed by a full-auto rapid spray that tore through the targets and the air between and around them.

He turned back to us, looking incredibly pleased with himself, and tapped a small touchpad on the frame's forestock. "The second is the sniper config." The upper barrel with the protruding muzzle extended out telescopically about a foot and a half in a smooth slide, and the reflex-sight-style scope clicked up a notch, split, and then elongated to form an adjustable long-distance scope. As Flak leaned down on the table to shoot, two bipod arms automatically split off the side of the frame and braced against the surface. He exhaled slowly and put a shot clean through the head portion of the farthest oval target.

"That's how it's done," he muttered, probably mostly to himself, but we all heard it.

He stood and turned to face us, tapping the touchpad again and collapsing the rifle down to assault mode. "Lastly…" He gestured to the sealed port below the primary barrel. "We call this the melt shot." Flak aimed down range and squeezed the smaller trigger. We heard a rapid clinking sound, and then the lower port opened and glowed a bright emerald. When he released the trigger, a golf-ball-sized metallic ball tore out of the lower barrel, engulfed in green flame like a small meteor. It exploded on the target in the center of three others and disintegrated all of them. So, it was basically a grenade launcher. Rather than it being an explosive we had to load manually, it channeled the small BB ammunition from the clip into a lower chamber that cooked them into a larger solid projectile. "This is capable of accepting other special ammunition too, but they'll have to be loaded manually," he added. Lesson for another time, I guess.

When he finished demonstrating the various modes the rifle could operate in, he held it in front of himself and let it go. A few in the front dashed forward to catch it, but the rifle magnetically snapped to his chest. He chuckled at the ones trying to save it. "Just like the Warthog, magnetic clips here and…" He pulled it off his chest and threw it over his back, the rifle rapidly clipping to the center of his spine. "…here."

Will leaned over to Frank in front of me. "Didn't think there was anything wrong with a sling," he said quietly.

"Mhmm. Chest carry is nice though."

"Yeah, wouldn't want your old arms to get tired," Will said, jostling Frank.

"Ah…fuck you!" Frank fake sneezed back. "Aghh." He held his chest again, groaning in pain. Will chuckled, and Flak glared back, making Will pretend like he was coughing.

"Keep it down over there, Reach."

"Yes, sir. Sorry, sir."

Flak shook his head but continued demonstrating. I couldn't help but smile. Will glanced back at me with a grin and wink.

"Behave," I whispered in a mock stern reprimand. Will purred and made a claw with his hand like he was a sexy cat, the classic Austin Powers response.

"Holy shit. Reach! Shut the fuck up back there!" Flak yelled, incredulous that he had to repeat himself so soon. An angry grade-school teacher.

Will snapped back around to face the front. "Roger that, sir," he said seriously, standing straight. He gave me a quick sideways smile. Someone was in a good mood, getting to play with guns.

CHAPTER XI

There Goes The Neighborhood

Six months aboard the *Albatross* flew by in a haze of information over-load and exhaustive routine. Even for me, a career student, it seemed like a lot for any of our minds to fully grasp. With twelve months still to go, I was sure most of this would remain in the realm of CliffsNotes; half remembered. Maybe that was the point; jam it all in, sort it out later, much like university back home. That was my theory anyway, but I doubted many of my classmates' retention capabilities.

On the other side, our physical training was progressing at breakneck speed. New synapses fired relentlessly, building our muscle memory for violent action and increasing our capacity for energy output. It was like holding our breath underwater in a pool until eventually we could sit on the bottom while minutes passed. Our bodies' tolerances built to levels thought impossible as the tech harnessed every cell and maximized their production capabilities. We even started regularly supplementing with high-caloric nutritional gels between meals to keep up with our output demands. They tasted like smoothies—which was good for the fruit-flavored ones, not so good for the full-meal ones. Something to get used to either way since they'd essentially become our deployment MREs.

Besides our training, life aboard the *Albatross* was becoming more comfortable. We were more accustomed to the ins and outs of the ship and the confines of space. We didn't give the food a second thought anymore, and the uniforms, which originally felt strange and restrictive as everyday wear or just plain alien, now felt like a second skin. Our rooms felt like home, each person putting their own touches to the space.

The few personal items I'd brought along lined the shelves and filled the drawers (took me a while to unpack): pictures of Mikey and me and our parents, my diplomas (useless now), several books from Earth, my old dog tags, the first science fair ribbon I ever won, a metronome that one of the few good foster parents I had gave me (not for any sort of musical inclination but because I found it calming), my dad's old Dodgers baseball hat, some aromatic perfumes and candles, and a tennis ball I liked tossing against the wall. I had also brought some sweatpants, a couple of hoodies (including the ones from my alma maters), and a few other small items of clothing that I liked to wear inside my room to relax or when we were off duty outside.

The aviary had been taking on a life of its own too. Some people had packed flags, which now hung from balconies, reminders of a home we might never see again. In fact, one of the first nights Megan and Will spent in the brig was due to one of the flags—a Confederate one some clown had decided deserved real estate. I wasn't there when it happened, but apparently Megan had noticed it first, reasonably took offense, and what began as a heated discussion about removing it escalated into a brawl when Will showed up to support her. The flag hung for all of five minutes. It may not have been a very diplomatic process, but the message was clearly received. This was a new tribe, and the prejudices of the old ones wouldn't be accepted. Will made that clear, and few had the courage to oppose him. Plus, he was right, and most naturally agreed. Still, they got a night in the brig to condemn the fight.

Access to synthesized paint allowed some doors to be painted and approved graffiti to begin decorating the walls around the complex. The circular area beneath the central column had colorful canvas stretched out from the pillar, creating a sort of covered market space. Lanterns hung from the poles that supported the edge of the tented verandas and lined the bridge and pathways throughout the courtyard, and Macau-like lanterns floated in the ponds, giving it a Chinese garden atmosphere.

Some people had brought along different instruments. Others had improvised them from things they found around the *Albatross*. They played on an elevated stage constructed beneath the tower, often creating a street-like music that echoed through the complex during our simulated nights.

When we first arrived aboard, small groups had gathered in the halls and messes and down in the parks, cliques of comfort, but now it was constantly alive with people mingling, dancing, singing, playing games, and drinking. It had become a colorful tribute to the cultures of home and grew more diverse every day. It wasn't perfect. People still got in fights from time to time, and there was crime, but it was mostly petty (and inescapable with so many humans in a tight space), and neighbors still occasionally bickered about unimportant little things, but for the most part, people seemed happy.

There was no currency aboard the *Albatross*, but a trade had developed. Everything from Earth trinkets to chores, handmade goods to sex. There was no designated brothel, but there was a ring that ship security had tried to crack down on a few times—if there were instances of violence—but it only seemed to make them more discreet. Besides, we mostly policed ourselves. Outside of any attacks, which obviously required attention, it was a delicate matter. Not everyone on the ships came from countries that banned sex workers, and we had to try to be understanding of this new cultural mosaic. What it came down to was making sure the people involved were protected and not abused. I felt like it was an awkward matter for the Lumenarians as well since sex work wasn't considered taboo for them. My understanding was that no one was trafficked on Lumen, though.

Individuals slung the White Bird alcohol (which had originated in the Delta aviary but was now more refined) straight and in cocktails pumped out from dispensaries moved to the market. Originally a bootlegging operation, it had been sanctioned and monitored by the *Albatross* command and was now given out freely to those who were finished their training for the day. As much as some might have wanted to throw three sheets to the wind, it was never much of a problem. Our training didn't allow it mentally or physically. It was a miracle that Will had kept it up as long as he did.

To be honest, it was surprising how much the upper echelons of leadership let us get away with, but at the same time, they had learned a lot about us in their hibernation period above Earth. It occurred to me that one such observation might have been humans' resistance to micro-management or dictatorships. Any problems that may have arisen from allowing the distribution of alcohol or other contraband were probably considered minute compared to the potential ramifications of stifling the freedom of a naturally chaotic and oftentimes violent species.

I awoke at my normal time and went about my usual morning routine. Freshly showered and dressed, I settled in front of my desk and opened a file on my display glass. The military history of the Forsaken war. A topic spanning over 150 years and originating on one of the Lumenarians' outer worlds named Ourea, a rocky planet around an un-(human) mapped star about fifteen lightyears from Lumen. It had been a vicious attack that left the planet decimated and nearly all of its fifteen-billion inhabitants either dead or possibly abducted, save for a handful of ships that managed to escape. It was a completely unexpected slaughter, the enemy appearing with no warning and disappearing immediately after the conquest. The responding Lumenarian fleet arrived months after the fires had already burned down to simmering coals. That was the problem with such distant colonies. Thread drive or not, and with time-dilation effects, transit between was not immediate.

For another ten years, nothing was seen of the mysterious force. It wasn't until a resettlement attempt began that they saw them again. The accompanying protectorate came face to face with an armada like nothing they had ever experienced. The Forsaken had claimed Ourea and weren't letting it go.

The space battle that followed was known as the First Fall. The loss of the planet was without significant military resistance and considered a cowardly strike against a civilian population, but the attempt to re-establish the colony was supported by ground and air forces in the millions, the first real conflict against an unknown enemy. While the Lumenarians tried desperately to evacuate their people from the planet, Forsaken ships rained hell upon them, tearing apart the orbital fleet and flooding the ground with thousands of invasion troops. In fact, according to records, of the millions of settlers and military personnel, only two survived. I read that fact several times to make sure I was seeing it right. It had to be propaganda. Either way, it stated the only survivors were two young soldiers aboard a ship named the *Tide*. One went on to become a member of the Lumen war council and the other a commander of several warships before landing on his current post on the *Albatross*: Arthur.

Someone knocked on my door, drawing my attention from the file. I didn't want to tear myself away from this new information, but I got up and went over anyway. When I opened my door, two Lumenarians stood facing me with big, sharp-toothed smiles. It wasn't uncommon for our hosts to cruise through the aviary from time to time, but it was strange that they were in front of *my* door and so early in the morning—with big grins.

"Uh, hi…" I said.

"Hi! My name's Kilo, and this is Cash," one of them said while extend-ing his hand. It was always hard to tell the ages of their kind, but I would have guessed these two were somewhat younger, maybe around a hundred. They didn't have the same cracks in their skin as someone like Flak, and neither bore scars from war, which was all too common among the older generations of their species—or maybe they were just lucky. Kilo was a deep charcoal with a mix of ashy grey and nearly black striations and green eyes with blue streaks. He stood a few inches taller than Cash and was slightly leaner. Cash was a sooty slate color with crimson and navy patterns etched across his body, and his eyes sparkled with hues of red and gold.

I reached out and shook their hands in turn, still unsure what they wanted. "Nice to meet you. Is there…is something wrong?" I asked, looking them up and down.

"No, not at all. We're going to be your new neighbors! Moving in a few units down," Cash said enthusiastically. I stared at them in surprise and then leaned out and glanced around the aviary. Lumenarians on all levels were moving things into rooms and knocking on doors to introduce themselves.

I turned back at the smiling ones in front of me. "Oh, OK, well…hi. I'm Sarah. Welcome to the neighborhood, I guess." I tried to salvage the skeptical expression I had on my face when they arrived.

"Sarah Li. Yeah, we've heard of you," Cash said eagerly.

I felt a blush stain my cheeks.

"Arthur decided it was time to end the segregation and help get everyone more accustomed to living and working together," Kilo said. "So, here we are."

Just then Will walked over. "Hey. What's going on?" he asked, wiping sleep from his eyes. Kilo and Cash turned and extended their hands to him, big smiles on their faces.

"These are our new neighbors, apparently," I said, gesturing between them all.

Will stared at me for a second while it clicked. Then he turned back to Kilo and Cash. "Huh, no kidding. Super cool. Welcome to Charlie. Sorry I don't have a pie."

Kilo and Cash looked at each other, confused.

Will glanced at me with his charming smile.

"That's OK," Kilo said. "Hey, you're Will Reach, right?" He stared curiously at Will, whose face fell, not sure he wanted the attention.

Will shot another glance at me. "Uh, yeah."

Kilo and Cash looked at each other and then turned back to him, smiling even wider with their lizard mouths. "We've heard some things…" Will's face fell even more, no doubt worried that his bad habits had filtered through the ranks. "Good things!" Kilo added. "Can't wait to spar with you."

Will looked relieved, though still a bit stressed, but he smiled to cover it. "Careful what you wish for," he said, jabbing the air. The soldierly bravado connected across species. "There isn't a Tango out here too is there?" Kilo and Cash both laughed, smacking Will on the shoulder, but they clearly didn't get the reference.

I got the impression that although they knew my name, Will was the main attraction. Our Lumenarian instructors and those who didn't know our group as well generally fawned over Will. His mystery and power was a constant draw—the golden boy with a heart of darkness. It also helped that he was, for the most part, friendly and approachable. I didn't like the small pangs of jealousy I felt, but I was smart enough to know where I stood with Will and where my skills outshone his, and that was enough. I could feel moments of envy without allowing it to consume me in an unhealthy way. It was the basis of competition. It's how we had progressed as far as we had as a species. A conversation I had had with Sky a few months earlier showed me how similar that made our cultures.

"Intelligences capable of scientific and creative endeavors seek the advancement of their species ultimately because of an instinctual desire to connect with those around them," she said. "Otherwise, no one would ever remember their names." It was a strange paradox that spoke to the duality of people, where one element craved the love of others while the competing half loved itself equally or more. The angels and devils on our shoulders.

Kilo and Cash introduced themselves to others on our level and then moved into their units. A silent lottery had been conducted aboard the ship, relocating groups of people to new housing assignments and allowing roughly 10,000 Lumenarians to move into each of the other five human-dominated aviaries and the original human occupants heading over to the sixth previously alien-run complex. Some people were upset about having to move their lives to an entirely new section, but lucky for us, no one from our tight group of friends had to relocate. I was starting to think that was by design.

From then on life would be fully integrated with our hosts, and the lines of separation would blur, which was a good thing. The first six months had been reinforcing an *us and them* mentality, like adults and children or the borders between countries. The more we learned about each other, the more effective we'd become. Now not only would we be living side by side, those Lumenarians not directly occupied with the running of the ship would be training with us too.

The instruction for the day had been cancelled to allow time for everyone to move dorms, and we took advantage of the opportunity to lounge in the market and the fields. Frank and I sat at one of the tables below the central column and sipped from synthetic Long Island iced teas.

"Not quite like home, but it'll do," Frank said, holding his cup out for a cheers. I clinked his glass and took a drink. We both watched Will, Miguel, Jiro, Megan, and the others play soccer in one the fields. Instead of the usual matches that often took place, several Lumenarians, including Kilo and Cash, played with them. They were incredible at every physical feat we had seen them do, and they were too big to push around, meaning they picked up soccer quickly—frustratingly quick for some of the humans playing, but they laughed it off and worked harder in the spirit of competition. Will took a fall, getting dangled by Kilo, but rose to his feet, breathing hard and smiling. He glanced over at us and gave a quick salute, which we returned. He seemed so different from when I had first met him—happier, more consistent. Frank and I sat quietly for several moments watching them.

"Will is a complicated guy," Frank said, breaking the silence.

I nodded. "Yeah, sure seems to be." I stared out at the field. I felt Frank watching me. I turned back to him. "What?"

"Will ever talk about our time in the service?"

"He's told me some stories about you and some of the other guys in your unit but nothing about combat or anything," I replied, not sure where Frank was going with this. "Why?"

Frank went quiet for a moment. "This one time our team was tasked with taking down a high-value target that intel said was hiding in a cave somewhere in the Bolan Pass outside Quetta. We'd been crawling those mountains for days looking for him. Now we were good. All twelve of us were at least three or four tours deep, a couple had more, and Will was our captain. No one else I would've rather had, but there's nothing quite like local knowledge."

Frank took a drink and collected himself, recalling the memory in detail. "The attack came at dusk. The whole time we thought we were tracking them, they were tracking us. We fucked up. Combination of bad intel and underestimating them. Ran into another group we had mistaken for our quarry while those on our tail hit us from the other side. It was a shit show, and we weren't in a good place. We lost half our team almost immediately. The rest of us were pinned down. It seemed like we were fighting the whole fucking Taliban army. Within the next hour, only four of us were left, and it was not looking good. Jonesy was bleeding out, Denton couldn't see out of one eye, and I'd just taken a round to the leg. Thought that was it..." Frank drifted off, taking another drink.

"Will?" I asked.

Frank stared out at Will playing soccer in the field. "Will. I remember him sitting there with his back against a rock staring at all of us, looking at the guys we'd lost. Enemy salvo never let up. RPG here and there. I thought he must've been hurt or shell-shocked, but that wasn't it. He was calm. Reflective even. Like he knew exactly what he needed to do but wasn't sure if he should. Best guess I have for what he was thinking anyway." Frank turned and stared into my eyes. "Then he got up and left."

I cocked my head to the side. "What do you mean? He ran away?"

Frank shook his head. "Will doesn't run away from fights. I heard the gunfire slowly die down, the odd burst here and there. Then yelling and screaming." Frank stared off, lost in the memory. "Will showed up a couple minutes later. He was carrying the long-range radio one of our guys had been wearing calling for an extraction. He was covered in blood—none of it his." I breathed out slowly, taking in everything as Frank took another drink. "Turned out we had accomplished our mission. Even though the target we *thought* was the target was never there, his fifteen-year-old son was."

"Jesus."

Frank nodded slowly. "Agency never told us that was the real mission. None of us had any idea he'd be there. After that, they gave us medals, and we gave them our papers." Frank downed the last of his drink. "Listen, Sarah. Will feels everything, good and bad. And he doesn't feel it softly. You've seen how he deals with all that. He's the best guy I know…and scary as shit when he's protecting the ones he cares about."

I suddenly understood why Frank was telling me all this. He wanted me to fully understand what I'd be getting myself into with Will. He knew Will would never hurt me or any of his friends, but being unsure of how I felt about him could do serious harm to Will. It also helped everything else make a lot more sense. Will's drinking, his mood swings, the darkness behind every smile. I knew a bit about Will's wife and daughter, but from what I'd been piecing together of his timeline, this had happened before them. It was a deep part of who he was.

When I looked back at the field, Will smiled as he dribbled the ball around Kilo and passed it to Cash, who wound up and took a powerful shot. The keeper sparked up the tech in his hands to dampen the blow. Everyone stopped and stared with their mouths hanging open. Then Will led the slow laughter as they got over their surprise and embraced the change. They all high-fived and took a break to get some water and rest.

Will grabbed a towel from the edge of the field and came over to us. He sat down and wiped the sweat off his face and neck. "Hey. What're you guys talking about?" he asked, glancing at our drinks. As far as we knew he hadn't had a drink since the incidents with Frank in the sim field and me in the hallway, but I could tell it was clawing at him. Saw it whenever people were drinking or when he was drinking his morning coffee and not tasting alcohol. I stole a sideways peek at Frank, who maintained eye contact with Will.

"I was saying you haven't gotten any better at soccer," Frank said.

Will laughed and threw his hands up. "Hey, you know football is more my game. Welcome to join the next game though, old man. Show us how it's done."

"Ah, wouldn't want to make you look bad, golden boy," Frank replied with a grin.

Will chuckled, but I could tell the "golden boy" comment irked him. "Asshole." He looked over at me and smiled warmly. The look made me feel like I was the only one in the courtyard. "How about you, Sare? Kick the ball around?"

"Never really could get my heart into soccer. Too much diving and flopping around like a little baby," I said, grinning back at him.

He nodded. "Fair enough." The story Frank had just told me flitted through my mind, and I looked away, uncertain how I felt about it. I think Will noticed because he looked back toward the field. "Well, I'm definitely not suggesting football with those guys playing," he said gesturing to the hulking Lumenarians. "Maybe we can get them with some baseball next time."

I felt Frank's eyes pass over me, noticing the awkward tension. "Well, you know I'd definitely be down for some baseball," he said. "Not as hard on my knees." We sat quietly for a few moments, taking in the day and the life around us.

I looked over and saw Mikey walking along the outer ring of the atrium with Seyyal, deep in conversation. They held hands briefly but then released them, glancing around to see if anyone had seen them. Relationships aboard the *Albatross* weren't forbidden, but there was a stigma about dating people you might fight and die alongside. And the issue of rank became involved, even though technically none of us really had a rank yet. "Hume trainee" was probably the closest, according to

Flak. Most, like Miguel, ventured to other aviaries for relationships to mitigate the chances of command structure and deployment overlap. That didn't mean local hook-ups weren't frequent though. We were still living in the idyllic bubble that a new adventure without the fully comprehended consequences brings, but each day and each step up in our training brought us closer to the realities of what was coming, and that seemed to keep things light. Maybe I was just projecting my own worries, though. Either way, I was happy for Mikey if he was finding something in Seyyal and she in him.

"Sare?" Will asked.

"Sorry, what? I was a little zoned out."

"I was asking how it felt to be responsible for naming an entire alien race."

"Florii? Oh, it's not very creative. I'm sure someone else would have thought of it or something similar. They do look like plants." Alien race number three, now the "Florii" (Floor-eye), were an incredibly old species that resembled a moss and shrub-covered centipede—only about six feet long. To be honest, almost immediately after I said it, I thought Florii sounded a little too delicate considering how creepy and insect-like they looked under the plant cover, but I suppose it was decided now. It'd be interesting to meet them in person.

"Still, you thought of it first, and everyone agreed on it." Will winked at me, and I felt a warm blush run up my neck and face.

Just then Kilo and a Lumenarian female we hadn't met approached the table. "Hey, Will, mind if we join you?" Kilo asked.

"Uh, yeah man, for sure. Pop a squat," Will replied, gesturing to the free chairs.

Kilo and his friend sat down and looked at us. Then Kilo reached out his hand. "Oh hi, sorry, I'm Kilo—"

"Yeah, Sarah and Frank. We actually met you first thing this morning."

"Right! My apologies. We've met so many new people today. This is Tash, by the way," Kilo said, introducing the female alien with him. She smiled and shook our hands but was very quiet, maybe not super happy about the move to Charlie complex or just shy; I wasn't sure yet. It was the first time I ever would have described one of the Lumenarians as mousy. There was an awkward couple of moments while we all spun in our heads trying to think of something to talk about. The gap between human and alien suddenly seemed huge despite the last six months living aboard the *Albatross*. It had been a teacher-student relationship so far or like coworkers in different departments. Now we were being forced to look at each other as actual people, the academic period of learning about our cultures having passed. It was time to experience them directly.

"You are Sarah Li, are you not?" Tash asked me suddenly. I was surprised to be recognized again.

"Yeah. Sorry, have we met before?"

Tash shook her head but held her stare, studying me. "You scored in the top half of a percentile for intelligence during your initial screening. It was very impressive for a human." I tried not to take offense to the "for a human" part.

"Well, thanks. That's still like a thousand people on the *Albatross* alone though. How would you know who—"

"I have a very good memory," she said quickly. "Have you ever played Commander's Die?"

"Commander's…Die?"

"Yes," she replied with a nervous nod.

"No. It's a Lumenarian game, obviously?" I asked. She nodded again. Tash reminded me of a shy little kid. Even her voice seemed young and nervous. "Maybe you could teach me some time," I said, trying to lead her further into the conversation.

"Yes. I could teach you now, if you want?"

I got the feeling she was trying to get a measure of me. "Sure. Do we need to go somewhere or—"

In reply, Tash pulled a small obsidian cube from her robe pocket and set it on the table. It looked like a Rubik's cube. She tapped the center tile on the top face. The cube hummed and floated about six inches off the table. Then it clunked apart like a Transformer and expanded to a larger cube with sixty-four tiles to each of the six sides, eight by eight. I pressed on the cube, always curious about the perfected mag-lev technology that several of the Lumenarians' tech seemed to utilize. It didn't even budge. *Cool.*

"The objective of the game is to win as many points as you can by building armies on the cube's surface and dominating your opponent's armies," Tash explained. She ran her fingers up the center two rows from her side to mine, a light-green energy pulsing from her fingertips as she did. The tiles lit up as she touched them. "Tutorial mode," she said. The tiles returned to their original onyx color. "An army is at least two tiles joined together. You can select one, two, or three tiles every turn, but if you select three, they have to be adjoined." She touched two separated tiles individually, then dragged her finger across three that were touching, each tile glowing as she did.

"Do the corners count as connected?" I asked.

Tash smiled. "Good question. No, they do not. It has to be the sides or faces of each tile." She selected a few more tile configurations. "The number of tiles connected properly gives that army a ranking and can be as large as you like. If it is unopposed that still only counts as one point at the end of the game though. Points are scored throughout the game by the skirmishes and then tallied at the end by what armies remain in dominant or uncontested positions."

"OK. So, how do the skirmishes actually work?" I asked, increasingly intrigued by the game.

"Numbers. If I have an army that is three strong, and you have an army that is also three strong against it, they are null. Stalemate points. If one of us decides to reinforce our army with more tiles, that army gains the dominant position. If the opposing army doesn't match their strength or exceed it within three turns, a point is awarded to the dominant army." I could tell she was getting excited talking about the game.

"Does that army get wiped off the board?"

"No. You can always come back to it later, but at that stage you will just be winning back a point you already lost."

"Or you could use that army to tie into another one and win a skirmish elsewhere," I realized, getting the feel for the strategy.

"Yes! Yes you could!"

"Do you play on the bottom face?"

"Yes, but it's blind. You have to play by feel and memory. Same with each of our sides. The only difference is our sides remain blind to our opponents all the way through the game. After sixty moves each, the cube will expand again and rotate the top face to the bottom and vice versa. So, remember what was on top." The others, who had been chatting about something else, gravitated over to watch and listen to the rules. Will leaned on the back of my chair and peered over my shoulder, his hand ever so slightly grazing my back. It was such a small touch and probably unintentional, but I liked it.

"Mhmm. So, it's kind of like Battleship meets Go meets Chess. I think I got it. Let's try one," I said, keen to give it a go and maybe even impress Will.

Tash jumped slightly, surprised I was already confident in the rules or at least willing to dive in. "OK!" she said with a big smile.

She wiped the tutorial layout and pinned in the match start. By then an even larger group had leaned in to observe this new game. Tash let me lead off, my tiles highlighted in a cobalt glow. Her plays shone scarlet. It didn't take long to get the hang of the game's general principles, but Tash obviously had a much more advanced handle on the strategy. I had also not anticipated the sixty-move expansion and rotation very well. With no move ticker to clock our progress, it was based purely on memory.

After Tash's sixtieth move, the cube hummed and vibrated, mechanically separating and spacing new tiles between each row, making the game become fifteen by fifteen tiles per face and then flipping the bottom blind side to the top. I had ventured a couple of moves on the blind side to establish at least a few armies down there, but as it flipped, I realized I had misremembered their positions and set myself up for several attacks that were hard to defend against. After another sixty moves the match was over and the points tallied in holo projections over each face and then totaled above the cube. Tash beat me handily.

"Good game!" she said. She didn't boast or rub it my face at all, which was nice. She just seemed excited to have taught a human something and possibly have a new opponent to play.

"Yeah, you too!" I said, shaking her hand. I'm very competitive with games, but it was my first try. Next time I'd do better. So far I liked our new neighbors.

With the relationship between the humans and Lumenarians increasingly cemented aboard the ship, training sessions took on a new life. Our new neighbors were integrated into almost every aspect of our routine. Not only did this initiate exciting new challenges and experiences, new formations and strike teams were introduced, possibly orientations that would carry through to the war itself. Several humans throughout the ship were even given leadership positions on these teams. All of them were ex-military who had previously commanded troops. To no one's surprise, Will was given a squad. I knew he didn't want to lead, but apparently Arthur had refused to let him off the hook. After what Frank had told me, I could understand Will's hesitation regardless of how natural he was at it.

My squad leader was an older Lumenarian named Dredge. He was a very competent soldier, but he was also rigid in his tactics. That led to significant amounts of frustration, especially when our squad went head to head with squads like Will's during training. Dredge didn't adapt well to unorthodox methods, which Will often deployed. Will, being Will, never took it easy on other teams during training either. I could understand it from a learning perspective, but it could be hard on morale when he'd wipe the floor with people. His team was good to begin with, but once Will began pushing through his resistance to lead, they became nearly unstoppable.

"I know you have some weird crush on him, but he's a dick," Mikey complained to me over dinner (after a particularly bad ass-kicking from Will).

I chuckled. "Mikey, it wasn't personal," I said, eating some of my grey grub. "Damn. I grabbed the meatloaf, not the brisket," I muttered, glancing over at the food queue. That was the trouble with food that all looked the same.

"Well, he could take it easy on the other teams. Not all of us have freakish power."

"The Forsaken aren't going to take it easy on us. Will being a *dick* is just preparing everyone for what may be coming. You've heard the way the Lumenarians talk about them. It's like they're Voldemort."

"Yeah, yeah," Mikey grumbled, his arms crossed.

"Our deepest fear is not that we are inadequate. Our deepest fear is that—"

"Oh my God, shut up!" Mikey said. "You say it all the time."

It was one of my favorite quotes. Marianne Williamson. "And you still don't get it. You or me or Will 'playing small' doesn't serve the world. It all works here. His team is made better by his example, and everyone who fights him has to learn to adapt—also becoming better."

"Jesus! You don't always need to defend him."

"I don't."

"Yes you do."

"No I—"

"Yes, you do."

"No I don't, Mikey," I said with a glare. We had both dug our feet in despite being aware I was arguing like a child. *Siblings.* "But I believe what he's doing has its benefits. This isn't for fun. This is to survive a war. You're just being a baby because he spanked you."

"Fuck you!" He stared off, and we sat in silence for several moments. "He didn't spank us. Just…beat us…badly." He fought a grin and went back to eating.

I smiled and went back to my synthetic meatloaf. "What scenario were you guys running?" I asked. I wanted to learn as much about Will's tactics as possible, so when the time came, I wouldn't get caught with my pants down either.

"Boreal forest. Classic head to head."

"What'd he do?"

"He retreated," Mikey said, staring off in remembrance of the battle.

"Retreated?" That didn't sound like Will.

"It was a feint. Bottled up in an urchin formation, so we couldn't tell how many of them there were. Turns out half his squad were up in the trees. Soon as we passed, they dropped down behind and slaughtered us." Mikey exhaled loudly. I couldn't help but smile. It was a good move. Something I was sure my own squad leader, Dredge, would fall for. Easy to judge in hindsight, but I was pretty sure I would've seen through it. Will wouldn't retreat unless he had no choice.

"Don't smirk. You guys would have done the same thing."

"Well, we won't now."

The next day my squad was paired against Will's in a series of scenarios. Essentially, each scenario pitted teams against each other in large simfield battles that resembled the objectives one would find in paintball matches—capture the flag, storming the castle, defending positions, and so on.

We were just beginning our third bout of the day. The first two were fairly crushing and predictable defeats—an even-strength head to head and a night sim capture the flag where Will's team emerged unscathed and unseen, which was doubly impressive considering Will basically glowed in the dark. I guessed his work with Arthur was paying off. For us it was a frustrating exercise in obeying orders...and failing.

As Dredge took his place in front of us, he outlined the round's objective. We all listened somewhat wearily, knowing the likely outcome. Dredge wasn't doing much to inspire our confidence. He still refused to take a broader view of the battlefield, and it was costing us. He had too much tunnel vision for the objective, was too fixated on the target, too stubbornly locked in old transparent stratagems, and unable to factor in...Will.

"So, this time we're going to be attacking their bunker." Dredge's words were met by a collective groan, all of us considering this task particularly daunting. Even though Will's team would be down to half strength, a handicap for having the fortified position, it was still a large advantage for a team that didn't need one in the first place. "Hey! We can do this!" Dredge said, glaring around at all of us. "We're going to divide into three strike teams and flank up the sides." I instinctively rolled my eyes, which Dredge saw. "What, Li? You have a problem with that?" He glared at me. Behind his back, Jiro gave me an *Oh shit, stepped in it now* look.

"No, sir. I'm sure that's what the book would say to do," I replied, knowing that Will would tear us apart with his half team.

Dredge narrowed his four eyes at me and turned back to the rest of the group. "Left flank will be Jake's squad. Right flank will be—"

PHHHT!

Dredge was floored by a blue concussive blast. We all spun quickly and looked up the slope. Will was 200 meters up behind a tree with his rifle braced against its trunk. Miguel was behind another one to his side.

"Hey guys!" Miguel waved.

"We doing this or what?" Will shouted with a cocky grin.

"Return fire!" I yelled, turning my rifle toward Will and Miguel. Green and blue shots rifled up toward them, peppering the trees and ground in diffused bursts of energy. Will and Miguel were too quick though. They ducked behind their trees for cover and zig-zagged toward their bunker.

I glanced down at Dredge. Once someone was tagged in a battle, his or her communications were shut down, and they were mostly paralyzed until the action left their area, and they could depart the field. So, as much as Dredge wanted to bark orders at us and vent his anger toward Will, he was silent. He looked like a child throwing a tantrum.

"Sorry, Dredge. We'll take it from here though," I said, doing my best to keep my face neutral. Jiro suppressed a laugh. I was the number two, which meant it fell to me now.

Will had crept forward and isolated Dredge on purpose. It was a strategic play to take out the commander early, but knowing Will, I was pretty sure he did it for me. They were on defense for this one, but he took a reckless opportunity to go on the offense. It could have easily gone another way if we were more prepared.

I looked around at the rest of my team and was happy to see they all looked as relieved as I did. Maybe now we'd have a chance. It was still a difficult objective, but at least we could try a new approach—*my* approach. When I glanced at the ground again, Dredge was trembling with rage.

The bunker sat in the middle of a plateau at the top of a gradual slope through lush alien forests. The vegetation was large and prehistoric looking, dark shoots of navy and maroon rising toward the sim-field ceiling, a re-creation of the wilds on a planet named Ares. The structure itself was more of a fort than a bunker. Square with four walls of heavy concrete-like blocks and two entrance gates, one in the front and the other in the rear. The jungle around it was cleared for sightlines 360 degrees. Not a super-fun approach. Luckily, as per the simulation, the alien sun was setting and pitching everything into darkness, possibly our only advantage.

I led the column forward into the no-man's land between the jungle's edge and the bunker. We stayed tight and huddled low, moving quickly and trying to cover as much ground as possible before being spotted. About halfway across, the first shot tore over our heads, followed by a heavy salvo of emerald and sapphire blasts. In a flash we drew our kite shields and braced ourselves, collapsing into a circle, a glowing shell in the middle of the dark field.

The kite shield was a relatively new addition to our arsenal. The first time Flak demonstrated it to us, we were transported back to the Los Angeles Coliseum. It was the same device Sky had used to save our lives (except she had overloaded hers). A palm-size cylinder mag-clipped to our hips, which could be deployed as quickly as we could grab it. Telescopic bars shot out vertically and horizontally creating a roughly 2 ½-by-5-foot cross. Our bioenergy arced across the points and filled in between, creating the appearance of an electrified kite.

We pushed forward as a unit, stepping into the maelstrom. Peeking up through the cracks, I saw most of Will's team flocking to reinforce the front, committed to raining fire down on us. I ordered my team not to return fire. I wanted Will's team to be confident they had us pinned down. Several of the soldiers on the wall leaned out a little farther to get an angle.

"Sauce, now!" Four clean shots tore across the opening and dislodged four of Will's men from their perches. I had left my best marksmen in the tree line to pick off their wall sentries. Gowon, a Nigerian on our squad who had garnered the nickname "Sauce," led them. The guy *always* doused his food bricks with a synthesized hot sauce that clocked somewhere in the million-plus Scoville unit range. He and my other snipers would keep Will's troops ducking, and just like Will's tactics against my brother's squad, our formation veiled our numbers. "Second team, go!"

Just then a blast came from the back of the bunker, and the wall guards spun to investigate. A chaotic flurry of blue-and-green blasts reflected in the dark inside the fort. Just the distraction we needed to bridge the gap. My back row lobbed a volley of melt shots to rock back the sentries who weren't distracted.

"Levee!" I yelled. Our block of shields flattened out into two lines, the rear line retracting their kites and placing their Tempest rifles between the gaps. From there we pushed hard to the wall, hammering the upper parapet. At the doors we split into two groups and stacked on either side. The Lumenarian behind me, named Rocky, dipped past and placed a breaching charge on the gate. I was excited. I felt like we might actually have the drop on them. With a nod, we all braced, and the explosive seared through the door and exploded out the other side.

As we swept inside, I called in my marksmen. "Tree line, bring up the rear," I ordered through comms.

"Roger that," came the response in my ear.

"Jiro, Rocky, you know what to do."

"Rodge," they said as they peeled off.

The firefight inside the bunker was fierce but quick. Will's team took out over half my people in the ensuing battle, but amazingly, we won. I looked around, somewhat stunned. My team high-fived and cheered. I turned just in time to see my tree line team enter the complex, except it wasn't them. Will, Kilo, Miguel, and Megan stood there holding a Tempest in each hand—clearly my marksmen's.

"Honey, we're home."

Each of them also wore cocky smirks because they had us dead to rights—or so they thought.

"Now!" Suddenly, Jiro and Rocky popped up next to the gate, having played possum. The sudden lateral distraction pulled apart Will's flanks. Violent flashes lit up the space until everything went still. Will and his troops managed to take down a few with them, but in the end, it was Jiro, me, and five others from my team still standing. It was as if Will thought I wouldn't notice the core of his team wasn't present during the main fray. Maybe he thought the chaos of it all would hide that fact. His misstep; we had won.

"Lights dammit. Reach! What the fuck was that?" Flak growled at Will after the simulation had disintegrated back to the empty shell of the sim field.

"I mean…guess we lost," Will replied with a shrug.

Flak glared. "You're still treating this like a game, Reach! Grow up! I expect better!" I had never seen him so angry. He turned to the rest of us. "Yes. Here you can explore new tactics, learn new formations, and expand your skills, but it should never come at the expense of your people or the objective. Here you risk to learn, not to showboat! The only thing you learned today, Reach, is that Li is significantly smarter and more disciplined than you." I glanced at Will, who bowed his head and clenched his jaw, staring at the floor. "Training's over today." Flak marched toward the door and stopped next to me. "Good work, Li. You found the flaws in your opponent, adapted, and executed. Keep it up." He turned and left the field. It felt good, but it also felt like a hollow victory.

As everyone milled out, Will came over to me, looking sheepish. "Shit, huh?" he said. "Always knew you were smarter though."

"Flak's right."

Will looked up at me, then nodded slowly. "Yeah, I know." We stood there awkwardly for a moment. I was still irritated with the feeling of a partial win and the cavalier way in which Will had handled it. "You did great out there though—"

"Jesus, Will. Mikey was right, you're being a dick."

Will recoiled. "Wait, Mike—what?"

"He said you made them look like fools the other day, and I defended you. I get it. You're so much better at this than everyone else but you're not trying to lead by example. You're just fucking around!" He stared at the floor. "Everyone else is really trying here. To learn, get better, compete. It'd be one thing if you destroyed all the other teams cleanly, but instead you do it in a way that makes us all look like assholes. I won this time, and you still made it feel shitty. You're too cocky, Will." I knew

I had hurt him, but in the moment, I didn't care. He needed to hear it. It wasn't just that he made us look bad and made me feel humiliated. I knew all that arrogance was going to get him—and probably others—in serious trouble in the real war one day, and the kicked puppy look he was giving me only added to my anger.

"I'm sorry, Sarah," he said without making eye contact. "I should've taken it more seriously. Won't happen again."

I stared hard, trying to hold on to my indignation. Finally, I nodded. "Well, yeah. Do that from now on," I said, realizing my anger had almost melted away, but I couldn't give in that fast. Unfortunately, Will didn't miss much, and I saw a smile tug at the corner of his mouth. "Don't smile at me, William Reach."

"Sorry," he said, tightening his lips. "In my defense, the tree tactic against Mike's team was a good move regardless." I stared at him and shook my head slowly. If he hadn't had that stupid charming smirk on his face, I would've cuffed him.

"Dick."

"Hey, *you* beat *me*," he said, holding his hands up. Charming asshole.

CHAPTER XII

Meat

I was starting to get frustrated. It had been a year since we left Earth, and Will still hadn't made a move. *A year.* We still ate together almost every morning, were in all the same classes and training sessions, and slept only steps away from each other. I knew he felt something for me beyond friendship, and I was pretty sure he knew how I felt, but he couldn't make the next step. And knowing his history, as much as I wanted to take that leap for him, I couldn't. I deserved a damn medal for patience. I was even playing stupid games to try and rally his courage. Every time I pulled away to try and send the message, the bastard would flirt and charm back my attention. It was infuriating, and it was driving me crazy. I wasn't sure how much more I could take. It wasn't like he was my only option. It seemed like every day I had to turn down someone else who was actually willing to make a move. But my thoughts always returned to Will. It felt like some juvenile high-school-crush drama. I was too smart and too strong for it all. On top of that, did I really want to put back together a broken man? I wasn't sure he could do it himself. He seemed more together since I had first met him, but he still had a ways to go. Every time I thought about that, considered how I'd been doing that in some way my whole life, struggled with the responsibility, I still came back to…yes. For Will I would. Dammit.

After a particularly rough CQC training session—breaching and sweeping a building for hostile Forsaken simulations—I lingered behind to stretch my leg. I flexed my foot against the wall and leaned my hips in to stretch my hamstring. Noticing me, Will stopped at the entrance and gestured for the others to head off, saying we'd catch up.

"You OK?" he asked, coming over to me. The two of us were the last ones in the sim field.

"Yeah. Just tweaked it a bit on the last set of stairs," I said, switching to a quad stretch. I lifted my foot up behind me and grabbed my ankle. I stumbled slightly, losing my balance—or at least made it seem that way.

Will lunged in to steady me, putting his hand on my arm. "Careful," he said, staring into my eyes and smiling. Guys like to feel like the hero. Poor unbalanced damsel me. His smile took on a bit of a smirk though, which made me think he probably saw through it. I was far from a trapped princess, and he knew it. "Falling over while stretching would have been embarrassing."

I couldn't help myself. I was done waiting. I let go of my ankle and grabbed him by the back of his neck, pulling him into a deep kiss. The kind of kiss that feels electric and sun-like (or maybe that was the biotech). The kind that stops time. It surges through your lips and ripples across your body, raising hairs and goose bumps. The kind of kiss that you remember in your whole body. So much for letting him make the first move. When we parted, slowly, I opened my eyes, a bit nervous to see his reaction. His eyes were still closed and his lips slightly parted. When he finally opened his eyes, the whites flashed with arcs of cobalt fire. I sank back on my heels. His expression was…difficult to read. A combination of shock, confusion, awkward joy, pain. I didn't know, but it wasn't particularly good.

"Uh…" he droned. Wasn't exactly the reaction I was hoping for.

"I-I'm sorry. I—" I looked somewhere between his neck, chest, the floor, my hands, the walls, anywhere but his eyes.

"No, it was…um…"

Just then Codec materialized in a static flash beside us. We both stepped back from each other as if we had been caught in some dirty act. Shit.

"Ms. Li, Mr. Reach. Good evening."

"Hey, Codec, what's up?" Will said hastily.

Codec hesitated a moment, as if the AI was also aware of the immense awkwardness in the room. "Will, Arthur would like to see you in his quarters at your earliest convenience."

"Yep, OK. I'll head right there," Will replied. Too quickly. It felt like a knife to the heart. I couldn't look at him and only caught the faintest sideways glance back. I thought I had felt a fire in the kiss, but maybe I was wrong. My cheeks flushed a humiliated crimson, like a little girl whose Valentine's crush hadn't even noticed her.

"I'll let him know. Catch you crazy kids later." *Goddammit, Codec.* He disappeared, leaving the silent ocean-like void between Will and me.

Will hesitated, looked like he was going to speak, then put his head down and turned to the door. "Uh…yeah. I…have to go."

"Yeah, no. Don't keep Arthur waiting."

Will stood awkwardly still for a moment. "Yeah…I'll see you later." With that he turned and left the sim field, vanishing down the corridor and leaving me in the large empty space. Alone.

Shiiiit.

By the time I got back to the aviary, I had already rerun the event through my head a thousand times. The looks before, the kiss, the reaction. I felt like an idiot. How had I misread things so thoroughly? Had I been schoolgirl crushing on Will so badly for the past year that I had disregarded all sense? It wasn't like me to crush on anyone, let alone someone who seemed so ardent in playing hard to get or not interested at all. Goddammit. I was smarter than that. Much smarter.

I sat down in the market below the center spire, people bustling around after their training; chatting and laughing and drinking and playing games. The cherished forgotten moments between the realities imposed by our relentless instruction. I couldn't go back to my room to stew in secluded misery—my intellect railing against the melodrama of it. I felt robotic. So, I did my best to push it from my mind and observe the life around me. Lumenarian and human now seamlessly integrated in the housing complex, the beautiful mosaic of it all, some great new art on the walls, another soccer game.

It wasn't working. I couldn't focus on anything but the dreaded moment.

Suddenly, Megan saddled up a chair next to me, drinks in hand. "Jesus, Sarah, nobody's buying that half-ass smile you've had on your face the last ten minutes." She set one of the glasses in front of me. "Drink."

"Nobody—what?" The thought of a group studying me from a distance in my current state was horrifying. How obvious was I?

"Naw. It was just me. The boys weren't paying attention," she said, gesturing over to Miguel, Jiro, Kilo, and Cash, who were absorbed in animated discussion. Mikey and Seyyal must have been off somewhere, most likely together. Happy. "Fuck is wrong with you?"

"Nothing. I'm fine!" I felt and heard my voice over-pitch the lie. Megan stared at me with an unconvinced raised eyebrow. "Megan, I'm fine," I said, steadying my voice.

"Wow. You almost sounded convincing on that one." She chuckled. Then her gaze softened, and she glanced around. "Sare, it's me. What's up?" I shook my head, avoiding her eyes and trying to shirk it off. "It's Will, isn't it?"

I looked up at her. "You know what? Everyone is always talking about Will. It's not always about Will."

She held a long, still stare. "Did you guys bang?"

"What? No!" I said loudly, a few people glancing over. I sank farther into my chair. "No, Megan. We didn't…bang."

"OK. I believe that. It's definitely still about him though."

"Goddammit."

"I know you, Sare. What happened?" I glared at her, infuriated that she could see through my veil. Then it broke in me. I couldn't be angry with her for seeing exactly what was happening. She was blunt, but she also saw a lot. "Did he finally make a move?"

"No…I did." If I couldn't tell Megan, who could I tell?

"Fuck yeah! How'd it go?"

I cocked my head to the side. "How do you think it went?"

"Right. Sorry. But, like, what happened? Is he a shitty kisser?" She leaned in close, unable to hide her curiosity.

"No. Good kisser. Just..."

"What?"

"I think it was a huge mistake. He seemed so...off afterwards," I said, feeling an embarrassed prickle in my cheeks.

"Oh. Maybe *you're* the shitty kisser."

"Hey!"

"I'm kidding! Pfft." She jostled me. "You probably just knocked his goddamn socks off. What did he say after?"

"He didn't really say anything. He got called away by Arthur."

"Huh..." She looked up in thought. "Well, that doesn't mean anything. Not like he woulda told Arthur to give him a date bail call." She narrowed her eyes at me. "And you do realize Will is fucked up, right?"

"Jesus, Megan, he's not fucked up."

"Uh, yeah. He is. But that's OK. Just means he's gonna be a hard nut to crack. You two are perfect for each other. I mean, you have your shit together, and you're way smarter than he is, but you're smarter than everyone. And he only seems to like you more for that. Far as I can tell, it doesn't intimidate him at all, which happens with a lot of guys. Insecure jackasses. Hell, you should've seen the last guy to hit on me. Told him I was a lesbian, and he got offended as if his charm had failed to convert me or something. Anyway, Will's totally secure, besides the part where he's so fucked up and you're not really. But he obviously likes you. You could see that from space. He's just really, really fucked up."

"OK, you can stop saying that," I said, feeling both uplifted and annoyed.

"I'm just saying. It's like a nuclear bomb between you two. Right now you both have radiation sickness. At some point you're either gonna become a mutant or die."

"What does that even mean?"

"I think that's one of those things that made more sense in my head before I said it. Something about time and proximity—colliding objects in space or something. Never mind."

I shook my head in response but smiled. It did help talking with Megan. We sat quietly for a few minutes sipping on our drinks, Megan conceding to let up on the conversation.

Two Lumenarians set up a game of Commander's Die next to us, and I watched them play for a couple of moves. They were playing a speed game, and it seemed too quick to actually read and form strategy, but I saw it piecing together slowly.

"Sarah," Megan said, suddenly drawing me back.

"Megan."

"You need to go find Will and kiss him again."

I stared at her for a moment and then laughed. "Oh yeah?"

"Yes," she said in the same tone. "Force him to make a choice. It'll drive you mad otherwise." She wasn't wrong necessarily. Maybe a bit blunt, but she cared.

"I could also just talk to him."

"Sure. Fine. Whatever. If you want to pussy-foot around it," she said with a cheeky grin. "Go get him, Sarah. But remember, it's not too late to like girls."

Just then Seyyal left Mikey back with the guys and arrived at our table. She glanced between Megan and me, narrowing her eyes. "Is this a Will thing?"

I'm not sure if it was that I knew Megan would hound me relentlessly if I didn't go or whether I fully believed this was the best action, but I made my way to Arthur's quarters to head off Will as he left. I walked down one of the aft-section corridors playing out everything I wanted to say in my head, all the ways it might go depending on how he responded.

I rounded another corner and faltered a step when I saw Will at the far end of the corridor walking with his head down. I hadn't expected to run into him so soon. I didn't feel ready. About halfway between us, three Lumenarian engineering-crew members were working on a panel that looked like it had been pried off by force or possibly blown out by some sort of surge, the edges bent and scarred. Will looked up and saw me. After a moment of surprise, his face spread in a shy smile, the sight lifting my courage as we got closer. Three people were walking slowly in front of me, another three in front of Will.

"Excuse me," I said as I brushed past. It took me a second to realize they were wearing armor under their robes and had Warthog pistols clipped onto their legs. I looked up and saw Will realize it at almost the same moment. His face dropped suddenly.

"Sarah!" he yelled. Everything seemed to move in slow motion.

One of the humans on Will's side of the corridor pulled his weapon and fired on the Lumenarian workers. The first shot ripped the back half of one of their heads apart in a vicious splatter of black blood, tissue, and bone. In a flash, Will had tackled the one closest to him and grabbed his gun.

I only saw the bright glares of light out of the corner of my eye as I turned and engaged the ones closest to me. The two remaining Lumenarians were unarmed and ducked under several more blasts. I struggled with the first human, pinning his gun hand into the air as several shots hit the ceiling. His elbow glanced off my cheek, and I felt blood pour from a cut there. I gritted my teeth and fed him two uppercuts to the gut, hunching him over and twisting his arm behind his back. I barely dodged a shot aimed at my face and without even thinking pulled up the one I had under my control. Two shots tore into his chest as I held his body up for cover. Reaching down I brought up his arm and snatched the Warthog before it fell from his grip. Two powerful blasts disintegrated my would-be assassin's torso in a torrent of crimson blood and entrails. I ducked my head behind my body shield again as the last man opened fire, sending three more rounds into the meat and one that passed clean through and grazed my hip.

"We are the OnSpec motherfuck—" someone shouted from somewhere in the corridor, the words cut off by a loud commotion of bodies and a bright flash of light.

Suddenly, it was silent. I peeked around the shredded body in my arms and saw a headless form slumped down on its knees, unnaturally propped up by a rigid locking of its armor. I heard footsteps running toward me, and I spun my gun arm down the corridor to stop them. I found myself aiming straight at Will, who held his hands up. He had a pistol in his hand and blood streaked across his torso.

His biotech, which was flared up in a bright sapphire glow, faded back to normal. "Sarah, it's me! You're OK. It's over," he said, creeping toward me, his hands still out in front of him. I realized how hard I was breathing and that I was still aiming the gun at him. I lowered the pistol and dropped it to the floor. It landed with a clank that seemed to echo for longer than it should. I stared at the tattered mass of flesh in my arms and then shoved it away. It landed with a sickening squelch. I glanced over and saw the two Lumenarians getting to their feet. One had been grazed in the leg and stood on it uneasily. Both wore the dark oil-slick blood of their fellow crew member, now splayed out on the floor.

"*Albatross* command, there's been an attack. We need security and medical personnel to aft corridor Bravo-8 section 22. Combatants down. Seven dead," one of them said into comms. Suddenly, the hallway lit up with pulsing red lights and drawn-out alarms.

"*Albatross* crew, report to general quarters, and remain there until notified. Repeat. Report to general quarters, and await further instruction," a voice boomed over the ship-wide comms. I looked around in a daze. It was loud, but it seemed like it was coming from a long way away. Will stood in front of me, staring into my eyes, concerned. He set down the pistol he was still holding and put his hands on the sides of my arms.

"Sarah, are you OK?" he asked, looking me over, then staring back into my eyes. He tore off a piece of his robe and held it to my hip, glancing down to make sure it was in the right place. I thought he looked scared, but I don't think it was for himself. I felt myself shaking under his hands. Tears welled up in my eyes, but I choked them back. A by-product of the adrenaline spike in my system slowly ebbing away. Or maybe because I had just killed two people. *I just killed two people.*

"I don't...I...they were..." I looked down at myself, realizing I was covered in blood.

"I know. I know," Will said, a slight waver in his voice. Then he pulled me in with his free arm and squeezed me in a hug. I held onto him like he was the only anchor saving me from being torn away by a hurricane. I felt the blood and gore on my exposed skin and in my hair and between our bodies. I didn't care. I couldn't let go.

Just then Flak and six other Lumenarian security personnel swept onto the scene, weapons raised. "What the hell happened?" Flak growled, staring at the blood and carnage and blast scoring on the walls. A moment behind them, the medical personnel showed up, and the corridor suddenly seemed very crowded. "Reach, Li, you OK?" he asked.

I kept my face buried in Will's shoulder, but I felt him nodding. "Yeah. Sarah needs someone to look at her though." Will gently pushed me away from his chest but kept his hands on me. Everything still sounded like it was coming to me from a distance or through a long tunnel. I focused on Will's eyes as he hunched over to look at me.

"I'm alright," I said.

"I know you are. But Medical is just gonna look after that cut on your cheek and the one on your hip," he said gently. I looked down, having forgotten about the graze on my hip, even with Will's hand still applying pressure. It didn't look serious, and it didn't hurt, but I saw a slow ooze of bright red blood.

"OK," I said quietly.

"I'm not going anywhere. They're going to patch you up, and then we'll go home."

"Home sounds nice." I almost felt drunk. Outside myself. The levitating stretcher was divided into three sections, and the medical personnel folded it into a reclining chair, sitting me down while they looked me over. Will stepped aside to speak with Flak.

"They killed two of my men in the nearby armory. Took the weapons and armor. Probably sabotaged the panel too. Fucking cowards," I overhead Flak say, staring at the place where the engineering crew had been working.

"One of them yelled 'We are the OnSpec' before I clipped him."

"Lights dammit," Flak cursed. "Thought we weeded them out." Flak pushed the headless corpse with his foot. The body tipped over and clanked to the floor, the armor collapsing back into its prism pucks.

"Yeah. That would've been nice," Will began but was silenced by a raised hand as Flak cocked his head, listening to his comms.

"Deploy security teams. I'm on my way." Flak signaled to his team.

"What's going on?"

"More attacks."

"You need help?"

"We got it covered. But…thank you, Reach. You and Li saved lives." He nodded to Will and then to me. Then Flak and his team took off down the corridor.

My wounds didn't require me to go to a med bay, so they dressed them right there. A few minutes later, more crew arrived to deal with the bodies. Will didn't leave my side. I realized I had tears running down my face, but I couldn't remember when I had started to cry, and I didn't particularly feel like crying. I wiped them away and glanced up at Will. "I'm sorry," I said, not sure why.

Will crouched so he was level with me and smiled sadly. "You have nothing to be sorry about," he said. He turned to the medical crew. "We good here?" They indicated that I was OK to leave, and Will helped me out of the chair. "Is it clear to return to Charlie aviary?"

One of the medical crew paused, listening to his comms device. "You're clear."

Will picked up one of the armor discs from the nearest body and placed it on his hip. The hex plates spread around his lower half. He picked up a Warthog and clipped it to his leg. "Just in case." Then he grabbed another one and put in my hand, raising it to my chest. He sent a gentle trickle of energy through me to activate it. It never hurt when someone else linked with me like that. It was more of an energizing buzz, almost comforting. The armor wrapped around my body. He looked me in the eyes again. "You ready?" I nodded, and we walked side by side back to Charlie aviary in silence. The corridors had been cleared for the alert, and the only crew that passed us were Lumenarian security and medical personnel. The ship was on lockdown.

When we got to the mouth of the housing complex, Will stopped and took my hand. He looked at the floor for a moment, then looked me in the eyes.

"Will—" he cut me off with a passionate kiss. We separated and stared into each other's eyes, seeing everything we needed. Then I pulled him back in. There was no hesitation in him. No withdrawal or uncertainty. If I had thought the first kiss felt like a fire, this was like a volcano. He held me tightly, and we backed against the wall, pressing into it as we thrashed against each other. It was clumsy and beautiful.

The aviary was a ghost town. Everyone had retreated to their dwellings to await the end of the alert and release from general quarters. We stumbled through the park, up the lift, and down the landing in each other's arms, as if separating meant we would float away into space.

Inside my unit, our armor disks and Will's Warthog clanked to the floor, and we stumbled to the shower. We got in fully clothed, the warm water washing the blood away in crimson raindrops and pink swirls around the drain. He stripped off my suit, and I peeled off his, letting them fall to the shower floor. After a few minutes we broke into laughter when we noticed the water pooling up to our ankles around the clothes-clogged drain, and we tossed them out in a sopping pile on the floor, resuming our exploration. He ran his fingers through my hair and tilted my face up to his. If his face hadn't been dripping with water, I would have thought he was crying—some twisted relief there, a burden lifted. He took several deep breaths with his mouth wide open, the way you do in a shower so you don't inhale water. Then he pulled me in and kissed me more tenderly than I would have thought he was capable of.

His hand grazed my hip wound, and he recoiled, worried he'd hurt me. "Sorry," he said. I held his eyes in mine and took his hand, pressing it against my hip. It throbbed with pain, and I felt tears welling up, but I felt like I needed to feel it all.

Later, when we both lay on my bed, tangled in each other's arms and legs, I stared at the pile of wet clothing on the floor. A small trail of residual blood ran snake-like from the puddle. I had almost forgotten. Somehow. I'd never killed anything before—*anyone* before. I had signed up for an intergalactic war, and the first thing I killed…was a human.

CHAPTER XIII

Abandoned

Since that first turbulent night together, Will and I had been alternating back and forth between each other's rooms almost every night. It was a clumsy passion in the beginning, each stumbling around the other's body and resistances. We both had locked pain away in the tension of our muscles and the depths of our bones, and we hadn't allowed anyone to unlock it.

And we weren't just having sex. As good as it felt sometimes, there was always a sliver or a canyon of detachment in a hook-up with someone I didn't really care about. It filled a need I thought I had until the repetition of it showed the empty shell—the pleasure almost purely physical and lacking that extra chemical that turned lust into ecstasy. Despite what some players might say, the best sex in the world isn't complete without that something you feel deep in your chest. Sometimes you can be fooled into it or fool yourself into it, but in the end you know. Maybe some can live without it, and that's fine, but it wasn't for me anymore.

Will needed to be the one to take that leap. Even though I had kissed him, he had to get it right in his head and follow through. So, when it happened, Will went deep, all the broken pieces bare behind his eyes, and I followed him. We squeezed each other so tight it was like we were trying to melt the cracks closed. The unfamiliar ground became firm under our feet, and the more we gave in to each other and explored, the firmer it got. Thankfully, the walls of the units were fully soundproof— I'm pretty sure they were anyway.

I had fallen asleep in Will's arms again, the tufts of his chest hair brushing against my back and the stubble of his five-day beard scratching the side of my neck. He was always very warm, which I imagined being a problem on summer nights back home, but in the mellow cool of my unit, he was the perfect temperature.

The room rumbled slightly, and I perked awake, barely opening my eyes to take in where I was. I thought I had felt something, but the room was still. Maybe I had imagined it. The faint glow from a light band along the floor threw shadows around the room and illuminated it like dull fog in underpowered headlights, shapes but no real detail.

I reached up and ran my fingers along Will's shoulder, tracing the lines of his shrapnel scars and the thinner lines of his biotech tattoos that rose slightly off his skin. He was sound asleep, a slight snore and whistle coming from his nose, apparently caused by a break during his original military training years before. His breathing was deep, and every breath pushed the front of his firm body gently into me. Any sign of the booze paunch he had when he first boarded the *Albatross* was long gone. His thunderous but comforting heartbeat pulsed into my spine. Feeling it, I closed my eyes and tried to get back to sleep.

Suddenly the room shook again, enough that I heard a few things shift on my shelves. I opened my eyes, sat up and looked around. It was silent save for Will's whistling nose. Nothing moved. Just as I was about to lay back down, the room trembled again, a low grumble, like tires driving over a cattle guard. I brushed off Will's arm and stood up, seeing if my feet felt anything more.

"Will," I said in a whisper. He mumbled to himself and rolled slightly but didn't wake up. "Hey Will—Will!"

He twitched awake and groggily wiped his eyes. "Hey, what, uuuh... what's up?" he asked, trying to blink and stretch his eyes through the sleep.

"The room was shaking."

Still half asleep, Will smiled. "Yeah, it was," he said with two cheesy finger pistols.

I couldn't help but chuckle but then snapped out of it. "I'm serious. It felt like—" Suddenly, the room jolted violently, causing me to lose my balance. I caught myself on the edge of my desk. Will rolled out of the bed and landed on the floor.

"Son of a bitch," he groaned, climbing to his feet. Just then red lights filled the room and pulsed an alert. I saw Will's face harden in the blinking light. A command call should have been broadcast, but there was none.

Fully awake, Will clicked into soldier mode. "Codec." Nothing happened. "Codec!" Suddenly, the image of Codec flickered in the room but seemed to be disrupted. We could make out his face moving, but only a garbled nonsensical sound came out.

"What's going on?" I asked, grasping at any information we could squeeze out. Codec flickered and then disappeared. Will and I shared a quick look and then threw on our bodysuits.

Will raised his forearm. "Combat," he said into his band. His bodysuit tightened and padded out into the underlayer for our armor, his blue circuit lines glowing through. I followed his lead and initiated the preset. We didn't have any weapons or body armor in our rooms. We had returned the equipment from the OnSpec attack several months earlier, but at least the suits provided some basic protection.

Will went to the door and glanced back at me to make sure I was ready to go. I took a deep breath and let it out slowly, then nodded. Will held my gaze for a moment and then gave me a tight-lipped smile. I knew what he was thinking because I was thinking it too. *Be careful.* He turned to the door and paused before edging it open and stepping into the hallway.

Thousands of others had flooded the complex to see what all the commotion was about. Frank, Mikey, Miguel, Megan, Jiro, and Seyyal rushed over to us.

"What the fuck is going on?" Miguel asked. "Codec's glitched out. Couldn't get anything from him." Just then another ship-rattling BOOM caused us all to brace ourselves.

"This isn't good. Something's very wrong," my brother said. I glanced at him, worried he might be on the verge of a panic attack. It was probably just me being a big sister since he hadn't had one in months, but either way, I watched him closely.

"Kilo? Cash?" Will asked, glancing around the aviary. Miguel rushed over to their rooms to check on them. Will looked concerned but calm, scenarios probably spinning through his head. A large crowd had started to form around us, Will being the beacon that he was. People throughout the complex gathered around the other leaders who had been popping up throughout training, everyone looking for answers. As I looked around, I realized none of the Lumenarians were present. And it wasn't just the aliens. It seemed like we were missing a substantial portion of Charlie's occupants.

Miguel returned and shook his head. "They're not here. None of them are," he said, noticing what I had. There was a loud murmur as people began to give in to their fear and uncertainty. I think everyone had expected our hosts to come out and magically fix everything. But for some reason, they were gone. Another BOOM shook the ship as the red lights continued to flash.

"Where is everyone?" someone shouted. Yes, where the hell were they? I tried to think about all the possible reasons their absence could be explained that weren't negative, but any way I looked at it, it seemed like we had been hung out to dry. There are never quite enough lifeboats on a sinking ship. Had the Lumenarians warned their own and a portion of the others, so they could make it off the ship?

"They left us! They went to save themselves!" someone yelled through the commotion, mirroring what I had been thinking. Panic set in as paranoid thoughts swirled in everyone's minds. I was outwardly keeping it together, but inside a swarm of bees was fighting to get out.

"Quiet down," Will said firmly but not loud enough to reach the whole gathering.

I leaned in close to him. "You're going to need to be a lot louder than that," I said, a smile hiding my fear.

Will turned and stared into my eyes, telling me without a word that it was going to be OK. He was steady, and it looked like he had decided on a course of action, a look that was not echoed by many. Then he winked. "Maybe this'll do the trick." He energized all his biotech, creating a bright blue flare that pierced through the apocalyptic flashing red lights. "Quiet!"

Our crowd went silent instantly, and that silence spread throughout the aviary, all eyes drawn to the sapphire beacon. He let his tech fade and then cleared his throat. "We need to find out what the hell happened. Doesn't matter right now where everyone else is. Either we find them along the way, or we don't. Simple as that. But right now we need to move. Get to the bottom of this." Everyone listened, and most of the crowd nodded in acknowledgment. "I don't know about all of you, but I'm feeling a bit naked without armor and a gun."

"Who put you in charge?" Tariq asked.

Several turned and stared at him.

The awkward silence was broken by Frank. "Shut the fuck up, Tariq," he said, instantly stripping Tariq of his confidence. Frank rarely spoke up in a large group, but when he did, it was either well thought out, direct, or just forceful, leaving little to no space for argument. Frank turned his attention back to Will. "What're you thinking?"

Will nodded to Frank and glanced around the aviary. "Everyone stand by." Suddenly, he whistled through his fingers. Several of the others around the dome who had been trying to wrangle the masses looked over. Will held up his fist for a moment to make sure they were paying attention and then circled his finger over his head before pointing to a place on the central structural column. He was calling a meeting to coordinate the next steps. Once he got the message across, he turned back to Frank and me. "OK, I'm gonna try and coordinate some stuff here. Check if anyone has any weapons in their rooms—batons, knives, baseballs, a fucking branch, I don't care. Anything is better than nothing. I'll be right back." He shot each of us an intense stare, saying all he could in it.

"Roger that, *sir*," I said with a nervous smile. Will winked and then took off toward the central spire. I turned to Frank and exhaled slowly. A series of smaller impacts shook the aviary, causing us all to brace again.

"Well, let's herd the cats," Frank said. We started spreading Will's orders to search for weapons throughout our group, which was now several hundred people along our level and the one or two above and below that had been looking toward Will's zone for guidance. "Anything you've got! We need to be prepared for anything!"

People darted back to their rooms and then returned moments later with everything from batons to pocketknives to chairs to broken pieces of memorabilia from home. The red pulsing glow of the alert made it all look like a strange scene from the movie *The Warriors*. Everyone huddled together, muttering as they awaited the next order. When Will returned from his tactical meeting, he didn't waste any time laying out the plan.

"OK, everyone quiet down!" he said, raising and lowering his arms to silence the group. "We're going to be breaking up into our training squads, and you'll get direction from them. So, find your squad leaders and rally. If you can't find any of your team, tag onto the nearest one." Hundreds of anxious faces stared at Will, not moving. "Now! Move into your teams now. Bravo squads 1-0 through 9-0 with me!"

There was a jumble of flailing bodies and apparent chaos as everyone jostled around to find their squads and figure out what was next. I was Bravo 4-1. With Dredge absent, I was in charge, so I gathered my people and hung out close to Will, Frank, Miguel, Megan, Mikey, Jiro, Sauce, and Seyyal. Frank was 2-1, Seyyal was 5-1, and the rest took up number two and three positions on the squads. My brother was Bravo 2-8. I was glad Mikey was on Frank's squad because I knew Frank would take care of him. Jiro and Sauce took spots three and six on my squad, and I knew they'd cover my back well. Apart from Will, who was Bravo 1-0, we were all without our squad leaders, and except for probably Frank, we were all feeling the pressure of it.

Will turned to us once we had fallen in. "OK, we'll be making our way along starboard corridor Charlie Golf 5 toward armory six to gear up and rally with Charlie 1-0 and Delta 1-1." Will said each designation clearly and deliberately, so everyone was certain of the details. "From there our objective is the command deck. Get some fucking answers. We obviously don't have comms yet for whatever goddamn reason, but our suit bands are working, so use those. Everyone good?" There was a collective nod. I was nervous, but I was glad our team looked the way it did and had Will leading it. "Alright. Let's kick some ass." The red-alert lights blinked steadily, their ominous glow filling the *Albatross* as we headed out.

As we made our way out of the aviary in tight formations, I glanced around, seeing most of the other groups diverting off in different directions and to different objectives. It wasn't perfect. We definitely weren't prepared for anything like this yet. It was a ragtag resistance, but at least we had points to move toward. Nobody looked comfortable, the nervous twitches rippling through the line as we made our way toward the armory.

Our squads broke in two and moved in staggered single-file columns along each wall. It was eerie how quiet and empty the corridors were. The regular cacophony was silent except for the occasional boom and shake of whatever was happening elsewhere on the ship and the soft rustle of our footsteps and clothing.

Looking ahead I noticed the last soldier in Will's stack, a young guy named Joey, leaning against the wall. I tapped him on the shoulder. "Six inches to a foot," I whispered.

"What?" he said, turning to look at me. His face was sweaty, and it looked like he was struggling to keep it together.

"Shots like to hug and skip along walls. Stay six inches to a foot off."

"Right, thanks." He nodded and turned forward, stepping away from the wall.

It was strange wandering toward the unknown. Half of me was relieved I hadn't come across anything, and the other half spun wild fictions and fears of what was ahead. I was thankful for the quiet, but like they say, it was too quiet. *Get it over with!* screamed through my head. Despite the feeling of dread, we moved steadily through the corridors without incident and with no sign of what was affecting the ship.

In fact, all the way to the armory, we saw nothing. All the same, we stacked at the door and breached the room like we were armed with more than Stone Age weaponry, flooding in with full force. Dead silence. The armory was untouched, save for a few weapons that had fallen on the floor, presumably from the impacts on the hull.

"Gear up," Will said. He didn't have to tell anyone twice. People shoved their way to the gear. I engaged the hex armor and clipped a Warthog to my leg and a Tempest to my back. I had no idea what we were walking into, so I loaded a shoulder sling pack that doubled as a bandolier with jolt shots and extra clips. I tossed in a few grenades as well. Lastly, I clipped a kite shield onto my hip, though I hoped I wouldn't need it.

Jiro tapped me on the shoulder with a small case and handed it to me, all business. Opening it, I took out the Raptor-eye contact lenses, nick-named "Raps," and put them in my eyes. I blinked a few times to configure them, switching rapidly between layers of infrared and bringing up the HUD. With most of the *Albatross* offline, there wasn't an abundance of local information, but at least they'd highlight immediate threats.

Charlie squads showed up a few minutes behind us and went about organizing their loadouts. They had had the same eerie, quiet march from the aviary with no opposition. We were still waiting on Delta squads, the tense minutes stretching by with no sign. I went over to Will, who had positioned himself by the armory entrance to scan for them, tapping on his forearm band.

"Nothing from Delta?" I whispered.

He looked up and shook his head. "No. They should've been here by now—"

"Bravo 1-0, Delta 1-1, copy?" crackled over the comms. How the hell did they get comms back up?

"Delta 1-1 go ahead. What's your twenty?"

"Had to divert to armory four. Barely made it." He sounded out of breath. "They're everywhere. Foxtrot is gone. All of them. Slaughtered." Will's mouth set in a hard line. "Found some sort of jammer en route and took it out, but not sure how long we'll have before they get it or another one up and running."

"Is it—"

"Forsaken. They've boarded." The words echoed through the room. Everyone stopped and turned to stare at Will and me, each face a mirror of terror. They must've found out about our mission and come to cut us off. "They're outside the armory!" We heard searing blasts of energy reverberate on the other end of the comms. "We're not going to be able to—"

"Delta 1-1?" Will asked. The only sounds that came through were grunts, the sounds of a large scuffle, energy blasts, and concussive booms. "Delta 1-1?" Nothing came through. Will looked around the room, every eye skittish. "All *Albatross* teams—" There was a loud squeal over the comms and then dense static, followed by silence. "Shit." Didn't take them long to get the jammer working again.

"Foxtrot's mission was to secure the reactor," I said, "right?"

"Yeah." Will looked around, obviously trying to think of some new course of action.

"I need to go secure it."

Will's eyes snapped toward me. "No."

"Will—"

"No, Sarah. You're not going to—"

"Yes, Will," I said, matching his glare. "It makes the most sense for me to go. I know far more about it than anyone else you could send, and you need to secure the command deck."

Will turned his back to the rest of the room to face me. He stared for a long moment. "Sarah…" In his eyes I saw all the things he wanted to say but couldn't. He took my hand and exhaled slowly. "I'm going to send Frank's team with you. And the Charlie teams."

"That leaves you short-handed two squads," I said. "That's crazy."

"We'll be fine—"

"Will, you can't—"

"This isn't a debate. That's an order." Will glared at me. After a moment he softened. "It's closer to the command deck for us. And we know for sure there's harm in your way. You're taking the extra people." Without waiting for my response, Will turned back to the group, all of them anxiously waiting for direction. "Bravos 2-1 and 4-1 teams will take Charlie teams to secure the reactor. The rest of us are continuing on to the command deck." Will looked around. No one moved. "This isn't what we expected our first engagement to be, but it's here. This is our home. The *Albatross* is *ours*. We have uninvited guests. Show them the door in the most violent ways possible. They wanted a look at humans; make them fucking regret it." If there was any doubt in anyone's mind about how dangerous Will was, it vanished in that moment. The look on his face was cold and merciless and his eyes flickered menacingly with blue fire. Despite finding it somewhat worrisome, it had the effect of driving courage into the ashen faces around us.

The two teams stacked on the inside of the armory doors, Frank's and Mikey's team in my line. We had our plans, knew our routes, and were armed to the teeth. It was just a matter of crossing the threshold and going at it.

Halfway back in Will's line, I noticed Seyyal staring at Mikey and nodding encouragement. She was guiding him by taking several deep breaths and exhaling them slowly. Mikey matched her breathing and nodded back with an appreciative smile. Everyone else was too distracted with their own worried thoughts to notice, but I saw the love pass between them.

I looked across the entrance to Will. He had his eyes closed and one hand pressed against a wall panel. I knew he was feeling the ship's pulse; I'd seen him do it before—did it myself from time to time. It was always comforting. As if we were part of a larger living thing. When he opened his eyes, he looked so steady and calm in the face of everything while I felt my hands shaking on my Tempest. I didn't want to let go and touch the wall for fear that my other hand would rattle my weapon too hard.

"OK, everyone good?" he asked the group, receiving nervous nods.

"Wouldn't mind stopping by the mess on the way," Miguel said from behind Will. "Feeling a bit peckish." Everyone stared for a second and then chuckled.

"Could lend you some *hellfire* if you want to spice it up a bit," Sauce said from a few slots behind me.

"Oh, hell no! I don't have a death wish, Sauce," Miguel replied. I smiled at Will, who seemed to take the levity as a good sign. He locked eyes with me and smiled wryly.

"Think you could use a few less trips to the mess, pal," he said.

Miguel chuckled. "Make you pay for that one later, Willy." The laughter died down quickly, and Will leaned into his rifle. I did the same.

"All teams on my go." Will nodded to me.

"See you on the other side," I whispered.

"Not if I can help it…Go!" Will tore through the doors and turned left down the corridor, his team tight on his heels. I led my team right, toward the reactor access, Frank and Mikey close behind.

Wherever the battles onboard were happening, we seemed to be skirting them. In the distance, we heard the odd scream and blast shake the still air, but nothing was in our direct path. Then we rounded another corner, and the sight stopped us in our tracks.

We had found Foxtrot—what was left of them. The white and space-grey walls and ceiling were coated in thick crimson blood that dripped into pools on the dark floors. When the alarm lights pulsed red, the corridor looked like it had been painted black. Not a single body was intact. Limbs and chunks of flesh were scattered in haphazard piles throughout. A few people retched and vomited at the sight.

"Jesus Christ..." Mikey muttered behind me.

"We have to...we have to keep moving," I said. The only way forward was through. I glanced at Frank, who nodded, his face stony.

I swallowed hard and stepped toward the carnage. There was no avoiding the mess. Our boots squelched and squeaked as we marched through the human soup, more than one person slipping in the gore. "Stay sharp," I said, forcing my voice to stay even. Dead eyes and horror-stretched faces stared up at us, some not attached to bodies. What the fuck could do this?

We made it to the nearby stairwell (since the lifts were non-responsive) and down four levels to the reactor floor. It was mostly a straight shot to the access doors, another ten minutes or so at a steady clip. So far, everything seemed abandoned. A ghost ship.

"Hold," the Charlie lead said in a hushed whisper. His name was Don. I'd seen him around the aviary and knew him in passing. We all froze and listened. A strange clink of metal on metal reverberated in the hall. It seemed to be close but was hard to pin down. I heard it again and turned slowly to look at the wall. A small tremor vibrated the panels.

BOOM!

Both walls of the corridor erupted in red lightning and shrapnel, right in the middle of our line. The blasts launched me forward like I'd been shot from an air cannon. A jumble of bodies slid away from the impact in uncontrolled rolls and flails. Frank landed next to me and painfully rolled onto his hands and knees to push himself up. He had a cut above his left eye and a sheared piece of the wall paneling sticking out of his right leg.

"Son of a bitch," he grunted. I glanced around for Mikey but couldn't see him. Jiro and Sauce hobbled up a little ways over, shaking off the concussive fog. I sprang to my feet and turned to see several hulking figures step through the holes in either side of the passage, each seeming to swell in the relatively narrow spaces. Their obsidian armor glinted in the white-and-red light, and a crimson glow pierced through the cracks in their suits. If we had thought the holo displays of the Forsaken looked terrifying, the real thing was ten times worse. Without hesitation, they tore into us. Don, who had been close to the blast location, crawled forward in a shell-shocked daze, only to receive a vicious dropkick in the side. It lifted him into the air, blood spraying from his mouth. Another Forsaken soldier tore Don apart with several well-placed shots before he hit the floor. After a moment of stunned shock and horror, I saw one of the enemy turning its large mech-suit head and glaring in my direction, raising his arm to fire.

"Engage, engage, engage!" I yelled through the smoke and chaos. Blue energy blasts ripped out from the unorganized bunches that had been blown to either end of the corridor, catching the Forsaken in a crossfire. The exchange was quick and violent. The last few sapphire shots hit the wall above my head from the other side. "Hold your fire!" The shooting stopped, and everything went still.

"Sarah?" a voice echoed from the side of the corridor.

"Mikey!" I rushed over to meet him in a desperate hug. He was OK. I hadn't seen him in the chaos, but he had crashed into the wall to my side, only managing to get up after the shooting stopped. We separated, and I took stock of the damage. I reached up and felt blood dripping from my left ear. I thought I had ruptured an eardrum. Everything sounded tinny and muffled.

Walking forward with rifles raised, we checked the enemy bodies to make sure they were fully down, firing a few shots for good measure into their lifeless shells of armor just in case. The breach explosions had taken out eight of us, the quick exchange another four. I couldn't linger over our people motionless on the ground, two of them from my own squad. Devon and Tilly. Good soldiers. Friends. Young. Dead.

"We have to keep moving—"

"We need to go back to the others! They're going to kill us all!" one of the Charlie squad members said, starting to panic.

"Listen, we need to—"

"We need to get the fuck out of here! Back the way we came or to the—"

"Hey! Hold it together!" I shouted. I couldn't have people losing their shit. Not now. The Charlie squad grunt looked like he wasn't going to quit, but Frank stepped forward to silence him.

Another guy, stark and pale, spoke up. "No, he's right. We should—"

"Can it!" Frank growled before giving me a sideways glance and nodding. "There's nothing voluntary here. Follow your orders from Sarah, or curl up and die. But if you're choosing the latter, stay the fuck out of the way." Another example of Frank demonstrating his *not to be fucked with* vibes. Anyone who was unsure who to follow, quickly looked in my direction. The two broken soldiers who had complained shied away from Frank, lowering their eyes. "That's what I thought," Frank said, hobbling back to stand behind me.

"For all we know, more have looped back the way we came," I said. "We need to stick together, and we need to protect the reactor. That's our lifeline, and that's our job. Keep it tight, and let's keep moving." I turned toward our destination.

My words were met by a brief pause that felt like an age as I worried no one except Frank, Mikey, and the rest of my small squad would follow me. Then I heard them all fall into the stack behind, followed by the ratchet and clanking sounds of guns being checked and primed and armor butting against them as they were pulled tight to the shoulder. A firm squeeze on my shoulder signified they were ready to move.

We were attacked three more times before we reached the access doors to the reactor. Small four-and-five-person fire teams. Each Forsaken went down hard, taking several of us with them, including Sauce, but

I couldn't dwell on it. There wasn't time. It wasn't like the simulations. There was something about the simulations though. I couldn't put my finger on it. It must've been the way shots glanced off the Forsaken more here than in the sims, or the fact that everything seemed just a bit less effective. They were faster, and it took more energy, more of a direct hit to drop them. They weren't major skirmishes, but they chipped away at our numbers and our stamina. We were down to only fifteen people.

There was another bend in the corridor and then a straight stretch of about a hundred meters to the access. We caught our breath for a few anxious moments, and several of us used our first round of jolt shots to replenish our bioenergy. The stim coursed through my body, setting every nerve on fire and peaking behind my eyes. I blinked away the electricity and exhaled slowly.

"Everyone ready?" I asked, turning to look down my battered line. Nervous nods returned.

We rounded the corner and clipped toward the access with rifles raised. At the far end of the hall, three humans appeared, sprinting toward us. Bloody and terrified.

"Go! Run! Go!" they screamed, motioning for us to turn around. Behind them a wall of Forsaken soldiers marched out of an offshoot passage. A full platoon of them flooded the corridor.

"Behind you!" I yelled as the enemy opened fire and shredded the three runners into sacks of gory mulch. Their torn bodies slid nearly to our feet. "Shields!" More shots darted toward us. I drew my kite and holstered my Tempest, snapping up my Warthog instead. The shield's bright sapphire glow filled the space and hummed with a static fizzle. The front six, Frank and I included, linked into a wall while the back rows aimed between the gaps to return fire. Mikey was right over my shoulder, laying down suppressive fire.

We were only twenty meters from the reactor doors, but it might as well have been miles. The enemy advance had stopped us in our tracks, even forced us to slide backwards as we braced against the crimson onslaught. One person in our line stumbled just enough to cause their shield to waver, and a red blast tore through it. A Charlie squad member behind stepped in to fill the gap. For every hard-fought step we took, we were hammered back two. The Forsaken dropped in droves but trod over their dead like they didn't even notice them, getting closer and closer.

I leaned into the impacts, and Frank did the same, teeth clenched in a strained scowl. He shook his head quickly. "There's too many of them," he said. "We have to fall back."

"We have to secure the reactor!" I shouted over the chaos. It was a desperate plea more than anything. Our numbers were falling too quickly, and there were too many of them.

"We'll come back, Sarah. We have to—" The shield bearer next to Frank got belted back just enough for the energy field to tilt in. The next shot glanced behind the line and straight into Frank's side. His eyes widened in shock as he stared at me.

"Frank! Frank—no! No!" He looked down at his side and then back up at me. Somehow, he still managed to keep his shield energized, but he collapsed onto one knee. "Frank!"

"I'm good, I'm good," he muttered, but his eyes lolled strangely in his head. I wanted to reach down and lift him up, but I had to hold the line.

"Frank!"

"Sarah, you need to go—"

"I'm not leaving without—"

"Sarah! Go!" Suddenly, by some sheer force of will, Frank powered his way to his feet and stepped forward from the line, someone filling in behind him. "Go!" He snapped off his Tempest and braced it against the edge of his shield, sparks etching off the metal from the energy sear. Then he ripped into the encroaching Forsaken line. I felt Mikey's grip on my arm, pulling me back.

Jiro backed up quickly next to me, firing relentlessly into the enemy. "Sarah, come on! We have to go!" His words reverberated in my burst eardrum.

"Fall back! Fall back!" I heard myself yelling, but it seemed to be coming from somewhere outside of me. I watched as Frank, amazingly, continued to step forward against the barrage. Red fire flared out around the edges of his small blue wall. We hurried backwards, still shooting around Frank. Just as we reached the corner, one of the Forsaken got close enough to bat away Frank's shield with a vicious swipe. Frank stumbled to his knees and looked up as three others tore into him, his lifeless body dropping to the floor.

Around the corner we latched the shield cylinders to our hips and drew our primary assault rifles. Then we ran like we'd never run before. I couldn't believe it.

Frank was gone.

Every feeder corridor was teeming with the enemy, each vector channeling more of them to our retreat, each opening a torrent of scarlet firepower that ripped into our flanks. We had nowhere to go. Each time we thought we were clear, more came and funneled us another way. Only ten of us were left, none of whom I knew well except for Mikey and Jiro. We bought a couple of moments ducking into a ready room.

"What the hell are we going to do?" one of Charlie company shouted. My head was spinning as I tried to formulate any semblance of a plan. Everywhere we had turned, the Forsaken were there, converging on us like a deadly game of cat and mouse. We were drastically outnumbered and cut off. Frank was gone. Will might be gone too. If the rest of the ship was experiencing the same amount of carnage, everyone could be dead. It was hopeless, and this wasn't one of our simulations...*a simulation!* If we made it to a sim field, we could program whatever scenario we wanted and lock it out. The physics in there were nearly perfect, and we could hole up there until help came. It might be our only shot.

"The sim field. We make it there, and we can punch in the fortress sim. Lock it out. Force them to meet us on our own turf."

"The whole *Albatross* was our turf," someone said.

"Well, if anyone else has an idea, I'm all ears." I was met by blank faces etched with concern and fatigue. Jiro reloaded his Tempest and stood up, silent but ready. Mikey nodded to me. I knew I had their full support at least. "OK. Sim field it is."

When we left the ready room, the halls were oddly quiet, as if the Forsaken had made quick work of the *Albatross* and its crew and moved on. Only occasionally did we hear distant echoes of fading horrors as other pockets of resistance were tamped down. We crept down the corridors toward the nearest sim field, hoping to avoid any more full-scale attacks until we could fortify. The once-pristine passages were marred with scorch marks, blood, and shrapnel. Bodies lay in failed skirmish patterns and haphazard tangles of ambushes along the route. At one intersection, the dead were piled so thick that it almost looked like a barrier of butchered meat had been erected, streams of blood forking out in a river delta of crimson.

"Our father who art in heaven, hallowed be thy name," someone muttered behind me. Apparently, his god wasn't listening.

"Keep moving."

At the sim-field doors, we stacked up for entry. Mikey keyed the access code, and the doors shot open. Bright yellow light and heat flooded the corridor as we poured in. Someone had programmed the "Oasis" sim, a massive landscape of golden sand dunes under an oppressive sun. A small outpost of green-and-brown palm trees and ruins was hidden in the distant middle. A trail of dead Forsaken and humans lay half buried in the sand leading toward it. Someone had already tried to hold out here.

"Who the fuck set this? This is a kill box!" a member of Charlie squad said.

I turned to my brother. "Mikey, get us the fortress sim. And close these doors."

"Roger that." He went to the panel next to the entrance. I scanned the area to make sure nothing was coming for us from the rolling dunes. The horizon and the bluebird sky had the faint artificial shimmer of the simulation, but the sand felt grainy and visceral and compressed and shimmied underfoot as if we were in a real desert. "I can't alter the sim. Says I'm locked out. Can't close the doors either," Mikey said.

"What?" I rushed over and looked at the panel. Something seemed to be corrupting it. I tried a couple of bypasses, to no avail. The panel wasn't responding. "Shit!" I said, punching the display.

The oasis had no fortifications. The central landmark was a small outcrop of trees and lush vegetation around a shallow pond set in a bowl of surrounding dunes. Old adobe ruins were also there, but they were hardly adequate cover. It was also an exposed dash, almost a quarter mile through sand, which was terrible to run through.

Suddenly, a rush of red blasts rang through the open doors. The remainder of my team took cover on either side and returned fire.

"We can't stay here!" Mikey yelled. I dipped into the opening to shoot back and to get a look. Hundreds of Forsaken were converging in the corridors and making their way toward us.

"Well, we are sure as shit not going that way!" a member of Charlie squad shouted.

"Look!" Jiro pointed into the sim. Rising behind a row of dunes were several large sapphire shots, like flares. There were other survivors in there. It would be a tough sprint, mostly open ground to cover the distance, but it looked like our only chance.

"Alright! Let's peel off and make for the oasis. First one over the last dunes, fire a couple shots, so they know it's us coming. Ready?" Everyone nodded, determined to get the hell away from there. "Go!" I shouted, shooting through the door.

The team rolled off and sprinted through the sand. The slack footing was a frustrating obstacle as each foot fought for purchase. On the face of every dune, vermillion blasts peppered the sand and arced around us, the far slopes a temporary shield from the barrages. On the last dune before the final drop into the gulley, Mikey shot off a few warning rounds to let whatever team was still alive know we were close. We half-jumped and half-rolled down the descent while the entrenched team fired over our heads at the Forsaken pursuers cresting the dunes.

The oasis was vivid green amidst the gold, and several of the fallen palms provided at least a bit of cover. Dead humans, Forsaken, and charred, glassy craters ringed the haven, as if whoever was there had been holding them off for ages. Blood curdled in brown pools and spatter patterns throughout the battlefield. We trundled over the fallen, using their bodies as solid footing to propel us forward.

"Sarah!" a voice echoed ahead. I looked up to see Will standing up from behind cover, eyes flaring a bright blue and his Tempest raised. "Run!" I glanced over my shoulder to see the obsidian flood of Forsaken pouring over the dunes. A shot grazed my arm, hot and sharp. I ignored it as best as I could and sprinted for Will and the others.

Mikey ran by my side, matching my speed. We were so close. Then suddenly he wasn't there. I slowed to a stop and turned. Mikey was laying face down, a massive hole in his back, blood seeping out into the sand. Random impacts showered the desert's golden flecks onto his back. Everything slowed. *Mikey? Mikey? Mikey, get up!* I thought it but couldn't say. My feet trudged toward him. I needed to pick him up. Dust him off. Get him to cover.

"Mikey?" I whispered, unaware of anything else around me. Suddenly, I felt rough hands at my side turning me around. It was Will and Jiro, shaking me back to reality. Everything sped up, and shots whistled past us.

"Sarah! He's gone! We have to move!" Will yelled. They half-guided me, half-dragged me back to the oasis. We tumbled over the downed tree, and then Will and Jiro snapped up to return fire.

"Sarah! There's no time now! Shoot back!" I looked around in a daze. Seyyal was lying on her side with her eyes closed, not moving. Miguel sat with his back against the tree a little ways over, staring at nothing. He was missing part of his leg below the knee. Only Megan and four other members of Will's team were left, as far as I could tell, and they all shot relentlessly into the dunes, fighting desperately to hold back the onyx-and-crimson tide. "Sarah! Snap out of it! We need you!" Will yelled, jostling me. I looked up at him. He had blood running down half his face, and I saw an oozing wound in his side.

"Frank's dead," I said. I wasn't sure why I said it, just figured he'd want to know. Will didn't look down, but I saw his jaw clench. Then every line on his body cranked to an even brighter glare, and a demonic blue fire erupted out. As he shot, waves of energy ebbed from him, more than his weapons could channel forward. Something guttural and violent exploded from him, an animalistic sound of sheer rage. It was terrifying. It was *hate*. It was also enough to shake me out of my shell-shocked daze.

I crouched next to him. The Forsaken attack wasn't in the hundreds; it was in the thousands, and they bore down on us with no regard for their losses.

Suddenly, a red blast lasered straight at me. The shot didn't seem to move me, just moved through me. I stood up straight and stumbled back several steps. I blinked in surprise as a second round tore through my stomach, this time launching me backwards in an uncontrolled roll, concluding with me staring up at the artificial sky. There was something surreal about it all. Something not right. The next thing I knew, Will was crouched over me, trying frantically to stem the bleeding. It didn't hurt. The sounds seemed dampened too, and not just because of my ruptured eardrum. If I couldn't see the shots raining overhead, it would have seemed like I was sunbathing. The fire that had engulfed Will was gone, and only his eyes shone with blue electricity.

For some reason, even with all the chaos, all I could think about was how much I was going to miss him. *I love you—loved you.* I had found so much more on the *Albatross* besides adventure and knowledge. I had found a new family, and they were all dead or dying. All their faces flickered in front of my eyes.

"Will...Will, I'm sorry," I choked out. My mouth seemed to be filling with hot fluid.

"Shhh. Shhh. Just stay still. I'm going to—" Will cut himself off, tears welling in his eyes. I felt my body go still, and my chest stopped heaving. I couldn't blink. Couldn't feel my heart. Was this death? Could I actually feel it all just...stop? Then, with a wave of sudden head-spinning lightness, I rose from the ground and looked around. The pieces were still moving, clunking toward the inevitable, but everything was quiet. I looked down at Will, hunched over my corpse. Holy shit. I had died. Everyone was dead. Will was the only one still alive. Surrounded by piles of bodies. Jiro folded over the downed palm tree. Miguel sitting there. Mikey face down in the sand. Seyyal. Megan. All dead. The Forsaken were close, on all sides, but none quite had a shot at Will's hunched position. Or maybe they knew they had him dead to rights with no escape and no chance for survival. They tightened the noose, a cautious creep toward the last beacon of resistance.

Will reached down and closed my eyes, which could no longer see. He pulled a jolt shot from my bandolier, then another from his own. He staggered to his feet, and the nearby Forsaken readied their weapons to cut him down. The first stim sent a twitch through his body that wrenched him violently. Who knows how many he had already used. The second one didn't convulse him as much, but his every fiber ignited in blue fire again. He slowly turned in a circle, staring out and through and beyond. He looked numb as he dropped his rifle into the sand. The Forsaken inched toward him.

Then, almost calmly, he balled his hands into fists and hunched over, tightening all his muscles and shaking. The tension reaching a breaking point. I wasn't sure if it was the second jolt stim killing him or whether he was just succumbing to his hateful rage, but in a blinding flash, he straightened up and released a nuclear-bomb-scale explosion from every cell in his body. It washed over everything around him, filling the sim field with a sapphire tsunami, destroying everything in its path.

It was over. Everything went black.

PART III

(ARTHUR)

At length did cross the Albatross,
Thorough the fog it came;
As if it had been a Christian soul,
We hailed it in God's name.

—"The Rime of the Ancient Mariner"
by Samuel Taylor Coleridge

PROLOGUE

The Beginning is The End

The ceiling rose above me in arching vaults of color and shadow, each rafter exposed and dropped down from the brushed lumenium shell that made up the roof. The ribs from the peak curved in waxing and waning crescents to the bottom, joining with the patchwork mosaic of stone tiles on the floor. The dim vermillion glow of perpetual dusk shone through the full-height windows that lined one side of the room, offering a view of the street far below.

I remembered the first time I saw the chambers with my father. Holding his hand as he walked me in, bathed in the same light that shone now. I could barely see over the thick slabs of dark stone that made up the U-shaped table running most of the length of the room. We walked up to the head table, which was constructed of brilliant white marble with dark veins, slightly elevated above the others. My father's seat behind it was a climb that left my feet dangling over the edge, a wild abyss or gravity-less space in my imagination. He had told me the history of the place and its importance to everything we held dear, the sacred duty we had to protect it. He explained the significance of the black leaves and vines that crawled up around the frame of the massive ancient entrance doors through which council members and citizens alike had to walk.

Everything seemed to move in slow motion as I stared up into the space above. I saw the scorch marks painted along the walls and ceiling. Cracks and debris etched off and between the impacts. The odd flash of blue, green, gold, and red energy blasted across my vision, bringing me back into the moment. Shouts and the percussions of battle came to me as if I were underwater, strangely muffled and muted. My hands trembled as they felt down my torso, searching, seeking the wound I could not feel but knew was there. I brought my fingers up to my eyes, seeing black blood drip off them in thick glossy threads. I rolled my head to the side. Staring back at me were two of Flak's glazed unblinking eyes. Half his face was a gaping void, mulched carnage steaming from the shot.

Just then a pair of hands reached down and shook me. I looked back up to see the human who had grown to be like a son to me kneeling at my side. How did we get here? He glanced from my stomach to my face. The blue fire that had consumed his eyes raged for a few moments before it gradually faded to reveal his crestfallen stare. I could tell in that look that the battle was over. My battle.

The last thing I heard before everything faded to black was Will calling my name. "Arthur. Arthur. Stay with me. Arthur!"

CHAPTER XIV

Bocce

26 MONTHS SINCE LUMEN DEPARTURE (LD)
– 8 MONTHS SINCE EARTH ARRIVAL (EA)

"It really is a beautiful world."

"They haven't been treating it so well."

"Hopefully, we can help fix that."

"If they get out of their own damn way," Flak grunted. We both stared down at Earth from the command deck's main viewing display. The shiny blue ball rotated calmly beneath us.

"How are the engineering crews coming with the transfers and upgrades?" I asked.

"They call them secretaries down there. I'm not one of them," Flak said. "How should I know? Can tell you how many grenades are in Armory 1 though."

I shook my head and turned back to the rest of the room. "Hera. Progress?" I asked one of my bridge officers.

She looked up quickly from her console. "Agricultural and hydro processors are coming along, but we're not going to be finished the energy upgrades before you'd like to leave. Much of their technology is proving too…primitive to integrate fully. Engineering is recommending we build new particle-fusion facilities altogether and upgrade the infrastructure later."

"That would take even longer," I said, unable to hide a note of frustration. We were already losing so much time. We needed to get back. The war would not wait for us.

Hera glanced down at her console for a moment. "Opus is returning to the ship in two hours. He would like to discuss the matter with you directly," she said.

"Very well. And the other upgrades?"

"The thread-drive research has been downloaded to their systems. It'll take them a while to make sense of it and longer to adapt without lumenium and fostrogen, but it's there. The terraforming tech and habitable world catalogue are transferred, and they've already begun construction of the planetary defense systems. Should be complete long before the near-Earth object they've named 4179 Toutatis hits. They were a little off on their calculations—"

"Guess it was lucky for them we showed up," Flak muttered.

"The weapons research is also ready to transfer whenever you give the go-ahead. They seem particularly interested in that, but our crews are assessing the best distribution procedure."

"Good—"

"I want to say again that I disagree with giving the humans weapons tech," Flak cut in. "They'll destroy themselves. It's dangerous."

I exhaled slowly. We had had this discussion before. "I understand your position, Flak. But we cannot ask for their help, to have them join us at our side, and yet treat them like children."

"They *are* children." I felt other eyes on the command deck staring at us. It was possibly a shared sentiment, though most did not have the courage to speak out as Flak had.

I turned to face him. "That is enough. The matter is closed." We stared hard at each other. For a moment I thought he might argue the point further, but then he nodded.

"Arthur, you'll want to see this," my comms officer, Trig, said from his console on the side. It was an excuse to break the standoff with Flak. "It's the footage from the terrorist attack in Los Angeles."

"Told you we should have had our own people armed down there," Flak grumbled.

"Send it to the main console," I said, walking over to my central hub. The holo display flickered up and showed one of the compatibility testing facilities on Earth. "No Lumenarian will be armed on the planet," I added. "We are not an occupying force. They have their own police and military."

Flak followed me over and leaned against the edge of the console, watching. "And our people are still getting killed. They should be able to defend themselves."

"They can naturally defend themselves better than any human. An explosive kills indiscriminately. They lost many more of their own in the attacks. Lumen weapons would just make them trust us less," I said with a sideways glance, then turned back to the display.

Like thousands before them at the stadium—millions around the world at that point—a row of humans stood behind the firing lanes and received their biotech. It looked like a strong group, only a few tech rejections. Sky and Herb. *Herb.* I had known him since he was a fresh recruit aboard one of my older posts, the *Anvil*. Smart, strong, and kind, if not a little naïve. Gone. Thank the lights Sky was alright.

Herb and Sky paced down the line explaining the situation and then instructing the humans to place their hands on the read-out cubes. The cubes did not simply provide a target and focus point but also logged data, scientifically tracking outputs throughout the day. After Sky did her demonstration, the humans took their places and attempted to move the drones. One by one they interacted with them, a wide range of capabilities. The last one, a male, seemed to be struggling to operate the tech. Sky stood behind him and tried to mentor a reaction. Not everyone who accepted the tech could operate it. It looked like this one might be—

"Damn," Flak said, straightening up. In a violent outburst of sapphire energy, the human blasted the drone like nothing we had seen. The cube data spiked along the side of the feed and then cut out. The box limped back to the ledge but was no longer providing information. I dragged my finger through the air to rewind the display and played it again. Impressive.

"How many others have shown these levels?" I asked.

"That was the most powerful we've seen yet," Trig said. "Only an incredibly small percentage of others have been close." I stared at the display, zooming in closer on the human's face. He looked more surprised than anyone. Then again, he should be. No one could have anticipated that. I studied his face. I saw something. Something dark behind his eyes. Something afraid of itself.

"If he decides to continue in the program, make sure he gets assigned to the *Albatross*, and send his personnel file to my console," I said to Black, one of the other officers. He nodded and returned to his terminal.

"The *Albatross*? Is that what we're calling it now?" Flak asked. "Thought it'd at least be a predatory bird."

"The albatross is symbolic."

"So is an eagle or a hawk, if you're set on Earth birds."

"Well, you do not get to name the ship," I said with a smile. "I do. You should read more of the humans' literature."

"I read some. The material on war anyway," Flak said. "And for such a short history, they've sure had a lot of it." I was not sure if he respected the warrior in them or found it troubling. "I'll leave the poetry to you," Flak added, then tapped the console and watched the rest of the feed— Herb being held hostage, the standoff, the bomb going off and tearing through the room, Sky barely getting her kite shield up in time and overloading it.

"But you still recognized it was from a poem," I said with a sideways glance and a smile.

A few hours later, I was sitting in my quarters reading the book of poetry from which I had gleaned the inspiration for the *Albatross*.

The weathered anthology was a gift from a diplomat on Earth with whom I had had several meaningful conversations. He was a kind old man who seemed more interested in what I thought of the world than what we could give them (which was refreshing). I enjoyed the tactile sensation of paper pages and the sound they made as they turned. The yellowed leaflets and creased spine were a testament to time and the many different eyes that had laid upon the volume, something lost in digital renderings.

If Lumen had ever had physical books, they had been gone for millennia, the memory of them lost as well. I had taken to accumulating a small collection during my time on Earth, something to carry across the stars, to take in the knowledge slowly and thoroughly. I had books about prominent figures of human history, classic tales of fiction, military strategy, art and culture, and several poetry collections. The poetry struck a chord for me. More than anything it seemed to show glimpses of the human heart and soul. Voices from ages past. Passions and pains.

"Arthur?" a voice sounded gently from my doorway, pulling me from the depths of "The Ancient Mariner." It was Opus, our chief engineer down on Earth.

"Opus, please come in." I gestured to the seat in front of my workstation.

"Thank you for seeing me," he said, taking the seat. I waited for him to speak. It seemed like something was weighing on him. He fidgeted slightly.

"You wanted to discuss the progress on Earth," I said, prodding him.

"Yes. I apologize. It's a…difficult thing to propose."

"To propose?" I asked, slightly confused. I knew the process was taking longer than anticipated but did not expect something significant was needed to overcome the delay.

Opus straightened up, his face serious. "As you know, the upgrades won't be complete in time for our planned departure."

"I am aware."

"Well…a small group of us…we would like to volunteer to stay on Earth. To complete the integration and help the humans adapt our technology."

I stared at him, unable to hide my surprise. "You want to stay on Earth?"

Opus nodded slowly. "Yes. We've given it a lot of thought. We would like you to petition for a permanent Lumen Embassy on Earth. We would stay and oversee the adaptations. Teach the humans. And learn from them."

I could not help but feel proud. One of my greatest fears was that other Lumenarians would see humans as something less than, feel superior to them despite the sacrifice they were making for us, and that it would create a divide. Not everyone saw what I did, that in their adolescence they had strength and beauty. What they lacked in technological development they made up for with hope and determination. They were what I imagined us to be in the beginning, a flawed species striving to reach great heights. They were Icarus, and we could give them better wings. "We don't want you to think we're trying to run away from the war—"

"No, of course not. I know you. It had not crossed my mind," I said. "However, you realize we may not return in your lifetime…"

"We know," Opus said. The solemn look of determination on his face made me believe they had given it serious thought. "We think it could be an important show of faith. It's to be a union after all. But all some of them will see is us taking their people away. If some of us were to stay…"

I nodded, mulling it over. I did not oppose the idea completely, but with the recent OnSpec activity on Earth, it made me wary. It was not something I could ask of my crew. It would have to be fully voluntary, and it would need a cap. We were fighting a war, after all. I could not leave half my crew behind.

"How many of you wish to stay?"

"Ten of us."

"There are still a few weeks before we depart. I will think on it. This is a big decision."

"I understand." Opus rose from his chair. "Thank you for speaking with me, Arthur." I nodded, and Opus reached over and placed his hand on my forehead. I placed my hand on his. He turned and left me to my thoughts. Ten children of Lumen left amongst the billions of Earth, some of whom passionately wanted us dead.

27 MONTHS SINCE LD – 9 MONTHS SINCE EA

The next few weeks passed in a blur of diplomatic meetings and logistical planning sessions. Critical adaptations to the *Albatross* and the accompanying *Osprey* and *Pelican* were also undertaken. Flora and fauna from Earth were brought to the living quarters to help alleviate what we knew would be a psychologically trying journey for our new allies. Crews worked with little time off to adjust the basic utilities throughout the ships—lowering seats and tables for the average human height, installing the necessary facilities for human waste disposal, inputting the new human food-processor formulas, fabricating uniforms, and modifying our weapons and equipment for their smaller stature.

Outside of the physical changes throughout, teams of our scientists also continued to conduct biological research, curing most human diseases (in time I was sure all of them), studying hypothetical long-term effects of the biotech on human anatomy and nanotech-induced evolution, among other things. There was a high probability that our new recruits, should they survive the war, would live significantly longer than their ancestors.

The new Lumen Embassy was approved by world governments and given a site outside a city named Reykjavik in the nation of Iceland. In the end, eight of my people decided to stay on Earth. I worried for them but admired their bravery—pioneers in a way. We left them with a shuttle and enough supplies to continue their work for a time, but eventually they would have to make do with the resources available on Earth. A food processor would also convert sustenance into something more palatable for them. Much of Earth's flora and fauna was edible to us, but we found the taste repulsive (something I had to tolerate during countless diplomatic meetings). In this case we left them with weapons as well. In the event of the OnSpec launching an attack, I would not leave them undefended. Earth militaries would also ensure their safety, but just in case, I would leave it in my people's hands to defend themselves.

They had directives regarding dissemination of information, but it would mostly come down to their own judgement. I trusted them. The only real directive for which I expected full compliance was the protection of weapons research from nationalist advantage. I did not want to see the wealthy and power-hungry use the advanced technology for their own ideological agendas. They were meant to be used for peacekeeping and planetary defense only, should the need arise. Luckily, because of how dependent our technology was on biology, the process would be a slow adaptation. I hoped it would help unite them into a global force rather than a band of individual factions. It gave me hope that there were already talks to establish a United Earth Alliance, as it was tentatively being called.

It was hard to say goodbye to my people, and I spent as much time as I could afford with them before leaving, but what they were doing was important. The first ambassadors on an alien world inhabited by an alien race.

When he arrived on the *Albatross*, I had William Reach assigned to Charlie aviary. It was not announced, but we drafted that complex to have the most promising recruits in terms of strength, experience, and intelligence. Some were also there specifically for Will; people who, in our brief observation, would make him feel comfortable and, in time, would challenge him. I knew he could be a beacon, a light that others would follow and grow in. In addition, we could not rely solely on Lumenarian leadership and expect the humans to consider themselves equal. They needed their own. According to his military records, Will had done it before—and had run from it. We just needed to teach him not to run. Regain what he had lost. We would build a team around him, and when the time came, if they proved to fill the hopes we had for them, we would ask worlds. The other ships would do the same, channel together targeted groups of gifted individuals—experiments in potential. When we arrived back home to the war, they would be the tip of our spear.

29 MONTHS SINCE LD – 1 MONTH INTO RETURN TRIP (RT)

A month after our departure from Earth, I called Will to meet me in my quarters. From the first moment, I knew I had made the right choice. He was quiet except with the people who were closest to him. But almost immediately others seemed drawn into his orbit. I saw his stubbornness and resistance as well. To be honest, I saw glimmers of myself in Will. I wanted to begin learning about him, from him. To build a relationship of trust. Only so much could be gleaned from a distance.

When Will arrived he knocked on the frame of my open door before entering. "Sir?" he asked, standing at attention, the soldier's discipline immediately present.

"Hello, Mr. Reach. Please come in. And it is Arthur. No need for the 'sir' or standing at attention," I said, gesturing to the seat across from me. He relaxed but still looked uncomfortable.

"Thank you, sir—Arthur. And it's Will," he said with a small nod.

"Will." I stared at him for a moment, trying to get a read. He buried his darkness well. A certain charming façade that flickered faintly at something insincere—something hidden. I imagined he had his share of commanding officers whom he'd had to grudgingly obey. I could tell he was taking the time to analyze me. A barely visible smirk creased the corner of his mouth. I got the feeling he saw through most psychological tests, taking the deeper purpose in stride and possibly even balking at it. He had been, at one point, one of Earth's most elite special forces soldiers, after all. His science and mathematics aptitude tests were not exemplary, but he did well in logical thinking and reasoning. I could tell he knew people, and he obviously knew combat.

"You must be wondering why I called you here," I said, breaking the silence.

He exhaled slowly, a faint smell of alcohol wafting across the desk. He had been hiding that well too. "I am curious," he admitted.

"Your compatibility test data was interesting. Then when you underwent the full-body biotech integration, Sky provided updated scans. Seems you are a bit of an anomaly."

He already had blue eyes, but something more seemed to flicker there. He looked away suddenly, glancing around the room. "Well, Mom always said I was special. So did Dad, but he didn't mean it in a good way." I could tell it was a lie, a sarcastic deflection from some insecurity. "Don't suppose you have any idea why?" he asked with a suspicious glance in my direction.

"We are still trying to find correlations."

"Mhmm." I got the impression he was curious about me but not yet trusting. Which was fair. It must have seemed strange that with all our technology we still had not figured it out. I was not satisfied with my answer either. It was a mystery I also wanted to solve. Regardless, trust would take time.

I stood up. "We should take a walk."

The nanoparticles formed in rippling waves, taking their shapes and filling out in vibrant colors; a wide green field under a clear blue sky, the grass shorn at the equivalent of a golf course fairway on Earth. I knew this from a particularly unproductive meeting with a pompous world leader in the United States who had tried to teach me the game.

Will took in the scene and breathed deeply. "Would almost be convincing if it weren't for the air."

"Even we have our limits," I said, setting the case I had brought with me on the grass. "This were a gift from a German ambassador. He did, however, inform me that his country did not invent this game." I opened the case and turned it to face Will. Inside was a set of red-and-green balls and a small, white pallino ball.

Will stared in surprise. "Bocce…You want to play bocce?" He glanced up from the set to me.

"Yes. I quite enjoy the game. Requires control and learning to play to your strengths."

"I always thought it was just a summer game you got drunk playing."

"Shall we play?" I lobbed the white ball about fifteen feet in front of us. Will stared at me for a moment and then picked up the red set of bocce balls. I took green. I threw mine, and then he threw his. His first toss landed just shy of the mark—I had expected an overthrow.

"So, why Arthur? Didn't you have a name before?"

My second throw arced well with a backspin and landed a few inches closer. I caught Will smiling slightly. "I enjoyed the stories of Camelot," I said.

Will's second throw was short, meaning he had to throw his remaining two. His last shots grouped well, and he bowed out of the way for my turn, confident in his placement. "But I am still called by my *old* name," I added. The first of my remaining two knocked away Will's closest and landed mine nearly against the white jack. In my peripheral I saw Will's jaw clench.

"Dammit," he mumbled. I could have thrown a shy safe ball to lock the victory and not risk knocking away my other ball, but that was not the point of the exercise. I threw my last ball in a perfect line that stood it an inch from the white marker. I had the two closest placements, winning the match. "Nice shot," Will said grudgingly. We walked over to the balls and picked them up. Will palmed the white pallino and shot a sideways glance at me. "Winner throws again," he said, holding out the ball.

"You throw this one," I said, bowing aside.

"OK then." He pitched the ball approximately sixty feet away and nodded approvingly. "What do you mean, you're still called by your old name?" he asked as we began throwing our balls.

"Certain words—times, dates, names—are manually assigned in the translator bank. Not everything translates over, and we have different system values. For all the Lumenarians on board, they still use our measurements, automatically equated over, and call me by my Lumen name, but you hear it as Arthur. Likewise, when you say 'Arthur,' I hear my true name."

"Huh. So, it's just for our perception."

I won that round with all four of my shots closest to the white. If Will was going to beat me, he would have to do it squarely and earn it. I would not coddle his ego. He stood with his hands on his hips, staring down at the defeat.

"Well, there it is." He shot me another peripheral look and held it. Then he smiled. "Thought you might let me win for a second." He narrowed his eyes, and his left one twitched slightly. "Glad you didn't."

I shrugged. "We often learn more from losing."

"So, you want to be my teacher. Is that it? Trying to figure out why I'm here," he said, a cold barb in his half smile. I took a moment to study him. I wanted him to feel uncomfortable. To have time to overthink. He was quick enough to keep up with sarcasm, but maybe the quiet would force him to look inward. Then again, I think he saw through it. He did not flinch.

"Why *are* you here? What do you want, Will?" I asked finally.

"What do I want?" He looked unsettled but covered it quickly. "Real maple syrup would be nice." This time I held the unflinching stare. If I had to guess, I would think he was contemplating another sarcastic response. We stood there staring at each other, and then he looked away. It seemed as if he was looking at something, though only grass lay around us. His eyes tracked it along the edges of the room. "I don't know," he said quietly. I imagined a sort of respect to the directness of my question that was rewarded with a shred of honesty. Perhaps that was the key with Will. No sideways approaches. Just straight on. "I'm here to protect my brother for one thing."

"You mean Mr. Frank Farr."

"Not all family's blood."

"I understand," I said as I picked up the bocce balls and returned them to the case. Will brought over his and I stored them neatly away. I turned to him, "My son…was not my blood."

"You adopted him?"

"Not exactly. It is incredibly rare for our children to be biologically our own on Lumen. We believe that as a species we share blood. The blood of the individual is not important. Children are raised by the state until they are ten years of age and then assigned to families. It has been so since before any of us can remember. Nonetheless, we feel deeply for family." Will listened intently. I saw my son's face flash behind my eyes. He was always quick to smile. Much more vibrant and outgoing than me. "We lost the planet Cerberus fifteen years before we departed for Earth, and that is where I lost him."

Will stared at me and then looked away, clearing his throat. "I'm sorry," he said, his eyes darting down from mine. I returned a nod of understanding. If nothing else, we were two fathers of fallen children. He traced the path of another invisible specter then stared out across the field. "He was a soldier?"

"Yes." I saw it all play over again in my mind's eye. Seeing him on Forge for the last time, his hand upon my forehead and mine on his, then receiving the reports from the battle. Cal, my son.

My ship at the time, the *Anvil*, had been sequestered to provide escort for a supply convoy to the planet Stormwater to restock. The *Anvil* was an old vessel, set for decommission in the coming years, and was deemed a potential liability in combat. I knew it was sturdy and would have held up in battle, but when it came down to it, good ships were needed for escort duties as well. Being in thread-drive travel, I had heard three months later about the slaughter on Cerberus and the withdrawal of the orbital support for the ground personnel—of which my son was a part. They had been left to die when the Forsaken fleet arrived and overwhelmed them. However, many supposed that the retreat had been premature. According to the brief, even before the last ships jumped, the planet looked like a glowing orb of orange fire. The enemy bombardment scorched every surface. No one could have survived, I was told.

The news had been spread via general channels and then, a few weeks later, Sky arrived to tell me in person. She had been serving as chief medical officer on a ship named the *Sickle*, which had been engaged in the battle. "He's gone," was all she could get out at first upon facing me. She and Cal had an intimate relationship and cared deeply for each other. She had violently objected against the retreat order, her protest verging on mutiny. In the end she was quelled, and the ship jumped. In the aftermath she had been reprimanded, demoted, and then forced to transfer off ship. She had been by my side ever since, the closest thing to a daughter I had.

The initial report had been a devastating blow, but having to hear it from Sky was worse. She nearly collapsed when she first saw me, and when she eventually told me about the battle, I felt lost. Like the floor had fallen out from under me. I held her quaking body in my arms, not sure who was shaking worse.

"Arthur?" Will asked gently. I must have drifted off in memory longer than I thought.

"My apologies," I said, shaking away the spectral thoughts. "Almost every Lumenarian crew member of the *Albatross* has lost someone in this war. We would not have wagered the time lost to come to Earth if we did not hope beyond hope that you could help shift the balance."

"Why?" he asked incredulously. "Why…how can we possibly make such a difference?" He met my eyes again, unsure.

"We are not a people of war. In all of our recorded history, this is our first major conflict. So, in that regard, you have tremendous experience." Will bobbed his head side to side in dubious agreement. "Besides that… love and power," I said. Now Will sported a skeptical expression. "It was a gamble. A terrible wager. But when we sat above Earth, learning about you, that is what we saw most. We saw a people consumed by passions, sometimes destroyed by them. There is strength in passion, Will. A fierce pursuit of knowledge—sometimes misguided but always there. Humans who, long before we arrived, thirsted for the stars, driven to understand the mysteries of the universe. Those who are fighting desperately to save your climate. The ones who live for the betterment of others."

"Sometimes it feels like they're pretty outnumbered," he said.

"But they are there, and they are in all of you," I said. "Then with humans like you…we saw the biological capabilities." I saw concern flit across his face, the fear of his own power. "You do not need to be afraid of that strength, Will."

For a moment it looked like he was going to argue. An ego push of bravado, a cover and deflect, but then he looked down. "I'm not afraid for me. It's for everyone else," he said quietly. He had an almost childlike look to him. I suppose loss has a way of aging people in some ways and regressing them in others. It made me think about how I handled it myself.

"Then, more than anything else, we will work on control."

32 MONTHS SINCE LD – 4 MONTHS INTO RT

Once a week, Will and I met in private to train. We began slowly. I brought drones similar to the ones he had fired against in the compatibility testing and got him to focus on controlled bursts. His power could dismantle them, but I wanted him to give them a gentle push. Five feet, ten feet, then back to five. I could tell he was getting frustrated as he struggled to force them only a short distance, constantly blasting them away. The more agitated he got, the less control he had. The Earth weapons he was used to had a set velocity and stopping power; he just had to be on target. The biotech was fully dependent on the user. Before he ever got one of our weapons, he needed a closer handle on his primary weapon: himself.

He rifled another drone clear across the room. "Dammit!" he yelled, pacing in a circle and breathing hard. We had been at it for over an hour. He was getting worse; or rather, his control was not increasing as quickly as his biotech capabilities were. I watched him quietly for a moment. Before and after the attacks he looked filled with rage, like he was focusing on some hidden hate.

"What do you think about when you release your energy?" I asked.

He looked at me and then averted his eyes, as if to hide his shame. "I don't know. Nothing." He stared at the destroyed drone, his chest heaving. Then he looked around the edges of the room as if he was seeing something that wasn't there. A thing he did often. "Everything," he said finally, closing his eyes and suddenly looking very tired, beyond physical fatigue.

"Anger?"

"Rage."

Thought so. "Perhaps nothing would be better," I said.

Will stared at me and then chuckled, finally breaking out into a full laugh. "Yeah, that'd be nice," he said. I waited until his laughter died down.

"Your problem is not physical control, Will. It is mental."

"You're not the first one to call me crazy. Trust me."

"I do not think you are crazy, Will. I think you have a past." He looked over at me, the brokenness bare behind his eyes. Exhaustion had the effect of stripping away the layers. I let him see my own, and he nodded in acknowledgement, offering a wincing smile.

"How do you keep the past…in the past?" he asked.

"I live with it every day," I said. It was true. I saw the lost in many things while awake and when asleep. "But I do not let it control me. I control it."

He stared at me. "So…become a Jedi. Awesome. Good chat." I would have to look up what a "Jedi" was.

"One of your famous civil rights activists on Earth once spoke of darkness and hate. And how it was not the solution. Only love was. Martin—"

"Martin Luther King, Junior," Will said. "Great ideas. Wish people had listened to him, but look where America ended up."

"So, *you* listen to them. I believe they are not words solely for society as a whole but for individuals as well. It all begins there. Love is as powerful inward as it is outward. Hate only consumes one way in the end."

Will exhaled loudly, apparently thinking that was going to be difficult.

"You have those good memories," I continued. "The ones about love. The ones before all the loss. Because when it really comes down to it, we do not feel loss without loving something first. Try to remember that. Try to live in that. Do not worry. Eventually, it will become like a muscle memory. It will take very little thought."

"Well, thank Christ for that."

Regardless of his frustration and slow progress, Will returned week after week for our training. Gradually, he opened up more, and the more he did, the less prone he was to losing control. Some symbiotic effect of physical labor and psychology. Training in hand-to-hand combat helped as well since he was more aware of the potential damage he could inflict. On a target drone it was more difficult to tell—a biotech-laced punch to a living being was a different matter. However, even with the dampening technology in the sim fields, I felt each blow when he managed to connect. I might not have been as spry as I once was, but I had not lost many steps. On the odd occasion, I had to wave a hand to pause, so I could catch my breath and recover.

"Shit, sorry!" he said, rushing to my side. "I keep trying to pull my punches, but whenever I give it some juice, it fills the gap." He looked guilty and concerned, breathing hard, his face sweaty.

I caught my wind and stood up straight, trying not to show the pain. "As it should. That energy cushion should prevent any significant damage to your hands in a fight. The trick is not to use all your energy at once. Pace it for what you need and when. You look tired, Will," I said with a smile and a sudden lunge back to action.

Because of his strength, he lasted longer than I thought he would, but eventually his jabs and crosses became sloppy and slow. He was burning himself out, each hit draining him joule by joule. By the end of the fight, he stood in front of me swaying side to side, his eyes hazy. I pushed him on the shoulder, and he stumbled back and fell. For a moment he lay on his back, sucking deep breaths into his belly. Then he rolled over and got up on one knee. "Son of a bitch," he said breathlessly. I helped him to his feet and steadied him as he wobbled. "You sure you're two hundred and fifty years old?" he asked.

"It is easy to lose count these days." I materialized a bench, and we sat down. Will dug a canteen out of his bag and took a drink, then offered it to me. I shook my head. "No, thank you."

He smiled, wiping the sweat from his face. "You're not tired at all, are you?"

"It was a good session. You are getting better," I said with a smile. In truth, I could not have gone on much longer.

"Yeah, feels like it," Will said, one eyebrow arched in disbelief. We sat in silence for a few moments. He looked over at me. It seemed like he was about to say something but then held back.

"What is it, Will?"

"Sarah—one of the other humans in Charlie…" I knew the woman he meant. I had observed them getting close. He clearly had feelings for her. She was also a genius, scored in the top half percentile on all the aptitude tests. She had been an easy choice for Charlie aviary. Her budding relationship with Will was a bonus. "She read in the history files that…that you were in the first major battle with the Forsaken."

"The First Fall. Yes…" I drifted off into memory. It was not a good one. After the sack of Ourea, an attempt to retake the lost world was made. So many lights extinguished. It seemed like a lifetime ago, and for humans, it would have been almost two of them.

"If you don't want to talk about it, I understand," Will said, looking away.

I thought about it for a while, picturing the battle—or at least the limited view I had of it. I understood why this story was of interest to him. It may have been on a much smaller scale, but his service jacket had outlined one of his final missions with the United States military. Perhaps he wondered if I shared the same survivor's guilt he did.

"I would have been around your age at the time—or at least the Lumenarian equivalent," I said, the thought making me smile. "They struck the planet out of nowhere. Massacred the civilian population and then vanished back into space without a trace. And we searched. By every means available to us—nothing. Ten years passed, and it was decided to attempt a resettlement of Ourea. At the time the largest Lumenarian fleet ever assembled positioned there to secure the territory."

I remembered the feeling of pride and the desperate lust for vengeance I felt being aboard the *Tide*—the first ship on which I was a crew member. Back when Harden and I were inseparable. Looking out at the massive collection of warships hovering above the quiet world, it seemed like nothing could stop us. I almost hoped the Forsaken would show up, so we would have a chance to get retribution for all the Oureans lost.

"They were waiting for us. Somewhere out there in the dark. Once the new settlers and defense forces were committed to the ground, they attacked. It was just a small skirmish at first. They ignored the ships in orbit and ran to the surface, took the fight to the ground. So, we sent more of our forces down to protect the settlers." Every tactic was a lit tile on the face of Commander's Die. I was part of the engineering crew at the time and had to listen and watch the reports on displays from orbit. "For three days a battle was fought down there. Their *small* advance force massacred hundreds of thousands before we finally managed to suppress them and capture five."

"You took five prisoner?" Will asked, surprised.

I nodded slowly. "It was the biggest mistake we made. Each of the five went to different ships for interrogation. We thought it best to keep them separated. One came to the ship I was stationed on."

When the shuttle carrying our prisoner arrived, I was doing repairs on one of the other transports. Harden nudged me to draw my attention to it, and the whole bay stopped working to get a glimpse of our shadowed enemy for the first time. The ramp lowered, and twenty elite LUMSET soldiers marched out with their rifles trained on a lone Forsaken soldier shackled in energy restraints. He seemed so unfazed. He looked around the shuttle bay, almost casually taking in the room, then walked forward at his own pace. Any jostling by the guard seemed only a mild inconvenience. When the prisoner's helmeted head turned toward me, it felt like ice piercing me; a cold, dead compassionless stare, though I could not see through his visor. I had to shake off the chilling sight once they cleared the room.

"They never made it to the brig."

"What happened?"

"All I know for sure is that the five ships that had the prisoners were the first to fall. Some sort of cascading failure at the reactors. The Forsaken fleet arrived in force shortly after." The chaos of the day still rang in my ears.

Will shook his head. "I don't understand. You were on one of those first five. How did you survive?"

I saw the wall of fire and electricity billowing toward me in slow motion. Felt the heat of it boiling against the skin on my face. Heard the sound like water crashing into the obsidian rocks at the bottom of Lantern Falls on Lumen. "Luck," I replied with a shrug. "The shuttle I was working on was nearest the bay doors. The explosion slammed me and one of the other crew members into the shuttle and out into space."

"Shit," Will said, exhaling slowly.

"Yes. The shuttle was badly damaged and ignored in the ensuing battle, so we simply floated away." Floated away for months in the cold lonely darkness of space.

"Only the two of you survived?"

"That is just propaganda," I said with a half-hearted smile. "Something to stir the masses. Half the fleet jumped away before they were destroyed. We were just the fortunate two who survived a sinking ship. We were rescued sometime later."

I drifted off again in remembrance. The flickering glimpses in the shattered displays of the carnage and debris around us was a crippling sight. The countless frozen and torn bodies of our people floating through space a constant reminder of our bad fortune and inadequacy.

For reasons I understand but never liked, we were hailed as heroes of the first fall. Victors of failure. The lone survivors of a terrible battle in which we did not even fight.

"Thank you for telling me," Will said quietly.

I nodded. "I think we are done for today." I got to my feet stiffly (very much feeling my age). Will stood too. "I will see you next week. And Will…it is quite obvious how you feel about Ms. Li. Perhaps there is something there."

Will's eyes widened, and then he grinned in an uncharacteristically sheepish way. "Don't know what you're talking about." I smiled and bowed my head. Will shook my hand, nodded, and then left the sim field. Handshakes still seemed like an odd custom to me.

I stared at the door through which Will had left. He reminded me so much of myself in the decades after the First Fall. Lost. Searching for something. But then again, perhaps I was *still* looking for something.

CHAPTER XV

Assignment

"I have an assignment for you."

"Of course. Anything."

"It is time for the segregation to end. I am going to transfer you into Charlie aviary, and I would like you to choose a close group of others to join you. Put forward some recommendations."

"Wasn't the plan for everyone to be mixed throughout the aviaries?"

"That is still the plan. But Charlie is special. Elite. In time more will be asked of them than any other division."

"Seemed like Charlie was getting a lot of attention. Well, many of us have been looking forward to getting to know the humans better, and I look forward to the challenge."

"There is one in particular I would like you to meet."

"William Reach."

"Yes." So, word *was* spreading. "Kilo, you are one of the best we have."

"Thank you, Arthur," he said with an appreciative nod.

"I think together you could make a formidable team. That is what I am doing with Charlie. Building a team. Will is…an enigmatic individual. A leader."

"I think most of us have heard about Will Reach. Is he as powerful as they say?" Kilo asked. I could tell he was asking as a measure of himself as well. Some youthful competition. Good. He seemed excited.

"More. We have never seen anything like it. By the time we reach Lumen, I anticipate he will be more powerful than any of us. However, right now he is separate, unchallenged. He needs someone like you, and you need someone like him."

"I understand."

"I am going to send you Will's dossier. I want you to learn about him. He does not trust easily." Kilo stirred uncomfortably in his seat. "What is it?" I asked.

He seemed to be searching for the most diplomatic words. "With all due respect, Arthur, I think...it would be better just to get to know him. If someone has trust issues, researching them beforehand doesn't seem like the best approach." I smiled. It was the response I was hoping for. Will would have seen through the other tactics. Only honesty would break through his walls. "But...you knew that," Kilo added, seeing my reaction.

"I know you are the right one for the assignment, Kilo. I look forward to seeing what you can do."

"I won't let you down," he said, rising from his seat.

"I know you will not. Try to get me those recommendations by the end of the day."

"Yes, Arthur." I placed my hand on his forehead, and he placed his on mine, then he went to leave.

"And Kilo, Will is not *just* an objective, and his growth does not come at the expense of your own." He smiled in understanding and then left my quarters.

I sat back down and looked at my desk display, going over the general rosters for the new housing assignments. Will's group had been given the most experienced instructors and had the most intensive training schedule. Now they would get the last piece of the puzzle: the best and brightest Lumenarian teammates.

It was encouraging to see how quickly the humans took to their new cohabitants. Within days our two species were playing games in the common areas of the aviaries and eating meals together. Kilo and several of his most trusted comrades had been inserted into units only a few doors down from Will, and they seemed to bond immediately. I knew Will's inner circle would be difficult to pierce; however, I also knew if any Lumenarian could do it, it was Kilo. He was young and powerful and, more than anything, honest and always spoke his mind—traits that I knew Will would respect.

In the training rooms, they challenged one another and flowed well in team drills. There were obviously growing pains. The humans, being quite a bit smaller, made maneuvers with them awkward at times. The differing heights also made organized shield walls difficult for one party or the other. Close-quarter room clearing often led to Lumenarians stepping into humans or vice versa, and hand-to-hand training had to be taken in steps, so we would not hurt them—with the exception of Will and some of the other more elite recruits. Eventually, all these things were ironed out until they moved as one, learning the strengths and weaknesses and how best to work around them. For every trait lacking in one species, the other complemented well.

When Kilo and Will sparred, Kilo had an obvious reach advantage, but when Will got in close, which he often did, Kilo struggled to compete. Their matches often drew an audience. Other training slowed or stopped altogether, so people could observe them. I made a habit of watching them whenever I could on the displays or in person. When it seemed Kilo's ability to challenge Will had been exhausted, Will was matched against several Lumenarians and humans at a time. No matter what we threw at him, he seemed to adapt to it and excel.

"It's almost scary what he can do," Kilo said, shaking his head. "If all the humans could master what he has, this war will be over quicker than we thought." As with Will, I had a weekly arrangement with Kilo to meet up for briefings.

"We can all learn from Will," I said. I was glad Kilo was impressed with him, but I did not want him to doubt his own abilities or to accept that they had a limit. Will obviously had not. "I have observed how much he has learned from you."

"Yeah. Not sure how much more I can teach him though. He adapts to everything, and his style is incredibly unorthodox. He definitely doesn't fight fair— I mean he fights brutally. To win. Every time." Kilo chuckled.

I smiled, thinking back to the first time when I would not let Will win at bocce, the idea that nothing would be learned by treating an opponent like they were better than they were. Boosting confidence had its benefits, but so did provoking the natural competitive spirit in someone who wanted to be the best.

"He punched me in the shin the other day when Cash and I were sparring with him," Kilo said. "It wasn't even a hard shot, just enough to knock me off balance and block Cash. It was all he needed. I never would've thought to do that. He sees all the angles, all the openings. Pure combat improvisation."

"It is what we observed in the Forsaken," I said quietly. Kilo stared at me and nodded. We sat in silence for several moments. It was true. In the close-quarter conflicts where our people had managed to escape, all the reports detailed a seeming lack of consistent tactics. Something flexible and violent. "Perhaps we were wrong to assume we would be doing most of the teaching," I said. "We have more to learn from the humans than we could have imagined."

It was a sobering thought and a good check on our egos. Despite our technological advancement, there was no substitute for that Earth theory of fierce Darwinian instinct, something I felt was lost on us from thousands of generations of tech dependence and relative peace. None of the humans fought like they had biotech; it simply enhanced what they already had. They would be adept fighters without it. We, on the other hand, had never really been without it and as such had a harder time adapting to the pure form of combat. In truth, before the Forsaken, our military had been more akin to a police force. Large-scale conflict was something from our long-forgotten past, if it had ever happened.

"How does Will's…mental state seem?"

Kilo shifted uncomfortably in his seat. "He's good," was all he said, holding my stare. I took it as tenuous, a slight twitch giving it away. Will was excelling at his training, mostly happy, but probably a little restless and bored, and I imagined that was when his demons spoke loudest. At least he didn't seem to be drinking anymore. I was surprised at Kilo's curt response though. His loyalty to Will was already strong, just as I had hoped. And Will was not one to take loyalty without returning it.

37 MONTHS SINCE LD – 9 MONTHS INTO RT

"What am I looking at here?" Will asked as he read over a list I had transferred to his forearm band.

"It is your new company," I said with an eager smile.

"What?" Will looked up at me, anger striking across his face. "I don't want a company."

"It is a promotion, Will," I said, unable to hide my disappointment.

"I figured all the company commanders would be Lumenarian."

"The plan was always to have human captains eventually. Only those with prior military combat experience, of course. It could never be a true union if we did not permit humans to also lead. You are simply among the first."

"Well, with all due respect, no thank you."

I blinked several times as I registered his refusal. "Will, you are ready to—"

"Great. Put a rifle in my hands, and get someone else to point me toward what needs doing." I stared at him for a long moment. "Look, I'm just not the—"

"No."

"Yes, no. Glad you see I'm not the guy for—"

"That is not what I—"

"See, I'm more of a blunt object kind of soldier, and—"

"That is enough," I said firmly. Will went silent and looked down. I watched him, waiting for my irritation to settle. "I thought you would be ready to step into your role willingly, Will." He made like he was going to argue, but I held up my hand to silence him again. "So now it is an order." He clenched his jaw. "You have been leading this entire time anyway, and now it is official."

I stood and walked over to my shelf of books; I always found them grounding. "Eventually, we learn that it was never for us. The best leaders do not lead for themselves; they lead for everyone else. Because everyone else is made better by them. Made safer and more powerful. That is your responsibility, Will. Anything less serves no one."

Will shook his head slowly, tiredly. "I can't lose anybody else." We both fell silent in the face of his admission.

"You are going to lose people no matter what, Will," I said gently. "All we can really do is give them the best possible chance." Will looked up at me and I saw the storm inside, the fear and doubts that he hid so well laid bare. "You need to make peace with that," I said.

40 MONTHS SINCE LD – 12 MONTHS INTO RT

Flak looked like he was on the verge of going on a rampage, or so his body language would suggest. He stood with his arms firmly crossed, biotech lines glowing faintly, his stare fixed on the bodies in the hallway (or what was left of them), and an expression of barely contained rage ebbing out in small twitches. It was a gruesome sight, and the motive behind it was even more disturbing. Xenophobic hate.

He had just returned to the site after his security teams swept through the other incidents. I could even make out the faint silhouette, like a clear shadow, of Sarah's body on the wall, where blood had splashed around her as she held her terrorist shield, an outline where the spatter couldn't reach.

"Fucking OnSpec," Flak growled. "If it hadn't been Reach and Li here, it could have been a lot worse."

"Mhmm," I mumbled, still stunned by the scene and not really listening. After months aboard the ship, we'd had no idea the terrorist faction was operating. The perpetrators had blended in completely and bided their time for an attack. It was not particularly successful, but coordinating a strike of any magnitude under our gaze would have been incredibly difficult. It meant they communicated solely by word of mouth and discreetly at that. It also meant they had some way to identify each other. The human inhabitants of the *Albatross* had been drawn from all over the planet, meaning the chances that the different cells would know each other was incredibly unlikely. These six alone were from the nations of Canada, Turkey, Costa Rica, Spain, India, and the United States. Completely random geographically.

A concussive BOOM snapped me back to attention. Flak withdrew his fist from a large dent he had just created in the corridor wall, his rage boiling over. Several of the other crew stared and shied away. He wound up for another strike.

"That is enough."

Flak froze mid-swing and exhaled slowly, turning back to face me. "If I get a hold of more of those OnSpec bastards, I'm—"

"Why were none of them taken alive?"

Flak gaped at me, his mouth slightly open. "They didn't exactly give us a choice," he said, crossing his arms again.

"We could have interrogated them."

"I understand that. Three of them shot themselves just to prevent us from taking them alive," he said. I saw his anger and frustration bubbling up again. "If you're suggesting I lost—"

"No, of course not," I said.

Flak nodded suspiciously as if to say, Better not be.

I was not really accusing him of anything; I had simply wished out loud for what could have helped; the ideal outcome for such a turbulent event. So far in the attacks on Earth and aboard the ship, none of the terrorists had been caught alive. It kept us blind to so many things. I pulled him aside from the other crew and leaned in close. "You are going to lead the investigation on this. Select a small team, and keep it quiet. I want you to go over personnel files one at a time if you must, double back over security feeds, find any connections you can. If there are any left on my ship, I want them found."

We shared an intense stare, and Flak nodded slowly. "I'll find them."

We both turned back to the mangled bodies on the floor. I had expected much, but I never expected this.

CHAPTER XVI

From This Light To The Next

The words echoed in my head like the fading resonances of a deep heavy bell tolling in a wide-open valley. I was suddenly aware of how comfortable this room and my seat behind my desk were. I always liked it, but now (strangely) it seemed especially warm. The old Earth books on my shelves had a certain aesthetic appeal against the metallic and opal-sheathed panels of the chamber walls, like a cultural time capsule. I thought about what words in what pages would seem the most fitting for this feeling that railed against the setting. Somewhere between numb disbelief and grief. Curious, the things that passed through my mind in such moments. To be honest, I was surprised it had taken so long for the first, but some glimmer of hope had stuck in the background of my subconscious, supposing we might get lucky.

"Arthur?" Sky stared at me from across the desk. Perhaps I had wandered off in thought longer than I realized. The words were escaping me: my response and the fitting few in the shelved tomes. I went to speak, but nothing came. "We're still asking around to see what his—"

"How?" I asked suddenly.

Sky looked down at the desk for a moment before glancing back up at me. "He…hung himself from a railing in the aviary." I closed my eyes, and the image of a body dangling off the parapets for the whole complex to see flitted through my mind. It was a disturbing thought, but the practical comprehension of the situation dashed ahead. Who had witnessed it? How could we mitigate similar instances in the future? Should counselling be mandatory for the inhabitants of Charlie? It always took longer than expected for the simple *why* to form. Why did he do it? What was the trigger? The final straw? I shook my head, trying to shake away the clinical responses.

"I am sorry. You were saying something before I interrupted you," I said, looking to Sky.

She observed me for a moment before continuing. "We are trying to figure out what his customs were..." Sky also struggled with the words. "Regarding death."

"Of course."

On Lumen, or anywhere on our colonies, death was always treated the same way. The body was preserved, wrapped in cloth, loaded into storage until the mortuary ships were full, and then launched into a star. In the event that the deceased was of particular esteem, he or she might receive a more expedited journey to the sun; however, that was usually reserved for long-serving council members or admirals. I would probably receive a private shuttle to my solar grave. It did not matter to me, but many still clung to tradition. It seemed familiar to the burials of Viking kings I had read about on Earth. More an issue of ego than necessity. If we died in a system that was not our own, efforts would be made to return us to the star we grew up around. It was in our cells; we would be returned to the light that created us. For the loved ones who remained, a funeral was traditionally celebratory rather than a tribute to grief—ending with the deceased's life tech being placed in the Hall of Memory. However, since the war began, the overwhelming amount of loss made it difficult to dwell on the good things—not simply the loss of life but also the loss of their life tech, which transferred their stories.

"Was he on any psychiatric watch?" I asked.

"No. From what little I've learned so far, his friends said he seemed a little distant recently but not enough for them to be worried about anything like this," Sky said, shaking her head.

"What was his name?"

"Travis Dayton." The name was familiar to me. He had been chosen for Charlie aviary because of his biotech and personality test scores. He was strong and proud. I had anticipated that he and Will would butt heads. But in being an opposition to Will, it would challenge Will to be patient and to earn the trust of someone who felt superior to him. It was easy to lead people who were looking for a leader, another thing to lead other leaders.

"He was in Will's training group," I said absentmindedly.

Sky stared at me. "Yes…" She stirred in her chair. "I don't think that's particularly important right now. News of this will be felt throughout the ship regardless of what squad he was on." She looked irritated. I stared down at my hands, ashamed that my obsession with Will's training had been so apparent. "I'm sorry, Arthur. I didn't mean to suggest—"

"You are right." There was an awkward moment of silence between us.

"With your permission, I'd like to go to Charlie and offer counselling."

"Please do," I said with a nod. Sky rose from her seat, and I did likewise. She placed her hand on my head, and I placed mine on hers. "Thank you, Sky." She bowed and then turned, leaving my quarters.

I sat back down and stared at the books on my shelves. "Ah, distinctly I remember it was in the bleak December, / And each separate dying ember wrought its ghost upon the floor. / Eagerly I wished the morrow;—vainly I had sought to borrow / From my books surcease of sorrow—sorrow for the lost Lenore— / For the rare and radiant maiden whom the angels name Lenore— / Nameless here for evermore," I recited aloud to myself. The Earth poet, Poe, spoke to me from the pages.

Though Travis had many friends, none of them could tell us what his preferences for burial were. It was an understandable oversight. Few of the volunteers were actual family, and such conversations usually happened between family members, to my understanding. That and knowing what we were marching toward generally favored lighter vocal fare. Not that I could not see deep bonding between the inhabitants of the *Albatross*, but morbid discussions admitting the possibility of a destructive end were generally avoided. I was sure after this incident that more conversation would occur around the topic, but for the moment, in the case of Travis Dayton, a decision had to be made. We could not transport his body back to Earth, so now we had to choose a method of burial for him.

I called a meeting with several of the Charlie aviary residents to discuss the issue. Travis was not, by all accounts, a pious man. He had believed in a god but had not participated in any religious services. Two of his human friends, a man named Tariq and a woman named Karen, assured me that he was in no way devout. It did not shed much light on his preference. It was a passionate discussion that I feared was argued on each participant's bias rather than what Travis might have actually wanted. With no way of knowing for sure, they simply took a vote. In the end it was decided that he would be laid to rest in the Lumenarian way. It was essentially a cremation, so it also paid tribute to Earth. The first human ever to be interred in a star.

"If nothing else, it'll be a really cool way to be laid to rest," Tariq said.

Though Sky and several of the other medical personnel stressed repeatedly that it was not my responsibility, I still carried the weight. I knew what they meant, but it did not change the fact that I had recruited them all. So, I took on the burial rites myself.

One of the terms for a medical table in a mortuary or coroner's office on Earth was a "slab." For some reason the crude word jumped out at me as I stared down at Travis's body in the morgue off the Charlie 6 medical bay. We called everything in a mortuary room "guidance apparatus" due to the idea that we were simply preparing the deceased's light travel from this place to that—guiding it to its final resting place. "Slab" seemed like such a cold, impersonal term, but perhaps there was some merit to it. To place each corpse that passed through a coroner's life upon a pedestal would be a devastating tally on their minds, especially when dealing with the multitudes of dead in war, such as Sky had. There was something to be said for not connecting with every form that passed through. But this was not war. Not yet. There was time to feel every ripple of Travis's choice.

His body had already been washed and prepared for the wrapping. The bruising and discoloration around his neck was vivid against his milky white skin. Though his head had been realigned from the broken neck, a medi-gel sealed line was visible on the side of his neck where the vertebrae had protruded through the skin. I thought suddenly how fortunate it was that his head had remained attached to his body, for the witnesses at the time and now for me staring down at his remains. All death is gruesome in some way; bodies do what they do when everything relaxes for the last time. But the hypothetical image of his head coming off was a disturbing thought. The table's energy field encasing his body slowed decomposition and stifled the smell, but the field's faded emerald color gave the appearance that he was wearing a mask, something akin to Frankenstein's monster. He looked waxen and artificial, as if he were a mannequin.

I walked to the side of the room and opened one of the drawers. Inside was a large woven roll of traditional Lumen cloth. The fabric had the look of burlap but was smooth and soft, like velvet. Various colors represented the different worlds in the Union. The dead were generally wrapped in the color of whatever planet they were born on. An injection of programmed nanoparticles would change the hue from the base stark white. White was also the representative color of Lumen. Considering the design of the UN flag for Earth, I programmed the sheet a royal blue. It was soundless as I pulled it from the rack and stretched out an adequate length. It always felt like a fluid when I touched it. The room was perfectly quiet, ringing slightly in my cochlear structures. I stood and stared at the cloth in my hands. It had been quite a while since I had to do this, and I was having trouble turning to face the body. The first human I had ever seen dead, or at least dead in a state of relative peace. The OnSpec members were a different matter. I had not dealt with their bodies. How many more would lie upon tables like this in the coming months and years?

When I did finally turn, I could not help but feel a new wave of emotion. The biotech striations on the back of my hand glowed lightly, and I knew they would be shining everywhere else as well. I felt my jaw tighten instinctively as I set myself to the task of wrapping the body.

I programmed the energy field to levitate Travis's body six inches off the table and slid the sheet under his form. As the body floated off kilter in the zero gravity, I guided it flat to wrap it properly. Generally, this was done with two or three Lumenarians, and I saw why. It was awkward on my own. Once I had the cloth positioned well, I lowered the body in the field and disengaged it. The fabric ends folded over his face to his mid chest and feet up to his knees. Then the cloth wrapped around the length of his body. When he was fully covered, metallic clasps held it all together, so it wouldn't shift during transportation. I stared down at the blue shroud and found the way the fabric settled in the ocular cavities somewhat haunting, like a specter staring up at me. The nose intensified the effect. Our Lumenarian faces appeared more featureless under the coverings because of our lack of a nose.

In three days we would be passing a blue giant star and stopping for the funeral ceremony. Until then the body would stay there, preserved in the stasis. There was no rush to dispose of the terrorists' bodies, but Travis was different.

I placed my hand on the forehead of his shrouded body. "I am sorry you felt this was the way," I said. "May your light find peace." I left the room and the dead behind.

I held up a hand and backed away. I needed to catch my breath. I still had some tricks in my repertoire, but Will was combating most of them with relative ease. At this point our sessions were mostly just good exercise for me. Physically, he had exceeded most of what I could teach him.

"He was kind of a pain in the ass to be honest," Will said during our weekly training session. He wiped some sweat from his face. "But I liked him. He was a tough son of a bitch."

"Did you know him well?"

"No. I mean, he was in my training section, but we weren't close. Competitive against each other, yeah. Seemed like a good guy for the most part, though. Just stubborn." Will walked to the side and took a drink from his canteen.

"Him stubborn?"

"Yeah, yeah," he said with a grin. I got the feeling that he was deflecting slightly. Something lay beneath it all.

"Suicide is incredibly rare among Lumenarians…"

"Uh-huh."

"It is not something I am particularly familiar in dealing with." Will did not look over from the side, his eyes frequently tracing the movements of ghosts as I continued. "Before we left Earth, we were warned about certain statistics among humans, even studies conducted by space agencies regarding long-term space travel and—"

"Yeah, yeah. Fragile up here sometimes," he said, tapping his temple. He still wouldn't look right at me. He drained the last of his water and tapped the top of his canteen. The funnel condenser spun up with a faint green glow, sucking water out of the air.

"Fragile…" I said. I watched him closely, noting the struggle in his body. Finally, he shook his head and looked at the floor.

"I shouldn't have said 'fragile,'" he said. "I mean, yeah we are, but, well, People are just…fucked up. Especially guys, it seems. I mean there's a whole world of shit for women too, but…" He looked up at me with a weak smile. "Our whole lives people tell us to be tough. To be the man of the house or that boys don't cry or to always protect your family." He stopped abruptly and stared at the floor again, then blinked and shook his head. The biotech lines across his body began to glow a deep cobalt. He glanced sideways again, following the path of another unseen thing. I wondered how many spirits haunted his mind. "Or any of that bullshit," he said through clenched teeth.

I watched him in silence. Part of me was curious whether he was going to keep it under control. The thought made me feel guilty, like I was using Will as some sort of academic study—which, in a way, I was. I knew where his pain was coming from. Just as I was about to speak, he continued.

"Doesn't seem like we're ever really taught how to deal with it all." He took a deep breath and exhaled slowly. The biotech lines faded back down to their tattoo black. "It's an injury no one sees on the outside. Deep damage." His smile was sad, and he suddenly looked much older than he was. It was a strange thing to see someone so obviously hurt smile so much. Maybe that was as much of the problem as anything else. It reminded me of another Earth saying I had heard; "Grin and bear it."

"Soldiers often carry that burden more than anyone else," I said. "Have you spoken with any of the counselors?"

Will shook his head. "Talked to one, you've talked to them all." I was surprised to hear he *had* spoken with someone. He must have noticed my expression. "Forced. High school for...someone. And Afghanistan. Guy in our squad and a few others. You may be a stranger to this, but I'm definitely not."

"I see." We sat quietly for several moments. "I would like you to start a group."

"A group?"

"To talk."

"Yeah, that's what I figured." He looked uncomfortable. "Christ. First you force a squad and then a company on me, and now you want me to hold their hands." I ignored that last comment, the hypocrisy of it apparently lost on him.

"Just for humans. As close as we are becoming, I think it is important that you have a dialogue amongst yourselves. As I said, Lumenarians are unfamiliar with this issue."

"If Frank was here right now, he'd piss his pants laughing. I'm not exactly a group kinda guy."

"Leaders often have to conduct tasks they do not like for the sake of their teams."

"I keep telling you, I'm not the leader you want."

"Yes you are, Will."

"Well, maybe I don't fucking want to be. I don't know how many times I have to say it."

We stared at each other for several seconds.

"Will…perhaps that is why you are best suited for it." He looked away, clenching his jaw. "All of this," I said, gesturing to the sim field and the ship in general, "is to help you become what you are meant to be. People flock to you, Lumenarian and human alike."

"You put them there! You surrounded me with them!" He glared at me.

"I put them in your path. They decided to walk it with you. Do you not see, Will? Without trying, without wanting it, even trying to prevent it, they follow you." He broke the stare and looked at the floor. "Power and skill draw people in. Good leadership keeps them there."

Will stood and turned his back to me. "Find someone else. We're done for the day." He went to leave. For a moment I thought about letting him go, then decided against it.

"No, we are not," I said, my voice echoing in the space. Will stopped and turned to face me. "The training is over when I say it is." As he glared at me, the lines began to glow their familiar blue again. He looked furious. "Come, William. Show me you have nothing left to learn."

He lowered his head and stepped toward me with clenched fists. Will fought with a berserker's flurry that I was barely able to dodge, each strike grazing closer and closer, but I managed for a time. I was purely on the defensive, in survival mode. A jarring shot to my stomach reeled me in. I could not go toe to toe with him for long and expect to win. To give myself a half second of space, I slammed him hard in the chest with an open-hand blast that just skirted his guard. The impact rocked Will back two or three feet, just enough. The whites of his eyes flared with sapphire electricity, so much so that his irises and pupils disappeared in the storm of blue. Everything slowed as he wound up for a power blow. It would be crippling. I matched his haymaker with my own but crouched lower and swung my left hand behind me. At the moment of contact in the middle, I emitted a burst of raw energy a fraction of a second early (interrupting most of his potential build) while also releasing my backhand with another powerful burst of uncontrolled thermal energy. The concussive boom would have been enough to discombobulate anyone nearby, and my backhand projected force that braced me from flying backwards. The effect was like a squeeze in a vise as two walls of energy cocooned me, but it redistributed both our energies entirely into Will. He flew backwards into the wall with a crunch and fell onto his stomach.

I was breathing hard but did my best to control it. I did not move to see if he was alright, I knew he was hurting. He pounded his fist into the floor, sending out crackling blue energy. The rest of his lines erupted and engulfed him in a brilliant but terrifying fire. I had never seen anything like it. He rose to his feet, consumed and seething, and took two menacing steps forward.

"Now we are done," I said. Will froze in his tracks. I saw how much he wanted to keep fighting, but he also knew it would be trouble if he did. He relaxed his fists and stood glaring at me, his tech lines calming to their tattoo black, but the blue fire didn't leave his eyes. Without a word, he turned and marched toward the door.

"Will." He stopped in the entry but didn't turn. "I did not have a choice either." His head turned slightly, then he continued out of the sim field. I stared after him and then looked down at my hand. The skin had cracked at my knuckles, and the cracks streaked up toward my wrist. Black blood oozed out. That was everything I could have given, and Will would not have let me get away with it twice.

The blue giant star was brilliant in the displays broadcasting the view around the ship. Lumenarians and humans alike flocked to the observation decks to stare in wonder. It was the first glimpse of stationary space in over a year, and it was a sight to behold. Even my crew, so accustomed to the cosmos, was constantly amazed by the beauty of it all. The system had no habitable planets, only a few gaseous orbs and molten rocks revolving in the stellar orbit. The star itself was in the middle of a massive solar flare event that shot fiery cerulean arcs into the surrounding dark in a wild and fierce display. It was a beautiful day for a funeral.

The *Osprey* and the *Pelican* loomed around us in loose formation. They had had their own casualties. A handful of training accidents and several suicides. That was also to be expected; they had significantly more souls on board. I felt lucky that we had had only one casualty. The other ships would be holding their own funerals and launching their own dead into the star.

Thousands gathered in the main aft shuttle bay for the funeral procession, mainly the inhabitants of Charlie aviary since Travis had been one of their own. Everyone else held vigil in the aviary parks and ready rooms throughout the *Albatross*. Out of respect for many of the humans' customs, the affair was more somber than something one would see on Lumen. One of the crew, a man named Jude, who had been training to be a priest before our arrival, read some passages from the Christian Bible. We still did not know whether it was something that Travis would have wanted, but we felt it would not hurt.

After Jude's sermon, the metallic coffin that held the blue-shrouded body was carried by six pallbearers to the center of the room. Earth's international flag was draped over the casket, and then the escort stepped back. We were still agreeing upon a new sigil for the Union forces, which I would have liked to fold over as well, but nothing had been decided yet. In time perhaps there would a single, unified flag.

I took my place at the holo-feed recorder, looked out over the thousands gathered, and thought about the hundreds of thousands more who were watching. "It is easy to forget that in our journey toward war, some us are already fighting wars inside and that the scars we bear are not always visible," I said. "Travis Dayton was a son of Earth who sacrificed everything to help us. His fight is over." I stared down at the coffin, feeling all the eyes upon me. "We often think we are all alone, holding our suffering inside to save others the burden." I found Will's eyes in the crowd and saw the weight in his face and his shoulders. "There is a saying on Earth. 'No man is an island.' We will never completely understand why someone would choose this. We can assume, but we can never know for certain." I looked out at all the eyes again, focusing on as many as I could. "We all come from different backgrounds, different faiths, even different worlds. However, when I look around at all of you, I see an amazing union. The people around you, Lumenarian and human alike, will always be there for you. You are never alone. 'Never an island entire of itself.'" The crowd stirred, each glancing to the souls next to them, many exchanging silent nods. "Travis Dayton will be missed. From this light to the next."

The lights in the shuttle bay were dimmed, and I raised my hand into the air and flared up my biotech, a glowing green beacon in the semi-dark. Throughout the bay, and I hoped the entire ship, everyone raised their hands and did the same. The emerald and sapphire lights filled the area.

As the casket was carried to a drone for its final send-off, several humans reached out to touch it. As they did, they pulsed some of their energy onto its surface. Soon every person it passed reached out to transfer some of their own into it, an ebbing flow of bodies reaching out and swirling away in its wake. The sight made me proud as much as it reflected my feelings of guilt and sorrow.

The coffin was loaded on the shuttle, and the doors closed behind it. We all stood in silence as it hummed to life, rose into the air, and passed through the bay's hydro barrier.

Once it was clear, a gentle murmur spread through the collective, and everyone began to make their way back to their aviaries. I wondered if the feeling that I had not quite said enough, that my words had not been resounding enough was common after Terran funerals. In traditional Lumen ceremonies, little was said at all, and what was said was mostly a standard proclamation for the dead. The more intimate eulogies were spoken in private or shared in less formal settings.

As the attendees filtered out, I caught a glimpse of Will staring back at me. Once I met his eyes, he gave me a subtle nod of understanding, which I returned, and then he went on his way.

From the command deck, I watched the dim light of Travis's shuttle and a second light carrying the OnSpec dead drift toward the blue giant. I may have vehemently disagreed with their choice and not fully understood it, but even the terrorists deserved to be laid to rest. We had no ceremony for them, but I could not bring myself to simply evacuate their bodies to some random cold expanse. Several other small lights from the *Osprey* and the *Pelican* joined them in procession. In time they faded from view, lost in the sapphire brilliance. I stared at the massive orb, the display filter preventing it from searing my eyes. The first burial of the mission, and it certainly would not be the last. Finally, I turned to Harper at the helm. "Count us out please."

"Yes, Arthur." She toggled her console for thread-drive initiation and switched comms to a ship-wide broadcast. "All stations. Thread drive engagement in five…four…three…two…one."

In a blink we were back in the milky blur of faster-than-light travel and continuing on our way to Lumen. On our way to war.

CHAPTER XVII

Where Were We...?

42 MONTHS SINCE LD – 14 MONTHS INTO RT

The holographic display fired up around me, blasts of red and blue rifling past my vision. The dark shapes rushed forward like a flood, washing over and through the halls of the *Albatross*. I raised my hands and controlled my omniscient sentinel view to zoom in on certain areas of the battle and oscillate around to others. The humans moved well despite the onslaught. Their choices were strong and tactical but ultimately futile.

"Arthur," Flak grunted next to me, gesturing to a section of the display in his field. "Reach's group is making their last stand." He slid the view toward me, and we both watched intently. "What's left of Li's squads have been funneled there too." I tried to glance between the other fire teams slowly being overwhelmed, but I could not restrain my curiosity. Flak and I leaned in as the final wave descended on Will and the others in the oasis sim-field scenario.

His companions dropped around him one by one. I zoomed in close on Will as the last of his team fell beside him, then Sarah. He held her as she took her last breaths, disregarding everything else going on around him. I had hoped they would remain apart during the scenario. I knew seeing her die would echo within him for some time. He closed her eyes and then took one of the jolt shots from her bandolier, palming one of his own as well. I studied his face. A cold twitch spasmed across it for a moment before his jaw clenched, and his eyes hardened. The first stim shook him, and the second ignited him—every biotech line on his body flaring up in a devastating blue fire, encasing him in a torch of electric energy that arced into the sand at his feet. Over the dunes, hundreds of sprinting Forsaken charged down, feeding the ranks encircling him. Will dropped his Tempest rifle in the golden sand and stood to face his imminent destruction.

"Wouldn't have thought he'd ever give up," Flak said.

"He is not," I replied as Will clenched his fists and tensed every muscle in his body. In a searing flash, he erupted every cell in a massive cobalt explosion that washed through the sim field, wiping everything away. Flak and I stared in stunned silence.

"What the hell was—"

BOOM!

We stumbled off the shaking holo-display pad and looked down the adjacent row of escape pods that had been temporarily retrofitted as "imsims" (immersion simulation pods). Several pods down, the door had blown from its hinges in a sapphire burst and slammed into the nearby wall. We ran down to find Will climbing out, still engulfed in the electric glow. He was disoriented and flailing, still half caught in the artificial scenario.

Flak rushed forward and grabbed him by the shoulders. "Reach! Reach!" he shouted, shaking him. The transfer of energy from Will to Flak made Flak's biotech glow a bright green, and I saw his eyes widen not in pain but like his body was a battery connected to a high-voltage charger. "Will!" he yelled again, trying to rattle sense back into him.

Will breathed hard, grasping at Flak's arms and the air, his lips parting in a teeth-grinding growl. "Where were you?" he rasped angrily.

"A simulation, Reach!"

"Will. It was not real," I said firmly, trying to wrangle his focus. Finally, he seemed to realize where he was, taking in the details of the room and Flak standing in front of him. He looked over at me, his face bathed in sweat. His biotech gradually faded as he calmed himself.

"Shit, Reach. Make a TO proud," Flak said, gruffly patting him on the shoulder and nodding his approval.

Will looked over at me. "The uh…it was…the…" he panted, searching for the words but still confused.

"That is right, Will. A combat simulation. We told you, you would not remember being in it when it started. Gives it a realism different from the sim field," I said, trying to reassure him that he was, in fact, alive.

"Everyone else—"

"They are fine. They should be waking up in their pods any moment." On cue, several of the pod doors swung open, and their inhabitants groggily climbed out, filtering into the hallway.

"Holy shit sir—I mean, Arthur," Will fumbled, looking lost. "Just—"

"It is very real," I said with a nod. I looked up to see several of the humans hugging each other and rejoicing that they were alive. They had the look of trauma, the wide-eyed nervous laughter that kept them from weeping, one of the side effects of the body dumping the excess adrenaline out of their systems. A fevered mix of fear and joy.

Frank came up behind Will and spun him around, embracing him tightly. "Jesus Christ. I didn't think we were walking away from that one," he said.

"Thought I lost ya, man," Will replied, his voice shaking slightly. Suddenly, his eyes widened and reached past Frank, grabbed Sarah, and pulled her into a tight hug. She returned it, closing her eyes and exhaling unsteadily. After a long moment, they separated awkwardly. Will glanced over his shoulder at me. Then he turned and muttered something to her that I did not quite hear before he turned back to me. I saw he was about to say something when Miguel came up behind them.

"Sarah, Frank, Will. Holy fuck—sorry, sir." I nodded to him that it was alright. "When I—I…died, it was like I became a spirit, watching everything else happen. That shit was crazy, man." He turned and gave Flak and I and accusatory glare. "Did you just Kobayashi Maru us?" Flak and I looked at each other, not understanding the reference.

"There wasn't any way to win, was there?" Will said.

"There was one way." I glanced at Flak, who stepped forward.

"Evacuating in the lifeboats and detonating the thread-drive reactor," he said. Several in the crowd began murmuring to each other, clearly unsatisfied with that answer.

"Doesn't seem like winning..."

"It wasn't about winning," Flak said. "It was about surviving. It was about saving as many of yours as you could and killing as many of theirs as you could. In war sometimes that's the best you get. Keeping as many alive as possible to fight another day." The room went quiet, and I saw everyone thinking on this, trying to decide if they would rather die fighting or retreat. Many would boast about their desire for a Valkyrie end (as I had read in an Earth book on mythology), but in my experience, hindsight left most survivors grateful to be alive even if only for a few days longer.

I looked at the many troubled faces and saw the weight of their ordeal. They looked tired and shaken. The first time someone went through it, the simulation was indistinguishable from reality. Groups were selected, and the role of the pods was explained, but the sedatives administered before the program was initiated erased the previous day's memories, allowing the subject to fully absorb the fantasy. Subsequent journeys into the false world were susceptible to rejection since subjects were more aware of its possibilities; however, it was such a flawless re-creation that while inside, participants could never be certain it was not real until they were withdrawn from it, which was why it was considered a dangerous, reality-fracturing technology. For this reason it was rarely used except under specific safety and training protocols. There was a time long ago, back home, when such simulations were not monitored and were frequently used for leisure or a desire to escape a world crumbling after the great fall of memory. But that "freedom" became a cage, a prison of the mind that saw many Lumenarians trapped in the virtual reality or their tether to real life so frayed that they could not separate one form of reality from the other.

"Time has been allotted for a break from training over the next few days. I know it will be difficult, but try not to dwell on the scenario too much. Get some rest. Flak will be conducting an after-action review with all of you after the time off."

They stared blankly at me as Flak took up the reins. "It might not feel like it, but you all fought well. Be proud of that." As I watched them take in Flak's words, there was a swelling in the group. Despite their fatigue, each stood slightly taller, determination or sparks of pride flooding their faces. Flak was not often forthright with his praise. "Now go get some rest," Flak concluded.

The humans walked past us, nodding as they filtered out of the room. When the last of them made their way through, Flak and I stood facing Will, who had stayed behind.

"What is it, Reach?" Flak asked. Will looked hesitant, like he could not quite figure out how to say what he wanted to say, his eyes teeming with uncertainty.

"Why?" he said finally. "Why me? How can I do what I do?"

Flak and I glanced at each other. We had been asking that question since the beginning, and we still had no answer. We knew that one common trait among the humans—those who proved compatible with our technology—was a higher percentage of Neanderthal, Denisovan, and archaic Homo sapiens genealogy, but some had very little. Most had higher neural activity, but many were average, and a few were below. Some had low insulin levels, some had denser bone mass, and some had type O blood, but many did not. There were patterns, but every pattern had an exception, a cosmic jumble of genes and synapses.

"We still do not know," I admitted. He stared at me for a moment, then broke eye contact, nodding and looking at the ground. "I am sorry, Will. We are still learning more—"

"It's OK," he said with a tight smile, deflecting his disappointment. "Just curious." He stared back at me with his intense blue glare. "May I be dismissed, sir? Could use a shower."

"Of course." Will nodded and walked past. "Will," I said. "Good work." He stopped and nodded again before turning and leaving the chamber.

Flak and I stood there watching him go. Flak shook his head and smiled. "If we ever do figure out what makes Will, Will, give me a shot of it. He'll be as strong as any of us by the time we reach Lumen," he said, staring at the blasted-open pod. "Hell of a thing." I looked at the empty doorway through which Will had left. Flak turned and tapped his forearm band, shutting down the holo-display and powering down the pods.

"Stronger," I said quietly.

"What's that?"

"He will be stronger than any of us." I didn't tell him what I was really thinking—Will already was.

Flak smirked and turned back to the display to review the footage. I stared down at the crumpled door of Will's pod. One of the pod's features, to increase the likelihood of rescue in space, however slim, was to initiate a preservative stasis for the occupant. This was maintained to allow the simulation to function without the occupants involuntarily acting out the scenario, like the way some kick or punch in a dream. Will should not have been able to blow the door off its hinges. Just another layer to the mystery that surrounded him.

I wandered back toward the command deck, replaying the recent events and going over the tasks of the day in my head. As the commander of the *Albatross*, I had nothing particularly exciting to do during the long months of travel. Monitoring the ongoing training, checking maintenance reports, doing research, and acting as the primary liaison between us and the humans took up the bulk of my days. The training sessions with Will were a nice reprieve, though incredibly trying at times. When I thought about it though, I realized this probably would have been more the pace of my life had war not broken out.

As a younger male of ninety Earth years, I had been studying to be a historian and teacher, my days spent combing through Lumen's memory banks. A great hall that was made of glass and light, a lumenium skeleton holding it all together that hardly seemed capable of supporting it. Down the center of the long, brightly lit room were hundreds of glass chambers equipped with terminals to access the specific lives we were researching and imsims to experience them. Billions of souls were catalogued in perfectly vivid detail, each memory of the departed accessible and viewed as if through their own eyes. The challenge was siphoning through the massive archives to find the right subjects and then homing in on the critical moments of their existences to glean the relevant information. That had seemed to be my future. A peaceful life of study. Then the Forsaken sacked Ourea. I, like many others from Lumen and the outlying colony worlds, heeded the call to action. The call to get retribution for the billions of lights extinguished in the blink of an eye. I spent the next ten years training and waiting to fight a hidden enemy that we knew nothing about but who had to be stopped.

With the academic schedule pushed back to allow the humans to recover from their ordeal in the imsims, I knew several of the sim fields would be vacant. I walked to the closest one and programmed one of my old settings. As the doors opened, the nanoparticles finished taking their form, and I strode across through impossibly dark space and the twinkling lights of distant stars. The floor sucked up all the light, as if I was walking in the void. The planet floated in the simulated beyond, a small cerulean globe with sparks of crimson igniting on its surface. Clouds of debris drifted past—bits of scorched lumenium, broken nano-glass from displays, frozen and crystallized fluids of differing hues, mechanical tools, equipment crates, and then the biological masses. I sidestepped an arm as it hurtled past, not giving it a second glance. I had seen it all so many times before.

The shuttle hung in front of me, ravaged by the destruction of the *Tide* and flickering its last embers of power. I opened a slot in the side with my forearm band to pass through the replicated hull and stepped inside. I ducked under some mechanical shrapnel and sat down on a heap of debris next to an engineering access panel—the panel that would decide whether we lived or died. Above my head was a cracked display that showed diagnostics and output. The energy levels fluctuated and dwindled, dipping into complete failure zones. I reached into the mess of gel electrical circuitry, the lifeblood of our ships. Pulsing some energy through my hand, I looked up and watched the levels somewhat balance, maintaining our life-support systems.

"They're all dead," the voice echoed from behind me.

"Yes, they are," I replied, not turning but focusing on the engineering panel. There was never any other way to repair it, not with what I had available, but I still tinkered.

"But help will still come?" the voice asked, coughing weakly.

"Yes, of course. They could be here any moment," I said, knowing the truth.

"Arthur, I'm not a fool—"

"You will become one," I muttered. The simulated memory would not have heard me anyway. Some simulations, such as combat programs, were free to react within parameters while others, such as this one, followed a narrative. This one I had recreated as close to how I remembered it, every horrifying detail. It was a nightmare, but I needed it as some obsessive attempt to hold on to the truth as I knew it—and feared it. A painful reminder.

"It has been six weeks…and it is time," the voice said.

I half turned in my makeshift seat and looked over. "It is not. Not this time, Harden." He sat leaning against the opposite wall. I had treated his wounds as best as I could at the time, but he was very weak. His eyes were scared and pleading. "There is still hope," I said, repeating the words I had said a thousand times, knowing they did not matter. What would pass had already passed.

"You can't keep this shuttle going much longer, my friend."

"I will sustain it for as long as I can," I said, putting my hand back into the panel and jolting it. An effort in futility. We sat there in silence for a while.

"How do you do it, Arthur?" he asked. I remembered how I had replied back then: "*I am just that powerful.*" Some small flicker of ego to lighten the doom. However, I could no longer mimic the words or the tone. Maybe that was part of the reason I went there, to discover new truths in myself.

"It is all I have left."

Harden chuckled as if I had spoken the original words. "Well, even you have your limits." It was as if a spectral play was overlapping the simulation. Even now, so many years later, I remember exactly how everything felt. How exhausted I was. How every ounce of my energy was draining into the shuttle. Knowing it would not be long until I failed to keep us going. I knew Harden's eyes were boring into the back of my head. He was mustering the courage to put words to the thoughts we had both been having. "We can still survive this," he said quietly.

She will never recover. It would be a mercy—

"She will never recover. It would be a mercy—" Harden's words overlapped my own.

"That is enough."

"Her body could sustain us for weeks longer!" Harden shouted. I closed my eyes and took my hand out of the conductive gel. "Arthur, you know this is—"

I keyed my forearm band and paused the simulation.

For the first time since arriving in the sim, I allowed myself to glance at another corner of the shuttle. There, heavily bandaged and wrapped in thermal blanketing, was our third survivor, a young Lumenarian named Lira. The third survivor no one was ever told about. I stared at the frozen figure, so close to a death that had passed before my eyes a thousand times. My greatest shame.

"Arthur?" a voice called from outside the shuttle. I dismantled the simulation with a wipe of my forearm band. The room returned to its empty default setting. Sky waited at the entrance as I walked over.

"Yes, Sky, what is it?" I asked, still somewhat distracted by the journey into simulated memory. She stared at me for a moment and then nodded toward the center of the room where the shuttle had been.

"There are better ways to spend your free time. Better places—"

"I have no free time. Only moments when no one is looking," I said with a tired smile. Sky knew about my frequent visits to this old horror, but not even she knew what was truly inside the shuttle.

"Speaking of which, the second group in the imsims is nearly ready to initiate. Should be about an hour."

"As I said, no free time. Thank you for letting me know." We left the sim field and walked down the corridor. "I would also like you to run advanced diagnostics on Will's pod. Bio and technical. If something was wrong with it, I would like to know."

Sky glanced at me from the corner of her eyes. "If Will was involved, I doubt it had anything to do with the equipment."

"My thoughts as well. But I would like to be sure. See what else we can learn from it."

"I'll get right on it."

"Thank you, Sky."

Sky and I conversed all the way back to the imsims, speaking of lighter fare and home. It almost distracted me from the darker thoughts and memories.

Within the hour the second group of humans were dropping into their simulated worlds of chaos while Flak and I and a few of the other command personnel resumed our observations.

They did not make it nearly as far.

CHAPTER XVIII

Project Swift

38 MONTHS SINCE LD – 10 MONTHS INTO RT

I enjoyed showing off new toys, possibly as much as the humans enjoyed playing with them. I experience a glow of pride as we so often took for granted the technological marvels we had created. The undisguised excitement I saw in Will's eyes on several occasions was what made the reveal fulfilling, like how I imagined humans viewed their children on Christmas or birthdays. This was something a little different though, something over a hundred years in development.

Will met me in the lower levels outside the access doors that led to the surprise, a quizzical, uncertain expression on his face as he approached. "I've never been this deep in the ship before. Been trying to avoid using Codec, so I get used to finding my own way, but I definitely needed his help to find this place," he said, gesturing with his thumb over his shoulder.

"Thank you for coming. I think you'll like this." I opened the doors, and we walked along empty, winding corridors and lifts before arriving at another sealed doorway. I keyed open the access, and we stepped onto a near replica of the *Albatross's* command deck. I watched Will as he took in the space.

"I don't understand," he said. "Did I just get fully turned around or something? Swear I was paying attention." As he examined the control panel, I chuckled at his disorientation.

"This…is Project *Swift*," I said proudly.

"Like a shuttle?"

"Not exactly. This is an entirely separate ship." I activated the control console and brought up a holographic display of the project's schematics. It reflected in Will's eyes as he studied the design. The *Swift* followed the basic look of the Lumenarian vessels he was familiar with but was significantly smaller and had a more aggressive shape. A thread drive still ported from the fore to aft sections, but the teardrop was more pointed at the bow and flattened through the body. The wings were not fully retractable like the larger crafts but swooped up gently, giving it a slight manta ray appearance toward the rear—but as if the aquatic creature was oriented backwards. Four railguns extended forward from each wing and two more off the nose; large energy cannons trained ahead for aggressive maneuvers. And those were just the obvious offensive capabilities. "It is among the next generation of fighters. One of six originally built on the planet Forge. Constructed into the lower levels of the *Albatross* with the ability to break away during attacks and for separate missions."

"It's beautiful," Will said, still staring unblinkingly at the display and running his hands along the edge of the console.

"I thought you might like it," I said. "The other warships, including the *Albatross*, are designed mainly with strong defensive capabilities. Though we are well-weaponized, more than the carriers, we are made to withstand significant trauma while remaining relatively still. Too big and slow in close combat to outmaneuver anything during a fight. This..." I pointed to the display, "is the opposite. Built for offense. Fast and agile. Small crew, only ten thousand. Capable of landing planet-side. The thread drive is limited due to its size. Shorter jumps topping out at around six months, so it could not make the Earth run in a single go, but it can handle most deployments between local systems."

Will nodded enthusiastically. "So, when're we taking it for a spin?"

I paced around the command deck. "It is not ready yet. Still under construction. The *Albatross* was assigned to me while still in dock. The *Swift* Project took second priority. When the approval came to embark on the Earth recruitment voyage, they had not quite finished, but I wanted my ship. So, here we are."

"How much more does it need?"

"We have been checking items off the list during the voyage, but it most likely will not be finished for another year or so. Still needs some materials from Lumen and the planet Forge when we get back," I replied, going over what remained to be completed in my head.

"I know a few people who would love to see the engineering that goes into this. Sarah Li for one. She's about as smart as humans come back home, probably a lot smarter now. And hell, I can work some tools. Anything we can do to help in our off time?" Will asked. I had not considered humans being part of its construction. However, it was never a bad idea to have an enthusiastic crew working on a project. It would mean a steep learning curve in addition to their regular training, but it could also be important symbolically to have humans involved. The first spacecraft built in a joint effort between our two species.

"It would have to be voluntary duty," I said. "And your other training takes priority."

His eyes lit up. "Of course. And trust me, you'll have to be turning away volunteers for this."

I nodded my approval, and then we took a brief walk around the interior structure of the completed sections, discussing the ship's potential and a basic list of what tasks needed to be done. I did not expect Will to remember it all or even to lead in this aspect, but I did enjoy showing off the new toy.

42 MONTHS SINCE LD – 14 MONTHS INTO RT

Will was right. The engineering crews had to pick and choose from a horde of human volunteers who all wanted to take part in the ship's construction. Certain labor-intensive tasks were given out freely while the more technical aspects were assigned primarily to those with engineering or trade backgrounds. All of it was an apprenticeship of sorts, a unique work-study program that introduced the volunteers to new tools and skills that could be applied later to ships throughout the fleet, wherever our crew ended up being stationed.

I had received some grumblings early on from my own engineering crews that it was slowing down their progress and frustrating having to teach while working—not every Lumenarian crew member had signed up to be an instructor, after all. I overheard a woman on Will's squad named Megan Daniels, who was a mechanic back on Earth, joke about a mechanic's fee being increased the more a customer wanted to be involved with the repairs. Many of my crew seemed it was a fitting analogy at the start; though Ms. Daniels seemed oblivious to her position in the joke when she told it. The moaning subsided when they realized how quickly some of the humans picked things up, and they could not deny the logistical support of so many extra hands.

Will had also been correct about Sarah. She soaked up knowledge like a sponge and was soon working alongside some of our most expert technicians. I had no doubt that, given time, she would know the inner workings of Project *Swift* as well as anyone. She and I had also begun playing games of Commander's Die on a weekly to biweekly basis. In this regard she was a significantly more fulfilling challenge than Will.

I stuck my head in from time to time to monitor the project's progress and to observe the interactions between our two races. It filled me with hope to see the consistent and growing bond between our peoples. The humans choosing to dive further into the endeavor, beyond their already exhaustive training schedules, demonstrated a forward-looking and encompassing vision for the future. A desire to be more than just weapons. A true union. That simple gesture paid dividends with the rest of the crew.

It had been a sleepless night, so I made my way down there again to peruse the work.

"Sarah," I said, looking down at her. She was lying on a levitating dolly, half underneath a console on the command deck, like a mechanic under an Earth vehicle. She slid out and looked up at me. It was late at night and quiet, only a handful of crew putting in hours on the project.

"Arthur, hi!" she said, a little flustered. She stood up and then teetered slightly. I put my hand on her shoulder to steady her. "Whoa," she said. "Sorry. Been down there for a while. Stood up too fast."

"Quite all right," I said. She looked tired but also energized by the work.

"The computing power of these ships is incredible. Beyond quantum. The calculations for the clock alone are amazing. And that's just one small thing of a billion others." She laughed. "It's more like a cosmic barometer than a clock. How it can be calculating and accommodating the linear time during space-time fluctuations in thread-drive relativistic travel speeds, taking into consideration all the varying celestial objects with gravitational lensing effects we skirt, all the—that sort of computing back home would shatter our systems." She stared off for a moment, factoring all the variables. "It's crazy. And here I am getting all worked up over a *clock*."

I chuckled, seeing how fascinated and enthralled she was with it all. "Well, we have had some time to perfect it. Sometimes I feel we forget how amazing it all is."

"Yeah, it really is. I hope I never stop feeling this way. Don't imagine I will though. There are lifetimes of knowledge available here," she said, glancing around the command deck.

I nodded. "More than you can imagine."

"Was there something you needed, Arthur?"

"I just wanted to remind you to take breaks. Hera says you have been down here more than anyone else. Even more than Ms. Daniels, who has now taken to ordering around the engineering crew." Sarah chuckled. "Hera wonders when you sleep." Sarah shrugged and made like she was about to argue, but I would not let her. "Even you have limits, Sarah.

The mind is an incredible thing. However, combining all this with your physical training can strain even the keenest of them."

Sarah nodded reluctantly, as if I had told her to stop reading a good book. "I probably should take a break, to be honest," she said with a sigh.

"The ship is not going anywhere." Sarah nodded and began cleaning up around her workstation. "Perhaps a game of Commander's Die soon?" I asked.

"I'd like that," she said with a smile. "I'm getting better."

"I have no doubt."

She loitered around the area for a few moments, glancing in my direction from time to time as she packed up the tools. "Are you waiting to see if I leave, so you can keep working?" I asked.

Sarah chuckled. "No, no. Not that."

"What is it?"

"You and Will seem to be getting very close," she said. "He talks about your sessions sometimes—not with many people, but he's mentioned it to me."

"Yes. Will is an interesting individual."

"You know...it's also interesting the types of people who have surrounded him. Frank being assigned so close by, his only semblance of family. Odds of that are...low. Unless someone was looking out for him. The instructors our class has received—*chief* medical officer, *Albatross* quartermaster, *chief* engineering, *chief* communications officer, etcetera. Not that I'm complaining, but..." She had pieced together the manipulation. Not that it would have been hard for anyone looking close enough. I would not play her for a fool.

"I wondered if someone would notice."

"I think most in Charlie know we're special. They just don't see the orchestration," she said. I paced around the command deck, reflecting on the plan. "People are happy to take it as luck or serendipity, all of us being together," she continued. "I've always been a little more skeptical of compounding coincidence." She held an intense stare. "Charlie is an experiment. Will is." She never ceased to impress me.

"Will is a weapon," I admitted. "An incredibly powerful one at that. And our most immediate needs are for instruments of war. We chose to surround him with the best, so each would feed the other. The time may come when you are not all together." Sarah twitched slightly at the thought. "And if that time comes, you will all become the beacons of your stations. Lights to rally around. The *Osprey* and the *Pelican* are doing the same thing with certain individuals. Power fostered well disseminates a thousand-fold." I stopped and smiled. "And they do not just surround Will. They surround you as well, Sarah."

She smiled shyly and nodded, grateful for the compliment. "Just…" she struggled to speak the words. "Be careful with Will. There's already one war going on in his head. He's more fragile than he looks." I saw how much she cared about him. I knew how much I cared about him.

"A responsibility, I believe, we both share."

Sarah gave me a tight-lipped smile and nodded. "Goodnight, Arthur."

"Goodnight, Sarah."

After she left, I stood alone in the room and glanced around, reflecting on everything that had passed so far in our journey and everything that would come to pass. It was all coming together. All my hopes. I smiled to myself and drummed my hand on the console under which Sarah had been working.

45 MONTHS SINCE LD – 17 MONTHS INTO RT

With only a month left of our journey home to Lumen, the results of the training had exceeded expectations. My people and the humans moved as one during exercises and subsequent imsim scenarios. The sim pods were not as easily accepted by the mind after the first endeavor. Humans like Sarah and Will saw through the façade, but they still provided useful training opportunities. We had to send several to Medical after the most recent foray into the digital world due to psychological trauma. It was to be expected after repeated simulations and the exhaustive training for the last seventeen months, but it was a difficult thing to watch. People pushed past their breaking point. Mental injuries when the body was still intact were sometimes the most devastating. Trauma-induced psychosis and post-traumatic stress disorder were not monopolized by the humans; however, in this case, aboard the *Albatross*, it was. We were more accustomed to long voyages in space, even though this one was longer than usual, and we were returning home, not heading hundreds of thousands of light years away from it. That, coupled with the fact that we were not having copious amounts of new information pounded into our heads, made most of us especially sympathetic to the humans' plight. I just hoped we would not break them in the long term.

The memory of Travis Dayton jumped to mind. There had been ten more suicides aboard the *Albatross* in the months since his departure, and each one was felt deeply. It seemed the farther we made it, the harder it was for them to bear. We made an effort to increase dialogue. Support groups and therapy sessions were frequently attended. After Travis's funeral, Will had even followed my suggestion and initiated one, an informal weekly gathering of mostly military veterans. Others attended as well, I suspected in part due to Will's natural charisma, but I did not think that was particularly important. There was discussion and that was what was critical. Even so, although the humans were sharing, some fell through the cracks. At least with the winding down of our journey back, those who were feeling the strain could take more time to recharge. There was always more to learn and more training to be done, but with the time passed back home and the status of the war, I was not sure what kind of a break we would have upon our return. I did not want my people to be burnt out before setting foot on a battlefield.

Perhaps because of these factors it seemed the work on Project *Swift* was in resurgence. A happy and fulfilling distraction from other problems. For a while, particularly when the training was at its most intense, labor on the project had dwindled. Humans like Sarah, Will, and Megan maintained consistent shifts, but they were some of the few. Now with more time and less intensive training, extra hours were filled tinkering with the prototype vessel. By the time we reached Lumen, significantly more progress would be made than I had hoped. Requisitioning and installing the remaining materials and components would be a matter of weeks rather than months.

I was making my way down to the *Swift* for a status update from Hera when my forearm band pinged a message. Apparently, Sky had an urgent matter to discuss on the bridge. I was already in the lower levels and anxious to see how the progress was coming along; however, current *Albatross* operations took precedent. So, I turned around and made my way back up the ship.

When I walked onto the command deck, Flak, Sky, Hera, and several other members of my senior staff were there waiting. They all turned to face me when I approached.

"What is this? Did I forget about a meeting?" I asked. They all looked at each other, confused. "I received a message saying you wanted to see me, Sky," I said.

"You received a message from me?" she asked, a look of surprise on her face. "I didn't call you."

I turned to Hera. "And I was supposed to meet you on the *Swift*, Hera."

Hera shook her head, confused. "Yes, but I received—"

"We all got a message from you saying we were needed for an urgent meeting on the bridge," Flak grunted impatiently. I stared at them for a moment, then looked over at Trig.

"Trig, have any comms been sent from my personal channel?"

"Yes, Arthur. Twenty minutes ago. General priority call to all senior staff to meet here," he replied. I rushed over to my command console and brought up the ship holo feeds, flipping through them.

"Arthur, what is it?" Hera asked.

I scanned the data log and examined the messages. Something was going on. The display blurred, whipping through the halls and chambers of the *Albatross*. Nothing. Everything appeared to be business as usual.

"Trig, scan for groupings of weapon signatures not within scheduled training areas."

"On it."

I continued scanning private channels and looking for any clues as my senior staff leaned in. "Arthur, what's going on?" Sky asked stepping around the console. I did not look up. "We need to—"

"Got something," Trig said. "The only cluster anomaly is in…" He double checked his monitor, then glanced over at me. "The *Swift.*"

"What the hell are weapons doing down there?" Flak asked, shoving his way around one of the other bridge officer's terminals. I opened the feeds on the smaller vessel. Several of them were out of commission in the construction areas, which was normal. Empty corridors, empty corridors—there! The images hit like one of Will's punches.

"Flak."

"That…that's not possible…" Flak muttered in disbelief, leaning in closer.

"Flak!"

"I'll scramble teams." Flak glared at the display for another moment and then ran out of the room.

"Flak!" He paused and turned back to me. "Lumenarian teams only." He nodded and continued out.

The feed showed several groups of armed and armored humans securing the auxiliary vessel. They had full loadouts of Tempests, Warthogs, kite shields, and grenades. Several bodies lay in the adjacent halls. There was only one main access into the craft from the *Albatross*, since it was designed to be its own fighter. The other entries were through the ship's shuttle bays, which were inaccessible while the *Swift* was attached to the hull. A detachment of the renegade humans was barricading the entry and rigging explosives. In one of the hallways, several Lumenarians and humans were on their knees with their hands behind their heads, facing a wall. Armed combatants patrolled behind them, ready to execute them at a moment's notice. The OnSpec.

Just then an emergency alarm sounded, and crimson lights flashed through the room. Several of my staff stared up at the blinking lights. "Shut that off," I said. The alarm was silenced on the command deck. "What triggered the alarm?"

Harper flipped through her controls. "They're trying to separate from the *Albatross*!" A low rumble was followed by a vibration that rippled through the ship. If the *Swift* separated while the thread drive was engaged, it would be catastrophic for both vessels, essentially like dropping a geosync anchor while going full speed in a harmonic propulsion boat but much worse. The shaking must have been from the locks trying to disengage and a slight gap forming between the hulls.

"Lock them out, Harper. Black, help her." Black, another bridge officer, rushed over.

"I'm trying!" she said as she hammered on the controls.

"All *Albatross* crews report to general quarters. This is not a drill. I repeat. All *Albatross* crews report to general quarters. This is not a drill," I said over ship-wide. I opened the *Swift's* command deck feed. I froze as I stared at the images. Three armed Lumenarians marched with the armed humans on the bridge. They seemed to be working with the humans, perhaps even leading them.

"What...what are they doing?" Sky asked. I had theories, but it seemed impossible. It also was not important now. All that mattered was stopping them.

Several bodies lay strewn throughout the chamber, and another group of hostages knelt with their hands bound in energy restraints. Sarah was among them, as were several other faces that I recognized. I suddenly noticed one of the bodies lying face down on the ground and zoomed in. I could only make out the back of his head, but I was certain. It was Will. A small pool of blood had formed around his head. The sight brought the familiar feeling of the floor dropping out from beneath me.

"Arthur! I've locked them out for now, but they're wreaking havoc on our systems," Harper reported. "There's something interfering with our data communication to the *Swift*. I still have control of the latches, but they're trying to break free manually."

It snapped me out of my shock. "Do what you can."

"What can I do?" Sky asked urgently.

"Rally medical teams near the access, and await orders."

"On my way." Sky hustled out of the room.

"Trig, can you get me comms on their command deck?"

"Negative. They've severed everything. We could lose the feeds soon too. They're not looking to negotiate." Trig shook his head, worry etched in his face.

"Harper, drop us out of thread drive as soon as possible."

"Already on it. Five minutes for spool down," she replied. The room shook violently again, and I braced myself against the console. They were rocking the *Swift* in its cradle, attempting to break the mechanisms holding it on to us. Luckily, its thread drive was not fully operational yet.

"Make it faster." They must have known we would disengage the engines as soon as we realized what was going on, which meant their big move was to separate suddenly. Failing in that would force them to take a more improvised and brutish approach. However, they had clearly planned for contingencies in the event they could not break away cleanly, hence keeping hostages alive.

The ship rattled hard as the clock ticked down for the thread-drive drop. At any moment the *Swift* could snap the tethers and kill us all. Each second grew more and more tense as the shaking intensified.

"Harper!"

"Dropping out now!" With a sudden lurch, stationary space appeared in the displays, and the rough vibrations ceased.

"Good work, Harper." She nodded back to me and exhaled loudly. "Dispatch fighters and repair drones to secure the *Swift*. They will most likely still attempt to break away."

"Yes, Arthur." Harper turned back to her console.

"Flak, status on breaching teams?" I asked over comms.

"Four teams at the main access, and I have a breaching shuttle with another four positioning outside the hull for a lower entry," he replied.

I pulled up the schematics in the lower sections of the *Albatross*. I knew the structural layout of both ships like any of my engineering crew, but I had an idea and wanted to be sure. One section of escape pods on the bottom of the ship had been rendered inoperable during the *Swift's* construction. Normally, the entire auxiliary vessel would be an emergency raft, the second line of individual pods releasing in sequence.

"Flak, send two more teams and an engineering crew to meet me at the decommissioned escape pods in the lower sections of Delta..." I zoomed into the plans. "Section 37."

"We have it under control. You don't need to—"

"That is an order."

There was a slight pause over comms. "Yes, Arthur," came the gruff reply.

I hurried over to the weapons and armor locker at the side of the command deck. I had nearly forgotten the feeling of hex armor as it clinked over my body, snugger than I remembered. I clipped a Warthog pistol onto my right hip and a kite shield on my left. The tactile sensation of the Tempest rifle in my hands instantly transported me to another time. There was no shred of peace in these weapons.

As I turned to leave the command deck, Trig called out to me. "Arthur, I found a back door into the *Swift's* systems. Should I shut it down?" I knew why he asked. With their capabilities neutralized, and realizing there was no escape, they might start taking it out on the hostages. On the other hand, the longer we left them functional, the higher the chance they would break away.

"No, not yet. Can you cause problems to keep them occupied?"

"I believe so."

"Good. Do what you can. Stand by for my order to kill their systems. Also, contact the *Osprey* and *Pelican* and appraise them of our situation." Trig nodded and went to work. I took one glance around the command deck and then departed for the bottom of the ship.

It took half an hour for the engineering crew to remove the escape pod, whose launch tube we would be using for access, and to run a tether down to the lower vessel. From there they would cut a hole in the *Swift's* upper hull for us to enter. We all crammed around the last engineer as he made the final incisions.

I felt like a relic standing next to the rest of my team, each young and fit for duty. But what I lacked in vitality I made up for with experience—or so I told myself. I needed to be part of this mission. It was my people held hostage down there. I had recruited them, and I had missed the ones who had turned. Nothing could stop me, just as I knew nothing could prevent Flak from leading the main breaching team. I was tired of dealing with these OnSpec terrorists. This ended here. I glanced at Kilo, who was the only member of the team I knew well, and he shook his head, obviously not enjoying the experience either.

Inside the tube we braced against the flexible walls as the *Swift* bucked in the latches below. The tether was a makeshift solution beyond its normal functionality, and just outside its walls was the cold vacuum of space. It was a small mercy that it was not translucent. We were in the gap between the two vessels, and I felt very exposed. If they broke away, we would be sucked out into the dark.

"Trig, has there been any response from the other ships?" I asked into comms.

"Negative, Arthur. Nothing yet," Trig replied.

"Copy, keep trying."

"Yes, Arthur."

I did not like feeling so blind. Where were Hatcher and Block?

The glow of the laser torch faded, and the engineer placed four charges around the perimeter. He swiped the detonator code to Kilo's band and nodded to me before climbing back up the chute.

"Flak, are all teams ready for breach?" I asked over comms again.

"On your mark," he replied.

I took a deep breath, exhaled slowly, and then glanced between the members of my team. We all wore green bands around our arms to differentiate us from the enemy. They all looked nervous but eager to get it over with.

"Trig, kill it now."

"Done," his voice crackled in my ear.

Suddenly, the violent writhing of the ship below stopped, and my team and I gripped our weapons. A moment later the charges around the breach point blew, severing the last holds on the entrance, and we dropped into an upper corridor of the *Swift* with a jarring thud. The hall was dark, save for the dim flicker of the emergency lighting. We stepped out of the way, and a second group dropped through the hole between us.

"Bravo team proceed along foreship sweep. Alpha on me. Weapons free."

"Roger," the teams echoed back at me.

"Remember, at least three of our people are aiding the terrorists. Take no chances." They nodded, and the Bravo team took off down the corridor with rifles raised. My team corralled around me, and we headed in the opposite direction toward the command deck.

The corridors were eerily quiet and empty as we moved through them. The prototype ship was never bustling like the *Albatross* proper, but it was still odd for it to be so dark and vacant. From the feeds we had counted twenty-five humans and three Lumenarian terrorists as well as eighteen hostages. Because of the construction, some areas lacked visual coverage; however, they were the least important zones, so we did not anticipate the enemy to have anything more than the odd patrol rotating through.

As we rounded a corner, we froze, face to face with three armed humans. There were twelve of us, and all our rifles were trained on them, towering over them. We stood with weapons pointed at each other for what felt like ages. Seeing the hate glaring back at me, I lowered my rifle slightly. "You do not need to do this. There is still a way back from—"

The first shot came from the humans, and I bobbed just as the energy seared past the side of my head. Before I could bring my rifle back onto target, the rest of my team cut them down in a quick exchange of blue-and-green blasts.

I stared down at the torn bodies in front of me, crimson blood pooling on the floor. The senseless dead. I felt a hand on my shoulder and turned quickly.

"Arthur, are you alright?" Kilo asked, a worried look on his face. I was sure he would have preferred to lead this mission himself and felt somewhat burdened by me.

"Yes."

Kilo gave a small nod. "Keep your rifle up," he said quietly.

Flak's team would have the greatest struggle breaching the *Swift*. The access was a natural choke point laced with booby traps, and from the feeds we knew that was where the bulk of the OnSpec resistance would be. However, once Flak and his team were clear, they would converge with us on the command deck.

The team that breached on the bottom of the hull was sweeping through the lower decks, methodically working their way up and would likely not be close enough to offer support. The *Swift* was significantly smaller than the *Albatross*, but it was still no small task to secure it.

We moved quickly but cautiously through the corridors on the most direct path to the bridge. We encountered only one other group of humans along the route, but there was no hesitation in the firefight. Another five of them and five on my team lay dead in a scene of bloody carnage—the red blood swirling with the black blood of my people. Kilo and another had pushed in front of me, Kilo taking a graze to the arm and the other falling dead at my feet. We had trained the humans well, and they were proving it.

At the entrance to the command deck, my team stacked behind me on the right side.

"Flak, status?" I whispered into comms.

Just then Flak rounded the corner with rifle raised, a handful of his team in his wake. Bloody and rough looking, he nodded to me and then took up a position on the other side of the doors. Two old dogs leading the charge. Seeing my team operate, my confidence had waned in leading them, and I realized how egotistical it had been for me to come along. However, standing before the final and possibly most hazardous threshold, I would not let someone like Kilo take the risk for me. I had insisted on being there, and now I had to deal with it. I felt Kilo squeeze my shoulder, signaling that the team was ready.

"Now." The door whooshed open, and we flooded into the *Swift's* command deck. My team and Flak's flanked out into a flat line on either side of me, each with rifles raised and trained on their targets. Ahead of us were six human OnSpec and the traitorous three Lumenarians, all standing behind hostages, using them as shields. We had them outnumbered more than two to one. Out of the corner of my eye, I saw Will leaning against the wall with his hands bound in energy restraints. He was unmoving, but the fact that he was bound gave me hope that he was still alive. The Lumenarian in the center of the room held Sarah at arm's length in front of him, a Warthog pistol pointed at the back of her head. I recognized him; his name was Trap, a member of the engineering crew. That explained how they were able to manipulate the *Albatross's* systems so well. I was ashamed to admit I did not recognize the other Lumenarians or humans. My Raptor lenses highlighted their identities, but they were strangers to me.

"Hello, Arthur," Trap said, glaring out from behind Sarah, who looked shaken. My rifle was trained on his head, which weaved back and forth behind Sarah's. Humans were not the best cover for beings of our size.

"Dover, you son of a bitch!" Flak snarled, pointing his rifle at one of the other two Lumenarians.

"Flak—"

"He was on my OnSpec investigation team! He's the damn reason why we couldn't lock anyone down!" Flak tightened his grip on his rifle, and Dover leaned in behind his hostage with a sinister smirk.

"Whatever you think you can achieve with this—"

"Be silent," Trap said. Flak leaned further into his rifle next to me. There was a tense silence between all of us as both lines stared each other down. The look in the eyes of the OnSpec humans was that of fanatical zealots, a removed determination, hate. "You're a fool, Arthur," Trap said. "You see nothing. What you do not know would be the end of us all." They had obviously been deceived by something or someone. I did not understand. What could have possibly turned them this way? How could they find their purpose aligned with OnSpec? It made no sense.

"Why the humans?" I asked. "They have done nothing but help."

Trap cocked his head to the side and smiled. "As I said, you know nothing, Arthur. It's not what *they* have done." For a moment Trap seemed to be lost in thought. I took a slow step forward, and he snapped out of it, leaning in behind Sarah.

"Even if you succeed, the *Osprey* and the *Pelican* have six times our number of—"

"The *Osprey* and the *Pelican* will be having their own troubles right now. Hopefully, they've been more successful than us," Trap said. We held an intense stare for a long moment. I felt his loathing. I felt the same for him, but I also wanted to understand. My mind raced to the other ships and hoped beyond hope that they were alright.

"There is always a way back," I said. I knew the words would fall upon deaf ears, but I felt it needed to be said anyway, though I knew it lacked conviction. I did not know who I was trying to appease. I suppose I still had hope. Trap and the other Lumenarians laughed. The human terrorists grinned maliciously beside them. They all knew this was a one-way trip.

"There's no going back," he said. I saw the acceptance wash over him. I think Sarah sensed it too because she closed her eyes tightly. "Mason sends his regards—" Before he could finish, I sent a precise round over

Sarah's shoulder, straight through his face. A burst of dark blood shot back through the command deck, and his body dropped lifelessly to the floor. Suddenly, there was a fast and hot exchange of emerald-and-sapphire blasts. Bodies ducked and weaved through the chaos, and I saw all the hostages drop to the floor. I was not sure who had been hit and who was simply getting out of the way. Then everything was still and quiet. I rose slowly from my crouched firing position. There was a delayed PHHT and a POP, and I saw the last Lumenarian terrorist's arm fall to his side and his body slump over. He would not be taken alive.

When the haze fully settled, three hostages, eight members of our team, the Lumenarian terrorists, and three of the human OnSpec lay in bloody heaps on the floor. The other three human terrorists crawled away, crimson trails following them. Kilo and four others rushed over and disarmed them, weapons aimed at their heads.

I went to Sarah's side and put my hand on her shoulder. She was shaking forcefully and still had not opened her eyes.

"Sarah, you are safe. It is over." She opened her eyes cautiously and stared at me. Suddenly, she threw her arms around my neck and hugged me. Then she released me and hurried over to Will's side. I wanted to follow, but I needed to take stock of the room.

My team was releasing the rest of the hostage's bonds and double checking the dead when Kilo marched the three injured and bound OnSpec humans up to me. "Take them to the brig," I ordered. Kilo shot a concerned glance over at Will. "I will see to him, Kilo. Thank you." Kilo nodded and led the terrorists out. One of them spat at me and swore as they dragged him from the room. I wiped away the saliva and watched them go.

"Fucking scum," Flak said as he stared down at the body of Dover, whom Flak had personally dispatched.

"Flak, I want security to sweep every inch of the *Swift*. Make sure no one is hiding aboard. Send additional patrols to maintain lockdown back on the *Albatross*."

"Will do." He led the rest of our teams out of the command deck.

"Sky, three injured human prisoners are headed your way. See to it they're taken care of by one of your teams. Come to my location with another medical team immediately," I said over comms. "Trig, contact the *Osprey* and the *Pelican*, and request their status. Fill them in on our situation. Harper, dispatch remaining repair drones to assess structural damage to the *Albatross*, and begin repairs."

"Roger," echoed in my ear from all three of them. Finally, I went over to Will and Sarah. Will had a vicious wound across the upper side of his head that oozed blood but had mostly crusted over. It was slightly toward the back of his head, giving me the impression he had been taken by surprise, surely the only way they could have taken him down. It was surprising they had kept him alive after getting the drop on him. Everyone knew how dangerous he was. In fact, I doubted whether the restraints could have held him if he woke.

"Will, Will. Wake up, Will," Sarah urged, shaking him gently, her face streaked with worry. I went over to the medical cache at the side of the room and brought over a kit. The medi-gel seared the wound and stopped any straggling bleeds.

"This should wake him." I took out a jolt shot and handed it to Sarah. She pressed it into Will's leg. I saw the luminescent serum course through him.

After a moment, Will started awake, the whites of his eyes fizzling blue. "What…what happened?" he asked, reaching up to feel his head. Sarah intercepted his hand and held it.

"You're OK. You're OK."

He stared at her for several moments and then smiled drunkenly. "God, you're beautiful," he said, putting his hand to the side of her face.

"Will…" Sarah muttered awkwardly, glancing at me.

Will blinked and stared at her. "Wait…Sarah, are you OK?" She nodded and smiled back to him, but I could tell she was fighting through the shock. Then his eyes found me. They looked unfocused and confused, dancing between anger, perplexity, and a concussion. "Arthur… what's going on?"

I knelt down and tried to gain his focus. "There was an attack, Will. It—"

"What? Who?" Will jumped to his feet, but he had to steady himself against the wall. Sarah and I held him for support.

"Will, you need to sit down. Rest—"

"I'm good. I'm fine. I can fight," he said, shaking his head as if to clear the fog. His biotech lines flickered with arcs of sapphire.

"It is over, Will," I assured him, putting my hands on his shoulders and leaning in close. "We got them."

He blinked several times and then calmed slightly but he still looked agitated. He glanced around the room, finally seeing the chaos, bodies, and blood. "What..."

Sarah and I glanced at each other.

"OnSpec," I replied. It still seemed surreal. We had been moments away from complete destruction. The fact that the terrorists had been aided, even led, by our own was even more disconcerting. How much was I missing aboard my own ship? Perhaps my obsession with the "Will experiment" had clouded my judgement. Or maybe I had simply underestimated the humans' abilities and their capability for deceit.

"Shit. How many of these fucks are there?" Will asked.

I wondered the same thing. They were more dangerous than I could have imagined. I had thought they would peter out over time, deprogrammed with their experience aboard the *Albatross*. I was wrong.

"Wait..." Will shook his head, looked at the green band around my arm, and then stared at the three dead Lumenarian terrorists among the other dead humans in the center of the room. "Why are they over—"

"They were working with the OnSpec," Sarah said.

"That...that doesn't even make sense." Will stared at us. "How does that make any sense?" Sarah turned and looked at me.

I felt instantly uncomfortable, like they were blaming me. It was understandable. They did not know everything about life on Lumen. Just as I was about to respond, Sky and her medical team hustled into the room.

"Arthur, are you alright?"

"Yes. Look after Will and the others." Sky held my gaze for a moment, then nodded and attended to Will as the rest of her team checked out the other hostages and the security personnel. Will tried to insist he was fine, brushing her away, but Sky was firm.

"The prisoners?" I asked.

"Wait," Will said. "Some of the OnSpec survived?"

"They'll be fine," Sky replied tersely, focusing on Will's head wound as she avoided my gaze. Will winced and went quiet. I was fairly certain Sky was irritated with me for leading the mission.

I turned and took in the room again. Every bit of carnage piled on me like a sack of lead. Then, though it seemed like I had just blinked, the command deck was clear, and the last of the crews were filtering out. With the fray concluded, the injured being patched up, Will and Sarah and the other hostages safe, and the criminals locked in the brig, I needed to decide where to go from there.

"Arthur, I have Commander Hatcher and Commander Block on comms," Trig said in my ear. "They need to speak with you immediately."

"Copy. I am on my way back to the bridge."

CHAPTER XIX

Blood

Details about the incident on the *Swift* were kept, by and large, classified from the rest of the crew—for the time being. Obviously, they understood there had been some form of OnSpec attack aboard the ship, and the locking down of the *Swift* in the aftermath led many to infer that it had played a part. However, those involved were ordered to keep a tight lid on the information. The three human terrorist survivors were held out of sight in a secluded brig without formal charges, all record of them redacted. The fact that three Lumenarians had aided them was also kept secret. I did not want more fear being spread than was already being assumed. It did not help that we were stationary in space while the locks were repaired to reengage the smaller vessel. It involved fully separating the two ships, a fleet of repair drones, and two weeks of work to get us operational again, a delay that seemed to stretch time for much longer than it actually did. At least being out of faster-than-light speed meant we were back on linear time with home.

The OnSpec had obviously been planning the attack for several months, possibly since leaving Earth. The *Osprey* and the *Pelican* had suffered from a coordinated strike at nearly the same time, the difference being they did not have ships like the *Swift* embedded in the lower sections of their vessels. In their cases, the attacks were attempts on their reactors, hoping to cause a chain reaction that would cripple them. Luckily, and due in no small part to the efforts of each ship's security teams, the plots had been thwarted. The loss of life, however, was much higher aboard their ships. In some ways we were fortunate that the *Swift* was the target. It kept the conflict isolated. If the OnSpec had launched their offensive centrally, it could have meant much more collateral damage.

Similarly, the attacks aboard the *Osprey* and the *Pelican* had been orchestrated by rogue factions of Lumenarians. With their conflicts being more public, Commanders Hatcher and Block were scrambling to control the flow of information regarding that fact. The human crews would already be suspicious of their own; we did not want to add a fear of their hosts to the mix. Regardless, these new events wreaked havoc on morale. We were so close to home, and yet suddenly it seemed like we were just leaving Earth. Relationships were strained and tenuous. As much as we tried to suppress them, rumors were circulating, and tension spread throughout the ships.

The *Osprey* and the *Pelican* hovered in space around us during the repairs and loaned us their drones to speed up our recovery. Without their assistance, it would have taken closer to a month to become operational again. Meanwhile, a difficult decision needed to be made—what to do with the OnSpec terrorists.

The final say fell to me. However, I appointed a panel of humans I trusted, and Kilo as the Lumenarian representative, to oversee a trial. Because they had been witnessed and caught in the act, it was brief. In fact, to call it a trial would be a loose definition of the word. Each terrorist was allowed to make a statement before the panel, but none of them expressed remorse or begged for leniency, which also made the verdict easy. The deliberation lasted all of half an hour. *Guilty.* The difficult part was the sentencing. Even for their own kind, the humans were less than forgiving. The panel's recommendation: execution. It was not arrived at easily, but apparently they thought it might be considered a small mercy. The idea of xenophobic terrorists being kept for a lifetime on an alien world seemed crueler than death.

I had no desire to make martyrs of the terrorists; however, I could not ignore the recommendation if I wanted the humans to feel like they had a voice—a voice that was growing and would continue to do so over time. On our side of things, capital punishment was not permitted on Lumen or any of her colonies. Sentences for even the most heinous crimes were served out in orbital prisons. So, I had to decide whether we would follow an Earth "maritime" law of sorts or maintain our regulations. Either way, the decision would be postponed until Flak's interrogations were complete.

"Execute them," Will said flatly as he sat across from me in my quarters. He selected two tiles on our game of Commander's Die, and the cube vibrated, split apart, flipped over, and opened into the half-game expansion. "Shit. I'm really messing up that blind side," he commented, examining the game's freshly exposed top face. He was actually quite good with the strategy on the faces he saw, but whenever he tried playing on the sides he could not, he tended to forget his moves and clump his armies together.

"Many countries on Earth have abolished capital punishment," I said, selecting three tiles on my side of the cube, blind to Will.

"Well, pretty sure most of the world's population lives in the countries that still have it." His own country included.

"True." I studied him as he examined the three-dimensional board. His head wound was mostly healed, and the hair at the edges of the puckered scar was starting to fill in again. Despite everything that had happened, he seemed to be dealing with it well. I got the impression that the debate of it all was fairly simple for him. He saw the issue in black and white. They hurt us, so we hurt them. Despite his limited view, I was impressed with how far he had come. The Will I had known in the beginning would have been having a much more heated discussion of the matter, especially since I knew he felt guilty for not having done more, even though he had been rendered unconscious before the action. Now he seemed calm, even controlled. "In detention, over time, they would have the opportunity to change," I said.

Will chuckled. "Maybe." He selected two tiles on the top face, linking several armies that had been split by the expansion. "But no matter what, they'd never be trusted again. They'd always be a liability. Outcasts."

"So, they deserve to die because they will never be trustworthy again?"

Will looked up at me with a tight smile and cocked his head to the side. "Arthur, if you're gonna play devil's advocate, at least try to be convincing. No, they don't deserve to die for being untrustworthy. They deserve to die for murdering hundreds of us and wanting to kill all of us. The people who were supposed to be their brothers and sisters—human and Lumenarian. If they get the chance, they'll try it again." Will turned back to the match.

I stacked three more tiles against one of his armies on a side face. "They could live out the rest of their days on a prison vessel, in peace."

Will stopped short of moving again and shook his head. "That wouldn't be peace. Not for them. I guarantee you they'd kill themselves there. Maybe not right away but in a year, two, five…" He went to make a move, his fingers hovering over a row of tiles, then stopped. "In some weird fucked-up way, hope made them do this. Hope kept them going this entire time until they could make this attempt. Put them in an intergalactic prison, and all that goes away." Will finally decided on a move and selected three tiles on my most recent side, reinforcing against my attack. "Don't get me wrong, I wouldn't mind seeing them suffer. But it's all gonna end up the same way eventually. Execution is a mercy."

"Do you really believe that?"

Will looked up at me. "Yes."

As hard as it was to admit, I saw his point. It would be one thing if we could send them back to Earth to face punishment, but this was something else entirely. I suppose I held on to the hope that immersion in our culture, even a prison, would be reformative, but I was not a human.

"Look, I know it's not an easy choice for you, and there probably isn't a *right* one," he said, "but people want blood. And blood might be the lesser of two shit deals here. An example needs to be made."

I shook my head slowly. "Throughout your history, examples always seem to be made in blood. There are problems in that, and there are other ways."

Will shrugged. "You're worried they'll become martyrs."

"It has crossed my mind," I admitted, glancing up from the board.

"Well, decision is yours," he said, grinning. "Guess that's why you get paid the big bucks."

"I suppose so." I returned the smile and drifted off in thought, weighing the options. We played the rest of the match in relative silence. Will was getting better, but he still lost. "Do you remember when we spoke of Martin Luther King, Junior?" I asked.

I watched the portly little old man with a thin mustache and round glasses shuffle off the recently arrived shuttle and look around. He patted a satchel slung over his shoulder as if to remind himself he still had it and politely sidestepped several crew hustling past.

"Ambassador!" I called out through the bustling work of the shuttle bay. He turned and smiled warmly as he walked toward me, zigging and zagging around the busy bay personnel. I imagined he had to do that a lot being so small among the giants around him.

He shook my hand firmly and energetically. "Arthur, always a pleasure!" he said brightly.

"How was your time aboard the *Osprey*, my friend?"

"Oh, well, just fine. It's certainly not the *Albatross* though. It's dizzyingly large. So many more bodies. Creaks like a submarine too. Not sure I was entirely fond of that." He held the smile, but it was more tight lipped. "Then, of course, there's this recent business..." I saw a glint of sadness in his eyes.

"Yes." I gestured for us to leave the bay, and we made our way down the corridors toward his chambers in Alpha aviary. "How is the *Osprey* crew?"

"As can be expected. Troubled people in troubling times. But you know, I heard you led the teams in securing the *Swift*."

"Yes. It was a...a difficult task," I said, flashing back to the carnage and loss.

The ambassador nodded in understanding. His face took on a more somber look, and he stared ahead as if he were looking through the walls and beyond. "And now more difficult choices, I'm afraid." We stepped aside to let a group pass. "I don't envy the decision you have ahead."

"I would like your input on the matter, Frederique." I stared at him for a moment as he took off his glasses and cleaned the lenses on his robe.

"It's a complicated issue," he said as he put his glasses back on and pushed them up the bridge of his nose with his index finger. "In my country, capital punishment is a thing of the past, as it is on Lumen, I believe?"

"Yes."

"But many here come from countries that still support it. And now, in a time of war, maritime law, exigent circumstances, the entanglement of radical beliefs, and all that fun stuff...much to consider." He took a deep breath and then let it out through his mouth. We continued walking down the corridor. "I know that I'm mostly just a figurehead," he said finally. "I have no actual say in the matter—"

"Frederik, that is—"

"No, no, it's alright. I understand my place. I was not elected king of the humans." He chuckled. "Wouldn't that be a thought. No, I'm simply a resource for you. An advisor at best."

"One whose counsel I respect," I said. Frederique was the first human I had bonded with on Earth, and we had had many conversations since. I deeply respected the man. He was intelligent, kind, soft-spoken, and honest.

"Thank you, Arthur. You honor me."

Just then we arrived at the mouth of Alpha aviary and stopped. Frederique stared into the cavernous space, wonder etched on his face. "Every time I walk in here, it's like the first time." I joined him in marveling at the grand design. After a moment he turned and met my eyes. "Ways change, things evolve, and we humans must accept that there's so much we don't understand, that there are other ways, better ways." He smiled warmly again. "I have always, and hopefully will always, believe in the sanctity of life." He nodded, mostly to himself, as if he had made up his mind. Then he opened his satchel and dug around inside. "I brought this for you. One of the *Osprey* crew gave it to me, and I've finished with it." He pulled out an old beat-up book and passed it to me. In faded print the cover read, The Alchemist by Paulo Coelho. "I know you prefer poetry, but this is pretty close."

"Thank you, Frederique." He reached up with his hand, and I bowed low, so he could reach my head. I placed my hand on his, the Lumen way.

"A game of bocce soon?" he asked.

"I would like that."

He nodded with a smile and then turned into the aviary. I watched him go, a character so out of place amongst the younger, fitter human recruits and towering Lumenarians, yet so much a part of the soul of it all.

Three days later, on the eve of our return to thread-drive travel, I stood in front of a small gathering inside the empty shuttle bay. I had ordered it emptied for this occasion. Everyone else was watching on displays around the ship. It was a strange sight, seeing such a bustling hub aboard the *Albatross* so quiet and still. It seemed as if everyone was holding their breath. I felt the moment in my stomach like a molten ball of lumenium. Three humans and three Lumenarians stood in a line holding Tempest rifles and wearing black full-face environmental masks.

I stepped forward to a small podium and looked into the holo-recorder drone. "No journey is without its hurdles. And recently, we encountered a devastating one, one that has shaken the trust we have worked so hard to build here." I had to swallow the feeling of betrayal and the sense of unease I had with it all. "For the last year and a half, we have learned together, trained together, and grown together. I am saddened that at this juncture in our mission we should experience such divisive and destructive conflicts of belief." I glanced over at the unflinching firing line. Stone statues of justice and vengeance. It still made me feel uncomfortable. "I know these are the actions of a few, but they must make us all reflect. The coming times will be difficult, more difficult than most of us have experienced. Together is the only way forward." I stared into the holo recorder, summoning the courage to make the call. "For crimes of treason against the Union and the murder of one hundred and seventy-two *Albatross* crew, we sentence these men to death by firing squad." My voice sounded hollow and cold as it echoed throughout the chamber.

The three OnSpec prisoners were led into the shuttle bay and positioned in front of a wall by armed guards. All three stood tall with their hands bound behind their backs and stared out with contempt etched on their faces. One of them spat on the floor, almost casually, and then returned to the same glare of blank hatred. The tallest of the three stood in the middle. His name was Colter. He was British, an ex-SAS soldier. He had dark skin and darker eyes with a series of old scars etched across his scalp and face. The others were an Australian and a Brazilian named Peter and Carlos. Also imposing figures.

The black-masked firing squad took position, and Flak walked out perpendicular to them, ready to give the order.

"Do you have any final words?" I asked, hearing the waver in my voice.

All three prisoners stood tall and raised their chins in defiance. "We are the OnSpec," all three said simultaneously. Then they fell silent. If they were afraid, they hid it well. The final test of a true zealot, their absolute faith in their cause and willingness to die for it. Flak nodded to another officer, who walked up to the prisoners and placed a sack over each of their heads.

"Ready," Flak said. The firing line turned toward the prisoners. "Aim." They raised their rifles and sighted on their marks. The moment before the final call seemed to stretch for longer than necessary. I even glanced over at Flak with his arm raised, ready to drop. For a second, I thought I saw doubt flit across his face too. Apparently, we all regretted having to do this. "Fire!"

Six shots tore across the space and cut into the prisoners at center mast, ragged holes searing through their chests in perfect placement. A slow-motion moment later, the bodies dropped heavily to the floor with a series of echoing thuds. The sounds of the shots and the bodies falling coursed through my own body like a sickening poison. I could not hear the reaction around the ship from the thousands of watchers, but I knew it would be similar to that of us in the shuttle bay.

Dead silence.

After the holo recorder was turned off and the shuttle bay had been cleared, the only ones who remained were Flak, Sky, the six masked members of the firing squad, and me. I glanced toward the bay entrance to make sure we were truly alone.

"Well, I woulda bought that," one of the masked soldiers said. He took off his mask, revealing Will's smiling face. I could not respond in kind. The deception of it all still formed a pit in my stomach. The others removed their masks as well—Kilo, Frank, Sarah, Cash, and another Lumenarian from Will's squad named Tex. Sky walked over to the bodies of the prisoners and keyed her forearm band. The bodies flickered and then disappeared as the holograms shut down.

"The prisoners?" I asked Sky.

"Safely tucked away in their pods. They'll be asleep until Lumen, or whenever we decide to bring them out," she replied.

"Nightmare or two along the way wouldn't hurt," Frank said.

"Team moved them discreetly during the broadcast without incident. Pods taken to the *Swift* shuttle bay," Flak said, his arms crossed in front of him. "Whole area is locked off now, per your orders. Guards stationed in case anyone tries to wander in,"

"Thank you. All of you." I looked between each one. "I wish I did not have to include you in this deception, but I saw no other way."

"We're with you, Arthur," Sarah said, giving me a nod, which I returned gratefully.

"I mean, worst case, we can always shoot them later," Will said. A few of the others chuckled. At least *they* were handling it well.

I dismissed Will and the others and stood with Sky and Flak.

"Well, hopefully everyone got the message," Flak said.

"It may be our own people we have to worry about when we get home," Sky added. Reflecting on the three ringleaders of the attempted coup, I thought back on Trap's last words: "*Mason sends his regards.*"

"The rest of them?" I asked Flak.

"The other twenty-eight OnSpec we found were also podded and moved to the *Swift*. Cover story was they were transferred to the *Osprey*." Flak's interrogations had been fruitful.

"Let's hope that's all of them," Sky said, staring at Flak. His jaw went tight, and he bowed his head. I knew he still felt guilty about Dover and that the attack had occurred under his watch.

"Thank you, both of you." They nodded and then left the shuttle bay. I followed a few steps behind. Perhaps one day the outcast humans would return to us in one capacity or another, but for the moment, they were secure. We would arrive at Lumen in less than a month, and then they would be someone else's problem.

PART IV

(WILL — SARAH — ARTHUR)

And I had done a hellish thing,
And it would work 'em woe:
For all averred, I had killed the bird
That made the breeze to blow.
Ah wretch! Said they, the bird to slay,
That made the breeze to blow!

—"The Rime of the Ancient Mariner"
by Samuel Taylor Coleridge

PROLOGUE

The Beginning is The End

- WILL -

Blood. Blood blacker than oil. It dripped lethargically from every surface. So much blood. So much death. And I wanted more. My hunger was insatiable. I sat upon the pile of bodies like a throne, waiting…waiting…waiting.

I reached into my sling pack and pulled out my canteen, the metal scuffed and dented. The strong acrid aroma of Prima blood whiskey greeted my nose. It was no White Bird, but it got the job done. There'd never be White Bird again—or black or blue or green. I drank deeply, bludgeoning away the thought. Felt it course through me like acid and lightning.

"Don't look at me," I said to the dark corners of the room. I knew they were there. They were always there. Relentlessly there. Watching. Waiting. "I said…*don't fucking look at me!*"

Dead silence. Of course. They were all dead. I took another swig of the liquid fire. A quiet groan sounded from somewhere just outside the dim ring of light in the center of the room. I looked over. There was no rush. One of them wasn't quite extinguished yet, and he crawled painfully toward the exit, half his arm and one foot left in a black pool behind him. With a huff, I rose from my podium of corpses and walked over, stepping on and around countless more dead. I stopped a few feet behind the doomed male and stared. Stared and…nothing. I felt nothing.

"Well, you did make me like this," I said. He didn't turn around to look at me. To look upon death. I'm not sure he even knew I was there, to be honest. I glared down a moment longer before unclipping my Warthog and putting a powerful sapphire blast through the back of his head. Very little was left. Meaty chunks of torn flesh and shattered bone in a viscous pool of mush.

A few moments later, a dark eye, one of the two larger ones, with flecks of copper and emerald, fell to the floor with a squelch, right where the head had been. I stared for a second and then looked up at the ceiling.

"What the fuck were you stuck to?" I asked. Ah, whatever. I marched back to my throne of death, the sound of my wet, sticky footsteps echoing in the silent room. Picking up my canteen, I finished it in a heavy gulp, held the whiskey in my cheeks for a moment like a squirrel holding acorns, swallowed, and then tossed the canteen aside. My eyes watered slightly, and I breathed in slowly through my mouth, letting the dank, sickly air cool my tongue and throat. I glared into the empty darkness, soaking up the silence and wishing it would never end. I could make it be silent forever. That much I had power over. No. I still had work to do. I was still owed so much blood. So much suffering.

Suddenly, child's laughter echoed out from behind me. I spun to find the source, scanning the hazy black. Then it came again from somewhere to my side. Then from the other side. *No, no, no.* I closed my eyes, vividly aware of the alcohol heat creeping through my body from my chest and up my neck and face, pulsing in my temples.

"Evelyn. Sweetheart…please, not here. Please don't see me here," I begged the phantom. Again the laughter danced around me, playful and innocent and unaware. I felt hot pools forming in my eyes, threatening to burst from my lids, and forced them to stay shut. I felt the tension of holding it back mount in my shoulders and neck and constrict my chest, an uncomfortable panic rising. "Please, please, Evelyn, not here."

The laughter faded away, leaving a vacant ringing in my ears. I waited for several seconds and then exhaled, the air coming out in a ragged wheeze and my body relaxing slightly. "Thank you, baby."

"Will?" Sarah's voice echoed from the other side of the room. The hairs stood electric-shock straight on the back of my neck. I turned and slowly opened my eyes. *She* stood there amongst the carnage, a broken expression on her face. Somewhere between horror, disbelief, and love. I blinked several times, taking her in. Strange that she looked older than I remembered.

"I'm sick of ghosts," I said. I snapped up my Warthog and pulled the trigger.

PHHT!

CHAPTER XX

The City of Light

- WILL -

It felt strange to be wearing our dress uniforms, the only other occasions not being the brightest of days. Two-piece navy suits adorned with maroon trim around the cuffs and the cleft collarless neck. The pants were straight bootcut fit with a subtle pleat down the front of the legs and nearly invisible side pockets. The jacket was plain and smooth with a straight seam down the front that magnetically clasped for a clean solid look. The *Albatross* insignia was emblazoned on the left chest in silver, the bird overlaid on a plain outline of a hexagon. We were all immensely proud to be members of the crew and were especially happy that the crest resembled something more aggressive than the pudgy seagull look of a real albatross. The long wings stretched flat to the sides in mid-flight, tail down, the head and sharp beak looking straight up toward my collarbone, the small negative spaces cut out of the eyes showing the suit's blue background. Simple, sharp, strong. Below, my last name was stitched in the same maroon color as the trim. Despite the elegant and authoritative look the outfits gave us, they felt out of place. We had grown so accustomed to the lean second-skin combat and training gear that the looseness of the suit seemed unnatural.

I looked across the aisle of the shuttle at Sarah. She was chuckling to herself and smiling at me. I'm pretty sure she had noticed my somewhat skeptical and uncomfortable assessment of the uniforms as I fidgeted in my seat. I mimed adjusting an invisible bowtie and winked. I'd give anything to watch her laugh for the rest of my life.

It was always a slow and uneasy period switching gears from a soldier to civvy mentality. Back on Earth when Frank and I returned from our third tour in Afghanistan, I wore my fatigue pants anytime I left the house for weeks after. A stubborn grasping at pride or elitism so people would know what we'd done and not to fuck with us. A bristly standoffish and self-isolating mood that spoke of a knowledge that no one else had or could understand. Something sacred and dark. That clinging to a brotherhood far away. It felt adolescent in hindsight. I was different now, but I could still feel the familiar pangs—an anxious raising of the hackles. Then I focused on Sarah again, and it all faded into the background. God, she was beautiful. Looking into her green eyes quieted my demons. They still stood in the shadows, but they didn't howl as loudly most of the time, weren't as sharp and focused. It wasn't just that she was stunning; she was also smart, quick, and strong; and she had glimpsed the darkness inside me and not looked away. To be honest, I didn't feel worthy of her.

The shuttle departed the *Albatross* hangar and began its smooth descent from high orbit into the upper reaches of Lumen's atmosphere. The viewing panels illuminated around the walls and ceiling of the ship, giving us a 360-degree view of the planet as we dropped. Thankfully, Frank was over his shuttle sickness.

Dozens of large Lumenarian vessels hung in space above the planet. Each was similar to our three ships with only slight variations—different sizes, some more elongated and flattened out, others more bulbous and almost peanut shaped, and a few that looked more aggressive, like the *Swift*. Mingled amongst the Lumenarian ships were several crafts belonging to the other alien races: Florii caravan star cruisers (long flexible crafts that looked like interstellar freight trains), Jellian water shuttles (like space zeppelins made of lumenium-enforced glass and filled with water), and even a handful of Yáahlian solar skiffs (which looked like carbon-fiber croissants). The fourth race, which we had decided to name the Glowers (none of the nominated names seemed very good; we almost called them Energizers), didn't seem to be present in orbit. That was too bad. I'd been looking forward to seeing their ships in person. We were told the holo displays didn't do them justice—vessels that appeared to be made of pure light.

No land or sea features were visible through the glistening sphere of the planetary hydro shield. It looked like a droplet of mercury floating in the emptiness of space, broken only by a large cylindrical port that jutted out into space with revolving hexagonal rings around it, like a bolt secured with several hex nuts. It was a dock and customs area for non-Lumenarian ships that wanted to access the planet. The protective surface around the planet wasn't primarily for defense but to bolster the thinner-than-Earth atmosphere caused by higher stellar winds off the nearby star. Under the barrier, the technology minimized the temperature variances on the planet's shaded and lit sides. It was tidally locked to WOH S140, meaning that half the planet sat in perpetual night while the other was in eternal day. The Red Dwarf star shone on the port side of our ship, a fiery crimson and deep-orange orb that shimmered in the distance, reflecting off the aquatic surface below. As we approached the threshold of the barrier, everyone leaned forward or turned in their seats to look out the viewing panels. Like a hand dipped into a pond, we passed through with a ripple.

From what we saw of the planet during our descent, a massive Pangea-like landmass floated amidst vast blue-and-black oceans. Only small islands lay along the farthest reaches. Unlike the browns and greens of home, any acreage not covered by city structures and lights was shades of black. Vegetation under the red sun had evolved differently to maximize how it absorbed light, so photosynthesis could still occur.

The planet's only continent was one large city that, tens of thousands of years earlier, had been several cities that slowly grew together, their borders becoming indistinguishable from the main. Now Lumen was a sprawling metropolis divided only by day and night. The tidal locking split the continent in half, one side lying in the dark and the other in the light. The dark half twinkled with a billion fireflies of alien life. Towers and spires rose to dizzying heights, drones and shuttles buzzing relentlessly around them. On each side of the landmass rose an even more massive tower that reached right up to the hydro shield. Several other towers rose throughout the surrounding waters as well, each like the spokes of a wheel.

I turned to Kilo, who was sitting next to me, and gestured to them. "Hey, Kilo, what're those pylons that reach to the shield?"

"Ancient space elevators," he replied.

"Ancient?"

"Yeah. Think they're somewhere around forty to fifty thousand years old. Built before the great fall of memory. When the atmosphere started to erode, they saved our asses. The earliest most rudimentary form of the shield you can see above us. Now they're mostly just monuments to an age gone by," he said, staring out at the old structures, lost in his memories.

"You know, I've heard that mentioned in passing a few times now. What exactly is it?" I asked.

Kilo broke from the view outside and looked at me. "What? I forgot what I just said."

"The great fall of—oh, shut the fuck up."

Kilo chuckled. "Thirty thousand years ago the memory banks suffered some sort of catastrophic failure. All our history, science, culture—our memory—was lost. It was like a reset on our species. The years that followed were...dark. It took millennia to rebuild, and sometimes I wonder..." Kilo drifted off in thought again.

"Wonder what?"

"Oh, nothing."

"Kilo."

He stared at me for a moment before deciding to continue. "I just wonder sometimes whether things were lost that could shine light on our current situation."

"What do you mean?"

"The Forsaken aren't babes from the womb. They've been out there… somewhere for a long time. It's hard to believe we've never known about them until now." Kilo seemed worried about this thought but smiled it off. "Doesn't matter. Doesn't change what we have to do now," he said with a tight-lipped nod. I watched him for a moment, wondering if that could be true.

"Babes from the fucking womb? Really?"

"Shut up," he said, chuckling.

A grand thoroughfare as far as the eye could see stretched beneath us, straddling the line between the two sides of the city and intersecting at a building of epic proportions. "The Great Hall of Night and Day," they called it, the center-most point of the city and the hub of the Lumenarian government, where the main council sat. It stood out from the majority of the other structures, which rose in elegant, smooth lines and twisting architecture. The hall was a large slab, rectangular and wide with rough, dark, quarried walls made of something that resembled obsidian.

The shuttle took a broad loop around the middle of the city before beginning its decent to our designated landing zone. All over the city we saw shuttles from the *Albatross*, the *Osprey*, and the *Pelican* dropping down. Millions of little dots below lined the streets, milling about for the welcome home celebration. Each citizen of Lumen was curious and excited to see their own again after so many years and to catch a glimpse of the mysterious beings from another galaxy.

We all stood up, even before the shuttle touched down, keen to see the world through our own eyes and not the re-creations of a sim field or through the holo-display panels. As I stood there waiting for the door to open, I looked over at Sarah's profile. Her tan skin was smooth, and her bright, jade-green eyes shone, excited and a little nervous but veiled behind her strong calmness. Her lips looked soft and parted ever so slightly. I kept my right hand low and moved it out to the side, hoping she would sense it. For a moment it hung there, feeling the empty distance. Then, slowly, gently, I felt her fingers brush mine, and she took my hand. I smiled without looking at her and felt her do the same.

When the door finally stretched open, bright reddish light flooded in, making us all squint while our eyes adjusted. Our first real sunlight in almost two years. I closed my eyes and took several deep breaths, absorbing the light and taking in the fresh non-recycled air. Sarah and I released each other's hands but stole a sideways glance and a smile before flowing out with the throng of people.

The landing pad sat adjacent to the main thoroughfare, which was crowded with gawking, energetic Lumenarians. We marched forward, staring in awe at the massive structures around us, like gladiators on their first turn in the Colosseum.

"Welcome to Lumen, aliens," Kilo said with a wink and a nudge.

Despite the stark greys and whites of the *Albatross* and accompanying ships, the city streets were filled with color that ran up the sides of the buildings. Bright blues, greens, purples, and oranges sparkled like rainbow mosaics across every surface, and banners of light fabric fluttered in the breeze.

The crowd wore loose, linen-like tunics and robes, and each had a band around their forearms for their personal holo-displays, similar to the ones we always wore. Ours, however, were more advanced military grade, though. The civvy bands served several purposes, the primary ones being planetary comms and wallets for the digital currency accepted on any of the Union worlds, known as "un-coins," which we called "onions." Lumen didn't originally have a currency, at least going back several tens of thousands of years. It came into existence when the other races were brought into the mix. Un-coins were used primarily to regulate trade and for the marketplace. Currency wasn't required for the necessities of life: housing, basic amenities, standard food and water rations, and so on. It didn't matter for us planet-side; we weren't expected to pay for anything yet. We had service credit until our accounts were set up and a salary established and accrued. It sounded like we weren't going to have any financial worries for some time either way, maybe never.

The bands' third main use was as mobile polling stations for measures proposed by the government representatives. Apparently, Lumenarian politicians were more like lobbyists with no real power except to try and push their agendas as widely as possible. The passing or failing of bills and legislation ultimately came down to real-time voting from the public. A type of commie cosmopolitan democracy, Sarah had told me (I added the "commie" part when I learned they didn't pay for much of anything—eye rolling and head shaking from Sarah in return). The prime council and secondary war council, which were essentially the upper echelons of leadership on Lumen, only had real power as far as the emergency off-world war acts. Everything else was run by the people. This meant; however, that for the last almost 200 years, the war council had been running things. Kilo had told me that some of the council members had influence that bordered on intimidation, but for the most part the political system on Lumen had kept their people united and peaceful across all their worlds.

As we filtered from the side street onto the main thoroughfare, we joined up with other humans and Lumenarians from the *Osprey* and the *Pelican*, all parading toward the Hall of Night and Day. Cheers from the onlookers reached a thunderous fever pitch that vibrated in our chests and seemed to shake the ground. We all waved and smiled, and some of our Lumenarian shipmates reached into the crowd and placed their hands on foreheads or embraced those around us. I had to constantly keep myself from staring with my mouth open as I took in everything. The size and scope of our surroundings would make New York skyscrapers look like standing toothpicks.

Mixed intermittently into the crowd were several of the large cyborg jellyfish forms of the Jellians, each with a slight pink-and-baby-blue luminescent glow, their boneless tendrils waving gently in the air in a way that seemed to defy gravity. I couldn't see any of the Florii, but I figured that might be because such a large crowd was risky for them, being so low to the ground and all. The Glowers were also as absent planet-side, as they were in orbit. As amazing as Lumen was, I could tell everyone else was playing their own game of "I Spy" for the new alien races we'd only seen in holograms and sim-field nano-projections.

Suddenly, five Yáahlians swooped low overhead, their large dark wings casting a brief shadow over us. They soared in unison, just like a flock of birds from Earth, and landed on a nearby lower building to watch the parade. They didn't speckle the roofs like massive murders of crows I'd seen back home, but pockets of them were watching along the entire route, each one some chimeric hybrid between a raven and a six-legged black panther. In fact, they had been named by a Canadian First Nations member of the *Osprey*. "Yaahl" was the Haida word for "Raven." Even though they weren't fighters, I would've thought there'd be value in having them on the battlefield just for their intimidation factor. They may not have been aggressive, but they looked it. At the very least it'd be cool to ride into battle on one. Granted, that'd be an awkward conversation between sentient species; "Hey, my Yáahlian dude, mind if I ride on your back for a bit?"

"Hey, human dude, go fuck yourself."

Man, it'd be cool to have wings.

Lots of Lumenarian children were also present. I knew it was a parade with new aliens and all, but there seemed to be three or four children for every adult. Their developing bodies still sported tails that flicked haphazardly around their parents' feet. These would fall off at around age fifteen—yay alien puberty. I got a comical flash of Lumen parents stepping on their kids' tails as a human might step on a pet dog's; only now the dog could yell back. It stopped being funny when I saw Evie's specter walking amongst the crowd. It would have broken my heart if I stepped on her tail. Now that was a weird fucking thought.

As we passed a small alley, something caught my eye. A hooded Lumenarian dressed in black with a red armband stood against the closest wall and watched us flow by, neither cheering nor waving. His face was in shadow, but his eyes flickered with a light-green energy. Behind him a strange graffiti marking was etched into the wall. My Raps didn't seem to pick it up as writing. I don't know why, but it made me uneasy. Some old sense seasoned while patrolling cities like Baghdad, Kabul, and a number of other classified objectives. But here we were in a green zone.

Just then Kilo jostled in. "Incredible isn't it?" he said, grinning his lizzie smile from ear to ear.

"Yeah. No words," I replied honestly while trying to spot the stranger again. He was gone.

The shuttles had all landed close to the capital building, but "close" was a relative term. We walked in the parade for close to two hours before we reached the base of the monumental Hall of Night and Day. The perpetual shadow thrown by WOH S140 split the building in half, making the dark material it was constructed from as black as night on one side. A strip of dusk ran down the middle, and the other side glinted in the sunlight like volcanic crystal. The stairs leading up to the structure wrapped 360 degrees around it and rose what must have been close to twenty flights or several hundred steps. Each step was an awkward height for us smaller aliens, a fact that was clearly apparent as we watched Arthur and the two other ship captains climb the steps with three human liaisons. To our surprise, one of the humans was the little old man we had met briefly on the shuttle from Earth to the *Albatross*. The guy we had taken for some senile stowaway was, in fact, a fucking ambassador for our home planet.

Frank nudged me. "Isn't that the guy—"

"Yep. That's him."

"Son of a bitch." We both stared up through the crowd as the little ambassador smiled down and waved, pushing his glasses up on his nose. We laughed and cheered along with the parade. Several rows of council members stood on the stairs above Arthur and the others. Arthur embraced each in turn and said something to them that none of us could hear.

After the brief reunion, one of the leaders in the middle stepped forward and addressed the crowd. Her voice boomed through the streets by some technological projection. The crowd quieted down as much as several hundred million beings could.

I nudged Kilo. "Who's that?"

"Councilwoman Stone. Oldest member of the council. Close friend of Arthur's."

"Lumen celebrates the return of our travelled warriors and warmly welcomes the children of Earth," she said. "We thank you for your sacrifices and look forward to a future sharing the light. Dark days are not gone from us, but together perhaps there will be fewer ahead." Everyone cheered their approval as her voice echoed through the streets. "Too long have we feared the shadows in the night. With the Earth-born at our side, we will take back our worlds." The cheer that followed was like a sonic boom—the sound of people with renewed hope after decades of defeat.

Suddenly, I felt embarrassed. We had always dreamed about our place among the titans in the stars, but standing there listening to those words and facing a civilization so many light years (literally and figuratively) beyond our own, it seemed arrogant to assume we could make a difference. Their belief in us seemed foolish. That and the fact they had also saved us. At the rate we were going, Earth would've been uninhabitable within our lifetime. We, the volunteers, had jumped on the lifeboats, and the rest back home were being rescued by Lumenarian tech. We were small men and women among giants. Looking around our group, I knew I wasn't the only one who felt that way. Each person carried the weight of the task before us behind a tight-lipped smile. I made eye contact with Frank, and he gave me a sullen nod of recognition. When I looked at Kilo, he stared straight ahead with his chin held high. Clearly, humans did not have a monopoly on hope.

Once the main celebration of the parade had subsided, we were guided to our temporary living quarters a few massive blocks from the Hall of Night and Day. Three large beautiful skyscrapers shaped like DNA helixes rose around central columns of black vines and leaves as high as we could see. Our rooms were scattered throughout the three towers, meaning for the first time since Earth, we were mixed with people from the other ships. Not that we had gotten to know many outside of our own aviary on the *Albatross*, but now we saw others with the *Osprey* and *Pelican* sigils on their uniforms, human and Lumenarian alike.

The lodgings were welcoming but impersonal, and none of us knew exactly how long we would be stationed there before our first off-world assignments, so we didn't spend much time personalizing them. The rooms were four or five times the size of the units on the *Albatross*; they'd be comfortable one-bedroom apartments back home. They were decorated with the black and dark-navy plants of Lumen. Natural light flooded the rooms through large floor-to-ceiling windows that made up the rear walls with small patios beyond that either overlooked the city or the central column of dark vines. I was lucky enough to get an outer room high up in one of the towers.

From the balcony I could see for miles around the planet-wide capital. There wasn't a trace of smoggy metropolitan haze as I looked out at the amazing sights. The housing towers were located on the day side of the world. It was strange to look across at the twinkling lights of the buildings on the other side, knowing they'd never be lit by the sun. It looked like an entirely different city over there. Colorful neon banners and glowing streetlights sparkled energetically and chaotically through the dark. Blinking drones zipped around the buildings, weaving in and out. At any given time, I could hear the sounds from clubs and markets echo across, a percussive rhythm and faint otherworldly twanging that I felt deep in my chest. The day side had "nightlife" establishments as well, but they kept more conservative hours and generally lower levels of raucousness.

Technically, there was no class separation in Lumen culture. Everyone had an equal say in politics and under the law. Certain positions naturally came with more gravitas, but everyone's votes still counted the same, and everyone had equal opportunity. At least that's how it appeared on the surface; however, I couldn't help but wonder if the physical dichotomy of the city-world created some hidden divide.

Someone knocked on my door, drawing me away from the sights and sounds of the world below. When I opened it, I found Sarah standing there with a coy smile.

"Hey."

"Hey back," I replied. "Want to come in?"

Sarah feigned like she was examining the door and hallway, looking them up and down. "No. Actually just wanted to check out your door," she said with her sexy-ass grin and sparkling eyes.

I nodded to her. "OK then. It is a nice door. Have a good night!" I said as I closed the door and stood behind it for a moment, holding back a laugh. When I felt that if I waited any longer she might actually leave, I opened the door again. She stood there shaking her head with her arms crossed and her lips pursed, trying to hold back the smile. She was epically beautiful. "Get in here," I said, grabbing her hand and pulling her across the threshold, shutting the door behind her.

She laughed, and we squeezed each other tightly, pressing against the wall next to the entrance. She kissed me passionately, and I kissed her back. I ran my hand up the side of her face, feeling the softness of her cheek, and then gently bit her soft lower lip. I felt her mouth spread into a smile as she leaned back and then came in with even more energy, returning the playful nibble on my lip. I locked my fingers in hers and raised her hands above her head, pressing them into the wall. As I did, I flared the tech in my hand, transferring some of my energy into her. She took a sharp breath, and her eyes shot wide, glowing a fiery blue around her emerald irises. She stared into me and smiled. She brought our hands down and kissed one of my palms before interlacing her fingers again. I watched this tender movement, hypnotized, and then closed my eyes, feeling every fiber of her touch. When I opened my eyes, she smiled and sent her own jolt of energy into my hand, starting a sort of sexy mercy fight, her tongue ever so slightly licking her lips. She walked us back, our hands locked like the talons of plummeting eagles in a mating dive. We collapsed onto the bed, Sarah on top of me, still wrestling our energies back and forth and laughing. Finally, our fingers unclasped, and we fell into each other. Our bodies entwined, and we stripped off our clothes between the quick gaps in our grapple until we lay naked on top of each other. I stopped and pulled back slightly to see her face. I ran my thumb gently up her cheek and then brushed a strand of hair behind her ear. She stared through me, seeing into the darkness. She never looked away. We lay there gazing into each other's eyes for a long moment before she pulled me in, kissed me, and we made love.

Sometime later I lay with my head on Sarah's stomach just below her breasts while she gently twirled my hair. I listened to her deep breathing and her strong heartbeat. In that moment I couldn't imagine how I had fought so hard *not* to feel something for her. How the guilt had controlled me. Then one day it all broke like a dam. I broke. Every resistance gave way to a fiery passion. In the wake of it, Sarah had caught me and put me back together. I was still in awe of her. Impressed and amazed and confused why she would wait so long for me. I had seen something in her eyes from the moment we met, and I guess she had seen the same in me.

"I don't think we'll have much time here," she said quietly.

"They've been waiting over twenty years for Arthur to get back. I'm sure they want us to get started," I said, somewhat unenthusiastically but trying to hide it with a soft smile. We always knew war was coming, that it was the only reason why we were recruited in the first place. But it had been a long journey from Earth, and things were different now. We lay in silence for several blissful minutes. Then she crunched forward and kissed my forehead.

"Hey."

"Hey, yourself," she said. "If…if something happens to me—"

"Nothing is gonna happen to you."

"Will—"

"Sare, we're not talking about this," I said, sitting up on the side of the bed.

"Yes we are, Will." I felt her glaring into the back of my head and my biotech starting to glow. Then I felt her hand on my arm.

"I…can't think about that, Sarah." Images from our doomed imsim scenario floated across my vision. Staring down at her torn body, the light fading from her eyes. The crippling feeling of a final tether being severed and complete emptiness as she went still. It had shaken me more than I'd let anyone know.

"Just…watch out for Mikey if something ever happens." I stared at the floor and didn't move for a moment, then finally nodded. It was all I could muster as a response. It didn't prevent the haunting reflections or the demons crawling around the room. "Also make sure they ship me into a star."

"Jesus!" I spun quickly. She wore a smartass grin. "Pfft." I shook my head and exhaled, fighting back my own smile. She always knew how to quiet things while simultaneously setting my blood on fire. "You won't need a star. I'll burn down the whole fucking planet."

"For me?" I nodded quickly, and she pulled me in. I kissed her and started my way down her body until my face was between her legs, her fingers twisting in my hair again. I knew my tech lines were glowing, this time from something different.

"Oh Will, your tic-tacs are showing." Sarah chuckled between pleasurable gasps. "Tic-tac" was slang. Weaponized biological technology synapse lines—biotech lines—biotech tattoos—tech tats—tic-tacs.

I rested my chin on her thigh and cocked my head to the side. "You know, when I'm naked, I'd rather you don't call them tic-tacs. I don't want any confusion."

"Oh, there's no confusion on my part."

"Well, that's good—"

"Shhhh," she said, guiding my face back between her legs.

Suddenly, there was a knock on the door. We both froze and glanced over. "Will, it's me, Kilo. Come on, open up."

I looked up at Sarah. "Uh, yeah hey, Kilo. Just a second!" Sarah and I jumped up, and I tossed on my pants and jacket. Sarah grabbed her clothes and hustled into the bathroom. I went to the door and opened it, leaning through the crack. Kilo and Cash stood there waiting. "Gentlemen."

"You taking a nap or something?" Cash asked, seeing my disheveled appearance and trying to peek through the door.

"Uh, yeah. What's up?"

"The gang was hoping for a tour," Kilo said. "We were going to go for a walk and show off Lumen if you're interested." I stared at them for an awkward moment trying to think of an excuse, so I wouldn't have to abandon Sarah, but nothing that made sense came to mind.

"Um, yep. That sounds great. Let me just splash some water on my face, and I'll meet you on the ground level."

"Sounds good. Leaving in fifteen." Kilo and Cash turned to go and then hesitated. "Oh, and Will," Kilo said, "tell Sarah to come too."

"And shower quickly," Cash added. "You smell like human sex." They both laughed and patted each other on the shoulder before heading downstairs. I stared after them and then closed the door and smelled myself. What a couple of clowns.

Sarah peeked her head out of the bathroom. "Did they just say—"

"Yep." We stared at each other for a moment and then laughed it off. Even though we hadn't been publicly displaying our affections, I guess we hadn't been very discreet. The only people we had actually told were Frank and Mike. I was sure Seyyal knew too, but they all respected our privacy. Neither of us were ashamed of our relationship, but with training and fighting alongside each other, it seemed simpler if we didn't broadcast it. In reality, we were too deep into it to give a shit what anybody else thought. So, if it was out, it was out. An army couldn't have come between us, and we both knew it.

In the circular courtyard that ran between the three helical towers, Kilo, Cash, Frank, Seyyal, Miguel, Tash, Jiro, Mikey, Sky, Megan, and several others waited, chatting in a group. They greeted us happily as we approached—Kilo winking at me with two of his four eyes. Sarah saw it and glared at him, causing him to look away as if he suddenly noticed something up on one of the balconies. I looked at her as she smiled and suppressed a chuckle. She was perfect.

"Is everyone ready to go?" Sky asked.

"You bet," Frank said. "Thanks for giving us a tour," he added, holding eye contact with Sky and smiling. She smiled back. I wasn't a hundred-percent sure, because Frank hadn't mentioned anything to me, but it seemed like they were attracted to each other. Guess I had been too absorbed in my own shit to ask him about it. In the time I'd known Frank, which was a long time, he had never dated anyone. He had gotten married young, just before I met him. And she had died young. Cancer. Though he'd never say it, I knew Frank was one of those stoic and sometimes doomed romantics, the ones who believed true love only happened once. He didn't talk about her very often, and he didn't wander around in a constant state of heartbroken gloom, but I knew behind every smile was a shadow of memory that wouldn't let go. Just like me. I wasn't kidding when I said we were a band of orphans. From family and love. The ones who lost more than we got.

"It's been a long time since we were home. It'll be nice to explore a bit ourselves," Sky said, breaking from Frank's gaze and looking around at all of us. I saw the hidden sadness behind Frank's smile, but there was something else too. Maybe hope. He wouldn't be the first one to be attracted to a Lumenarian. Interspecies romance was a *scandalous* topic aboard the *Albatross*: taunts between friends that they were hot for teacher or ridiculous ideas that alien spawn would burst out of our chests (mostly certain it wouldn't happen), or that the Lumenarian females killed their mates. Jokes; however, eventually grew to people discussing the realities of caring for our allies more than just as the bonds of comrades at arms. Some of the narrowminded were disgusted by the notion of pairing with the Lumenarians (definitely those OnSpec fucks). Others were curious. Many just came to realize they didn't care. Personally, I didn't find the Lumenarians physically attractive, but they were brilliant. And love was love. Why the fuck did other people need to insert themselves between it?

Since it had been a full, long day arriving in Lumen, and the time would have coincided roughly with what had been established as night on the *Albatross*, we dipped into the dark side of the planet. City life had already returned mostly to normal since the parade a few hours earlier, but groups of Lumenarians still gathered around us as we walked the streets, trying to get a closer look at the humans. Some initiated the Lumen forehead touch greeting, and others excitedly tried out human handshakes and thanked us for coming to their aid.

When we arrived in orbit around the planet, the *Albatross* and other ships had downloaded a language patch to the Hall of Night and Day that pushed it to all the citizens, so we could understand them, and they could understand us. It made it convenient getting to know the locals and the locale.

Kilo, Tash, Sky, and Cash led the way to a side street transitioning through the dawn-like buffer into the dark sector. We couldn't help but gawk at the life above and around us. The horde of drones buzzing past, whipping from destination to destination. Lumen harp birds, which we had learned about on the *Albatross*, drifted through the sky in droves; their thin technicolor wings, which resembled the fins of Japanese fighting fish more than birds, fluttered in a smooth wave motion like they were underwater and reflected the city's many neon lights. Vendors lined the streets peddling trinkets, art, and food: black fruits and vegetables with deep crimson and navy veins and spines; and small elongated aquatic creatures, like eels, seared on grill-like platforms with a green glow. Onyx trees and vines were woven through every grate and up the walls of the buildings, giving it a wild steampunk jungle appearance. It was strange seeing what seemed like a primitive bazaar within such an advanced civilization. The colorfully clad citizens moved through the streets without care. Though the war was very real, it seemed the effect was felt less on the home world, the divide between civvy and soldier creating an isolating bubble of comfort for the general populace. Whether it was an intentional ignorance or arrogance, I wasn't sure.

As we made our way deeper into the city's dark hemisphere, the streets became increasingly crowded. The sounds and the air of the nightlife, or all-day life, thickened to a warm vibrating haze. People generally moved out of our way as we walked, both out of respect and curiosity, so they could step back a foot or two and get a better look. This was good for us too because those who didn't notice us posed a real threat of trampling us. That being said, the Florii seemed to weave their way through the crowd at ground level fairly easily without being stepped on, and they blended in a lot more than we did. Mike stepped on one accidently and got bucked off like a bronco rider, landing on his ass, face to face with the shrubby, pincered head of the trodden alien.

"Watch it, human!" the Florii grunted before scurrying away down the alley, the leaves on its back shaking chaotically.

"Sorry!" Mike shouted, dusting himself off. Sarah and I shared a smile.

"Narrowly avoided a diplomatic incident there, Mikey," I said with a grin, nudging him.

"Yeah, yeah."

There weren't many of the other alien races on the streets (the few Yáahlians seemed to stay on the rooftops, eyes glowing a refractive feline green as they stared down at us). Apparently, we had only seen so many during the parade because . . . it was a parade. They were fairly sparse on Lumen, as it turned out, especially since the war started. Those present were mostly from trade delegations, their ship's crews, as well as a few resident ambassadors. The days of Lumen being flush with other species had faded with the arrival of the Forsaken. None of them being warrior races meant they didn't want to unwittingly provoke an enemy that was decimating the more advanced Lumenarians. It didn't mean they had all isolated themselves back to their home worlds and abandoned their allies, but their aid was only in the form of resources and logistical support. Only the Glowers had fully cut ties in the time during the mission to Earth.

At one point, Miguel and I made the mistake of shaking tendrils with a Jellian. The result was both of us bursting into tears in the middle of everyone. They communicated via emotional transference, through touch rather than verbally. Turns out the Jellian—whose name we could only feel rather than say or spell—was *very* pleased to meet us. Before we could even react, the joy erupted in laughter and happy tears down our faces. (I guess we didn't know how to communicate our own feelings. Go figure.) The best way to explain the experience was like having some sort of synesthesia, the Jellian's "words" causing us to see music rather than hear it. Or maybe we just got hit with a massive DMT flood in our brains. Either way, Miguel made me promise not to tell anyone he had jizzed in his pants, which I think was the biggest takeaway. If he ever got married, I would save that "coming out" for then, pun intended.

In the shadows of the street, Evelyn pranced happily, taking in the sights as I imagined she would. She laughed and smiled and leaned in close to the dark flowers at the base of one of the trees. A Lumenarian brushed past, and the flowers quickly retracted into their pods, which lined the stem. Evelyn's face lit up, and she smiled over at me.

"Pretty cool huh?" I said, watching her.

"What was that?" Kilo asked.

"Uh, nothing." I stole a glance back toward Evie, but she was gone.

"Check this out," Kilo said, pointing to a second-floor perch above the street. Off the balcony, several cages hung with small jet-black birds within. I say "birds," but they looked more like miniature dragons crossed with bats: feathered wings, scaly backs, and round furry faces, chimeric creatures preserved and domesticated from the early wild days of Lumen. They had a predatory look that was different from the harp birds, which looked whimsical and butterfly-like in comparison.

Sarah stared up in wonder. "Are those—"

"Heart howls, yeah," Kilo answered. The small bird's breast heaved with a scarlet glow and powerful heartbeats that made an audible, even amplified purring sound. Nature's melody that accompanied the two Lumenarian musicians sitting on the terrace. One pressed his energized hands against the skin of a drum like he was doing high-tech CPR. A deep percussion sounded in our chests, and waves of gentle light wafted off, as if the light was infused with dry-ice smoke. The other player waved his hands laterally and vertically in the air like he was playing an invisible violin and a theremin simultaneously. It wasn't until I looked closer that I noticed he was wearing several rings on his fingers; which were the instruments. The result was hypnotic, wordless music and a light show that left our entire group transfixed on the stage above. I looked over and saw Kilo listening with his eyes closed, absorbing the sounds and being transported back into memory as he swayed with the rhythm.

"Where'd you go, man?" I asked, leaning in.

He opened his eyes and smiled at me. "Did you know that when we're born it's a lottery?" He gestured around to the crowd of Lumenarians. "Everyone you see here had their tickets drawn, so to speak. You see, each planet has a cap on its population. As that population dips, more embryos are brought out to be born, compensating for the losses. It's incredibly rare that anyone born ends up with their biological parents," Kilo said, staring back up at the beautiful alien music. I remembered Arthur mentioning that about his son.

"So, you never knew your parents?" I asked.

He shook his head. "Blood isn't as important for us here. We're all the same blood when it comes down to it. It never changed the way I felt about those who raised me or how they felt about me."

"You never wondered about your biological parents?"

Kilo smiled again and broke his gaze away from the musicians above to look into my eyes. "They lived and died over two thousand years ago."

"Wait...shit. What?"

Kilo chuckled. "Like I said, it's a lottery. More of a mass lottery now that we've lost so many in the war. That's why you saw so many children during the parade. My embryo sat in stasis for a long time, but I did look up my biological parents in the Hall of Memory. Got to see how they lived, the children they raised, what they did..." Kilo smiled, drifting off in memory again. He didn't look sad for not knowing them though; he looked proud. Some echo of living vicariously through the holo-reincarnations of his parents.

"What did they do?" I asked, curious to know what his biological parents were like even though they didn't raise him. Kilo grinned with pride and nodded up toward the balcony.

"They were musicians."

We wandered the dark and neon-lit streets with our Lumenarian guides for another hour or two before deciding to return to the helical housing complexes. I thought I was used to seeing incredible out-of-this-world wonders by then, but it was all sensory overload. There were seemingly endless new things to see and explore on the night side of the planet alone, and we'd only ventured a few blocks. But we were all feeling the jetlag of the arrival and subsequent parade, and I was pretty sure we weren't fully adapted to the higher oxygen and lower nitrogen levels in the air. Our systems were riding the turbulent rollercoaster of biological engineering we'd been undergoing since our departure from Earth. The embedded nanoparticles were still adjusting to the new atmosphere. I glanced over and laughed when I saw Cash smack a skewer of street meat out of Miguel's hands just as he was about to take a bite.

"Hey!"

"Didn't you pay attention on the *Albatross*, Miguel? Shale mites are poisonous to humans! You'll be shitting yourself for the next week," Cash said.

"Well, it smells really good," Miguel replied, looking sheepish.

Cash suddenly went stiff and straightened up, turning his head as if straining to hear something. Almost simultaneously I saw Sky, Tash, and Kilo do the same, able to pick up something we humans couldn't register.

"What is it?" I asked Kilo, looking in the same direction they were. The once-bustling thoroughfare had begun to clear as people hustled into the adjoining alleys, businesses, and households. Kilo held up his hand, signaling quiet. We all stood and stared. Then, faintly, we heard yelling in the distance. It was finally close enough and loud enough for our human ears to detect. I couldn't make out what was being shouted, but it didn't sound joyous. It sounded like a large angry mob moving in our direction.

"Should we be worried, Sky?" Frank asked, moving into a ready stance. Sky glared down the street, motionless. "Sky?" As the sounds of the mob got closer, we could make out the chant, but the strange thing was, one of the words was garbled, like our translators couldn't figure out the right equivalent.

"End the Shhbrtlap! End the Shhbrtlap!" The aggressive chant sounded increasingly close.

"Sare, your translator glitching out too?" I asked as the crowd encroached on our position.

"Yeah, getting gibberish," she replied, both of us fixated on the distant corner of the road.

"End the Shhbrtlap! End the Shhbrtlap!"

"What's going on, man? Why can't we understand them?" I asked Kilo. The Lumenarians shared a worried glance. My eyes flicked from one to the next. "What the fuck is going on?"

Kilo looked back at me. He appeared worried and confused. "It's—" Suddenly, the mob rounded the corner, bearing down on us. They wore hoods and had their faces covered, their clothing a uniform black with a red tag somewhere on their bodies, whether as a wristband, insignia, or headband. I fucking knew there was something shady about that Lumenarian I had spotted before. "I'm not sure," Kilo said. I believed him. He looked as unsure as any of us, but he seemed certain it wasn't good. There must've been about two or three hundred marching toward our unarmed group of twenty or so.

"End the Shhbrtlap! End the Shhbrtlap!" they droned on and on.

Sky turned to us. "Everyone remember how to get back to the housing complexes?" She was met by a collective nod. "Good. If we get separated, make sure you get back there. It's probably just a protest, but either way we should go—quickly."

A protest? About what? Sky looked like she knew something more, but there wasn't time to press the issue. "Lumen security, requesting support. Tracking on my location immediately," she said into a general comms channel. Then she led us away from the oncoming crowd and back toward the light side of the city.

We dipped into a tight side street and fell into line behind our chaperones. I brought up the rear, making sure everyone was together. Looking back, I saw our pursuers round the second corner and move quickly toward us. They were close enough that I saw some sort of weaponry in several of their hands.

"Sky! Not just a protest!" I shouted. "Move!"

She glanced back and saw what I saw. She said something to Kilo and sent him running back to me. "Everyone, let's go!" she barked.

Kilo arrived at my side and handed me a kite shield cylinder. "Why do you have these?" I asked.

"We are technically your chaperones right now. Safety first," he replied with a nervous grin. I slipped a fixed-blade knife out of my sleeve and held it in my dominant hand. Kilo cocked his head.

"Safety first," I said. After the OnSpec attack on the *Swift*, I wasn't about to blindly assume safety and venture out completely naked around Lumen.

Just then Frank, Miguel, and Sarah arrived at our backs.

"End the Shhbrtlap! End the Shhbrtlap!"

"What can we do?" Sarah asked.

I glanced back at them. "Make sure the rest of the group keeps moving forward. We got this."

"We're not gonna leave you guys."

"We'll be two steps behind you. Keep them moving," Kilo said. He nodded to me. "Like Will said, we got this." Just then a green blast ricocheted off the wall next to us. Kilo and I fired up the kite shields, emerald and sapphire side by side. "Go!" he yelled to the rest of our group as shots rained down around us. The first shot that hit my shield made a boom and shook me, sliding my feet back.

"Jesus, that was a hit!" I yelled over the blasts and shouting, that same garbled word ringing in my ears. Kilo slid back next to me from a shot.

"Black market or homemade. Looks like non-lethal rounds, but there's no restrictors. Hence the boom. They want us alive," Kilo said through gritted teeth. We took a couple more blasts and then backed up as quickly as we could to put more space between us.

"End the Shhbrtlap! End the Shhbrtlap!"

"You know, never liked hearing 'they want us alive.' Nothing good ever comes after that," I said, ducking behind my shield. I looked behind us and saw our team round a corner. Frank and Sarah gestured for us to hurry up.

A heavy barrage peppered our shields and the walls around us, causing us to brace and crouch low. "Got an idea," I said, grinning at Kilo. I leaned into my barrier and watched one of our assailants lining up a shot. Other shots glanced sporadically. I waited. Just as he launched his round, I sent a pulse of powerful energy through the kite shield and pressed it forward. The energy pillow arrested the shot and deflected it straight back at the crowd, a surge of my energy invigorating it. The blast tore into the group, sending a handful of Lumenarians onto their backs and causing several others to falter a step or two. I laughed and glanced over at Kilo, who looked surprised and impressed.

"Oh, we're definitely working on that later," he said.

"Yeah, right after you tell me what the fuck they're saying."

It was a small victory, but we were still staring down the barrels of dozens of weapons. Suddenly, a blast hit above our heads, taking out a small balcony. The rubble plummeted toward Kilo, who seemed frozen as he stared up at it.

"Look out!" I shoved him out of the way while throwing my shield above my head to block the falling debris. I dropped my knife as the material hammered down on me, some pulverizing on the kite's energy and others hitting the edges and pressing down on me, crunching me to a knee. Straining under the massive impact, I looked up just in time to take a powerful concussive blast to the chest. Everything went black.

"End the Shhbrtlap! End the Shhbrtlap!"

CHAPTER XXI

Old Friends and New Enemies

- ARTHUR -

I stared across the table, a mix of incredulity and rage seething behind my eyes. I tried to maintain an emotionless composure, but I was sure my biotech lines revealed my state.

"You want the Earth forces in the rearguard…months from the front," I said as flatly as I could. The council members stared back at me. Harden wore his all-too-familiar look of contempt, a smirk threatening the corner of his mouth. In my peripheral I saw Hatcher stir in his chair.

"Council members," Block said from the other side of me, "I believe you would change your minds if you could see what the humans are capable of."

"That is not necessary," Councilman Quill said. "We have adequate Lumenarian forces preparing for the incursion on—"

"Our teams are Lumenarian *and* human," Hatcher interjected, "and they are like nothing we've ever produced."

"Enough," Harden said, silencing the room. I had not taken my eyes off him. "The humans are unproven. They lack the training." He took his time as he spoke, enjoying the power. "Using them now would hobble our own troo—"

I keyed my forearm band and swiped data to the holo-projector in the middle of the table. The clip of Will blasting away the sensor drone during his compatibility testing flickered to life between all of us, cutting off Harden. All eyes focused on the vid as it repeated twice more. Then I played the footage of his final release in the ill-fated imsim scenario.

"That is Captain William Reach," I said, pointing to the display. "That was his first time using our biotech, and then only a few months ago." I glanced between the members of the council, each trading looks and murmuring to one another. I locked eyes with Harden, who returned an icy glare. "You have no idea what these humans are capable of. Only we know that." I gestured to Block and Hatcher, who matched my defiant stare. I knew they were also proud of their young and *once* untrained humans. "To not utilize this resource is to foolishly succumb to xenophobic dogma, arrogant pride, stubborn—"

"You will watch your words when addressing this council!" Harden said.

"We have sacrificed too much to be left in the—"

"You have sacrificed nothing!" he yelled, the room tense with the echoing crackle of his proclamation. "While you were off on your *mission*, we were here fighting the war." His words were channeled into me, cutting to the bone, striking at my guilt. But I balked at his notion of fighting. He had sent millions into the conflict, never to return, all from the comfort of Lumen, but the Harden I knew would not suffer their loss personally. I also did not point out that, in our absence, the war had been relatively quiet. "We understand the situation as it is, and we will allocate resources as we see fit," he said as we glared across the table at each other.

"Arthur," the calm voice of Councilwoman Stone cut in, drawing me away from the stand-off. Stone had been old when I left for Earth, and the twenty years that had passed on Lumen had not been kind. However, she still had the same kind, gentle look behind her eyes. She had always been the most reasonable and thoughtful voice on the council. "We all recognize that you and the other Earth mission commanders have sacrificed in other ways. It was a difficult mission on many levels, and we honor you for that." Block, Hatcher, and I bowed our heads in appreciation. "The time will come when we utilize the humans, and we look forward to seeing what you have made of them. However, now is not that time. We have already committed forces in preparation for the campaign on—"

"Perhaps if you hadn't taken so long," Harden began, but Stone glared and held up a weathered hand to silence him. I had a small impulse of pleasure at seeing Harden sulk before I returned my focus to Stone, who gathered herself before continuing.

"You will see the front with your Union forces. I promise you that. But for now you must be patient," she said gently. I bowed my head again, accepting the decree.

Stone put her hands on the table and creaked up to her feet, Councilman Quill aiding her. "I believe that concludes the council meeting for today. We will reconvene to go over the specifics of your assignments in two days. Again, we thank you for the success of your mission to Earth. May the others be equally successful. Welcome home."

We rose and began to leave the chambers when I stopped and turned back. "Councilwoman Stone." She turned to look at me. "They are *our* Union forces." Stone smiled warmly and bowed her head. Block, Hatcher, and I left the chambers. I sensed a rift in the way some of the council members had been regarding us, not just Harden. We had been gone a long time in the middle of the war.

Outside the chambers, I stopped in the hall and turned to the others. "It was to be expected that some would look down upon the mission. We knew that before we left, and now they have had time to stew in their reservations."

"I didn't just travel a hundred kiloparsecs to come back and 'sit on the bench,' as the humans say," Block grumbled.

"The Reach clips were a nice touch," Hatcher said. "I imagine they're downloading logs from our ships as we speak to get a better look. Footage of a few on the *Pelican* might sway them as well."

"Not if Harden has his way. Sure you had to save his life?" Block asked with a sideways glance.

"You both scrubbed the OnSpec data from your ship's logs, correct?"

Block and Hatcher glanced at each other. "Yes, we did," Block said. "I'm not sure we should be concealing—"

"We do not need to give the council any more reasons to doubt the humans," I said firmly.

"What about our people who collaborated?" Hatcher asked.

I glanced toward the council chambers. "I would like to discover what I can about the movement before bringing it to them. See how things have progressed here in our absence."

Block nodded slowly. "Mason."

"Yes."

Hatcher and Block also wore their concern. I wanted to know what we were bringing the humans back to, how hostile the climate really was for them, and how they fit into whatever Mason was up to.

Just then, as if by some cosmic joust of irony, Sky came sprinting around the corner. "Arthur!"

"Sky, what is it?"

She looked panicked. "There has—there's been an incident."

"What happened?"

She took several deep breaths to steady herself. "It's Will."

I had not expected to be wearing body armor again so soon, especially on my home world. It was also the first time in several thousand years that an armed military force was patrolling the streets of Lumen, and I felt the eyes of her citizens boring into us with a mixture of curiosity and suspicion. I would not leave this to city security. Sixty Lumenarian soldiers (all from the *Albatross*) accompanied me in the search for Will. It was the first tour of the city by our allies, and the movement had wasted no time in making their presence and power known.

The night-side streets of Lumen cleared as we passed and promptly swelled back to life behind us. Though there was some initial alarm and consternation with our presence, apparently, no one was too concerned about our search. Not that it would have mattered if they did protest; most civilians lacked the military-grade biotech to pose much resistance. Ours was regulated hardware reserved for military personnel and veterans, since it was a permanent enhancement. The only exceptions were the black-market bio-modifications, but they could be spotted easily. They had a habit of being glitchy and emitted uncontrollable flares along the tech lines. It was not a sign of power but of flaws. The odd citizen lit up with emerald sparks in the dark corners of the street but shied away as we approached. No one was going to face off against an armed force of sixty elite soldiers, movement or not. Instead they would watch and track us—shadowy eyes in every crook and corner. Lumen had a heartbeat that never ceased, an ever-watchful eye.

We marched in two parallel columns with me between the two lines. Everyone was armed with Tempest rifles, Warthogs, armor, and kite shields—the weapons loaded with non-lethal riot rounds and one clip of lethal rounds held in reserve. My instructions were to keep the weapons low unless absolutely necessary to show force or to mount an offensive. Dammit, this was all a foolish mistake on my part. I should not have let them venture out so unprepared.

I could not hide my stress, and Flak, marching in the right column, noticed. "We'll find him, Arthur. Knowing Will, he might've killed them all already, though." The thought was troubling. I would not hold it against Will. Being taken hostage in an alien city would be a difficult situation to manage, but I hoped that would not be the case. It could cause far-reaching problems for human-Lumenarian relations if he killed any Lumen citizens, even in an attempt to escape.

As we approached a side street, Kilo appeared. Dark blood had dried down the side of his face, and he looked on edge. "Arthur," he said with a nod. "I lost the ones who took Will, but I followed another group to a safehouse up ahead. I was just waiting for you."

One of my team stepped forward and handed Kilo a satchel of gear. "Are you alright?" I asked.

Kilo nodded as he dug into the bag. "Yeah. Let's get going. Can't waste any more time." He charged the hex armor over his torso and legs and clipped on his weapons and kite shield. Then he slung the pack over his shoulder and took hold of his Tempest. I was on the fence about allowing him to continue with us, worried his passions might get the best of him. However, he was one of the best, and he cared deeply about Will, so I could not refuse.

"I'd like to lead this one." Kilo barely waited for my nod of approval before he peeled off toward the target building.

At the entrance, Kilo stacked with four others on the right side of the door. Flak led four others on the left. I held back with the remaining soldiers. With a curt nod from Flak, Kilo's second placed the breaching charge and stepped back. A moment later, the charge bored through the door and shot into the adjacent room with a bang. In a flash the two breaching teams folded into the room, shattering the destabilized door. From outside I saw several quick bright-green flashes, followed by silence.

"Clear!" Kilo said over comms. I entered the building to find four Lumenarians stunned and dazedly looking around at the group of soldiers bearing their rifles down on them. Each wore the black-and-red robes of the movement, but their hoods and masks had been removed by Kilo and Flak's teams. They stared up at me, terrified. Not quite the stoic zealots we had seen aboard the *Albatross*.

"Where is the human?" I asked. I knew with this strike, word would spread quickly, and we would have to react fast to keep up before they could move Will. They shook beneath us, their fear rendering them mute.

I nodded to Flak, and he reached down and picked one of them up, slamming him against the wall. "Answer the question!" He threw a room-shaking hook into the protester's side, crumpling him over. Then Flak picked him up and pinned him against the wall. "Where's the human?" Flak's victim glanced urgently around the room, looking for any support or a way out.

I stepped closer. "I do not know what lies you have been told, but they are here to help us. You do not need to fear the humans." The terrorist squirmed against Flak, and Flak demonstrated his control by feeding him another stomach punch and tightening his grip, choking the terrorist's air.

"I...I don't know!" he sputtered through gasping breaths. Flak unleashed a vicious punch to his leg, the bone-snapping crunch echoing through the room. Flak let him fall to the floor as he writhed in pain. With a sudden and violent kick to the face, Flak rendered him unconscious. It was difficult to watch, but I would not interfere unless I thought Flak might actually kill one of them. Despite the violence, I knew he was holding back. Without hesitation, he nodded to Kilo. Kilo and two others pressed their Warthogs to the back of the other terrorists' heads, now positioned on their knees.

"I'll ask one more time," Flak said calmly. "Where is the human?" The switch in his tone was almost more intimidating than his implied threat. He walked over to the terrorist in the middle, crouched down, and drew his pistol, charging up the knuckle-guard blade with fiery emerald energy. With his other hand he grabbed the radical's arm and twisted it up. The soldier behind restrained the terrorist's other arm. He grunted in pain and stared up with fear. Flak held the blade millimeters from his wrist and glared, a sinister smile on his face. I did not blink.

CHAPTER XXII

Who The Fuck is Mason?

- WILL -

The world was spinning, flashes of light filtering in through the dark blur of my eyelids that, as much as I tried, wouldn't stay open. I felt the toes of my boots scraping along the smooth ground and pressure under my arms as two unknown aliens dragged me away. I didn't hear the chant from the crowd anymore, just ebbing sounds of the street pulsing between vacant silences as I was transferred in and out of buildings. My immediate captors were mostly quiet, but the odd garbled voice still murmured through it all. I wasn't sure if the words were the same as the ones from earlier, new ones, or just the result of a concussion.

Even the most fearless soldiers have a conditioned dread about being captured alive. It's one thing to fight and die in battle; it's another thing to have your death drawn out, paraded through the streets naked or videotaped at the end of a sword. It's the unknown, the sick spectacle. As those anxieties crept into my mind, the noises of the crowd and the street and the randomness of the transport dimmed to a consistent buzz until I could make out only faint echoes of the footsteps and my own body dragging through a large empty room. We came to an abrupt stop, and I was turned around roughly and dropped into a chair. My hands were folded in front of me and bound, and I felt them strip off my forearm band.

A splash of cold water hit my face like an electric shock, jolting my senses alive again. I blinked quickly, trying to clear away the fog and take in my surroundings.

The room was large and dark. I couldn't see the edges, but sounds carried, and it had a feeling of vacant space. I sat beneath a high light that only illuminated a small circle around me, leaving the rest of the room in shadow: a dramatic setting that would have fit in well for any mafia movie interrogation scene; which was what I figured was coming up next. Whoever had thrown the water in my face had stepped back into the darkness, out of sight, but I could sense eyes on me.

"Didn't get a close enough look during the parade, huh?" I said, my voice echoing through the room. I blew out sharply, spraying the water dripping down my face into a fine mist that reflected in the light and faded into vapor. "We come in peace, ya know." I stared into the black but couldn't make out anything. Maybe the faint outline of shapes but nothing distinct. I blinked again but couldn't feel my Raps. Must've been swiped out. I felt a small trickle of blood running down the back of my head and onto my shoulder. My noggin sure was taking a serious beating. I winced and went to touch the wound on my scalp before I remembered the device on my hands. It was some sort of energy-diffusing cube as far as I could tell. I focused a small amount of energy into the box, and it lit up blue but didn't emit anything, muting my tech. "OK," I muttered, examining the box a little more closely. Some sort of improvised version of the energy restraints I'd seen on the *Albatross*.

"You won't have any luck with that," a deep male voice said from the dark. I froze and then looked around, trying to see if he poked out into the light at all. I waited a few moments to see if he'd speak again. Nothing.

"Is my friend OK?" I asked. There was a long silent pause, as if to draw out my worry.

"He's fine," the voice said.

I stared in the direction I thought the sound came from, trying to pierce the darkness. "Well, if I find out differently, this little box won't save you," I said, raising my caged hands with an ice-cold smile. I expected a response, but none came, just the ringing silence. I rotated my head around again, trying to make out any details of the space or the person in it. Anything. "I'm guessing there's a reason you haven't killed me yet," I said, trying to squeeze out some information. "Look, I don't—"

"You should not have come here, human," the voice said. "You will find only death." The last words reverberated throughout the room.

"You realize we came all this way to help you, right, jackass?" I heard soft footsteps pace around the circle of light and followed them with my eyes as best I could. "What do you want? If it's information, do what you gotta do, but I got nothing for you." I really didn't have anything. We had no orders yet, so no tactical intel, and any information they could possibly want about Earth was easily accessible. Still no response. What happened to monologuing bad guys? I wasn't humoring him by keeping the restraints on for fun. "Can you get on with the waterboarding? Feeling a little parched. Oh, and if you don't know what that is, basically you just put a towel over my face and—"

"Be silent."

"Hey, what were you chanting in the streets by the way? That gibberish shit was—"

"You are not ready yet," the voice said calmly.

"What the hell is that supposed to mean?" I felt the eyes prying into me from outside the light. I was getting bored by this lackluster interrogation. "Listen, time to shit or get off the—"

"What is your name, human?"

I stared at the voice's origin for a moment, deciding whether I cared to answer. I could finally make out a dim outline. Ah, fuck it. "Will Reach."

"You will never make it home, Will Reach." There was such certainty in the tone. Oddly, it didn't sound malicious or threatening, like it wasn't meant to hurt or break me but to illustrate a truth. A touch of sadness maybe. It caught me off guard. Faintly, I heard a buzz. Out of the corner of my eye, I saw a forearm band light up. "There's a lie in the memory…" The voice and the footsteps trailed away, the cryptic message echoing behind them.

"Hey, what does that mean?" I shouted. In the far corner of the room, the opening of a door shot a sliver of light across the dark, silhouetting a large Lumenarian figure.

He stopped in the passage, turning back to me. "If you make it back to Lumen, find Mason," the mysterious figure said before turning and disappearing through the door.

"Mason? Who the fuck is Mason?" I yelled. Seemed like a lot of work for such a short chat.

A second after the door shut, a door at the other end of the room burst open, showering light into the darkness. A couple dozen Lumenarian soldiers rushed in with glowing weapons drawn and moved in standard CQC room-clearing form. They dipped their Tempest rifles into the corners of the space and then snapped forward, fanning out to secure the entire chamber.

"Oh, hey, guys."

After dominating control of the area, Arthur strode into the room and beelined toward me. "Will, are you alright?" he asked.

"Yeah." I held my hands up and flared my biotech, disintegrating the restraint in a flash of blue energy. "Flattered *you* came to rescue me."

"Don't get used to it, hume," Flak grunted, stepping into the light. "Well, get up. Not gonna sit around here all day." He looked down at the crumpled restraints. "You just waiting here for us to pick you up, Reach?"

"Well, I did have restraints on." Flak shook his head and rolled his eyes. I turned to Arthur. "Also figured I shouldn't hurt the locals too bad."

"Glad you are alright, Will," Arthur said quietly.

I nodded. "Everyone else made it back OK? Kilo?" I glanced between them.

"Aw, worried about me?" Kilo said, coming out of the dark and giving me a hug. He exhaled slowly and shook his head. "I'm sorry, Will. Should've had your back."

"Considering you guys found me, I'd say you did." I turned back to Arthur. "Not quite the welcome I was expecting, but doesn't seem they wanted to hurt us or me, just make some sort of statement. Arthur, we really should have a conversation when we get back," I said, giving him a firm stare. He returned the gaze and nodded. A faint flicker through the stoic look told me he was uncertain what information I had picked up.

Flak pulled some extra kit out of his pack and handed it to me; armor and a pistol. "You won't need these, but just in case. It's loaded, by the way, so try not to shoot yourself."

I tapped the armor puck against my chest and the second one against my hip. I held up the pistol and primed some energy through it, watching the bar on the side light up blue, then twisted the top half of the frame sideways for a visual confirmation, a habitual check.

"Everyone move out! Standard VIP guard!" Flak ordered. Arthur gestured for me to walk ahead of him. On cue, the soldiers formed around me as we marched out of the chamber, my own personal escort back to safety.

"Oooh, VIP, nice."

"Lights dammit," Flak said, rolling his eyes. Kilo chuckled.

"Hey, what are the chances someone picked up my knife?" I asked, looking around at the towering guards. "No? Man, I liked that knife."

The streets had returned to normal as we made our way back to the helical housing complexes, like nothing had happened. No sign of any of the black-and-red-clad protesters; and the hustle and bustle of sounds, sights, smells, and life moved in what I assumed was their usual relentless fervor. The odd curious look was thrown our way as I was marched along with the mountain of Lumenarian bodyguards but otherwise nothing sketchy or aggressive.

My captor's words swirled in my head as I tried to decipher their meaning. Despite the kidnapping, I never really got the feeling I was in danger. It seemed more like a warning that I didn't understand, and that made the riddle all the more mysterious. It was one thing for an enemy to spout some egotistical rant before the final blow, their verbal justification for the evils they did (or the good they did, at least according to their twisted minds). It was another thing when their only motive seemed to be being heard.

When I arrived back at the complex, Sarah, Frank, Miguel, and the others saw me from across the courtyard and waved, hurrying toward me.

Arthur stopped next to me. "I am sorry this happened, Will. We will have *that* conversation soon—about Mason and other things—but I have other matters to attend to right now. Also, expect a call for a meeting of the war council sometime in the next few days."

"Me? A war council meeting?" I asked, surprised I would be invited to one of the highest offices of Lumen. It would be all council members, generals, and admirals, and I was just a captain.

Arthur smiled. "You and the other human captains represent Earth. You have every right to be there." Arthur looked proud as he stared at me for a long speculative moment, as he often did. "I feel…" he drifted off, looking past me somewhere into memory. Then he smiled and returned his gaze to mine. "You have grown much since first arriving on the *Albatross*." I never dealt very well with praise. I always felt like it was undeserved, knowing the anger and darkness I held inside. But it mattered a lot to me what Arthur thought, maybe more than it should have, so I accepted the compliment with a nod. Funny where we find our surrogate fathers. He put his hand on my head, and I reached up and placed my hand on his head. Then he smiled and turned away.

As he walked off, Sarah and the others reached me. She wrapped her arms around me. I felt her body trembling as I squeezed her back. We separated, and I stared into her eyes, telling her without words that I was OK and how happy I was that she was OK too. Frank shouldered in and wrapped me in a bear hug, breaking the moment—and nearly breaking my ribs.

"Flashbacks, man," he said gruffly. I gave him a firm squeeze on the arm and a nod once we separated.

"Glad you guys are OK," I said, looking between them all. Over Frank's shoulder, a little ways off, I saw Arthur with his hand on Kilo's shoulder as he talked to him. Kilo nodded as they split and then made his way over to us.

"We tried to get to you, but security showed up and swept us away before we could get through. And we fought—"

"Hey, I knew you would. It's OK. I'm fine."

"Buddy had us worried for a bit there," Miguel said, clapping me on the back.

"Ah, you know it'd take more than that to bring me down," I replied with a wink.

Just then Kilo made it to the group. He had offloaded his gear and was back in his civvies. "Welcome to Lumen," he said, awkwardly waving his hands in front of himself.

"What was that, Kilo? Why couldn't we understand what the crowd was chanting?" Sarah asked, glaring at him.

Kilo shifted uneasily but tried to play it off like it wasn't a big deal. "It's just…it just doesn't translate over."

I knew Sarah wouldn't let him off that easily. "We're from different *worlds*, Kilo. Tons of stuff shouldn't be translatable, but this is *the first time*. There's something you're not telling us. We all turned our attention to Kilo's obvious discomfort. His eyes darted around looking for any reprieve, someone to rein back Sarah's prying. When his gaze fell on me, I shrugged and shook my head. We all deserved answers.

"It's a…a word from…an ancient banned language," he said slowly. As he spoke, he straightened up and garnered a stubborn expression. "And that's all I can say." There was a tense pause. Banned language? How could an entire language be off limits?

"Can't or won't?" Sarah asked, leaning in. I wasn't sure I had ever seen her so irritated—well, with anyone other than me. I had grown to accept Kilo into my small ring of friends, and since I'd known him, as far as I knew, he'd always been honest with me. He and Cash had become more than just neighbors on the *Albatross*; they were family. We ate together, trained together, spent our recreation time chatting and playing sports…twenty-four hours a day seven days a week we were next to each other. I didn't trust many people, but Kilo was one of the few. This sidestepping of some hidden truth was a weird shade on him, but I could tell Sarah's relentless stare was boring into his confidence, causing him to shuffle uncomfortably. If it had been just Sarah, Seyyal, Frank, Megan, Jiro, Mikey, Miguel, and me, I think he would've been quicker to divulge, but a small sea of curious faces was glaring up at him, and he was feeling the pressure.

Finally, he shook his head. "We're not supposed to talk about it—and not just to you. We just don't talk about it in general, and I don't know much. All I can say is the closest translation would be…" Kilo searched for the words. "False fall."

"False fall? What does that mean? Does it have something to do with—"

"I don't know!" he said, cutting Sarah off. "Look, I'm sorry. I don't have answers for you. It's literally tens of thousands of years old, and that's the first time I've ever heard it outside of…of ghost stories, let alone a fucking mob chanting it." The crowd moaned in discontentment and grumbled, some pointing fingers at Kilo, thinking he was still holding back. He bowed his head and gestured for them to keep giving it to him. I looked around at the faces demanding answers and then watched Kilo. He had obviously told us all of what little he knew, and I felt bad that I had been a part of cornering him. I should've trusted he'd tell us what he could. Everyone was fine, just shaken, and it was easy to let that feeling snowball into panic. Hell, I was the one who had been taken, and I was calmer than anyone else.

"Hey!" I shouted, quieting the group. Kilo glanced at me, unsure whether I was joining in or standing down. "I know Kilo—we all do. Anybody here gonna try to tell me you don't trust him?" I made eye contact with Kilo and nodded, which he returned with a look of gratitude. "Scratch that. I'm not asking. I do. If he says he doesn't know, he doesn't know. Now, I don't know about everyone else, but I'm hungry as fuck. And it's past my bedtime." I paused, thinking I should say more but decided against it. So, with a nod to the collective, I walked forward through the parting bodies. I stopped and turned to Sarah, who was still glaring at Kilo. "Hey, let's go." Reluctantly, she broke off from Kilo and followed me. The rest of our friends fell in behind us. I stopped again and looked at Kilo. "Jesus. You need an invite for chow now?"

"Yeah, food sounds good," he replied. A few people still glared but let him through.

I patted him on the back as he fell in line beside me. "Exciting day, huh?"

CHAPTER XXIII

Bright Eye

- WILL -

The "Mason incident" triggered a significant increase in security around the housing complexes and new policies regarding exploration of the city. From then on any human visitors wanting to wander out had to be escorted by a Lumenarian chaperone and go equipped with body armor and a personal sidearm loaded with non-lethal rounds. Though we were assured such an attack wouldn't be repeated, they didn't want to take any chances.

We had grown so close to our non-human shipmates on the *Albatross* and accompanying vessels that it felt strange to suddenly have our hackles up walking amongst the civilian population. It wasn't the welcome we'd been hoping for. We wore our armor under our dress uniforms to be more discreet, but there was no hiding the Warthog pistols magnetically glued to the outside of our pantlegs. They were too bulky for a concealed carry. We felt the same isolation we had felt when we first boarded the spacecrafts destined for Lumen, together but apart. Despite what all the Lumenarians who knew us and had travelled and trained with us said, we felt like fucking pariahs.

It all shook our faith in this new civilization. We had been picturing a utopia, but despite the dazzling setting and technology, we were already glimpsing cracks in the façade. We had put them on this pedestal, had hoped they were better than us, more attuned to a clarity of purpose. Sure, they had some cool new gadgets, but they also had many of the same old problems. Take away the starships and biotech, and suddenly we didn't look so different. Guess that's what happens when someone has a personality.

It had been a week since the incident, and I still hadn't had a chance to catch up with Arthur. He had been shuttling back and forth between meetings and planning for the rapidly approaching new campaign, with little time for individual sit-downs with personnel. Also, apparently the war council meeting had been postponed, or we had been deemed unnecessary participants (nobody tells me nothing), so didn't see him there either. But hey, not like I had been kidnapped recently and subsequently left in the dark as to why. Anyway, I did some digging. Unfortunately, either all our Lumenarian friends were incredibly good liars, or they legit didn't know shit. All I got were whispers of some movement, or faction, or other Onspecy-like bullshit equivalent.

For my part, besides my super un-fucking-fruitful detective work, I had attended numerous lower leadership briefings as well as community outreach seminars similar to the ones held on Earth before the recruitment process had opened up. My rough edges didn't make for a great public speaker, but I did tag along as extra security since Sarah had been elected to conduct several of the information sessions. Not that she needed the protection; she was fully able to handle herself in a fight, but I was there just in case.

She was a natural. Thousands of Lumenarian eyes were glued to her as she spoke, and her charismatic and approachable personality invited flurries of questions afterwards. She didn't tackle them like lectures but rather like conversations, a way to stay open and encouraging, connecting with everyone. The sessions weren't to provide information on our culture or planet so much as to show *who* we were and how we felt about where we were from. What drove us to join the mission. What made us uniquely human. Any of the citizens could read about the solar cycles, seasons, history, cultures, or sciences of Earth, but none could really know how our oceans smelled, what our sunrises felt like, or what lemon meringue pie tasted like—which, I learned during one of her endearing talks, was Sarah's favorite dessert. "It's like you get all the textures at once. A soft spongy cloud with a slightly waxy layer on top of a smooth Jell-O-like middle sitting on a rough crumbly base. A tart lemon sweetness mixed with an almost savory sweet taste in the graham crust and meringue top. It's the perfect pie. Not too heavy, not too light," Sarah had told the crowd, smiling and laughing. Some of the faces looked confused, but many laughed along with her infectious memory. Sarah could go on for hours about some fascinating technology or science that she loved and I didn't understand. I loved that about her, but it was amazing how fluidly she could also switch off the egghead and talk about anything and relate to everyone.

A hand shot up from the crowd. "What is…Jell-O?" someone asked. I locked eyes with Sarah and chuckled as she tried to describe it as best as she could.

After another seminar, at what would equate to a community hall on the day side of the city, Sarah and I walked back toward the housing complex together. The perpetual red day reflected off the surrounding buildings like light off a rippling crimson lake. Our Lumenarian chaperone was someone we didn't know, and he stayed several yards in front of us, paving the way while allowing us some privacy. Other humans were in our group, but we had managed to find a pocket of relative peace within the mass. Our hands brushed together occasionally as we walked, allowing the briefest of physical contact. In the seconds of grazing skin, it almost felt like we were a couple out for a summer afternoon stroll, sparks dancing between the tech in our fingers. Moments of normality in a way, only to be snapped back to reality by the buzzing drones and curious gazes of the aliens around us. Maybe one day even that would seem normal.

I felt a vibration from my forearm band. "You ever wonder…" Sarah started and then paused, drawing my attention from the display on my arm. "Go ahead, check that," she said, gesturing to the message.

"Sure it's nothing. What's up?" I asked, nudging her, shoulder to shoulder. She hesitated for a moment, looking up at the massive Lumenarian architecture around us.

"Do you ever wonder if we had met before all this…do you think we would have—"

"Boomchickawawa?" Sarah rolled her eyes at me. "Sorry."

"But yeah." She glanced at me from the corner of her eye. I thought about the question seriously, about who I was before all this. What I was. Then I thought about the best way to guide the conversation away. A small grin twitched in the corner of my mouth. "Don't deflect the question," she said, seeing right through me with those jade eyes. It was a playful jab but also a plea for honesty, and I took it in, disregarding another buzz from my forearm.

"No," I replied, looking at the ground. "I wouldn't have really seen you, and what you would've seen of me…" I cracked my neck, feeling the memory tightening there. "Well, you've seen glimpses. In a lot of ways, this thing we signed up for saved me."

We walked side by side in silence for several minutes, regret building up in my mind about being, what I thought was, too honest. The gap between our hands seemed like an ocean. Maybe I wanted the distance, felt I deserved the space between us. Then when I felt like my brokenness was catching up and consuming me, and the spirits were closing in around us, I felt her familiar gentle fingers on the back of my hand. I exhaled slowly, letting the dark thoughts subside. I glanced over at her, but she was staring straight ahead, clearly still reflecting on my answer. I wanted to say more, to tell her that it wasn't just the mission that saved me but her as well. But just as I was about to speak again, my forearm band vibrated. Frustrated with the interruption, I raised the display and looked at the message. I stopped in my tracks, causing Sarah to halt as well.

"Oh shit…" I said as I read the message.

"What is it?" Sarah asked.

Suddenly, Kilo appeared, running up to us from down the street. "Will, there you are!" he said, breathing hard. "Ignoring messages now, are we?"

"I'm sorry. Just saw it. Let's go," I said, clicking into business mode. Kilo nodded and turned to lead the way.

Sarah touched my arm. "What's going on?" she asked, searching my eyes for answers.

"Urgent war council meeting." I squeezed her hand. "I'll see you back at the apartments." I knew she wanted to ask more questions, but she also knew there wasn't time. So, off her nod, I turned and jogged behind Kilo toward the Hall of Night and Day.

Two doors sealed the great hall's main chamber. They rose forty feet high and ran around thirty feet wide. Each door was made of a massive slab of black obsidian-like stone and swung on heavy-duty gear-driven hinges that clunked loudly as the doors opened and closed—an archaic design preserved from the earliest days of the building's construction tens of thousands of years prior.

Kilo and I entered to a crowd of around 200 of the military's top brass and some civvy attachés. The room was centrally located along the building's dusky buffer. Crimson light flooded in through high pointed windows that ran from the ceiling to the mosaic patchwork floor, spanning the width of the long hall. In the center of the room, running almost the entire distance, was a blocky, heavy-duty U-shaped table made of layered basalt that opened to a slightly raised platform with an equally solid table of white marble streaked with dark mineral veins. The vaulted ceiling gave the feeling of walking into an old gothic cathedral with exposed stone arches that curved across and down from the peak. I rotated 360 degrees as I stood in the entrance, trying to take in every detail of the epic room. Black vines wove around the doors and windows like living trim. The etched edges of the glass threw multi-colored prisms throughout the chamber, the light flirting through the architecture's dark crevasses.

At the head table were fifteen chairs; ten seats occupied by the war council members and the remaining five by the top admirals, including Arthur. Around the longer U-shaped table sat the next leaders down the food chain. Everyone else crowded in the standing areas behind, an energetic and worried murmur echoing out from them. To my right, only one each of the Florii, Jellians, and Yáahlians were in attendance—probably their primary ambassadors. Even though they wouldn't be fighting, they were still allies, and I guess they deserved to know what was going on. To my left a group of twelve other humans were huddled together, chatting. I didn't recognize any of them, but I migrated over to them regardless. On the breast of their uniforms were the sigils of the ship on which they had arrived. Four others bore the mark of the *Albatross*, three from the *Pelican*, and the last five from the *Osprey*.

As I approached, one of the guys, a fit Chinese man with sharp features and a warm smile, turned to me. "Hey! Fellow *Albatross*. I'm Chen. I was in Delta aviary. This is Avery and Theo, both Echo. And Lauren was Bravo," he said, introducing them all and offering his hand. I shook it and then the others in turn.

"Will. Charlie aviary."

"Rreach? Will Rreach?" one of the *Pelican* officers asked, looking me up and down. He was a wiry little guy with orange hair, bright freckles, and a Scottish accent. The whole group turned and stared at me, causing me to shift uneasily.

"That's right," I said, a bit irritated that my reputation had preceded me.

The little guy practically bounced in excitement. "No shite! I've hearrd a lot about ya. You know tharr's only eight *brright eyes* in the whole human forrce! Well, so farr. They think we migh' all develop it at some—"

"Jesus. Why don't you suck his dick already, Hamish?" one of the women, also from the *Pelican*, asked. She was Spanish with amber eyes and wild black hair. The group chuckled as Hamish bowed his head in embarrassment. "Next thing you know, he's going to get trading cards made for the lot of you." Hamish narrowed his eyes and pursed his lips, wagging his head. "Anyway, thought you'd be bigger. I'm Sofia," she said, shaking my hand. "Hamish obviously, and this is James," she added, gesturing to the last *Pelican* captain. James reached out his huge hand. He was intimidatingly large, and his muscled frame seemed to take the place of two people. His buzzed head and beard also gave him an aggressive look, which made me think of a few special forces guys I'd served with.

"We should spar sometime," he said with a grin. "Show you how JTF-2 does it."

"Thought you looked like a moose-fucking meat eater," I jabbed back, immediately liking him and acknowledging the SOF recognition. "Know a guy named Charlie Fitzpatrick? Worked with him outside Kandahar. Good dude."

"Christ, you Americans all think the Canadian military's like ten guys," he said with a chuckle. Then he nodded. "But yeah. Chucky was a good dude."

I met the remaining captains with the usual cordial greetings. After I had done the full round, I turned back to the abashed ginger.

"It was Hamish, yeah?" I asked. He looked up at me and nodded. "What's a bright eye?" I was pretty sure I knew the answer, but he had such a kicked-puppy look that I figured I'd throw him a bone.

Just as he was about to speak, a loud jangling sound, like amplified electronic wind chimes, caused the gathered mass to quiet down. Our group at the back stepped out into the middle to get a better view of the front, trying to see through the tall rows of Lumenarian hulks.

I noticed it was Kilo right in front of me, and I jabbed him in the side, causing him to jump slightly. "Hey, move it, would ya? It's hard to see down here." Kilo laughed once he saw it was me, though several other nearby aliens looked scandalized.

"Could always put you on my shoulders, hume," he taunted.

"Yeah, yeah. Move it, lizzie." He chuckled and shuffled to the side, giving us a better view. I felt a couple of my fellow earthlings gawking at the close relationship Kilo and I had, possibly not being as tight knit with our hosts as some of us were.

Hamish leaned in and grinned. "We call 'em 'leatherrs' on the *Pelican*," he whispered to me. Kilo cocked his head and turned to Hamish. "Sorry," Hamish said. I chuckled.

At the head table, the council member sitting center right stood and raised his hands to silence the crowd. He was older and thinner than most Lumenarians with a somewhat sickly pallor to his ashy skin. Burn scars ran down the side of his face, and one of his larger eyes was slightly puckered shut from the scarring. Where the trauma met the corner of his mouth, it pulled up in tightened creases, making it look like he was perpetually sneering. His right arm was metallic below the elbow, and his mechanical fist clenched, pressing into the table. He went to speak and then stopped, his eyes falling upon me and the others in the back.

"Humans are not permitted in war council meetings," he said in a gravelly voice, glaring back at us. I didn't like his tone. It wasn't like humans had ever been to a council meeting to have ever been banned from a council meeting. If he'd said captains weren't permitted, that'd be one thing. The whole audience turned and stared—except Kilo, who just crossed his arms, silently defending us.

Arthur rose to his feet from his place at the table's end. "They are here by my request," he said, nodding to us and then turning to stare at the other councilman. They both stood their ground, sharing a look that spoke of a rocky history.

"You do not have the authority to—"

"Any council member may bring—"

"You are not a member of this council, Arthur. You are just an admiral, and as such—"

Another member at the far side of the high table stood, an even older Lumenarian whose body bent forward under the strain of almost three hundred years of life. I recognized her from the steps during the parade. Councilwoman Stone.

"Councilman Harden..." Her voice rattled yet strongly resonated across the chamber, addressing Arthur's opponent. I remembered the name from a conversation with Sarah about the First Fall. Arthur had told me more about it later but never mentioned the name of his fellow survivor, and I didn't press it. I saw then how difficult the memory was for him. Besides, I already knew the name from Sarah's research. I wondered what had happened since then that made them so combative toward each other. "Arthur cleared the request with me," Stone continued. "After what we have asked of them, they have every right to be present," she continued, glaring down the line. Her authority was obviously without question because both Arthur and Harden bowed their heads, acknowledging her words. The old councilwoman turned to us. "Welcome, humans. We *all*..." she glanced down at Harden "thank you for the tremendous sacrifices you have made to be here. We all owe you a debt of gratitude. And from what I hear, you are going to be a force to be reckoned with." I saw Arthur's chin rise slightly, an involuntary twitch of pride. We all stood a little taller and felt a touch more acceptance upon hearing the praise. "Councilman Quill, report."

The council member next to Harden stood and looked out at the assembly. I thought "Quill" was a good name based on his sharp pointed features, from the angles of his face to the more pronounced boney ridges that ran over the top of his head. "Thank you, Councilwoman Stone," he said as Arthur and the other two took their seats. "This message came in earlier today." Quill flipped a file from his forearm band to a large holographic display that hung in the middle of the room between the two wings of the U-shaped table.

A distorted female Lumenarian face appeared, frantic and bloody, her eyes darting around seeing things we could not, as if she were trapped and looking for a way out. Finally, she looked into the recording device, her voice crackling through in bursts between the static.

"I don't know if you will—*static*—most of the—*static*—destroyed." The image cut out for a moment and then flickered back to life. In the background were shouts and sounds of a fight, blasts from energy weapons, and room-shaking explosions. "Orbital fleet—*static*—gone—*static* We've tried to get as many people—*static* as—*static*'" She looked to her right as loud booms echoed next to her, fear etched across her face. "They're here." Just then a shower of debris and red sparks rained around her. She winced and braced herself before staring fixedly at something out of view. "No…No!" A large blade searing with crimson energy pierced through the front of her face and protruded out the back of her head. She hung there motionless for a long horrible moment, her eyes wide open and blood pouring down her body, until the blade was yanked back, and she collapsed to the floor.

Many in the audience looked away, but I stared unblinkingly, my heart pounding against the inside of my chest. The static crackled across the image and then a massive Forsaken soldier stepped into frame and blasted the terminal, cutting the feed. The room was frozen in stunned silence. Even the Jellian's luminescent glow seemed to fade.

"Holy shit," Chen whispered next to me.

"That message is two days old…from Stormwater," Quill said gravely. A worried murmur rippled through the large hall. From what I remembered, Stormwater was a mining planet chiefly responsible for extracting and refining lumenium. It was also within the second sector of Lumenarian-colonized space. Their galactic dominion was divided by imaginary lines, creating rings outward from the center, which was the WOH S140 system that Lumen sat in—a.k.a. Sector 1. Until now, only planets within the outermost field had been conquered by the enemy, six planets in total. But the middle ring that made up Sector 2 was sparser and only hosted four colonized worlds—the last line of defense before penetrating the inner hub of the three core planets of

Lumen, Ashwood, and Forge. If the Forsaken had sacked Stormwater, that meant they had taken over fifty percent of Lumenarian space.

As the chattering in the room intensified to borderline panic, Councilwoman Stone rose again and silenced the crowd. "Arthur has volunteered to take his ship, the *Albatross*, and a small advanced fleet to Stormwater to attempt a rescue of the remaining civilian population," she announced. The other human captains and I shared a glance, especially my fellow *Albatross* shipmates. None of us had expected to be thrust into the war so soon, especially under what appeared to be critically dire circumstances.

Harden stood and faced her. "We cannot waste valuable resources on a suicide mission," he said with a tone of tempered frustration. Several onlookers nodded in agreement. "Stormwater will be lost by the time any rescue arrives." Harden was referring to the approximately three-week travel time, a month and a half linear, it would take to reach Stormwater. It was a confusing dance between expediently getting there without achieving too high of relativistic speeds and going at full capacity, as Sarah had explained to me. We could technically get there faster by our perception, but it would stretch linear time on Stormwater significantly. There would still be a difference, but we could minimize it by travelling slower, a difference of hundredths of thousandths (maybe farther, I wasn't sure) of sub-light decimal points.

Arthur rose from his seat. "Have the Stormwater emergency protocols changed since before I left?" he asked Harden, somewhat condescendingly.

The councilman's jaw tightened as he figured where Arthur was going with the question. "No," he replied coldly. "However, it doesn't change the fact that what would be left is not worth risking our military personnel—"

"Millions of citizens could be barricaded in those mines. It would take the Forsaken weeks, months even, to get through all the emergency shut-off doors—"

"There is no strategic value in—"

"There is always value in saving lives!" Arthur and Harden continued to debate heatedly, both unable to control their passions. Their history was obviously more complicated than I thought. I had never seen Arthur waver in his steadiness, not even during our sparring sessions. I guess everyone had someone who could push their buttons.

"Enough!" Stone said, finally putting an end to the confrontation with a surprisingly firm boom in her voice. There was an awkward silence as Harden and Arthur re-entered the room, noticing the many eyes watching them. After several moments, Stone continued. "I agree with Arthur. An attempt must be made," she said in a tone that reinforced her word as paramount. Arthur and Harden nodded their acceptance of the decree, but I saw Harden clenching his fist in anger. "Three warships will—"

Arthur looked over suddenly. "Three?" he interjected but was shut down with a look from Stone. Harden couldn't hide a small sneer.

"*Three* warships will accompany two carriers to evacuate any survivors. However, due to the nature of this mission, I would like to ask the ship captains to volunteer. There will be no command order." Another murmur that spread through the room as the ships' commanders discussed the situation with their seconds.

"Hoorah," Lauren said beside me.

"Hatcher better sign us up," Hamish added. I had originally placed Hamish as being strangely timid for a captain. I now saw his fearlessness. He must have had combat experience from home.

"You're a carrier-class ship, Hamish. If anything, you'd only be tagging along to support us," Chen said with a smirk.

"I wouldn't get too attached to your sigil, Chen. I'd wager they don't keep all us humans on only three ships," Sofia said. "Most of us will probably be reassigned to new boats soon."

Most of us glanced down at the silver emblems on our chests. I hadn't considered the possibility of getting transferred off the *Albatross*. It had become a home, and even the days on Lumen hadn't dulled that feeling. I constantly dwelled on the desire to get back to the ship, a place where it felt like I had learned more about myself in a year and a half than thirty plus on Earth. And not just that, I was fucking proud to be a member of that crew. Arthur's crew. Glancing at the other *Albatross* captains, I knew they felt the same. The ship was a part of us.

Just then two Lumenarians rose from their chairs around the U-shaped table and nodded to each other. "The warships *Eagle* and *Shark* will accompany the *Albatross*," one of the commanders declared to the assembly. Arthur bowed his appreciation to them.

Then Hatcher stood. "So will the *Pelican*," he said with a nod to Arthur.

"Fuck yeah," Hamish muttered. There were a few moments of everyone looking around expectantly for the last carrier ship volunteer. I had thought the *Osprey* would jump to support Arthur, but Block didn't move from his seat.

Finally, the last one stood. "The *Chariot*, will answer the call," the female captain announced to the room. The roster was filled.

"I can't believe the *Osprey* didn't join us," Chen whispered. I glanced over at the five *Osprey* captains who stood off to the side. They all looked equally surprised and disappointed. I made eye contact with one of the female captains, a woman named Elora. She shook her head and shrugged while her eyes and tic-tacs flashed an electric blue.

"The pieces are set," Stone said. "Commanders, disperse your assignments, and prepare for departure. You leave in six hours."

Everyone stood and began moving with urgency to their tasks, filtering out of the great hall. Glancing up at the front, I saw Block and Arthur discussing something. Arthur nodded in understanding. I got the feeling something else was going on with the *Osprey*.

A few minutes later, Kilo, me, and some of the other human captains walked out into the adjoining hallway. Simultaneously, we all received vibrating alerts on our forearm bands.

"That was quick," Chen said. I brought up my display to read the message: "Captain William Reach. Report to shuttle dock 82 by e-21:00 hours for assignment to the *Albatross*." I breathed out a slow sigh of relief. I wasn't sure how I would have taken being transferred off.

"Shit," Avery muttered, staring at her orders. "I've been reassigned to the *Shark*." She looked devastated.

"I got the fucking *Chariot*," Theo added angrily, glaring at his message and then dismissing it with a swipe of his fingers.

"Well, at least you guys are joining the fight. I'm going to the *Osprey*," Lauren said. Everyone went quiet. Some hadn't got what they wanted, but at least they were being deployed. None of us knew what was in store for the *Osprey*.

Just as I was about to say something, Kilo nudged me. "We need to get going," he said.

"Rodge. I'm sorry, guys. Stay safe out there." I bid my temporary farewells to the others, and then Kilo and I made our way back to the Lumen housing complex.

As soon as we were out of earshot of the others I turned to Kilo. "Fuck, am I glad I didn't get transferred off the *Albatross*."

"Yeah, it's incredible. I kept telling them how useless you were. Still wanted to keep you," Kilo jabbed with a shit-eating grin.

"Guess your recommendations don't count for shit then, huh?" I said. Kilo laughed and then went quiet for several moments, a cold determined smile flickering across his face as he set his mind to the task ahead. "Hey, how's it comms get here so much quicker than we can travel there?" I asked.

"Planetary comms portals. Each world has a facility linking directly from there to here. Microscopic wormholes just for data transfer. Takes a lot of power but cuts the signal travel distance down to nearly nothing, relatively."

"Huh. Crazy."

Just then the *Osprey* captain, Elora, walked up to us. She was tall with deep-brown skin and bright green-blue eyes, and she spoke with a South African accent. "Looks like you're not gonna be the only bright eye on the *Albatross* anymore," she said with a smile. The whites of her eyes flashed cobalt again.

Back at the helical dorms, I sat down with my squads and relayed what little information I had and conducted general housekeeping duties associated with rallying everyone together for mission go. Afterwards, I started packing the few things I had brought down from the ship into my duffle bag, scanning the room to make sure I hadn't forgotten anything. As per usual, I somewhat neurotically searched through drawers I knew I hadn't used, under my bed, and went back and forth to the bathroom for my toiletry kit, always sure I was forgetting something. Same thing I used to do whenever staying in a hotel back home.

When I was satisfied that I had triple checked everything, I went to my balcony and gazed out over the city. For all I knew it would be a long time before we returned—if we returned at all. The dusk line that separated the two hemispheres of the planet twinkled with the familiar unchanging magic hour glow, fading between the technicolor night and red-washed day. A flock (Murder? Unkindness? Conspiracy? Yáahlock?) of Yáahlians flapped past, swooping wildly in an aerial dance. Guess I'd fly just for the sake of it too if I could. I tracked their progress until they faded into the distance and then watched the first rounds of shuttles take off from different docks around the metropolis, shooting skyward in smooth arcs to supply the orbital fleet and transport personnel, a steady stream of mercury drops ascending toward and through the planetary hydro shield above. I heard my door open and turned.

"Knock, knock," Frank said as he entered, walking toward me with his hands in his pockets. "You all packed up?" he asked, stopping next to me and leaning on the railing, looking out.

"Yeah. Finished a little while ago. You?"

"Yep," he replied with a nod. He tapped on the railing with his knuckles. I stared at him for a few moments. He wouldn't look at me. Something seemed off.

"What time is your shuttle?" I asked suspiciously. Frank tapped the parapet edge again and stared straight ahead. I saw his eyes darting along the horizon, searching for the words. He went to speak once but cut himself off. His silence and hesitance were making me nervous. "Just asked you what time your shuttle's leaving, not what—"

"I've been transferred to the *Osprey*," he said quickly. The words sent a jolt through my body, and my face prickled with unpleasant surprise. It was like getting punched in the gut or sacked. I was suddenly aware of how hard I was breathing and fought the impulse, taking several slower measured breaths. The idea of not having Frank with me throughout this journey was something I had never even considered. Panic juked through my mind as I tried to think of a solution. My tech lines were simmering blue.

"I can…I can talk to Arthur. Try to get you reassigned back to—"

"Will—"

"No, listen Frank. I'll get Arthur to—"

"No, Will," he said gently. A sad smile creased his mouth but not his eyes. I went to argue, but he raised his hands, gesturing for me to wait. "Lots of people didn't want transfers. I'm not gonna be the one asshole who pulls strings to dodge a shitty detail." Frank looked back out over the city. I stared at the side of his face, struggling to think of anything that might change his mind. But I knew it couldn't be moved. We stood there for what felt like an hour. "This is all fucking crazy, man," he said finally, the lights of the city flickering in his eyes.

"You're just figuring that out now?" I asked, forcing a half-hearted smile.

"We're gonna make it through this, Will. We always do." As he stared out, I knew he was picturing the same bloody past that I was.

"We've always watched each other's backs, though."

Frank laughed. "You didn't need anyone watching your back then, and you sure as shit don't now."

"OK, I meant more I watch *your* back," I said, mustering from somewhere a smile I didn't feel.

"Smartass." Frank chuckled, then we both went quiet again. I wanted to tell him how much he meant to me and how desperately I wanted him on the *Albatross*. Not because I wanted to protect him but because he had saved me from myself time and time again, helped keep the demons at bay.

I watched more shuttles rise soundlessly into the atmosphere. "What about Sky?"

Frank smiled, also tracing the ascending dots with his eyes. "I'll see her again."

My forearm band buzzed a notification: "One hour to departure."

Frank turned to me. "I should get going. You have to go soon, and I have an early shuttle."

"The *Osprey's* already getting deployed?"

Frank nodded. "Yeah. Shuttle's at 0400. Yay."

"Are you guys coming to Stormwater now? What's your mission?" I asked with a sliver of hope that he would be nearby.

Frank shook his head. "I can't say. It's classified," he replied seriously.

I stared at him for a moment and then narrowed my eyes. "You don't know what the mission is yet, do you?"

"Aaaaah no," he said with a grin. I couldn't hold it in any longer. I reached over and pulled Frank into a strong hug, holding him tight. Everything either of us needed to say was said in those few shared moments of the embrace. When we finally separated, we didn't speak. Frank headed for the door, stopping just before walking through and giving me a final look. "See you on the other side, brother." We nodded to each other, and then he left. I felt off balance and alone.

Fuck. Really wish I had some whiskey.

CHAPTER XXIV

Under Pressure

- SARAH -

It was the strangest thing. When Mikey told me he had been transferred to the *Osprey*, my first impulse was guilty relief, maybe even happiness. Not because he was going to be avoiding what was starting to sound like a suicide rescue mission on Stormwater but because I felt...free of him, like a weight had been lifted. I had been looking after him for so long. Of course, I still loved him, and I would still worry, but as cold as I felt sometimes thinking about it, there was something to be said for "out of sight, out of mind." I even thought it would be good for him. He wouldn't be able to call me up or come crash on my couch (or in my *Albatross* unit) on an anxious whim. And as much as I knew Will was hurting from news about Frank's transfer, it made me feel better knowing Frank would be there to look after Mikey. Plus, though the *Osprey* had some secret mission, it couldn't be more dangerous than ours.

Another thing that would have made me feel more comfortable about Mikey's reassignment was if Seyyal had been transferred as well. Their tearful farewell was almost harder to watch than saying goodbye myself. Mikey hadn't actually articulated it to me, but I knew he loved her. His first love. A quote from a poet back home sprang to mind, "our hearts were dominoes, spaced too far apart." It made me all the more thankful for having Will close. Unfortunately, it also meant Seyyal would be a constant placeholder for Mikey in my immediate world. I wasn't sure whether I felt that was a good thing or a bad thing.

Being back on the *Albatross* felt good despite our shuffled players. Of the original 200,000 or so humans who had boarded the ship at the start of our journey, only a fifth of that number remained. The others had been transferred to other ships that were part of the Stormwater mission, being held in reserve, or being deployed elsewhere. Of that 40,000, around 10,000 were replacements originally carried by the *Osprey* and the *Pelican*. It was some sort of secret league draft—the rest of the ship's capacity being filled by Lumenarian soldiers. This wasn't just for the mission ahead but to disperse humans throughout the entire fleet. In fact, comparatively, the *Albatross* had retained more humans than almost any other vessel, which I was sure was Arthur's doing.

There were no more lessons, no more casual soccer games in the parks, and the night gatherings in the makeshift market beneath the center spire of the aviary lacked their usual energy. We still had free time between the seemingly endless briefings, drills, and glass-house scenarios; but the reality of what was approaching hung heavier and heavier over our heads. Musicians still played in the forums of the housing complexes, but their songs took on a somber, reflective tone. We had fully switched gears from a training vessel to a warship. Each housing unit had a new locker installed during our time on Lumen. Now, as opposed to just the armory, our rooms were stocked with our personal firearms, gear, and body armor. Entering hostile space meant always having tools at hand in the event of a space battle and potential boarding. The simulated attack on the *Albatross* months earlier had prepared us for a worst-case scenario, but boarding us and taking the ship, in reality, would be much more of a fight for the enemy. They'd probably just blow us up.

For many people the first two weeks of our transit to Stormwater crawled by in a haze of anxious insomniac nights—the aviary ceilings now on four-hour evening by twenty-three-hour day cycles to simulate Stormwater's current season. We endured tiring repetitions of our objectives as we learned the ins and out of our new tactical layouts with, in some cases, drastically altered teams. This wasn't going to be a full-scale invasion to recover the planet. It was going to be a series of surgical strikes and special forces teams on the ground to recon and exfil any survivors within the urban centers while larger battalions secured key landing zones in the outskirts of the major cities and worked their way in.

One solid benefit to the personnel shuffle was Kilo. Dredge had been assigned to lead teams on the *Shark* (unfortunately for them), and Kilo had been transferred over to lead our company. I think the only reason Will didn't get angrier about it was because Kilo was with me. If he had been transferred anywhere else, I think Will might've snapped. At least he still had Miguel and Megan. Kilo had also made me one of his squad leaders, though not without some backlash. I was the only person in leadership who lacked real-world combat experience. I had never seen action in the air force and never fired a rifle at anything in battle on Earth. The only glimpses of it I had gotten were the goddamn OnSpec attacks; two of which I was practically a helpless victim and one where I barely strung together my defense. I knew I could lead the squad as long as I kept my confidence up, but it was a struggle when I thought any question, quiet mutter, or eyebrow raise was a direct challenge to my abilities. It didn't help that Will's advice for these situations was usually just to "show them who's boss." Easier said than done. Will was Will; he could have led however he wanted. His SOF moniker and hyperactive glowing tic-tacs left little to doubt. I was unproven—save for our one hollow victory over Will's squad in the sim field—and generally mild mannered, meaning an uncontrolled outburst to reckon file could do more harm than good for me, threatening my credibility. Joys of being a woman in leadership. Old prejudices weren't completely extinct here. Was I right or was I already losing control? We weren't even on the battlefield yet. Besides, overcompensating with force was never going to be my forte. Solving the problem with my mind was another matter. Some small part of me was eager to get on Stormwater and put it all to the test.

Kilo had booked us a slot in the sim field right after Will's time. We stood off to the side watching his team from a display panel as they moved through the schematic construct of the upper tower that led down to the mine elevators. Will stood ahead of us observing his team. It wasn't that he didn't need to run the scenarios (he alternated in and out), but this way nothing his team did would be missed. Any misstep or slow turn would be caught and addressed.

The towers were essentially venting stacks that had offices built around them to maximize space and hide the unsightly industrialization. Plan A for most of the objectives, since they shared a relatively generic structural design, was to drop onto the roof and secure the building, working down through the staircases and sabotaging the lifts. On the ground level was an atrium that miners filtered through to access the mine itself by elevators that dropped over six miles underground into a maze of tunnels that honeycombed throughout the planet. Because of the method required to extract lumenium and the potentially highly volatile reactions, heavy-duty blast doors were installed throughout the corridors at regular intervals. These were the only hope for the survivors.

Will's team had progressed smoothly and efficiently about three quarters of the way down the tower. We still had very little intel on how the Forsaken moved, but I knew Will would have programmed the simulations to be on alert and evasive and set to maximum difficulty. His guys were good, maybe the best, but even the best could improve. Miguel signaled for a stack outside one of the office doors, and ten others lined up behind him. Megan stepped past him and placed a core breach on the door, a breaching device that silently bored into the door and, on cue, molecularly dismantled the material like it was thin glass and then exploded out the other side. Starting at the back of the line, they passed a shoulder pat up the column, signaling they were ready.

Miguel looked at Megan and nodded. She activated the breach with her forearm band and turned away from the entry. The destabilizing explosive shattered the door and burst into the room. Miguel tore into the space first with Megan, another human, and two Lumenarians folding in perfectly behind him. Each knew exactly how to move in, digging their rifles into the corners and covering their sectors. The three Forsaken soldiers in the room didn't stand a chance. The others waiting outside zipped in and positioned on the next door. They were led by a young Lumenarian soldier named Ice. The second in his line placed the breach, and he nodded without waiting for the shoulder tap from his team.

"Too fast," Seyyal muttered next to me, shaking her head. The door crumpled, and he was three steps into the next room before the rest of his team followed. He was quick and precise, but one of the two enemies he popped wasn't in his sector, causing the second member of his troupe to double over an area, leaving an open unscanned quadrant. Before the Forsaken drone on the other side of the room was dropped it put a shot into the third man through the door.

"Freeze!" Will yelled, halting the simulation. He looked livid, obviously unaware we were watching or else didn't care. Everyone stopped in their tracks but relaxed out of their combat stances. Jeremy, the human who was hit, rose to his feet and looked around in frustration. Will walked through the nearest wall and stood in the last room. "Ice, what happened?"

Ice avoided eye contact but puffed out his chest. "I'm too fast for *some* of my teammates," he replied. It was a condescending comment that had been echoed by others a few times throughout our training. Many of the Lumenarians felt they shouldn't have to slow down, so the humes could keep up. I could understand their frustration; we had some of our own. It was difficult sometimes moving around the bulky aliens. As far as speed went, they covered distances faster, but we were quicker in close quarters.

Kilo shook his head. He knew what all the other Earth-transit Lumenarians had come to know: mixed teams that worked well together outperformed purely human or Lumenarian teams in almost every simulated engagement. It was tested and proven. But Ice and several others on both our teams hadn't been part of the Earth mission.

"Premature is a better word," Megan said with a grin and wink to one of the other women on Will's squad. A few in the room chuckled. Ice clearly didn't get it and just glared. Will gave her a scolding glance, to which she rolled her eyes. Will took a slow breath to control his frustration.

"Fast is good. Fast, unprepared, and uncoordinated is fucking useless. You didn't wait for the ready signal from your team, and when you entered, you went too far in without support. Not only did you leave yourself open, you confused the sectors for your tails," he said as he walked over to Jeremy and smacked him on the chest. "And then Jer died." Jeremy chuckled sheepishly. Ice glared down his nonexistent nose at Will, and Will glared right back at him for a long tense moment. "For all you new people," Will said, his eyes still on Ice, "you might think you're a bunch of badasses, but you got some big goddamn shoes to fill. We're not regular file. We're elite. And this sloppy shitshow ain't us. It's you. Pick up your game, or get the fuck out." Maybe because Will's original team had grown with him aboard the *Albatross*, he had seemed gentler before, but I had never seen him so cutting with his own team. Or maybe this was just that soldier mode we knew manifesting old habits. Now that the mission was rapidly approaching, he was turning the screws. "Listen, we're getting there. Ice, that was a fluid entry—quick out of the fatal funnel. Just slow it down that half second until your team is ready to move with you." He broke from Ice and glanced around the room. "We're gonna kick the shit out of whatever we face. But we become shit-kickers here first," he said, pointing at the floor. "Rodge?" Everyone nodded enthusiastically. "Hoo?"

"Hoo!" they all replied. The group swelled. Megan patted Ice firmly on the back, shaking some of the rigidity out of him. He reluctantly shared a smile. Sometimes all it took was reminding people they were part of a team and then telling them that the team could be awesome. Ultimately, people—and Lumenarians—just wanted to be part of something special. A good note to remember.

"OK! Let's run it from the top again," Will said.

"Oh no you don't!" Kilo yelled. Will swiped his forearm band and disintegrated the sim walls, looking over at us. "Our turn, Will. You're over your time."

Will glanced at his display and then shrugged. "Alright, guys. Pack it up. Back here at 22:00. Good work. Guess Kilo's gotta show his new team all the tricks I taught him," Will said with a wink and a shit-eating grin.

"Yeah, yeah. Move it out," Kilo said.

"Belay that!" a familiar voice growled from behind us. I turned to see Flak walking into the sim field with several levitating crates in tow. "I come bearing gifts. Fresh from R and D," he said, gesturing to them.

"Cutting it a little close to action, aren't they?" Will said, shaking Flak's hand. Then Flak shook Kilo's then my hand. He'd been absent the last few days on Lumen prepping the *Albatross* for possible transit. Then the Stormwater call came, and the last few weeks had been occupied strategizing the attack plan with Arthur and others in upper leadership. We had been so used to seeing him every day that I actually missed him.

"They wanted to make sure these were just right," Flak said as he opened the first crate with his forearm band. The top of the box pushed up along two telescopic poles. Between the poles was a rack lined with what looked like dark-brown leather trench coats crossed with plate-mail armor. Everyone gathered around. Flak grabbed one of the jackets off the stand and held it up for us to see. "These are your new battle uniforms. We're calling them…armadillo skins," he said dramatically, as if he'd come up with the name himself. Several of us cocked our heads to the side and looked at each other. "What?" Flak said.

Will stifled a chuckle. "Nothing, sir. Super-cool name."

"Alright, smartass, what would you call them?" Will obviously hadn't expected to contribute a name, so he winced, then gazed upwards as he tried to come up with one. I couldn't help but suppress a laugh. I'd seen him do it a few times when he couldn't think of a comeback. Drawing a blank, he gestured with his hand like he was about to share an idea, hoping it would come but ended up just waving his hand back and forth aimlessly until he bowed his head, conceding. "Mhmm," Flak grunted. Will looked at me and shrugged. I put a finger to my lips, partially covering my smile.

"OK, come get one and try it on," Flak said. Everyone stepped up in turn and received their new uniforms.

I held mine in front of me, examining the features and keen to figure out what else it could do. It was essentially a dark-brown leather trench coat or duster with slits up the side that ran to the hip. A series of interlocking brushed-lumenium hexagonal plates traced down the spine, along the tops of the shoulders, and down both forearms from below the elbow to the wrist, creating metallic sleeves. The silver *Albatross* sigil was embossed on the outside of the right arm, and on the left were the interlocking rings of Earth's flag, also in silver. For the Lumenarians, the left sigil was an eight-pointed star with more points silhouetted in the middle, giving it a 3-D look.

I pulled the jacket on and felt how it moved with my body. It automatically compressed to a comfortable fit, leaving flexible space in the torso and shoulders but a snug squeeze through the forearms. I felt a surge of energy run through my body as the outer layer synergized with my bodysuit and armor underneath. Looking over, I saw Will's tic-tacs glowing through the metallic elements. My hex plate forearms suddenly lit up like colorful LCD screens, transferring my band display to both arms—one side displaying an interactive hologram map and the other critical mission information. I noticed two symbols on my right pad, the symbol of a pistol and a rifle. I reached down and unclipped my Warthog. Priming some energy through it, I saw the display automatically highlight the pistol icon and show the ammo quantity: 100/100. I ejected the clip and watched the number drop to 0/100, then back up to full capacity when I reinserted it. I fiddled with the settings and accessed a detailed directory on my left sleeve. Suddenly, one of my cuffs lit up like a flashlight projecting around the room.

"Now that's cool," Megan said, looking over. She started playing with her own sleeve. I gave the jacket another once-over and noticed the firm, semi-raised collar. It felt too heavy not to have some other function.

"Does the collar do something?" I asked, trying to find some prompt on the display. Flak, who had been walking between us all pointing out features, came and squeezed the corner of my right collar. Suddenly, more hex plating split out of the seam and spread up the back of my neck and over the top of my head, creating an armored hood. I looked around at the others as they activated their own. The patterns gave off a scaly look that made me appreciate the armadillo skin moniker a bit more.

Flak turned to the rest of the group. "Add twenty degrees on either end of your temperature-regulation controls, and they provide extra tactical information, protection, and environmental camouflage," he said.

"Don't forget the extra pockets," Will added. Flak just shook his head.

"And we look fucking cool!" said Steve, a young guy on my squad and a recent *Pelly* transfer. Everyone went dead silent and glared at him. After a moment he realized he had cursed to a superior officer he didn't know, and he stared at the floor. "Sorry, sir." We let him stew for a moment, and then everyone chuckled. Kilo jostled him, and Steve laughed nervously with everyone else. Flak didn't laugh, but he didn't get angry either. If I hadn't known Flak so well, I might have been more irritated that one of my subordinates had shown such a lack of discipline in front of a superior. It was Kilo's company, but Steve was on my squad. It was also different aboard the *Albatross* from the military back home. The fact was, these ships were more than just a post; they were home for the foreseeable future. Action and relaxation would all be staged from here. Enforcing a strict discipline was a matter of time and place. During drills, scenarios, and missions, it would be paramount, but as soon as the uniform came off, it might as well have been a civilian apartment building. Steve's slip was borderline. It didn't help that Will notoriously danced that line too. But Will was Will; which meant he got away with a lot more than most.

"Take some time to get used to them," Flak said. "Before you know it, they'll be a second skin." He nodded to the room. "Any other questions, Codec can help you out."

Codec materialized next to him and began pacing around amongst the team, miming like he was examining the uniforms. "Ah, the series-eight high-versatility tactical combat uniform or armadillo skin, as Flak has named it." Flak shot Codec a glare and narrowed his eyes. "Hard to believe something so functional can also look so good," the AI quipped in his oddly human way.

"Last thing…" Flak reached into another crate and pulled out a small cylinder that looked identical to a jolt shot, only the normally gold plasma visible through the glass slot was jet black. He tossed it to Will. "Give that a go, Reach."

Will examined it and then looked at Flak, who gestured for him to get on with it. Will hesitated for a moment, then injected it into his leg port. There was a momentary pause and then Will stumbled slightly, throwing his arms out for balance. Miguel and Megan, who were on either side of him, lunged in to steady him.

"Jesus. What the fuck was that?" Will asked, breathing hard and slowly straightening up.

"Show us your little biotech trick for a minute, Reach," Flak said, crossing his arms. Will raised an eyebrow but then obliged. Rather than the sapphire glow that usually emitted from his lines and his eyes, they shot tamer white sparks and seemed to smoke. The whites of his eyes clouded over to a sooty black. It looked creepy, like he had suddenly transformed into a demon. A few people even stepped back.

"Whoa," Will said, looking at his hands.

"Ink-shots," Flak said, smiling. "As powerful as the tech is, it's not exactly stealthy. These stims will give you around an hour of darkness. Reach, how do you feel?"

"Like shit."

"Well, that's because it's essentially poison." Will stared at him, wide eyed. "Settle down, Reach, you're not gonna die. Just a bit of nausea, maybe a headache, some cramps. It's not easy to tamp down our natural hues. That's the trade-off. However, do not—I repeat, do not—take more than two of these within four hours. You *will* die. So, make sure you save these for when you really need them." We all glanced at Will, none of us looking forward to having to take an ink shot.

"I cannot believe you poisoned me, Flak. Especially without warning me first," Will said, exhaling slowly and hunching over to hold his stomach. "This suuucks."

Flak chuckled, then looked around. "The initial effects should fade in a minute or two. I want everyone to give them a try before end of day, so you know what it's like," he said, pointing around the room. "Four days to Stormwater. Now, company commanders and squad leaders, a word." We all nodded and followed him out to the corridor.

Flak folded his arms and glared at us seriously for a long moment.

"What's up Flak?" Kilo asked.

"How're you feeling? With your teams?" It was a simple question. Something any officer would ask, but I felt like Flak was fishing for something else.

Will shared a look with Kilo and shrugged. "Good. Ironing out a few kinks but solid. We'll be ready. Which I'm sure you've seen on the feeds when you check up on us," he added, trying to get Flak to reveal what he really wanted to say.

"That's why I like you, Reach. You're blunt."

"Well, I prefer direct, but thank you."

"You understand how important this mission is?" Flak asked. Will stiffened slightly, maybe not sure if Flak was accusing him of not taking it seriously. Wouldn't be the first time.

"Yes, I do. We all do."

"I'm not so sure," Flak said. I saw it hurt Will, but I had a feeling there was more to it than that. Just as Will opened his mouth to reply, Flak raised his hands to silence him. "This isn't just a rescue mission. This is proof. Proof that recruiting all of you was worth it. This isn't *just* for any survivors we find. This is to show everyone who you are, who we are together, and what we're capable of." Flak glanced between all of us. "Arthur didn't want me to bring this up, to put more pressure on you down there than you'll already have, but I disagree. Pressure makes you better, or it makes you worse. But worse is death, and that's what you absolutely need to see this as, living or dying. Help could be months, even years, away if you don't make it back to orbit."

"We understand," Kilo said.

Will crossed his arms. I knew he had seen some of the worst conflicts on Earth, and I imagined he hadn't really thought of this as anything more than the same with new weapons. I had understood from the beginning what was at stake, but even I had fallen into a pattern of target fixation. We didn't just need any win here; we needed a resounding victory.

"It's one thing for an individual to die. It's another thing for an entire cause," Flak said. We all glanced between each other, taking in his words.

"We'll do what we can," Kilo said.

Flak gave us an understanding nod, satisfied we had received the message. "Good. As you were. Li, hang back," he said. I felt the hairs prickle on the back of my neck as the others returned to the sim field.

"Oh, and Flak…" Will said. "Don't poison me again, please." Flak shook his head and chuckled. Will shot me a wink and returned to his teams.

"Fucking hume," Flak grunted with a restrained smile. He turned back and stared at me for a moment. "How are you feeling, Sarah?" he asked, his voice surprisingly gentle.

"Uh good, sir. You?" I replied, immediately regretting it. I was nervous. I knew what Flak was going to bring up.

"You're the only human squad leader without prior combat experience."

"I know, sir."

"I disagreed with a non-combat veteran making squad leader, but it was felt that your company lacked strong human leaders, so, here you are." I remained silent, the words stinging even though I understood where he was coming from. "However," he continued, "if anyone was going to get it, I'm glad it was you." I relaxed slightly. It still wasn't *really* a compliment, but the look on Flak's face made me think he thought it was. "Everyone's got a plan until the shooting starts."

"Not exactly how the quote goes, sir," I said, regretting my words almost immediately once again.

Flak stared for a moment, then moved on, ignoring my comment. "Your greatest strength is that brain. You're smarter than ninety-nine percent of these knuckle draggers. And that sets you apart. When everything starts going off, keep sharp. Your mind is gonna try to get cloudy, isolating what's directly in front of you. Don't let it. Take it all in like I know you can." I saw, for probably the first time, just how much Flak cared. How much he saw in all of us individually and as a unit. He was worried about me. About us. He had a gruff way of showing it most of the time, but everything he did was to make us better. "Do us proud, Li. Dismissed," he said with a nod.

"Thank you, sir." I nodded back and then returned to the sim field to begin running training scenarios. My palms felt sweaty. Pressure could make me better or worse. I hoped it wouldn't be the latter.

Twenty-four hours away from dropping onto Stormwater, Will and I sat in the aviary market listening to the musicians play their traditional and improvised instruments under the artificial starry night sky. Miguel, who we had discovered a few months earlier was a talented singer, sat with the players strumming a soft acoustic guitar riff and waiting for his cue to sing. The tinny percussion of synthetic marimba-like bars rattled and pulsed a slow, languorous beat while the strange theremin-violin rings instrument we had seen on Lumen hummed an otherworldly melody in the vein of "I'm on Fire" by Bruce Springsteen.

> *I saw you once*
> *From across the aisle*
> *And those eyes my God*
> *Girl, they made me smile*

But when I heard the church bells ringin'
The alarm on my bedside rang
And I knew that it wasn't real
It was all just make-believin'
And when I rose
When I ro-ooose…
I felt like dyin'.

Seemed too much for one man
Bound by the cold
So-oo far from home
Feelin' so damn old

Then a little birdy told me
There ain't no sorrow's song
That'll make the Albatro-oss
Flap or fly wrong
So when it all comes fallin' down
I'll lean against your walls
And you hold me
Yeah, you ho-oold me…
Far from dyin'.

Miguel sang beautifully and softly, his baritone voice drifting over us. It was strange watching someone like Miguel playing and singing something so gentle. He was a physically solid guy and a great soldier, precise and violent, and when he fought it was unrelenting and aggressive, like a wolverine. He always seemed kind of stiff to me, right from the first time I met him in the LA Coliseum during compatibility testing. But watching his fingers dance along the strings of his guitar made the soldier in him seem far away. Goes to show nobody is just one thing.

As I listened, my mind was transported back home. I glanced around at everyone else absorbing the serene sounds, many closing their eyes and cherishing the few moments of peace we had left before being thrust into the shadowy conflict. The cold reality of that drew me from any sort of contentment to the uncertain future. I did a mechanical breakdown of every stage of the upcoming operation. Every step and breach, drop alpha and secondary bravo, tower sweep and clear or street approach, the descent into the mine, the tunnel routes, securing the survivors, primary and secondary extractions: an intricate game of Commander's Die; move to countermove, adjustment, memory, reading our opponent, and adapting. I almost laughed at the realization of how quickly I had switched from enjoying the night to being a soldier. It came as naturally as breathing.

The thought made me look over at Will. I saw his mind dipping into much of the same and darker, his half-glazed eyes tracing the movements of invisible specters.

"Hey," I said, taking his hand under the table and pulling him back to world of the living. He blinked a few times and then looked at me, covering with a smile. "Stay here…with me."

"I don't know what you're talking about," he replied with a wry smile. "I'm always here." He knew he couldn't hide from me, but that didn't mean he wouldn't try.

"Mhmm," I said. He looked deep in my eyes, sending a warm flush up my neck and into my cheeks. He had a way of making it seem like he was looking through me. While some found this unsettling, I found it comforting. Something was given back and shared in the stare. He told me he felt much the same about how I looked at him.

Just then clapping sounded around us. We looked over at the musicians and joined the applause as Miguel's song faded out. He smiled and gave a self-conscious bow and wave. Having immersed himself in the music, the applause brought him back to his awareness of the audience. He sipped some water and then put his head down and started picking the beginning of another ballad.

"You're ready for this, right?" Will asked. I kept watching Miguel like I hadn't heard the question, but I felt Will's stare. "Sare?"

"You don't have to worry about me, Will."

"Oh, are you going to a different mission than I am?" he asked, a grin flirting with the corner of his mouth.

"No."

"Aren't you worried about me? It's gonna be, like, really dangerous." Feigned hurt and fear took over his face, which creased into a smile.

"Jackass." I shook my head and rolled my eyes. We sat in silence for a few moments. "Kilo is one of the best captains out there, and I can handle myself. You know that. Our squad is good. We'll be OK," I said, running my thumb against the back of his hand. He nodded. "Are you ready, Will?"

"I was just thinking..." he said, leaning in.

"Yeah?"

"We don't know what tomorrow might bring. How much time we might have left."

"Oh, we might not have much time left, huh?"

"I mean, who really knows?"

Before I knew it, we were back in Will's room stripping each other's clothes off, sparks literally flying as we spun around the room. I kissed down his neck and worked across his shoulder, tracing the edges of his shrapnel scars. I knew it was one of those spots that made his eyes glow and sent shivers across his skin. He pulled my face back up to his, running his fingers through the hair behind my neck. We found ourselves pressed against the outside of the shower glass, separating only briefly to breathe. I shoved him back with a two-handed burst of my biotech and a devilish grin.

Just then "Ain't No Mountain High Enough" by Marvin Gaye and Tammi Terrell started playing throughout the room. We both instinctively looked up at the ceiling.

"Stop fucking listening to and/or watching us, Codec!" Will said. The music cut out.

"Sorry," Codec replied.

"You can actually keep playing the song though," I said with a grin and a shrug. The music resumed. Will rolled his eyes and chuckled. I reached into the shower and turned on the water, looking back at him and slowly slipping off the last small bit of my clothing, throwing it aside with my toes. He stared, transfixed, breathing hard, mouth agape.

"Close your mouth, Will Reach, and get your ass over here," I ordered, gesturing with my finger. He lunged toward me, ripping the last of his clothes off. The hot water steamed around us and arced the blue fire of our ignited tech as we wove together. Two bodies became one, hopefully not for the last time.

Ain't no mountain high enough…

CHAPTER XXV

Stormwater

- WILL -

We all stared up at the dull greyish-white blur on the display panels. The air felt hot and stuffy from all the bodies in the tight quarters. The tension only added to it. I glanced at Jeremy as he wiped away a drop of sweat making its way down his temple. Popping his combat cherry on this one. Others fidgeted or tapped their feet. I felt my chest heaving with slow deliberate breaths, expectant but controlled. This is what I was best at. It was mostly quiet as we sat, waiting apprehensively for what was coming. Lumenarian and human side by side. If anyone did speak it was in hushed whispers to the person next to them, sharing some remembered joke to alleviate the anxiety or deflect the feelings of dread. The gentle creak of our synthetic armor and uniforms punctuated the near silence.

Miguel passed down a tin of dipping tobacco, which we called "bird shit." I packed it with a series of three flicks of my hand to settle it, took a pinch to place in my lower lip, and then passed it along. Genius goddamn requisition by someone on the *Pelican*—the formula transferred over during our post OnSpec attack repairs. All the invigorating effects and alertness of the real thing (and then some) minus the cancer. I tucked the dark substance into my lip on the left side, as I did in the service back home, and felt the buzz crackle behind my eyes. The flavors could still use some work, but it got the job done.

One of the command deck personnel sounded over a ship-wide inter-com: "All crew stand by. Dropping out in five...four...three...two...one." On cue, the panels around us snapped out of the milky blur to the dark void of space, showing us the *Albatross's* outside view.

Debris and shrapnel whipped past our displays like garbage in a dust storm, pelting off the hydro shield with electric cracks and fizzles—the wreckage of the Lumenarian defense fleet stationed there and the planetary protection systems. A slew of our allies' bodies, frozen by the cold vacuum, drifted into and disintegrated on the shield. Several people turned away from the view and grimaced. Others stared in horror and shock. The near-black orb of Stormwater loomed in front of us. No water was visible on the surface. The only things that broke the barren, windswept onyx were the ashy patches of cityscapes. Dark clouds of smoke billowed in the atmosphere.

"Contact ten o'clock!" the dispatch voice echoed, causing every head to swivel. The forward panels zoomed in to the distant hulking form of a Forsaken warship lurking at the far horizon of the planet. A single ship. A real ship. No more simulations.

"Holy shit," Miguel muttered next to me. We both stared with mouths open.

It was nearly invisible with its pitch-dark hull, save for the red glow that emanated between the seams of large patchwork panels and several ports around the vessel. It was made of two solid rectangular prisms in the fore and aft sections of the ship with protruding sharp-edged blocks that rotated around a smooth cylindrical core joining the two halves together, giving it an elongated dumbbell shape. It looked sinister and aggressive, blunt and violent. It was massive, as big or bigger than our carrier ships, like the accompanying *Pelican* and *Chariot*, which hung back from our warships.

The *Eagle* and the *Shark* pulled into our periphery, rounding out our flanks. The goliath Forsaken craft was in the middle of a slow lumbering turn as a cloud of drone fighters from all three of our ships swarmed out from the shuttle bays, and large emerald blasts tore toward them. They darted between the space rubble and lurched toward the enemy vessel.

A bright beam shot out from the front of the Forsaken ship into the black distance. The rotating blocks spun faster around the center, merging into a crimson blur as the rear drive sent a violent stream backwards.

Suddenly, the enemy ship disappeared into the void—a faint residual line visible along its departure path. I stared at the empty space. The process had looked uncomfortably similar to the thread drive. There was a brief stunned silence, then clapping and cheers pitched through the shuttle.

"Fuck yeah! They're already running from us!" someone shouted down the rows of seats. It was a nice thought, but I had a feeling it wasn't a cowardly retreat.

The command deck voice crackled again. "Shuttle teams go for launch." In an instant the *Albatross's* exterior feeds cut out and resumed the shuttle's natural displays. The inside of the shuttle bay disappeared as we dipped out and lanced through the hydro shield. The ride wasn't nearly as pleasant as our previous planet-side visits as we ducked and dodged around the field of floating jetsam. The shuttle lurched from side to side, up and down, avoiding major collisions and trying to drop us to our target as rapidly as possible—and that was damn fast.

Once we cleared the debris, our transports pelted into Stormwater's dense upper atmosphere, the shuttle's shield glowing from the strain. I clenched my jaw and held onto the straps of my seat as we rumbled through the trip, hoping it would be over soon. I had a strong stomach, but the jostling was intense. Several others vomited in the aisles. More ingredients for our fear stew. Finally, we cleared the roughest of it and dropped into a smooth arc toward the surface. The distant star, something similar in light spectrum to our sun, disappeared behind the horizon as we descended to the dark side of the world, embedding ourselves into the four-hour night cycle.

The obsidian-like stone, frozen in fields of wind-blown waves, hurtled beneath us as we flew at incredible speeds toward the nearest city. The only lights ahead came from the few fires still burning. A dozen other shuttles flanked us on similar trajectories, breaking off toward their targets only as we passed the outskirts of the dwellings. Unlike the immense skyscrapers of Lumen, the structures on Stormwater were low and blocky, like bunkers. The only tallish buildings were the entrance and stack towers of the mines, which were scattered across the sprawling cities in regular intervals like lighthouses. Rubble pyres burned, and large billows of dark smoke rose from many of the surrounding areas. Surprisingly there was no anti-aircraft resistance or any sign at all of the enemy below. No crimson dots peppered upwards toward our vessels. The streets looked abandoned.

"Bravo 1, we're approaching insertion Alpha," the pilot from our shuttle said into my personal comm. "Target in thirty seconds."

"Roger that," I replied, pulling up my personal holo-display. The panels along the walls displayed everything around us, but I could focus the small viewer where I needed. "Bravo squads, target ETA thirty seconds. Prepare for drop," I announced to the members of my team. We were the first of four groups onboard that would be dropped to separate objectives.

My crew unbuckled from their seats and stood, everyone fully geared out in their combat uniforms with Tempests, Warthogs, kites, jolt shots, and our cross-slung hip packs that doubled as bandoliers. They all stepped forward into the drop boots, which looked like heavy-duty ski boots and bindings. The boots latched onto their feet with a mechanical whir and click, then glowed blue and green.

I zoomed into my display to scope out our mine tower. My face fell as I saw the top half of our objective had been sheared off, the upper floors reduced to rubble and several Lumenarian bodies littering the debris. There was no spot for us to insert directly at the objective, so we'd have to adjust.

"Shuttle control. Primary drop site is a negative. Proceed to secondary."

"Roger that. Proceeding to secondary."

Shit. Our plan B was an insertion point a block from the mine entrance, a long block. It meant we would have to move through the open streets to get to our target; which was not ideal, but we had run through the scenario in the sim field.

"Bravo squad, primary is burned. Deploying in secondary. Pattern Charlie hotel dark on landing."

"Roger, copy," came the collective acknowledgement. Half my team pulled their Tempest rifles off their backs and held them at the ready. The other half unclipped their Warthogs and kite cylinders. Determined, rigid faces masked the fear. I stole a glance at the starboard panels and saw another shuttle about a mile away blinking in the dark sky, offloading its team onto the top of another tower—Kilo and Sarah's team.

Our shuttle swooped low, getting into position over the edge of a wide square with ruined intersecting streets. Scorch marks and fractured buildings lined the area, Lumenarian bodies strewn haphazardly throughout the thoroughfares with blood drying in large dark pools. I frowned instinctively at the images. It looked like a slaughter. I folded the holo panel and tucked it into my pocket, then unbuckled and stepped into my drop boots, rifle in hand.

"Rap two setting," I instructed. Everyone blinked the infrared setting on their contact lenses and nodded.

"Bravo 1 in position. Drop on your mark," the pilot announced. I took a deep breath and exhaled.

"Drop!" Circular holes cut away beneath our feet, and in an instant we were plummeting toward the ground, leaving the relative safety of the shuttle behind.

It was about an eighty-foot drop to the ground, everything rushing past in a blur. Fifteen feet from the street (which seemed entirely too fucking close), the ejection boots fired up and slowed our descent to a survivable fall, but it was still a jarring thud as we made contact, compressing into the planet. I preferred rappelling. The boots split and crumbled away as we touched down, and our armor and uniforms fluidly transitioned to a matte-black color. What I would have given for that kind of camouflage back home.

We collapsed into a circle. The outside of our group crouched with pistols up and shield cylinders in front of them, ready to fire up the tech in milliseconds. The second row stepped forward and aimed their Tempests over the outside's shoulders, scanning the streets and tops of buildings. It was dead silent save for the whistle of wind that wound between the structures, kicking up whiffs of black sand drawn in from the barren outskirts. The planet was hot and dry, an onyx desert on the inner edge of a star's habitable zone. The heat mixed with the strong odor of decaying bodies, making us wince and our eyes water.

"Fuck," Megan muttered next to me.

"You got something?" I asked.

"No. I swallowed my fucking dip on the way down."

"Christ, Meg. Stow that shit," I said, skimming along the building tops with my rifle.

"It was a fucking bloodbath," Miguel whispered next to me, his rifle trained ahead as he stared at a pair of bodies gunned down while trying to flee.

I stepped forward and then froze as my foot crunched and squished on something. Looking down, I grimaced at the charred remains of a Lumenarian leg. I clenched my jaw and looked back up toward our mission waypoint. "All teams forward. Secure northwest corner."

We fell into a column and hustled out of the square toward an adjoining street in the direction of our objective, moving as quickly and quietly as we could. We stacked against the wall, weapons sweeping in all directions.

"Jesus, my head feels like it weighs a hundred pounds," Jeremy whispered.

"You do have a big head for a human, Jer," Ice replied. Jeremy scoffed.

"Two G is a bitch," Megan said. "Feels like I'm hanging upside down." The nanites in our blood had been slowly strengthening our bones, muscles, and tendons during the trip from Earth, and our suits mitigated some of the planet's pull but not all of it. It seemed our heads took the brunt of it. "You probably barely notice it though, right, Ice?" Megan said. "You were fat to begin with."

"It's muscle. You know Lumenarians don't store fat the way—"

"Keep it tight, guys," I said. I was actually glad they were joking around a bit, levity being a good barrier against the despair that surrounded us, but I needed complete focus. "We've done this a hundred times. Let's move."

We marched forward, hugging the buildings at a quick and steady but not rushed pace. Our shield line holstered their pistols and kites and drew their rifles. We needed to be as much on the offensive as we could be for this rescue. If anyone was left to rescue. My left hand gripped the forestock of my Tempest, the inside of my metallic forearm sleeve lighting up a holographic map (infrared spectrum in the dark so it didn't give away our positions) that traced our progress and highlighted the route ahead. The mine entrance was a straight shot 300 meters ahead with only ruins and the dead in our path. Heat waves rose in mirage flurries from the solid stone roadway even in the shade of night, and smoke drifted past in whirlwind gusts.

One hundred meters out, a corner of one of the buildings along the edge of the large monument square that opened to the mine's front doors crumbled in an avalanche of metal and rock. I held up my hand, signaling the team to halt. "Megan," I said.

"On it." She slid her hip pack around and pulled out a hexagonal pocket drone, juicing it with a quick surge of energy, and tossed it in the air. It was self-powered, but the jolt synced it to her band. She pointed with her index finger, and the bot hovered toward the opening of the square. Structural fatigue from the battle or enemy tactics? I felt my heart beating in my temples as I narrowed my vision through the scope on my rifle, controlling my breathing.

"Anybody got anything?" I whispered into comms.

"Looks clear," Ice said.

"I got nothing," Megan answered, staring at the drone's feed on her sleeve. I sucked some air through my teeth with a quiet squeak, a mostly unconscious habit when I didn't feel sure of, or love, my options. The collapsed building created a choke point from the street into the square, which was already an exposed crossing to reach the mine. I didn't like it, but the city blocks were massive, and diverting around via side streets would be a serious detour.

"Alright, Meg, let's keep the drone in the air. Heads on a swivel. Let's go." We crept the last distance to the square at a more cautious speed. The feed had shown an all-clear, but we had been warned about the Forsaken's ability to avoid scanning tech, and the silence was making me uneasy.

At the mouth of the square, we crouched while Megan guided the drone to recon the opening with a swirl of her finger. Miguel, Ice, and I huddled around Megan's feed. Ford, Sea, Fred, and Tex, my Lumenarian squad leaders, rallied up front.

"What's up?" Ford asked. I nodded toward Megan.

"We knew the gap was potentially gonna be a tough cross, but..." Megan glanced at all of us. "There's the real problem," she said, zooming into the display and showing another collapsed building that had fallen into the square almost all the way to the towering statue of a Lumenarian miner in the center. The debris blocked our most streamlined route to the mine doors, meaning we'd either have to follow the wall to that point and then jut out into the fully exposed center before beelining it to the entrance or take the much longer route hugging the far side of the square, keeping us mildly exposed for longer. I stared at the options, weighing the risks.

"What're you thinking, Will?" Sea asked.

Both options really suck, is what I was thinking. "Original route. Still the quickest," I said. "Levee column to the midpoint and Urchin formation to the doors." They nodded, understanding the order. "And let's keep kites dark until we need them."

"Inks?" Tex asked.

"Negative. If they hit us out there, we'll need our shots traced. Plus I don't wanna feel like shit," I said, grinning.

"Roger that."

The orders were relayed to everyone else, and half the team holstered their rifles onto their backs and pulled out their Warthogs and kites again. We scrambled over the debris and into the square, fully committed to the forward push. The clattering rubble rang in my ears. Though unavoidable, it was an afront to my notion of stealth. We proceeded two abreast along the wall to our right. The riflemen, me included, hugged the wall while those holding shields and pistols marched on the inside of the ring. The far building tops, which had vantage on us, looked still, but we scanned them vigilantly.

Just as we reached the collapsed building about halfway along our path, a shot rang out in the distance. It echoed through the silence like an elastic band finally stretched past breaking. We all stopped instinctively, eyes darting through the darkness and the dense stillness, a quiet ringing in the stale air. Every sense was triggered to pin-dropping precision. The shot was a spark that would ignite a wildfire.

Then, in the static dark, the sound of a metal plate scuffing stone above us raised the hairs on the back of my neck.

"Shields!" I shouted as the first scarlet energy blasts rained toward us from the adjacent building roofs. In a violent flash of blue and green, the kite shields took form just in time to absorb and deflect most of the enemy's salvo. Each shield bearer in the wall strained under the heavy barrage, feet sliding on the dust layer over the stone street surface. The rifle line and I returned fire, aiming for whatever we could make out.

The Forsaken were everywhere, like they had appeared out of thin air. Black shapes scuttled along the building tops of two sides of the square, popping up from behind the roof parapets to shoot and then ducking out of sight just as quickly. The crimson, sapphire, and emerald energy trading back and forth in steady streams illuminated the square in an apocalyptic disco haze.

"We gotta move!" I shouted over the cacophony of battle noise. No sooner were the words out of my mouth than a large chunk of the structure to our backs exploded in a shower of red sparks. The debris fell toward our heads, giving us no time to dodge it. Everything seemed to move in slow motion as everyone who saw it coming braced for impact. I did the only thing I could think of. I dropped my rifle and threw my hands into the air, releasing a strong burst of unfocused energy from my bio tech. A thermal-electric cloud rushed upwards with sporadic arcs of lightning. The larger pieces vaporized into a fine sand that filtered down around us. Some of the remaining fragments fizzled and clunked off the kites. I collapsed to one knee. Raw releases could be powerful tools (well, for me—not many could do them with the same effect), but they were completely uncontrollable and drained my stamina fast. A desperate hail Mary move. The strength of my armor dimmed, letting me feel the extra gravitational pressure in a rush. I felt like throwing up. I breathed hard as Miguel put his hand on my shoulder and gave me a jolt through the hex plating, helping me recover and reenergizing my combat suit. "Thanks," I said, glancing up at him.

"Thank *you*. That would've knocked me the fuck out," he said as he ducked under a shot and returned fire. Earlier than I planned, I unclipped a jolt shot and jammed it into the port in my leg armor. The stimulant ripped through my veins like icy razors as it refilled my bioenergy. I clenched my jaw as my eyes erupted in blue fire and then shook my head as the adrenaline rush subsided to a background buzz.

"We're getting pinned down here. Keep them moving," I ordered, nodding to the head of the formation.

Miguel acknowledged and hustled down the line. "Suppressive fire! Move forward!" he yelled, peppering the far building roof with fast, light blasts. We bumped the shields along the rubble out toward the center of the square. Just then shots tore into us from the rear.

"Contact six o'clock high!" Ford shouted, turning and shooting back at the roof of the building we had just pressed away from. Our rear squad automatically folded around, closing our defensive wall while a second row stacked their shields above the first to cut away some of our enemy's high-angle advantage. A rapid, fleeting wave of pride hit me as I saw the team maneuver perfectly without my having to order it. My pride vanished when a blast found its mark in the middle of Lep's face, one of Sea's Lumenarian squad mates. An odd pop and a splatter was followed by a dark fountain of blood as his body collapsed into the dirt. *Fifty-nine.* The cold clinical thought jumped forward.

"Grenade!" Megan yelled as a blinking red orb dropped in front of the rear line. The shield bearers braced for the explosion. The blast came as a splashing wave of glowing magma-like fluid crashing into us. On contact with the kite wall, the burning liquid solidified into a steaming black mass, trapping our tech in its grasp. "Shit! Need support back here!" Megan called to the group as she wrenched her hand back from her stuck shield.

"Fire team two, fill in the gaps!" I barked. They rushed over, tossing their rifles onto their backs, drawing their barriers and firing their Warthogs through the gaps. Another scarlet round tore into Ryan center mast. He was dead before he hit the deck. *Fifty-eight.* There was no choice but to step over his body as we pushed on.

We made it to the center of the square, past the edge of the downed building. "Urchin!" The end of the line curled out into the opening, encircling the rest of us as we folded into the center. I tossed my Tempest onto my back and fired up my kite shield, filling in a second-row slot of the shell, the rest of the squad in the middle. Lumenarians took the taller roof positions. We completed the Urchin (or Roman style Tortuga), our shields interlocking to form the husk and our firepower the spines. "Nice work, guys! Push to the door!" We marched in unison toward the mine's large double doors.

The Forsaken attack surged around us like electric blood raining from the sky. A shot whipped through a crack, searing through Jeremy's armor and ripping into his shoulder. Blood splattered out. "Aaah!" He dropped to the ground, leaving a gap in the shell. "Oh fuck! Oh fuck!" he yelled, panicking as blood spurted from his gaping wound.

"Fill!" Two from the center stepped forward, filling the space left by Jeremy and taking over my spot. I reached down and grabbed him by the collar, dragging him with us, a thick trail of blood following. "Hold on, Jer."

We crawled up the stone steps leading to the entrance, Jeremy groaning as I hoisted him up the risers. At the doors we slammed against the sealed panels, pressing into them with our shields out like a bubble tucked in the corner of a glass of milk. Megan broke off firing and moved to the control display, hacking in to open the doors. I laid Jeremy down to the side and stacked against a door.

"Fire team one, right stack on me. Team three left. Second these doors open. Flash and clear." Miguel and two others lined up behind me while Ice initiated another column on the other side. We waited anxiously for the go-ahead from Megan, most troops bobbing on their toes and clenching their rifles.

"Anytime, Meg," Miguel grunted. "Sucks out here!"

"Ready?" Megan called out. I nodded across to Ice. Each of us primed advanced flashbangs in our hands with flares of blue-and-green energy.

"Let's fuck 'em up," I said as the heavy-duty doors cracked open. We lobbed the grenades in and then took cover. Each one emitted a three-series of shrill bangs and blinding multi-spectrum flashes that glared brilliant light through the open door. Within seconds we laced into the mine atrium and blasted away the twelve combatants inside, their massive dark forms flailing a resistance against the stun of the flashbangs. Three dead ahead, one in each of the near corners, two at the controls for the elevator lifts, one on the right winding staircase, another at the base of the left symmetrical staircase, and three on the balcony overlooking the hall. We paused as the dust settled and scanned the room for any other contacts.

"Clear. All teams move in. Rest of fire teams one and three provide cover fire at the door." The remainder of my people started flooding in. Occasional red blasts trailed through the open crack. Megan and Ford hauled Jeremy, who was covered with blood. Tank, our primary

Lumenarian medic, rushed over and took the reins. The second the last of us made it in, Megan closed the doors, which were now synced with her forearm band. I pointed up to the balcony. "Tex, take your squad and barricade the upper offices in case we have guests in what's left of upstairs. Ford, secure the elevators." Tex and Ford hustled past with their teams. Everyone was panting, finally having a moment to breathe. Loud booms shook the massive doors, unsettling the black sand that seemed to cover everything.

The room itself was eerily quiet apart from the thundering from outside, the echoes of weapons being checked, and canteens from our packs opening with the scraping metal twist of the lids. Everyone spoke in muttered affirmations and updates that they were alright, as if anything too loud might betray their courage. We were all mostly OK, except for Jeremy, but the shock of our first contact with the enemy was understandably fresh on everyone's face.

"It'll take them a while to get through these, but I'd rather not stick around for too long." Megan said, walking over to me and gesturing to the doors.

"Roger that," I replied, staring down at the huge Forsaken soldier lying dead at my feet.

"Jesus Christ," Megan whispered, "these things are fucking huge."

I nodded. "Yeah." We were immersed in our new reality, but looking down at the body seemed to painfully solidify the situation. Another one of those earth-shattering moments of awe that we thought we'd be used to by now, just not a fun one. Megan crouched next to the creature's head and ran her fingers along the edges of its prismed helmet. She pulled out her Warthog and seared the blade into the side until it made a click. With a hiss and a rush of gas, the compression seal broke, and Megan pulled away the front of the mask. The greeting stench was a combination of burnt flesh and raw sewage, causing both of us and a few nearby to cover our noses and shy away. Slowly leaning back in, I looked down at the soupy remains of whatever was inside the mech suit. They weren't kidding about the corrosive failsafe enzyme.

"Holy shit…" Megan said as she reached toward the gelatinous liquid.

"Whoa, hey! Don't put your fingers in that," I said, baffled that that's where her curiosity was taking her.

"Right. Probably a good call," she said, shaking her head as if to rattle away the thought. "What if that's all they actually are?"

"Huh?"

"Just goo in a suit."

"Feel like there'd be better shapes they could take."

"Good point…Like centaurs." I glanced over at her and raised my eyebrows, but she just stared at the mess below. *What?*

I looked around, taking stock of the room and the situation. The mine foyer was a large square space with an eighty-foot ceiling. The elevators down to the lower levels sat between the curving dual staircases that rose to an overlooking balcony, off which a series of doors led to the exhaust stack access and administration offices above. With the top half of the tower destroyed, I didn't expect much (if any) resistance in the surviving sections, but it was something to be wary of, hence Tex's squad securing the points of entry.

I went over to Tank, who was doing the best he could on Jeremy's injury. Taking a closer look, I realized Jeremy's shoulder was worse than I thought. It was shredded, the edges of his clavicle and upper ribcage visible in an unsettling bone-white against the dark carnage of bloody muscle and other tissue, his arm barely holding on to what was left. The nanites in his blood had been struggling to stem the flow, but even they had a limit. The med-gel agent that Tank applied stopped further bleeding, but it was a Band-Aid on a cracked dam. Thankfully, Jeremy was passed out. I knew better than to ask what his chances were in case he could hear anything in the dark recesses of his unconscious state. Hearing it out loud wouldn't change the facts. Tank took a sheet of lead-like med-skin material out of his pack, wrapping it around the wound and over the shoulder. A silver-lumenium patch that sealed the wound and refilled the armor. He gave it a small jolt with his biotech, and the pad compressed into the surrounding skin, lighting up the circuit board lines that laced throughout it.

"Do what you can," I said, patting Tank on the shoulder. He nodded, and I left him to it, walking to the middle of the room, where Ice approached me.

"One elevator is here," he said. "The other is down below. Ready when you are."

"Thanks, Ice. Gather the rest of the squad, and be ready to go." He nodded and went to it. "Squad leaders on me," I said into comms. Tex left his team up top and came down. Ford came from the elevators, and Sea and Fred came from tending to their battered squads. As usual, I felt like the short kid staring up at all the big kids on the playground—the tiny human among alien titans—but I knew my position, and so did they. "Alright, guys, easy part's over," I said with a dry grin. "I'm calling an audible. Fred, you're gonna stay here and support Tex and Sea. I want the upper levels cleared to get a better vantage of what we're facing on our way out of here and a solid plan for un-fucking this situation before I get back. Ford's squad and mine will clear below and exfil any survivors. Rodge?"

"Roger."

"OK. We know comms will be shitty in the mines, so set your clocks for three hours. You don't hear from us or we're not back by then, we're not coming back. Detonate the shaft and get to evac. Anything comes back up that isn't us, detonate and evac," I said, fully aware that going down into those mines might be a one-way trip.

"Three hours is tighter than we planned," Sea said with a worried expression. Just then another massive BOOM sounded against the entrance doors, shaking the building. We all glanced over at them.

"Yeah. Make sure we even have that long."

"Will do," Sea confirmed and then moved to notify her team. Tex and Fred peeled off as well. Ford smacked me on the shoulder, almost knocking me over. He looked uncomfortably excited, borderline manic. Crazy bastard. "Good day to die!" he shouted.

I raised an eyebrow and chuckled. "You and Tex have been watching too many Earth movies, Ford. Get your guys ready." Ford turned, but I grabbed his arm. "Hey, keep it tight. No cowboy shit, yeah?" He nodded and then headed back to the elevators. I gathered Miguel, Megan, and the rest of my team and followed. "*Albatross* Command, this is *Albatross* Charlie Bravo 1-0," I said, switching my comms to the *Albatross's* orbital frequency on my forearm band as I walked.

"Charlie Bravo 1-0, go for *Albatross* Command," the dispatch operator replied.

"We've reached the objective with heavy enemy resistance. I'm taking two squads into the mines for survivor extraction. Ground contact will be Charlie Bravo 2-0. Confirm?"

"*Albatross* confirms 2-0 contact. Good luck, Charlie Bravo 1."

Having completed my check-in, I switched back to local comms and loaded the elevator with the other twenty-two members of my team. Megan keyed the controls, and the doors whipped shut with a pneumatic whoosh.

And here...we...go.

CHAPTER XXVI

The Seventh Circle

- SARAH -

The lifts moved at incredible speeds, the levels flashing by as we descended. It was a substantial distance down to the mine's access tunnels, over six miles, which would be nearly into the mantle on Earth. I pulled out my Warthog and twisted the slide ninety degrees, checking that everything was clear and to see how full my clip was. The display on my sleeve was handy, but I still felt more comfortable looking at the gun directly; no doubt a bit of tech skepticism I picked up from Will. Satisfied, I holstered the pistol and pulled the Tempest off my back. Through the inertial dampening field, we felt the elevator slowing down, nearly at our destination. Without looking, I reached over and took Seyyal's tremoring hand. She squeezed my hand back, keeping her eyes forward.

"Ten seconds," Cash said, looking at the compartment's display.

"Front row," Kilo ordered. The twelve nearest the door pulled out their kites and pistols. The remaining twenty-four of us readied behind with rifles poised. We slowed to a stop, all of us tense, awaiting whatever was on the other side of the wide doors. Waiting, waiting, waiting…

The doors separated with a mechanical whir and whoosh. Three Forsaken soldiers stood casually around a fourth who was sitting on an equipment crate. Two others were carrying a Lumenarian body to be tossed on a tall pile of other bodies. Blood trails stained the floor in long oily-black streaks where others had been carried or dragged to their final resting place. They all turned just in time to see us cut them down in a hail of blue-and-green plasma blasts.

We flooded into the main junction room between the two large feeder mine tunnels. The room was wide with low ceilings and dim lighting, as if the dreary tone of mines was a universal trait. The walls were constructed of matte-silver, lumenium-laced concrete panels with embedded fragments of cobalt prisms. The tunnels were about thirty feet wide and smooth, lined with continuous strips of light running along the floor, walls, and ceiling. Harmonic resonators that carried trams to and from the access and main processing zones hummed dully.

"Charlie Delta 4-0, this is 1-0, copy?" Kilo asked into comms, seeing if we were penetrating the mine's depth at all. "4-0, 1-0 check." Nothing. Not even the Lumenarians' advanced technology could cut through the many layers of mineral deposits in Stormwater's dense crust. The direct mine to surface comms box next to the elevator doors was smashed and inoperable. "No joy on comms. Should have local though."

"Awesome. No tram either. Looks like we're walking," Tariq grumbled as we posted up at the entrances to both tunnels.

"We have ground to cover," Kilo said. Each passage was around a mile and a half to the mine-processing caverns. "Sarah, your squad take left. We'll take Right. Saff, your squad hang here and support as needed." Saff, short for Saffron, our other Lumenarian squad leader, nodded.

"Copy that," I confirmed.

Kilo took a deep breath and exhaled slowly. "Alright. See you in a jiff," he said, taking his team to the right corridor. I shared a nod with Seyyal as she peeled off and followed Kilo. Cash, Jiro, Tariq, Karen, and I stared after them.

"God, it still sounds fucking weird when you guys say shit like that," Karen said with a raised eyebrow to Cash.

"Yeah, it's like you've infected us," Cash jabbed back.

"Alright, Delta, let's do this," I said, turning to our route.

The descent through the mine tower had been pretty smooth. Clean drop on the roof, level by level sweep, then securing the atrium. All with minimal resistance. However, the tunnels provided their own set of challenges. The distance, negligible cover, long, straight, open stretches, and the narrowing of the tunnels provided a Thermopylae effect for us, as it did for them. It was too soon in our experience with the Forsaken to know whether we would turn out to be the Spartans or the Persians.

The first heavy shut-off doors were scorched and melted through the locks and forcibly pried open only enough to allow one soldier through at a time—another series of fatal funnel kill zones for us to pass through. Luckily, the passage stretched for a distance, allowing decent sight lines and not slowing us down too much, but it could be an issue if we were forced to withdraw quickly. Six emergency shut-off doors were spaced throughout the tunnel. After the first one there were no more Lumenarian bodies, which gave us hope that some citizens were left to rescue, the barriers having slowed down the Forsaken's advance.

We risked a slightly quicker pace through the first few breached doors to make up some time but slowed down as we approached the fifth set. We heard a loud banging echo from the distance. Concussive booms fizzled with a firework-like crackle at the end.

Hugging the walls, we crept up on the last forced opening, stacking to the right. I led the file followed by Cash, Jiro, Tariq, Karen, and the other seven members of my squad. Once the shoulder squeeze from the back reached me, I threaded through the gap with my rifle raised and the rest of my team hot on my heels. Silent and smooth.

The last stretch was 300 meters long with a forty-five-degree turn a hundred meters from the end. Straight ahead of us was one of the trams we had hoped would save us some time earlier; granted, the partially opened gates wouldn't have allowed us to pass anyway. It was a steel-grey and boxy levitating cart with slit windows along its sides and blurry waves of maglev energy under it, giving it a futuristic subway train look. We fell in line directly behind it. Upon reaching the back, we peered around the sides. Nothing was directly in sight, but we could hear the Forsaken working around the corner, the booms of whatever was trying to breach the final door a now-deafening blare.

I looked over at the tram with a sudden idea. "Cash or Bell, you can work this thing, right?"

"Yes, ma'am. What are you thinking?" Bell asked. Another one of my Lumenarian crew.

"Trojan horse." Most members of the group nodded, liking the idea.

Bell stared blankly at me. "OK, for us who didn't have years to study your history, I don't know what that is," she said, a little irritated to be out of the loop. It was easy to forget not every Lumenarian had a databank of information in their heads about us. Our comrades who had made the journey from Earth had so seamlessly, and sometimes eerily, taken in so many of the nuances of our culture, from movie quotes to historical references and idioms, that the newbies seemed a little stiff at times. Saving the full explanation of what the Trojan War was, I told Bell what to do.

A minute later the tram rounded the corner and sailed toward the forty or so Forsaken crammed at the end of the corridor, poised to enter the final chamber. The source of the booming was a ten-foot-tall, tripod-mounted battering ram with three massive pistons aimed at each of the three heavy-duty locks on the doors. A steaming core beam emitted out of the front of each ram, melting and targeting the points on the barrier for the repeated hammering, each impact sparking against the doors like a blacksmith's hammer on forged steel. Seeing it, I was amazed the gates had lasted as long as they had. The banging of the breacher shook in our chests, exacerbating our frayed nerves.

When the tram was about forty feet out, the Forsaken noticed it and fired at it, their shots tearing holes in the sides like Swiss cheese, tearing it apart until the maglev effect failed on one side, and it dropped lopsidedly to the ground with a crash followed by a hair-raising screech as it slowed to a stop. The enemy soldiers approached tentatively and surrounded what remained of it, scanning for anything alive onboard.

As they leaned in closer, from my sleeve I watched the drone's feed, which was stuck to the front of the tram.

"Now!" Bell tapped her forearm display. An instant later, a blast shook the tunnel with a thunderous BOOM. Before the sound had even finished rattling in the space, we were around the bend and unleashing hell into the dusty cloud, waves of blue-and-green shots ripping and crackling through the air.

We stopped firing as all movement ceased and we squinted through the explosion's fog. The banging from the tripod-mounted breacher continued to rail in my ears. As the smoke began to settle, a red glow emanated from just in front of the door. My eyes went wide as the glow took form, and I realized what I was staring at. Adrenaline surged and prickled at the back of my neck and up the sides of my face.

"Shield wall!" I heard my voice reverberate from somewhere in my stomach. Fifteen Forsaken remained, standing behind large, crimson oval shields that projected from their left arms. The cannons built into their right arms aimed around and between the interlocking edges. The first shot grazed my leg before I could get my kite out.

One of my squad mates, a young Lumenarian named Tar, collapsed in a mist of black blood as three rounds tore through his face and torso and severed one of his arms. I braced my rifle against my shield, sparks flying as it ground along the energy edge. In a strange flash of engineering insight and frustration, I pictured a future improvement in design for the kites but didn't have time to dwell on it.

The rest of my team fell in beside me, a David vs. Goliath scenario as our outnumbered wall battled against the colossal figures ahead. I focused hard for one massive shot, moving my hand forward to the second enclosed trigger, channeling the BBs into the melting pot of the lower launcher, a crashing semi-truck force that had decimated the simulations in training. I saw Cash and Jiro do the same out of the corner of my eye. The electric sapphire-and-emerald blasts soared across the gap, trailing phosphoric streaks. They collided with the center of the line and erupted in a flash of light, the concussive shock felt across the tunnel. My face fell, and my eyes widened again as the light dissolved, revealing the shield bearers only slightly pushed back from the wall and stepping back into place.

"Push forward!" I yelled through the strain of the oncoming torrent that followed. We marched slowly into the storm, each step a battle. Tactics raced through my mind as I tried to spot any break or gap in the Forsaken line. I had thirty feet to figure it out, which was closing fast as both sides stepped toward each other. The red wall and dark shadows behind looked impenetrable. We hadn't expected a mirrored tactic like this. None of the simulations ever formed shield walls. Nobody told us they even had shields. I didn't love our chances at that distance. They were too powerful and chipping away at us fast. Barry, a human, dropped next to me, blood spraying down my side. The line compressed together, stepping over his corpse. Getting in close was our only chance.

"What are we doing here, Sarah?" Jiro grunted.

Flak's words echoed in my head. *Your mind is gonna try to get cloudy, isolating what's directly in front of you. Don't let it.* I saw a large fragment of the tram to my right, about the size of a Volkswagen Beetle. The breacher was also a large piece of machinery that could do some damage if aimed the wrong way.

"Cash! Think you can send that for a ride?" I asked, leaning into my shield and nodding at the wreckage.

Cash glanced over at it and then looked back at me with a wide-eyed smile. "I can give it a shot!"

"Do it! Phalanx collapse on me as soon as it goes! Hoo!"

"Hoo!"

Cash rolled sideways, bracing his shield between himself and the wreckage and pumping his Tempest muzzle into the side of the car-sized debris, clanking together his melt shot.

BOOM!

The blast launched Cash backwards out of sight, but it also rocketed the twisted metal forward in a haphazard tumble through the air. It crashed into the Forsaken line, smashing two of them out of the way and opening up just the gap I needed. My shot rippled across the space and crumpled one of the breacher's tripod legs. It teetered sideways and pivoted. The massive glowing pistons extended violently and crushed two more Forsaken against the wall in a gory crunch. My flanks curled into an arrow behind me as we stormed forward to exploit the hole. It was like colliding with a brick wall at the moment of impact.

Once inside the line, a whirlwind of chaotic blue, green, and red blasts encircled us. Grunts of exertion and shouts pierced the rough, jarring sounds of combat, armor grinding on armor. Hot veins of light singed hair and sent streaking lines across our vision. Spurts of blood splashed across. Even through the cooling effects of our suits, sweat poured down my face. Sickening crunches and squelches sounded as impacts broke through armor, flesh, and bone. The breacher, now on its side, relentlessly hammered the wall and Forsaken pulp.

BANG! BANG! BANG!

They might have been significantly larger, but we were faster.

I got a shot off, searing a hole through the chest of one enemy soldier. I slammed forward as something crumpled into my back, my rifle snapped out of my hand as I collided with the wall. In a flash my pistol replaced it, the energy blade searing and slicing into an armored leg. Almost immediately, I heard a *schink*, like the sound of a blade across a whetstone, and the leg writhed and flailed away, collapsing the brute onto his side. I put one through its head without hesitation. The strange thing was, I knew my blade hadn't made it deep enough to cause any major damage, just enough to pierce the plating. I didn't have time to dwell on it as a large obsidian arm came crashing down toward my head. I got my forearm up just in time to deflect the blow but lost my pistol in the process. I blocked a second one much more solidly.

"Aagh!" My left arm raged with pain and tingled sharply. It was probably broken, but I swung my right arm around to glance off another axe-chop swing, this time a sharp edge of the plating slicing open a deep gash across my cheek below my eye. I felt the blood dripping freely down my face as I crouched low and fed a rapid-energy punch with my right to the side of my attacker's knee, which brought him down to my level. Twisting my hips, I swung my injured left hand around as hard as I could, connecting with its helmet and feeling the crunch in my own arm. Its head shook, obviously stunned, and I brought both my hands back up to finish the job. My palms connected on each side of its face with as much energy as I could muster. The helmet caved in like a tin can, and red blood shot out of the top. The blood arced in slow motion in front of my eyes, and within milliseconds it tarnished black. I spun around as a large mechanical hand gripped me by the throat, choking me. The squeeze tightened as I dropped to my knees, the edges of my vision darkening. I looked up helplessly as the final strike fell.

Suddenly, a stutter. A flash of brilliant light. Half a dozen well-placed shots tore my opponent to shreds. The iron grip slackened, and I dropped onto my back, sucking in several painful breaths. The air licked down my throat like fire. Then everything went quiet. The energy blasts stopped, as did the breacher and all other movement. I rolled onto my hands and knees. Hesitant to look up and see just how hard we had been hit, I winced, all at once feeling the various traumas to my body. I felt drained, weak.

Cash rushed over and helped me to my feet. "Sarah, you OK?" he asked, giving me a once-over.

"Yeah." I glanced around the tunnel's end. Half my team was gone. Bell sat up against the wall with Tariq pressing some med-skin around her leg, dark blood oozing around the edges. Karen's left eye was swollen and bloody, but she had already gone over to work on the door console. Considering how outnumbered we had been, we were lucky. I limped over a couple of feet, cradling my left arm, and picked up my pistol, clicking it onto my leg. Cash fished my rifle out of a pile of bodies and handed it to me. I tried to hold it but couldn't support the weight on my left hand.

"Sarah, your arm's probably broken. Let me look at it," Cash said, digging into his sling bag.

"I'm fine. Start getting that door open—"

"Karen's already on it. It'll take her a few minutes." He pulled out a metallic sheet of med skin and wrapped it around my forearm.

"It's going to disable my sleeve display if—"

"You'll manage. You need to be able to shoot more. Also . . . this is going to hurt," he said as he primed some energy into the pad. It compressed tightly and hardened. I sucked wind as the pain flared up again.

"Son of a bitch." The pain faded as the limb stabilized, but my hand still felt weak and tingly.

"You want a jolt?"

"I got it." I pulled a jolt shot off my bandolier and jabbed it into my leg. The stim tore through like a full-body submersion in ice water. The burst also took some weight off my body. I had barely noticed the increased gravity through the pain, but re-energizing my tech lightened the load. I looked up at Cash. "Did you get through that without a scratch?" I asked, noticing how unscathed he looked.

"Well, I think I might've bruised my ass a little bit on the knockback."

"Lucky bastard," I said as we both shared a tired chuckle. We were quiet for a moment.

"If only we had all been that lucky," he said with a tight-lipped frown as he glanced around. There was so much carnage. Black and crimson blood swirled together and pooled against the large failsafe doors like a reservoir to a dam.

"See if anyone else needs patching up. I'm gonna check on the door."

"Roger that," he said, leaving my side. I closed my eyes and took a few deep breaths to steady myself, then stepped through the tangle of bodies to reach the door panel Karen was working on.

"How's it coming?"

"They fried it pretty good, but I'm working around it. Five minutes, tops," she said, digging through the gel circuitry behind the panel.

"OK. You good?"

"That was fucked up, but yeah, I'm good," she said, clenching her jaw and nodding.

I walked over to Jiro, who was sitting on the backs of two Forsaken husks. Out of everyone, he looked the least rattled. As I approached, he tucked a pinch of synthetic tobacco into his lip and offered me the tin.

"No, thank you," I said, waving it off. Will and Frank often partook, much to my chagrin. "All the buzzworthy effects of the real thing minus the cancer," Will would say. Jiro spit out a large dark gob, right on the helmet of one of the Forsaken, making a metallic *ding*.

"Hey, can you help me?" he asked, standing up and walking over to another Forsaken body. "Peele's under here," he said, crouching to roll off the enemy dead. I knelt down to help, though my damaged arm made it difficult. The body was too heavy for the two of us. Jiro stood and stared, scratching his head.

"We'll get him out in a—" Suddenly, he snapped off his Tempest and fired several rounds through the Forsaken's middle, gruesomely cutting it in half. The enzyme-reduced mush inside spilled out with a nauseating stench. He holstered his rifle and smiled at me.

"That will do it." He leaned down and dragged the top half off Peele's body. I glanced around. Everyone else stood there motionless, watching him. Jiro walked around and cleared the lower half. Peele's body was underneath, half crushed with dozens of lacerations revealing fractured bones. Jiro reached down and grabbed his arms. "Well, take the feet." I glanced at the others and then lifted Peele's body with Jiro. I heard several sickening crunches, and his legs hung strangely in my hands, like a bag of gravel. I had to swallow several times to keep from vomiting. We walked him to the side, stumbling over the dead, and then laid him apart from the rest.

Cash and Tariq picked up Seraph, another Lumenarian, and brought her body over. We gathered the rest and laid them in a line. Seraph, Peele, Tar, Barry, Steve, Creek, and Cory, all gone. Steve was in pieces. The only way we knew it was him was by process of elimination. We did this in silence and then stood back, staring down at our fallen.

"Door's ready," Karen said quietly. We turned from our departed comrades and walked over to the door.

"Position on the sides," I said. "They don't know it's us, and no one on Stormwater will have our language patch yet or know what we look like. Cash, you're talking when the doors open." Cash nodded, and we took up our positions.

I signaled Karen and she opened the doors. The barrier clunked and whirred as the partially melted locks were forced apart. Then the two sides creaked and whined, grinding metal on metal as they started to separate. The moment a gap opened, a salvo of emerald blasts peppered through.

"Hold your fire! Hold your fire!" Cash yelled. "Union forces here!" The shots petered out, and we heard faint voices murmuring on the other side. The doors ground to a halt, open just enough for three or four abreast to pass through. Cash stuck his hand out and then leaned into the opening. "You're safe now. We've come to take you out of here." He held up his hands, gesturing for whoever was on the other side to stop. "Before you come out, there are humans with us, from Earth. Arthur brought them. Our new allies. Don't shoot them." Cash glanced over at me. "Trust me, you would regret it," he said with a tired smile. Then he gestured for me to come over.

I cautiously stepped into the shattered doorway and looked inside. I had to fight not to gag from the smell that greeted us. Sweat and waste and festering wounds and death stewed over the last few weeks of captivity.

"We're here to help," I said, trying to suppress a grimace brought on by the stench. The survivors stared back at me with a look of fascination and fear. I was the first human they had ever seen. Around 2,000 of them were crammed in the main mining chamber. They all looked exhausted and beaten; but each one was a light, a small justification for the dead who paved the way. My fallen gave it all for something, not just an empty room of bones and blood.

"It's time to get you out of here," I said. They just stared blankly back at me. Cash leaned over.

"They can't understand you yet."

"Right. Well, tell them it's time to go." I shook my head to clear the fog. Even with the jolt shots, my mind felt sluggish.

The others stepped out to reveal themselves. Tariq was not subtle about the smell. "Holy shit! That's the worst thing I've ever smelled." He glanced over at Cash and me, holding his nose. "What? You just said they couldn't understand us."

"Cash. You, Jiro, and Karen take point," I said. "Start moving them out. Tariq, Bell, and I will bring up the rear."

"Roger that."

I stood at the doors, ushering the mass of Lumenarians forward. Aliens of all ages staggered out, each one several inches shorter and quite a bit stockier than the Lumenarians we'd encountered so far; effects from the increased gravity. The children stared up, wide-eyed, their scaly tails flicking nervously behind them. Parents held the children's hands, pulling them along. They bowed their heads and thanked us, some even reaching out to touch us, placing their hands on our foreheads in the Lumenarian way or simply grazing their fingers along our arms and shoulders. We nodded and bowed and kept them moving with as gentle a push as possible. Half the battle was over. Now we had to get them out of there.

"They're so small. I thought they would be bigger," one of the survivors said as they passed.

"They're very strange looking," another commented.

"Cash, you want to tell them that we can understand them even if they can't understand us?" I said through comms.

"Roger that."

I shook my head and looked down the line. "Delta 3-0, this is 2-0. Survivors coming your way."

CHAPTER XXVII

Hellhound

- WILL -

When the elevator doors to the mine atrium finally opened, we were greeted by the anxious chatter of the 1,100 survivors huddled throughout the large chamber, up the stairs, and on the balcony. It had been hard to tell how many were down in the mine; but crowded in the forum, it made it seem like a stadium-full. As the group took notice of us, silence spread through the room, every eye glued in our direction. I saw the topside teams staring, some with mouths slightly open and the odd one with tears in his or her eyes. We must have been a ragged sight. The tattered leftovers. Twenty-three down into the mines, eight back up. Miguel and I helped Ford to his feet, supporting his weight under his shoulders—the lone survivor of his team. We stepped off the elevator with Megan, Ice, Crane, Jackson, Terra, and the straggling few Stormwater militia we'd recovered. The civvies parted silently to let us through. Tank double-timed up with one of Tex's guys, Freeman, and took Ford from us, setting him down on the side and going to work patching him up. I knew where Ford was; I'd been there. As bloody as he looked (and he was right fucked up), the worst wound wasn't going to be physical.

Sea waded through the bodies and stopped in front of me, giving me a once-over and closing her slack mouth. "Will, are you—"

"Rig the elevators, and send them back down." I didn't care if the bombs killed them all. However many Forsaken were left from Ford's tunnel were going to be buried alive down there. Sea stared for a moment and then nodded, brushing past me.

As we limped through the masses, the survivors reached out to take our hands or just touch us as we passed. Each brush was like a blade in my mind, a reminder that they were alive, and so many of my team were not. No amount of gratitude could lessen that feeling because in the end, the Stormwater survivors were just a number and a blank set of features. A job. An objective. I didn't know them. I didn't really give a fuck about them compared to my own people.

At the large main doors, Fred and Tex huddled together going over a holo display. The relentless pounding of enemy fire outside had slowed to occasional exploratory strikes. Apparently, they had given up trying to break through with brute force. They knew our only way out was through the doors. They just had to wait. I glanced over and saw Jeremy off to the side, propped against a wall. He was unconscious but breathing.

Tex looked up as I approached. "Shit, Will. You need Tank to—"

"He's looking after Ford." I felt blood dripping lazily off my flayed left hand. The sinuous metal fibers of my biotech, like braided steel cable, were exposed along the palm and inside of my fingers. A spasm twitched it, and I saw a quick spark of blue. I clenched my fist and ground my teeth. "Jeremy?"

Fred and Tex glanced at each other. "Lost a lot of blood, but he's stable for now," Tex said. "Tank did a good job."

"Good."

"Will, you need—"

"Update." Tex shook his head slowly, and Fred just stared. "Update. Now."

"The outer battalions aren't having much luck getting through the city. Heavier resistance than anticipated," Fred said, sounding dejected that he didn't have better news for us after our ordeal, but I got the feeling that wasn't the icing on the cake yet.

"And?" I felt the heat rising in my belly and chest and knew my tech lines hadn't stopped flaring since the mines.

"Three Forsaken ships dropped into orbit thirty minutes ago," Tex said. "They must've been staged close by. All the drones are occupied with that, so we have no air support." I stared at them for a moment. That was worse than I had expected. Shit on shit on shit. I couldn't help but chuckle, probably to prevent my mind from snapping.

"Enemy forces outside?"

"Our snipers above have been picking away at them, but still a full company, give or take," Sea said, arriving at the group. So, over a hundred, maybe two. Awesome. Despite the shitty situation, it made our next objective pretty clear. Help wasn't coming.

I switched my comms to the orbital frequency. "*Albatross* Command, this is *Albatross* Charlie Bravo 1-0."

There was a slight delay, but then the operator replied. "Bravo 1-0, go for *Albatross* Command."

"We're not going to make it to extraction Alpha." It was a hard thing to say out loud, knowing the way forward meant wading through a pile of bloody shit without the help of the outer battalions. The other squad leaders slumped slightly upon hearing it. "Bravo 1 squads will secure the local square for hot shuttle exfil. Have smaller birds prepped for twelve hundred survivors. Thirty minutes. Copy?" Tex, Sea, and Fred looked at me, surprised. Sure, the square was right outside, but it was going to be a bastard to secure and tenuously held if we did manage to lock it down. It wasn't big enough to land a shuttle capable of getting us all out at once, and time was not on our side with the battle raging above our heads.

Again, there was a delay in the response from the *Albatross*. Either because they were exceptionally busy or they understood the task ahead of us. "*Albatross* confirm."

"Copy 1-0. Shuttles inbound to your location in three zero minutes."

I switched comms back to local and looked up at my squad leaders. "If I thought there was another way, I'd take it," I said, looking each of them in the eye.

"Thirty minutes seems a bit tight," Fred said.

"Well, if we can't get it done in thirty, we're not getting it done. Three enemy ships in orbit means they might be getting reinforcements down here, and who knows how many more might be nearby. We hit them now, and we hit them hard." It was no time to second guess or falter. We had one chance, and every second of it was going to suck.

"You got a plan?" Tex asked with forced enthusiasm. I huddled them in close and pulled up the holo display of the square outside.

I stood with my back to the main doors, running a play-by-play over and over in my head of how I wanted the attack to go. Of the fifty-nine Lumenarian and human soldiers I had brought with me, only forty remained. Jeremy was out cold, and it was touch and go whether he would even make it. Ford was too broken and shell-shocked to risk bringing along, and Ice's leg was shredded enough that his lack of speed and mobility could be an issue. Of the available thirty-seven, I left four behind to look after the civilians and muster the Stormwater militia on the remaining upper floors of the tower to provide cover fire and sniper opportunities through the small windows into the square. The tower wasn't high enough to provide a great vantage down on the surrounding buildings, but it was better than nothing and maybe just enough to buy us the precious seconds we needed. I knew the clock was ticking as I stared out at the thirty-three geared to go. No one was a hundred percent, the remainder of my Bravo 1 squad least of all, but I needed everyone who could hold a rifle and move relatively well.

The civvies crammed as close to the edges of the atrium as they could, leaving an open path for us in the middle and to avoid any direct shots that would come through the doors when they opened. It was eerily silent in the echoey chamber. Everyone stared expectantly.

I dug my finger into my right chest pocket and felt the outline of Maria and Evie's picture, a small steadying force. Also in the pocket was my dud pistol round, a sort of *Memento Mori* totem. So, no time like the present. "You know I tell you how it is. Always have and always will. This is no exception," I said, looking at all the nervous, tired faces and trying to meet as many eyes as I could. They all seemed deflated. Hopeless. I exhaled slowly and focused on keeping my voice strong, steeling my gaze. "So, this is how it is…shitty. But I'm not worried. They're the ones who should be scared. What we do, we do like no others. And when we go through these doors, they're gonna learn that the hardest fucking way of all." Any lowered eyes slowly looked up, and a few nodded determinedly as they listened. "We're the good guys, but right now…right now I want the baddest motherfuckers the universe has ever seen. I want killers. Demons. I want fucking hellhounds." Maybe I'd seen too many war movies as a kid, maybe I was convincing myself, or maybe I knew the value of a group of soldiers who believed they were the meanest SOBs in the field. Sometimes they just needed a reminder. "I want blood. No stopping, no hesitation, no mercy."

"Hoo!" they shouted as one, causing a slight waft of obsidian dust to drop from the framework of the doors. Just what I was hoping for. In an instant the fear on their faces was replaced with a determined fire. A switch had been flipped.

I turned to face the entrance as my platoon fell in tight behind me. Slipping a jolt shot out of my bandolier, I injected it into my leg. Every tech line erupted in blue fire, and I felt it course through my eyes. Arthur had insisted I be a beacon.

"Shields." With uniformed precision, the shields were drawn in a flash of blue and green. Everyone was pulsing, ready to go. I exhaled slowly and spoke into my comms, signaling the contact upstairs. "Bravo 4-9…now."

The attack began in the upper floors with the militia and remaining members of our team showering the enemy with a relentless bombardment. A cascading series of BOOMS echoed outside.

I counted to five in my head and then nodded to the civvy who we had designated to operate the entrance. Daylight flooded through the opening doors in a brilliant glare that cut a strip through the atrium's dim atmosphere, reflecting off our shields in a dazzling kaleidoscope of colors. Then the wave of heat hit us. The sunlight hours scorched the temperature to over 50° Celsius (metric won in space). It felt like our lips were already starting to crack, the moisture being sucked from our skin.

Before our eyes could adjust, we were running down the steps of the mine. A large shadow crossed overhead as the massive hundred-foot miner's statue teetered over, the base crumbled by melt shots from my overwatch teams. It veered left in a lumbering fall, picking up speed. The top third connected at the lip of the east building rooftop with a ground-shaking rumble, sending a cloud of dust rushing across the square.

The rear fire team of three peeled off and split in two, ducking behind the two massive pillars that adorned the front of the building and firing up into the building tops. Once clear of the steps, our armored column divided into three smaller groups; twelve, twelve, and my remaining six. Being the smallest team, we cut to the closest building entry off to the right side. A crimson salvo rained around us, and explosions thundered shockwaves into our flanks.

I caught a glimpse of Fred's squad rushing a small fire team of Forsaken at the adjacent street, catching them off guard with the blitz. No stopping, no hesitating, no mercy. *Good job, guys.*

The second we slammed into the wall next to our target, Megan patched a breaching charge onto the door and took position. I nodded, and the breach ignited. Like a well-choreographed dance, we were in the first room. Thankfully, it was clear. We had rehearsed moving through these buildings as a contingency several times and knew the layouts like the back of our hands, though we had more numbers in the scenarios. The structure was a factory for mining equipment, and it was relatively open once we were inside. It'd be two more rooms through a reception area, an office, then a hallway, then the machining floor that rose three levels with a mostly open plan, apart from the equipment. Two lifts were along our route that we'd disable, so support from the top couldn't loop down behind us. Then we'd proceed to the south stairwell that accessed the roof.

The next two rooms through the hallway and into the factory floor were vacant. We covered Megan while she placed the charges on the first lift. I scanned the room, looking between the large high-tech laser CNC machines and presses.

"Ready," Megan announced as she linked the explosives to her forearm band.

"Second lift, let's go," I said. We folded together and moved toward the next objective. When we were about thirty feet away, the second elevator descended, and five Forsaken offloaded into the room. "Down, down," I whispered. Everyone ducked behind the machinery and waited. Simultaneously, the first lift shot to the roof. It paused at the top and then started dropping toward the machine floor. "Megan, blow one."

BOOM!

The first lift exploded behind us, incinerating the Forsaken inside. I popped up and picked off the lead Forsaken moving toward us. Crimson blasts tore past me and peppered the equipment around me.

"Flank right!" I yelled. We leapfrogged from cover to cover, closing the distance, as Miguel, Jackson, and Crane pushed to the right and forward along the side of the room. A well-placed grenade from Terra took out two, Jackson got another, and Miguel finished the last while it was firing at Megan and I.

"Clear!" Miguel called. With the second charge placed, Megan blew the last elevator, and we were on our way to the south stairs. The steps switch-backed up in the long, high rises and runs that we had gotten used to from Lumenarian architecture. We climbed in single file with rifles raised and pivoted around the corners in sharp, aggressive turns.

By the fifth flight, the alarm raised by the enemies dispatched on the factory floor showed its consequences. A wave of reinforcements came trundling down, ten in all. But as we'd seen in the mines, their size proved a disadvantage in the tight spaces. I collided with the first in line, ducking and taking out its knees, catapulting it over my back, the flailing body shredded mid-air by the rest of my team. It was a close game of speed and brutality from there. We hacked with the energy blades of our Warthogs and let loose with our Tempests, sometimes both at the same time. We were so squeezed in that corridor, body against bloody body, that it became like fighting underwater or some brutal rugby scrum, straining through the walls of armor and dead underfoot.

Half choked between the wall and a heavily plated Forsaken shoulder, I saw a large leg thrust forward in a vicious front kick. It caught Terra in the sternum with a bone-shattering crunch, caving in her chest and launching her backwards down the stairs. She seemed to move in slow motion as she flew through the air, black blood spraying from her mouth. She hit the landing with a thud and a screech as her spine guard scraped along the floor. Her head connected with the wall, snapping her neck in a final crack that I could hear through the fray. All four of her eyes stared blankly up at me. I punched furiously at the face of the body pinning me. It shifted just enough that I could get my other arm out. I brought my pistol to the back of the Forsaken's head and eviscerated it in a messy pop of bloody mulch and twisted metal. As the body fell away, I looked up into the barrel of an arm cannon. The red energy spooled in the chamber, and I felt its heat as it glowed against my face.

A sharp PHHT sound echoed in my ears. Then the arm shook and dropped away. Miguel had seared a hole clean through another Forsaken and into the one that was about to execute me. Behind the tinted eye slit of the Forsaken's helmet, I saw the enzyme swirl and melt away the tissue beneath. In the dark I caught a glimpse of two widened scarlet eyes staring out from inside before they succumbed to the acid soup. The body collapsed onto the pile at our feet.

"Making a habit of that," I said with a nod to Miguel as we looked down the stairs at Terra crumpled below. Crane stepped over the bodies and went to Terra's side, placing her hand over Terra's eyes. Another fallen comrade to add to the list we'd have to grieve later. I didn't want to rush the moment, but I had to.

"Crane. We gotta go."

The remaining steps to the roof were vacant, the enemy probably assuming those reinforcements would be enough. They were wrong, and we'd make them pay for underestimating us.

The roof was about a hundred meters long and sixty or so wide, flat with raised pony walls around the outside, giving it a large rooftop-patio appearance—well, a patio with no shade, vicious heat mirages, and thirty or so Forsaken soldiers huddled around the edges that lined the square. Five versus thirty. Awesome. There were only three points of cover along the surface: the structure that brought the stairwell to the roof and the two others for the elevators. Our only advantage was surprise.

The door from the stairs opened away from the enemy. Proceeding in a diagonal line from lift structure to lift structure would keep us out of sight from most of them. The problem was, while taking cover, many leaned with their backs against the ledge looking in our direction.

"Bravo 4-9, 1-0," I whispered into comms.

"Go for 4-9."

"Hold fire on west rooftop."

"Hold fire. Confirm?"

"Confirm. Divert salvo south and east."

"Roger. Copy." The concentrated fire from the upper floors of the tower stopped and cut across the square. Taking the bait, most of the enemy rose from their dug-in positions to fire on the tower.

Staying low so we weren't visible to the other rooftops, we darted from the midway cover and ran laterally to the cover nearest our targets. I signaled to prime grenades. After the mines we had divvied up supplies with the surface teams, so everyone would have more or less equal equipment for this assault, resupplying our all but exhausted ordinance.

I glanced between the members of my team. "Make them count," I said. We lobbed the grenades in a high arc along the enemy line. "Team 4-9, resume fire west. Give them hell." As the supporting fire resumed, the grenades exploded, and we were around the cover. It was a slaughter. The enemy was caught between two brutal onslaughts as they panicked, rising from their cover to engage us or second guessing their targets and firing blindly. We didn't falter a step, pressing forward with savage sapphire and emerald blasts. The grenades killed many, disoriented more, and we finished the rest. The result was carnage. Torn husks and limbs strewn haphazardly along the edge of the roof with black blood splatter. The few who tried to crawl away to cover were gunned down mercilessly as we dominated their position.

The kitty-corner building top, still controlled by the enemy, concentrated their attack on us, forcing us to duck behind cover again. I stole a glance between shots to assess the situation. The rooftop directly across the square had just been captured by Sea and Tex's amalgamated squad, and I counted nine of their team securing the objective. I looked over at Fred's team's target, but there was no sign of them.

"Bravo 5-0, 1-0 come in," I said. "Bravo 5-0, 1-0 copy? Fred come in." No response. I glanced at Miguel, who shook his head. "Fred, come on, buddy. Let me know where you're at." Still nothing. "Fuck." I glanced around frantically. We were already stretched so thin. An incursion into the last building would be nearly impossible while keeping our captured positions secure.

We skirted along the roof edge toward the southeast corner of our building. We played a matching game of whack-a-mole with the forces holding the building, but we weren't getting far. The mine tower was at the farthest point across the square, so their support didn't count for shit except to prevent the enemy from getting too cocky, which helped a bit. Our western building and Sea and Tex's eastern unit could keep the twenty or so of the enemy tamped down, but we needed it cleared to bring the shuttles in. We were out of time.

Shuttles all over the city were doing runs to and from the surface, extracting survivors or teams from different zones. Red dots pelted into the air, hunting their trajectories to take them down. That meant those engagements being freed up could rally enemy reinforcements to us. Our evac would be showing up in five minutes, ready or not. If we weren't ready, they'd be diverted elsewhere, and we'd have to hold the hostile area for even longer—provided the orbital ships could hold out that long. Looking into the sky, that was a serious concern. We saw the dim sparks of combat in space and the sunlit silhouettes of the massive warships, both Union and Forsaken, like daylight moons. There was as much chaos up there as there was down where we were by the look of it, maybe more.

"Will, we have got to get those fucking ticks off that building!" Miguel yelled from down the wall. I looked at the gap between the buildings. From the parapet walls, the outside edge of the roof sloped down toward the street, overhanging slightly. The space between was around twenty feet. *Shit.*

Then the first welcome transmission since we'd gotten down there crackled over my comms. "*Albatross* Charlie Bravo 1-0, this is Delta 1-0, copy," Kilo said.

"Delta 1-0, Bravo 1-0. Good to hear your voice, buddy," I replied. I wanted to ask if Sarah was with him, if she was alright, but I couldn't. Not yet. The answer could break me.

"Heard you guys needed some support. Delta 1 and 4 squads en route to your position." Hearing the broadcast, my team smiled with relief. Sarah was Delta 2-0. Why wasn't she with them? I shook away the thought. Could be any number of reasons.

"Roger that. We could use ya. ETA?"

"Ten minutes. Quickest we can do." My team's faces fell as we heard this, knowing it would be too late.

"Ten minutes. Copy." I looked to either side. My team looked crest-fallen. Jackson reloaded his rifle with a new clip and hurled the old one across the roof. I tried to muster as much confidence as I could despite a feeling of creeping dread. "Alright, guys, we knew it wasn't going to be easy." They nodded. "Don't suppose you can jump twenty to thirty feet, huh, Crane?"

"Not without a serious boost," she said. Jackson started laughing, and for a moment I thought he had snapped. Ruby blasts peppered the lip of our cover and zipped overhead. Then Miguel and Megan started chuckling too. Jackson's laughter was infectious, but we didn't know why. I couldn't help but join in. "What?" Crane asked, confused.

"I don't know," Megan said through her laughter.

"I just…I just pictured…" Jackson choked out the words "I pictured us locking our fingers together and trying to pick a Lumenarian up, like boosting fucking Shaq." He laughed harder, to the point of rapidly evaporating tears. It was kind of stupid, but the image was funny. Another one of those strange moments during conflict where those involved seemed completely detached from it all.

"Shut the fuck up, Jackson," Miguel said, trying to stifle his own laughter. Four minutes left until the shuttles arrived.

Crane stood to send some fire back toward the enemy. Suddenly, a large blast hit the wall in front of her, fracturing debris into her face. She writhed on the ground, holding her face. Jackson, who was nearest, crawled over and tried to get a look at her injuries. Any trace of laughter ended immediately.

"Jackson?"

He managed to pry Crane's hands away and look at her face. "She'll be OK," he said with an urgent nod, then continued to apply first aid. *Fuck, fuck, fuck.*

A boost… I froze as the idea formed in my head. It was fucking crazy, even for me, but it could work. Maybe…yeah, it could work. "Megan, you have any charges left?"

"One," she replied.

"Sync it and toss it here." She dug it out of her pack, linked it with her forearm sleeve, and tossed it over.

"Will, what're you think—"

"Jackson, give me your kite shield," I said, cutting off Miguel's question. Jackson barely looked up from Crane as he flicked his cylinder over. The team stared, trying to figure out where I was going with this. I held off telling them. I didn't need to be told it was crazy. "Give me some space," I said. "Move down the wall."

I placed the explosive on the outer slanted edge of the roof, praying a stray shot wouldn't connect with it, and crawled back about fifteen feet from cover. I breathed in and out sharply trying to psych myself up. *Fucking hell. This is stupid. Really fucking stupid.* I saw Miguel cock his head to the side, starting to piece it together.

"Will…"

"Megan, have your finger on the button. Second I clear that ledge, blow it."

"Rodge. Wait, what—" I had already started my sprint toward the edge. I saw my team yelling in surprise and scrambling to cover me, realizing what I was doing.

"Will, no!" Miguel yelled just as my feet left the ground. As I leapt, I tucked my knees up, crunched myself into a ball, and fired up Jackson's shield in front of me and my own behind me, creating a blue bubble of protection.

BOOM!

Megan timed the blast perfectly, the impact propelling me like a missile across the gap. Halfway across, I dropped the rear kite and unclipped my pistol. It wasn't pretty as I flailed across the distance, and I'd like to say I landed with a graceful roll to my feet, but it was more like a sack of potatoes dropping from one story up.

The collision with the ground knocked the wind out of me as I did my best to position my shield between me and the enemy. Three quick blasts found their marks before I had to crouch and hide behind the shield. The Forsaken response hammered into me, sending me sliding back along the fine layer of black dust on the roof. The shield cylinder grew hot in my hand, and the strain to keep it energized forced a steady stream of blood out of my left fist. Though the tech looked like fire sometimes, it didn't usually feel like it, but it sure as shit did then. I was clenching my jaw so tightly that it felt like my teeth were going to crack. I wasn't going to say I regretted my decision, but it might not have been my best idea in terms of self-preservation.

Just above the enemy's heads I saw another blue kite flying over. Son of a bitch. I didn't think anyone would be dumb enough to follow me. I should've known better. The difference was, Miguel didn't use a det charge to propel him, only a grenade. His arc barely cleared the lip of the building, and he crashed into two Forsaken soldiers, a jumble of flailing arms and legs. But it worked. The sudden surprise was enough of a distraction to give me a break in the salvo. Miguel bashed out with his shield and hacked with his energy blade. I didn't even bother holstering my pistol on my leg. It fell to the ground, and in the same motion I drew my rifle, covering him as best I could. Ten left...eight left...six left... Then two of the enemy stood to attack, disregarding their cover, and were gunned down by the neighboring rooftops. I closed the distance to Miguel and dropped behind his shield, firing over his shoulder.

"I told you not to follow me!" I shouted over the fray.

"What? No, you didn't!"

"Well...I meant to!"

"Wish you had!" he yelled through a strained grin. Megan nailed a throw across the street gap, taking out two more. The last two fought hard, pairing up behind their own shields, staying low. Miguel tagged the shield bearer in the foot, causing him to dip his shield just enough for me to get a clean shot through his head. When he dropped, the last one looked down at his fallen comrade, accepting he was defeated. Surprisingly, he lowered his firing arm and stared at us. For the first time, I hesitated, staring back over at the massive dark form. Cornered, completely beaten, he slowly stood to his full height, heaving with deep breaths. An instant later, shots from both rooftops turned his body into bloody black pulp.

Everyone on the surrounding buildings stood and scanned the area. Miguel and I were breathing hard, sweating profusely. He punched me in the shoulder. "Crazy fuck."

"Hey, you're the one who followed me, dipshit." He shrugged. He couldn't argue with that. "Tex, grab two members of your team, and begin clearing the south building from the ground up. Miguel and I will work down to you," I said through comms.

"Copy that," Tex replied. I saw him point to two of his guys and hustle off the nearby roof. I looked at Miguel and exhaled through puffed cheeks as the first of our shuttles buzzed low overhead, birddogging the line.

"*Albatross* Charlie Bravo 1-0, this is *Albatross* shuttle Juliet 8-2 Sierra, copy?" the shuttle pilot's voice came in over comms.

"Juliet 8-2 Sierra, Bravo 1-0 copy. Square secure and ready for the first round of civilian exfil." I glanced at Miguel. It was a risk calling the site secure without having fully cleared the south building, but missing the shuttle could mean not getting off the planet altogether. That and at least the roof was secure. If some Forsaken were still holed up downstairs, we'd make sure they weren't for long.

"Roger that. Coming into to LZ," the pilot replied.

"Bravo 4-9, maintain overwatch position until civilians are clear," I said to the tower contact.

"Copy."

"Bravo 3-0, Ford you on?"

"This is Tank. Go for 3-0."

In the midst of things, I had forgotten Ford's status. "Have half the civilians and the injured ready to move as soon as those shuttle doors are open and escort out on first ride. Copy?"

"Copy."

"Well, not getting any younger," I said to Miguel, gesturing toward the roof stairwell access.

"Just the two of us, we can make it if we try, just the two of us...you and I," Miguel sang as we walked over.

I picked up my pistol and clipped it to my leg. "Kinda hate how good that sounded." Miguel chuckled as we positioned outside the access door. "Ready?" I asked. He nodded, and I tapped the door panel, opening the access.

The shade from the sweltering sun was an instant relief as we descended the stairs. The sweat was slippery and cool against our exposed skin and between the layers of our suits.

It didn't take us long to figure out what had happened to Fred's team. At the bottom of the second flight, past the first switchback, the bodies began. They had been so close to making it to the roof. The walls were spattered with the deep reds and blacks of Lumenarian, human, and Forsaken blood. Scorch marks from repeated energy blasts painted every surface.

The building started vibrating, and we heard the hum of the shuttle's thrusters as it lowered into the square outside. We both looked up instinctively as if we saw it descending through the walls.

"Bird clear. Bravo 3-3 begin exfil," Sea commanded over comms. I glanced at Miguel and nodded. It was good to have the extraction beginning, but I wanted to fully clear the building. We stepped carefully and quietly over the dead in case more of them were farther down. We quickly cleared the top levels as we dropped, but the farther down we went, the more dead we found. Ours and theirs.

The epicenter of the engagement was on the fourth landing, the heaviest loss of life piled high, twisted into a distorted, gory mass like someone had taken a torch and welded them together. Fred stared lifelessly up at us, his head resting on his left shoulder, his neck severed almost all the way through save for a few sinuous cords. He was sitting with his back against the wall, two dead Forsaken lying haphazardly across his legs. Didn't go down without a fight.

"Jesus Christ," Miguel whispered, staring at the carnage, his jaw clenched and his brow fixed in a hard scowl to hold back the emotion. I nudged him forward.

"We have to keep moving," I whispered. After a moment he nodded, and we pushed on, climbing over the bodies.

The dead became sparser as we descended the next flight of stairs. Probably the ones who had been rear of the main impact and so were targetable over the shield wall—if a shield wall had even been possible. Or they had been booted or thrown down the stairs like Terra. It didn't matter how; they were dead all the same.

The next landing's doorway led to a hall of residential suites, a long row of around a hundred units. We wouldn't clear each one, knowing that each dwelling would be locked via the resident's bio codes, and the Forsaken wouldn't have had a way to bypass that like we did. So, we would only take time to clear the doors that were blasted open.

At the entrance to the hallway, Miguel stepped across to position on the other side of the door from me. As he moved, the door burst open. The two sliding panels, like pocket doors that would normally open into cavities in the wall, were forced into the stairwell, smashing out of their housings. The impact connected with Miguel's shoulder and launched him into the opposing wall, knocking him unconscious. The heavy arm of a Forsaken swung at my head. I ducked it just barely and brought up my rifle. The second swing came down midspan on my Tempest and shattered the weapon. There was a brief shocked pause as I stared down at the fragments and the brute wound up for another assault. *Fuck.*

I dodged three more strikes, pivoting around the enemy's lumbering form. As I turned and brought up my pistol, another blow knocked it from my grasp. *Jesus, Will, hold onto your goddamn weapon!* One more dodge, and then the next hit I wasn't so lucky. His forearm caught me in the chest and levelled me. I groaned, rolling onto my stomach, and tried to crawl away. I felt the shadow of it spread over my body, moving in for the death blow. This was it. He had me dead to rights.

My hand scuffed beneath one of Fred's teammates and grazed a Warthog pistol. Grabbing it, I rolled and put one through the torso and one through my attacker's head. He dropped to his knees, giving me a quick glimpse of his fractured arm cannon, the only reason he hadn't executed me instantly, I guess. Then his body tipped forward and fell onto my legs with a near bone-crushing weight. Son of a bitch, it was heavy. I tried to heave it off, but I was too drained. I just sat there, breathing. Suddenly, I heard movement on the stairs below. I snapped up the pistol and took aim.

"Whoa! Will, it's us," Tex said.

I exhaled loudly and lowered my pistol. "Get this fuck off me." His three-pack hustled up the stairs, Philips aiming down the open hallway and Tex and Boomer helping me roll the body off my legs.

"Thanks. Take your team, and clear the hallway."

"Roger that. Let's go," he ordered his guys, moving through the breached door. I went to Miguel's side and shook him.

He stirred awake and looked around. "What...what happened?"

"Just saved your life," I said. "Don't worry about it." Blood was dripping down the side of his head from a gash where he connected with the wall. "You good?" I asked, offering him a hand up. He took it, and I pulled him to his feet.

"I'll be feeling that tomorrow," he replied.

I chuckled. "Tell me about it."

A minute later, Tex returned with his team. "All the residential units are secure. Building is clear."

"Copy that. Nice job. Let's get back to the roof and hold overwatch."

We trucked our way back over the dead to the roof. I hesitated at Fred's body—I didn't even know what my team's death count was. I picked up a stray Tempest from the pile. I didn't like taking a dead comrade's weapon, but I needed it more than he did.

Stepping back out into the blaring sun actually felt good. The heat was still oppressive, but it beat the tomb-like atmosphere of the stairwell. At least we weren't breathing in the metallic stench of blood, sweat, and shit from the bodies below. Our friends.

As we reached the edge of the roof, the first shuttle was lifting into the air from the center of the square, its load filled.

"*Albatross* shuttle Juliet 8-2 Sierra, this is Bravo 1-0. Status on second shuttle?"

"Second shuttle delayed 1-0. ETA ten minutes," came the crackly reply.

"Copy. Safe return."

"Thanks, 1-0. Good luck down there." The pilot signed off, then rose vertically into the air and dove forward in an aggressive arc toward orbit. Ten more minutes to hold out. Nothing was going to be easy for us.

We all stood at the edges of the roofs around the square, one from each detachment positioned on the far side of the buildings to watch for any Forsaken reinforcements making their way along the side streets. We were spread incredibly thin, but at least we were secure for the moment. We were more relaxed, having established some semblance of control, but we still scanned the horizon and access points vigilantly.

"Bangarang Bravo. Let's just stay sharp and ride this out until exfil," I said into comms.

"Roger that, sir," came several responses.

"We letting the Bangarang slide? Sounds like a potential nickname to me," Megan said from the other building.

"Naw. Doesn't quite fit," Jackson said.

"Reach'll do fine."

"That's not a nickname. That's just your name. Besides, you can't pick your own nickname. Defeats the purpose," said Alex, who we called "Tips," from Sea's building.

"How about...Fireball? You know, because of his tic-tacs and shit."

"You're missing the point, Boomer. It's gotta be organic," Megan said. "Like the way we call you Dumbass most of the time."

"Aaah, fuck you." The laughter echoed around the square.

"Hellhound," Miguel said, standing next to me. I glanced over and saw him nodding slowly.

Tex also nodded. "Hellhound. I like it." A few others echoed the sentiment around the square.

"Guess that's it then, Hellhound," Megan said over comms and then howled. Miguel jostled me and joined in. I couldn't help but chuckle and throw out my own howl. Hellhound it was.

A few moments after the howling died down, Jackson piped up. "You guys figure Delta squad's gonna claim they saved us when they finally show up?"

"Not a fucking chance."

"Oh, hell no!"

"This is Bravo's house!" came the bevy of responses around the ring. Miguel and I glanced at each other and chuckled.

"Hoo!" Miguel yelled across the square.

"Hoo!" I and everyone else echoed.

"*Albatross* Bravo 1-0, Delta 1-0. Copy?" Kilo's voice sounded in my ear.

"Speak of the devil," I said to Miguel. "Delta 1-0, Bravo 1-0. What's your 20?"

"Approaching southeast corner of the square. Where do you want us?"

"We've got the rooftops secured. Let's keep you guys down there and secure the side streets. Copy?"

"Roger. Copy. Recommend bolstering overhead cover of the side streets over here. We passed a battalion about half a mile back. Weren't heading this way, but if they figure out the other mines are already cleared, they might turn around."

"Roger that." I signaled to the rest of my team, except for our scout on the far side of the roof, to move over to the east corner of the building.

When ten more minutes of sun beating down on us had passed, I looked to the sky in search of our shuttle. Nothing. It was strangely quiet. A few ships were still running the gauntlet from the surface to orbit, but traffic was thinning, and so were the sounds of combat around the city. We must've been one of the last sites needing extraction. I double checked my forearm display. Yep, pushing twelve minutes since the first shuttle departed. I was getting a nervous, expectant feeling that something bad was coming.

"*Albatross* Command, *Albatross* Charlie Bravo 1-0," I radioed to orbit. No answer. I looked up. The space battle was still raging, specks of green and red in a constant electric dance between the dim shapes of the larger crafts. I wagered it couldn't go on much longer. The flashes of light against the Forsaken shields paled in comparison to the massive impacts against our own ship's defenses. The Union forces were taking a beating. Luckily, I still saw only three enemy warships. The *Pelican* and the *Chariot* had moved in closer to receive survivors and provide additional support to the *Albatross*, the *Shark*, and the *Eagle*. The five Lumenarian vessels held formation in a wide wedge, positioned aggressively against the hulking figures of the dark Forsaken prisms. It was frustrating to watch the battle from the ground—not that we could've helped; but we all needed to get up there so we could get the hell out of the Stormwater system. If push really came to shove, the ships would be forced to flee with us still down on the planet, but I hoped we still had some time before it came to that. "*Albatross* Command—"

"*Albatross* Charlie Bravo 1-0, this is *Albatross* shuttle Lima 6-4 Echo. I am inbound to your position. ETA two minutes." A cheer went through the square as the message was heard on all the comms.

I breathed a sigh of relief and paced along the roof. "Good to hear that, Lima 6-4 echo. We were starting to get worried."

"Roger that, Bravo. See you soon." We scanned the skies and saw our shuttle approaching in the distance.

"Alright, guys," I said into local comms. "I don't want to stick around here any longer than necessary. Bravo 4-9, start moving the civilians out of the atrium. Roof teams, as soon as that shuttle lands, hoof it down to ground level." All the teams replied, and we waited tensely. If shit was gonna go sideways, that was the moment.

A minute later the shuttle buzzed in and dropped down between the buildings, creating an updraft of black soot. Miguel patted me on the shoulder, smiling, and we turned to leave the roof.

"Will—"

"Bravo 1-0, heavy contact east!" Kilo's said through comms. The adrenaline tingle shot up the back of my neck as I darted back to the parapet. A large crowd of Forsaken had rounded a distant corner about 400 meters back and were marching on our position—possibly by tracking the shuttle to our location. They kept a steady pace but were progressing cautiously.

"Of fucking course," Miguel muttered.

"Sea, hold position until civvies are loaded," I said, since her corner and ours had vantage on that street. "Megan, Jackson, Crane, head down and support Delta squad." They confirmed and made their way off the west building. "Kilo, doesn't look like they have a lock on us yet. Hold your fire until they're two hundred meters out."

"Roger." I looked over at the mass of civilians rushing out of the mine entrance and into the back of the shuttle. We just had to slow the enemy down; we didn't have to finish them. Miguel, Tex's team, and I hunkered down, propping our rifles against the edge and aiming down the street. Tex and I set our sniper configurations and picked our targets. The others kept their rifles on assault. A particularly ugly brute at the front (I assumed they were all ugly fucks under their armor) had a bullet with his name on it.

When they reached 200 meters, we unleashed hell. My first shot split the lead's helmet down the middle, and a dark fountain spurted up between the halves. The Forsaken column divided in two and hugged the walls of the buildings along the street, trying to reorganize their advance. It was the safe move, but it also meant their return fire was limited.

"Civilians loaded, Bravo 1," the pilot said over comms a minute later.

I confirmed and turned to Miguel and Tex. "Let's get the fuck out of here. All Bravo teams move to ground level." We pulled out and sprinted down the stairs, hopping over the bodies and whipping through the bloody abandoned corridors.

As we opened the street-level door, red energy blasts rifled past. I leaned out and returned fire down the route. To our right, Kilo's team was huddled at the corner shooting down line. Miguel and I held the door, laying suppressive fire while we sent Tex, Boomer, and Phillips across the exposed gap to the shuttle.

"All you, buddy," I said to Miguel. He was about to argue that I should go first, so he could cover, but my look silenced him. He took several quick breaths to rally his courage and then sprinted across. My turn. I did the same psych-up as Miguel and then took off across the street, shots ricocheting off the ground around me. Once I cleared the danger zone, I crossed over to Kilo's squad with Miguel and Tex in tow and Sea joining up with us partway along.

Kilo shook my hand when I arrived at his side. "Good to see you, Will," he said with a relieved and tired smile. He had a black bloody streak across his face that split through one of his smaller peripheral eyes. A metallic patch covered the center of the wound, but the edges were visible. Apparently, they hadn't had a cake walk either. I glanced around at his team. Seyyal turned from firing around the corner and gave me a nod. She was bloody, but I wasn't sure what of it was hers, if any. What about Sarah? Was she alright? Everything slowed around me. My breath caught in my throat, and even through the chaos around us, I heard my heart pounding in my ears with heavy, painful beats. I feared the worst. Kilo noticed and leaned in closer. "She oversaw the extraction of our survivors and was on the first boat out. Got the call to support you guys after she was already in the air." I couldn't speak for a moment, the tight knot in my throat slowly letting go. I nodded my thanks and Kilo nodded back.

"Take your team and get to the shuttle," I said. "We got this." He stared at me for a moment and then glanced at the rest of my team, each member battered as bad or worse than them but with a determined and unwavering look on their faces. He knew why we wanted to be last out, why it was important, and he didn't argue.

"All Delta teams, fall back to shuttle now," he ordered, holding eye contact with me. They had done their job, and they had done it well. The enemy was still a hundred meters from the corner. It was the space we needed. Kilo's squads pulled out with us filling in to give them time to move. As soon as they reached the shuttle, Kilo radioed me to confirm they were safe aboard.

One last wave of suppressive fire, and then we turned and bolted. Halfway between the corner and the shuttle, crimson blasts darted around us. They had covered the distance faster than I gave them credit for.

"Echelon left! Return fire!" Miguel, Megan, Jackson, Sea, Tex, Boomer, Phillips, and I flipped around and peppered the corner. "Peel one!" Miguel rolled off the front of the stack and repositioned at the back, inching us closer to the shuttle.

"Peel!" Miguel shouted. Each of us hoofed it off the line in turn and went to the back. Suddenly, Phillips took a round to the gut, a bloody burst that cut him in half. His mangled torso grasped at the air for several moments before going limp. *Fuck this.* I primed my melt shot, hearing the BBs clank into the chamber. I felt my biotech surge, enveloping me in blue fire. I didn't even aim. The sapphire meteor tore across the space and ripped into the side of the building. The corner exploded and collapsed into the adjacent thoroughfare. The force of it surprised even me, and I felt the instant energy drain of it.

"Go...get to the shuttle," I said through labored breaths. That wouldn't slow them down for long.

Overhead another shuttle screeched past, trailing smoke and fire and keeling over in an uncontrolled barrel roll. Shit. I heard it crash a ways off. Smoke rose in the distance. It was all chaos. Nothing we could do for them now.

We crowded into the back of the bird and yelled that we were on. With a sudden lurch, even before the door was fully sealed, the ship jumped into the air. I squeezed to the side and pulled out a small display panel, having lost my folded display in the mines. Looking at the ground, I saw the Forsaken forces had recovered and were firing wildly at the bottom of the shuttle, a last-ditch effort to take out as many of us as they could. The shots reverberated off the bottom of the hull, but nothing penetrated. After a few tense moments and heavy booms, we were clear and rocketing in a steep arc toward orbit.

CHAPTER XXVIII

Broken Wing

- ARTHUR -

"*Albatross* command, this is *Albatross* Charlie Bravo 1-0," Will's voice echoed from the side of the command deck.

"Charlie Bravo 1-0, go for *Albatross* Command," Trig replied.

"We've reached the objective with heavy enemy resistance. I'm taking two squads into the mines for survivor extraction. Ground contact will be Charlie Bravo 2-0. Confirm?"

"*Albatross* confirms 2-0 contact. Good luck, Charlie Bravo 1."

I brought up a holographic display of Stormwater and expanded the globe to a four-foot diameter. The image revolved slowly, and bright lights sparked along its surface. We still could not bring Forsaken units up through scanning; however, our own teams speckled the world scarlet in highlighted conflict. The capital cities of Thresher, Cascade, Levee, and Bay City were ablaze with combat. There were other hotspots of activity, but those four were the main urban centers where *Albatross* crew had been deployed. Some of the smaller rural and outskirt mining facilities were relatively quiet, our team's transponders emitting emerald dots as they secured the sites. Thresher looked like a wildfire, which was to be expected. It was the largest city on Stormwater and the most likely to be overrun with Forsaken. It was also where Will and Kilo's teams had been sent.

"Harper, deploy drones to the surface. Focus support on Thresher and Bay City."

"Yes, Arthur." A cloud of green sparks rained down from orbit, filtering through the attack sites.

"The battalions are going to have a hard time securing routes to the extractions," Flak grunted next to me, the lights from the display reflecting in his eyes.

"There is still some time before our teams make it back to the surface with survivors."

"If there are any sur—"

"There are." I saw Flak stare at me, then nod and continue watching the hologram. We had both been quiet since the drop ships descended on Stormwater. As much as we wanted this chance to prove our new union's capabilities, we were worried. There would be nothing easy about today. We had been lucky only one Forsaken vessel was there when we arrived. I did not anticipate that luck to hold out.

"*Albatross* Command, this is *Albatross* Echo Lima 1-0."

"Echo Lima 1-0, go for *Albatross* Command."

"We have twenty-four hundred survivors ready for exfil at extraction Alpha 3-2." A cheer went through the command deck, smiles all around.

"Good work, Echo Lima 1. Retrieval boats en route to your position. ETA five minutes." Even Flak allowed a small lopsided smile as he looked over from the display. I was too anxious to do anything but nod.

"Nearly five hundred thousand total so far," Trig announced to the room. Despite my worry, things were going better than expected. We had arrived just in time.

"*Albatross* Command, this is *Albatross* Bravo Sierra 1-0," a voice said from Trig's console. It sounded lethargic and beaten.

"Go for *Albatross* Command, Bravo Sierra 1-0."

There was a small delay before he replied. "We have…five Yáahlian survivors at our objective. Requesting dust-off at our location," he said tiredly.

"Confirm, Bravo Sierra 1-0. Five Yáahlians? No Lumenarians made it into the mines?" Trig asked, glancing over to me.

Again, the captain hesitated to respond. "No…About three thousand made it into the mines…They're all dead. They only left the Yáahlians alive." The room froze, and I froze with it. Slowly, all eyes turned to me, seemingly searching for answers. I did not know what to say. The fact that the Forsaken had slaughtered thousands of our people while leaving the Yáahlians alive was ominous—unprecedented behavior as far as I was aware. The complete implications of such an action could not be known for certain, but it made me feel uneasy. It could not be good for us. "*Albatross* Command, status of retrieval?" the captain requested.

"Priority," I said with a nod to Trig, who nodded back.

"Retrieval inbound, Bravo Sierra 1-0. ETA five minutes," he replied.

"Copy, *Albatross* Command." The shadowy meaning of the report did not seem to be lost on anyone on the command deck, and I heard a collective drawn-out exhale as everyone set it aside to continue on with their work. I glanced at Flak, who stared at the holo display, then stole a look up at me, worry and uncertainty etched on his face.

"Have any of the Thresher teams reported in yet?" I asked, attempting to refocus on the tasks at hand. The scarlet glow of the city had barely dimmed despite the air support.

"Only two teams so far."

"Have the battalions draw back to the shuttles and attempt re—" The proximity alarms suddenly filled the room with a deep pulsing red. I waved my hands above my head. The domed display panels all around the command deck became translucent, as if we were suddenly standing in the void of space. Directly above us, three leviathan Forsaken warships loomed, their engine trails still shimmering a crimson hue behind them. Each one dwarfed our carriers. "Brace!"

The first shots thundered into us with the force of a high-speed shuttle crash, sending us lurching around the room. I clutched the command console and spread my feet for balance. The barrages came from all three ships, each a steady stream of devastating firepower. Swarms of arrowhead-shaped attack drones filled the air between and started looping around us and targeting our returning shuttles. Obsidian and scarlet darts flew in the thousands.

"Harper, turn to and return fire. Trig, call in *Pelican* and *Chariot* for support." I glanced down at the Stormwater projection and all the combative sparks. "Withdraw planetary air support." I saw Black look over at me. Everyone knew what that meant. "Do it now. Prioritize shuttle escorts." The ground teams were on their own for now. More booms echoed along the hull and rattled the room, the hydro shield absorbing most of the impacts but heavily compressing for others, the force crumpling in some of the outermost layers of the *Albatross*.

"We can't take this for long," Flak warned.

I nodded. "We will hold out for as long as we can."

"*Albatross* command, this is *Albatross* Charlie Bravo 1-0," Will said. I was getting worried they would not return from the mines at all.

"Bravo 1-0, go for *Albatross* Command."

"We're not going to make it to extraction Alpha. Bravo 1 squads will secure the local square for hot shuttle exfil. Have smaller birds prepped for twelve hundred survivors. Thirty minutes. Copy?" I knew thirty minutes would be difficult for them to achieve, but it was going to be even more difficult for us to hold out up above. Trig glanced at me. I felt the decision prickle uncomfortably in my mind, manifesting in the form of a slight tremor in my hands and arms that I tried to stifle by gripping the command console even tighter. Another blast jarred the room. Several of the crew glanced up at the displays, which showed the first signs of cracking.

"We don't have time, Arthur," Flak said. "We need to—"

"No." My son's face flashed in front of my eyes. Receiving the news about the destruction of Cerberus. The rage I had felt about them being left to die. "We are not leaving them."

"*Albatross* confirm," Will said. I nodded to Trig, and he turned back to his console.

"Copy 1-0. Shuttles inbound to your location in three zero minutes."

"The *Albatross* can take it," I said. "Harper, have the thread drive spooled and ready to go."

"Yes, sir."

Flak stepped around the command console and stood at my side. "Arthur, I know why you're—" He stopped himself and glared up at the display panels and the Forsaken onslaught. He exhaled slowly and stared into my eyes. "Thirty minutes. If they're not ready, we need to go." I looked back at the display and nodded. A shuttle transponder rose from Kilo's location and I knew they were waiting for one more. They were relatively close to Will's position. I isolated Kilo's comms planet side.

"*Albatross* Charlie Delta 1-0, this is *Albatross* Command," I said. There was a slight pause.

"*Albatross* Command go for Delta 1-0."

"Kilo, as soon as your wounded and last survivors are on their way, I want you to take two squads and rendezvous with Will's team. Copy?" Again there was a pause. I knew Kilo would not hesitate to help Will, but I was sure they had taken their own beating, and he was assessing whether they even could assemble an adequate support.

"Copy that. Delta squads will assist."

The Forsaken attack rose to a roaring crescendo as the hydro shield was increasingly taxed and drained. Each contact was a brutal collision, and the command deck rocked back and forth. Half the display panels were shattered from the strain and compression (beyond the limit of the nano-glass's self-healing), and sparks rained down in fiery waterfalls. Conduit gel oozed from some of the cracks.

"The last two shuttles are airborne. ETA five minutes!" Trig yelled. "Scratch that! Echo-Zulu squad shuttle is down!" Elora Bhele's squad—a bright eye gone. Only Will and Kilo's shuttle was left.

Hatcher's form flickered into view next to my command console. He was bloody and obviously braced against his own console. "Arthur—" The image flickered out and then back in. "We can't wait. We need to leave now," he said evenly, but I knew how urgent it was. Hatcher was a commander through and through. He could always be counted on. If he said they were finished, they were.

"Thank you for holding out this long," I said. "Go." He nodded, and the projection vanished. A moment later, the *Pelican* thread drive ignited, and they were gone, their spectral drive trail all that remained. With one less ship to target, more Forsaken artillery turned on the remaining four.

I glanced at the shuttle's arc racing up toward us. It cleared orbit and darted through the shrapnel cloud, zigging and zagging around the horde of Forsaken attack drones in pursuit. *Come on, come on!* I tasked several dozen of our drones to break off and defend it.

One minute out I saw a large explosion pierce the *Shark's* shield into the fore section, just off the thread drive's iris. If it would have been slightly to the portside of the ship, they would have been finished. We had waited too long.

"All Union ships jump now!" I ordered over general orbital.

One by one their thread drives lit up. First the *Chariot*, then the *Eagle*, and lastly, with an exceptionally bright green flash, the *Shark* all vanished. I did not know how much damage the *Shark* had taken, but at least they got away, leaving only empty space, debris, and thread trails where they once were. All three Forsaken ships rotated slowly to concentrate on us.

Suddenly, to our port side, two more obsidian cruisers flashed into view. There was a stunned silence as everyone on the command deck froze at the sight of them. Their intimidating forms were aimed directly at us. Bright crimson flared at their ports and focused in their cannons.

"Shuttle's on!"

"Go, Harper, go!"

I heard the thread drive hum and felt it vibrate violently.

BOOM!

A devastating planet-shattering impact tore into us. It felt like we had been ripped in two as we slammed haphazardly around the command deck. The power faded to a dim flicker, the few remaining intact display panels showing us the end. I looked up from the floor and saw another devastating scarlet blast descending toward us until it filled the frame.

CHAPTER XXIX

A Hellish Thing

- WILL -

"Come on! We've got to go!"

"I'll be there. Go—"

"Not without you!"

"Sarah!" I grabbed her arms and stared into her eyes, the pulsing red alarm and flicker of the fires dancing in their depths. "There's no time to argue. I need you to go. Now. I'll be there. I promise. Take as many of our people as you can and go. I don't give a shit if you have to drag them kicking and screaming."

"Will I—"

"I love you." I meant it. Felt it more than I'd felt anything in a long time. I know why it had taken me so long to say it, but in that moment, none of it mattered. Carpe fucking diem. Maybe it wasn't the best time to say it, but I thought I might not get another chance. And if there was anything that might shut her up, it was that. She stared back at me, her mouth moving but no words coming out. It was all in her eyes, and that was enough.

Another massive impact jarred the bay, knocking many off their feet. It was chaos. The thousands of Stormwater refugees dashed around in a panic, seeking any semblance of safety. The *Albatross* crew did their best to direct them through their own fear and confusion. Panels along the walls crumpled, filling the air with more bright sparks and acrid smoke. The scarlet alarm throbbed through it all, blaring its sharp, haunting racket. Unlatched cargo slid across the floor and dispersed people in its wake. I looked around, seeking the other members of my team, now scattered. Just then Kilo stumbled into us.

"Will, Sarah, what—"

"Kilo, you need to get everyone you can to the *Swift*. Now."

He glanced around in a daze. "But there's—"

"Kilo!" I yelled, grabbing his bandolier and pulling him in. "The *Albatross* is *dead*." The words seemed to hit him like a ton of bricks. I felt it too. Somewhere deeper than my chest. I swallowed hard and glared up at him. Another explosion rattled our footing, and we braced ourselves. "Tell any civilians you come across to use the lifeboats, and get as many of our crew down below as you can."

"You want to leave the civilians—"

"There isn't room. And we need fighters. They still have a chance in the pods—"

"They have no chance in the pods."

"I don't care!" Kilo and Sarah stared at me. I saw the shock and loss in their faces. I really didn't care. I felt everything coursing through me and flaring through my tech. All I knew for sure was that I would have sacrificed every one of the Stormwater survivors just to get Sarah and my team onto the *Swift*. One clear thought. One devastating thought. "Go. Now. That's an order."

"You can't order me," Kilo said.

"Then I'm begging you. Please." There was a tense stillness between the three of us, even with the chaos surrounding us. My heart pounded in my chest.

"Where are you going?" Kilo asked.

"To the command deck."

Kilo stared at the floor. Then, after a long silence, he nodded.

"I'll get our people down there." I pulled him into a tight hug. Then I turned to Sarah and pulled her into a deep passionate kiss, one I hoped would not be our last. I didn't want to separate. I wanted to hold her for as long as I could, but time was running out. We pulled back, and

I looked into her eyes. All her biotech lines were glowing bright blue, tears running down her cheeks. The whites of her eyes flashed sapphire for a moment.

"Your tic-tacs are showing," I said with a sad smile. I didn't wait to see if she would smile back. I turned away and bowed my head, looking anywhere but her eyes. "Go."

The corridors rocked and tilted like a small skiff in the middle of a hurricane, the Forsaken bombardment keeling us from side to side. Frantic crew sprinted past me as I made my way up the ship. I felt like a goddamn salmon fighting its way up a waterfall, pushing through a throng of terrified faces, human and Lumenarian. I did my best not to look at any of them directly. I didn't want to see their faces later. I knew what was coming.

The farther up I made it in the *Albatross*, the fewer crew I came across, and the more damage there was. Entire corridors were impassable due to collapsed debris, and navigating my way to the bridge was becoming a frustrating rat maze.

I reached another dead end. Several lumenium girders had smashed through the paneling, and the ship's gel lifeblood circuitry pooled around the wreckage, a dozen mangled bodies beneath it all.

"Codec!" I yelled. He materialized next to me, his electric stick figure form flickering in and out in the hallway.

"Will, it's all going dark."

"Jesus Christ, Codec. That's morbid as fuck. Get me a route to the command deck."

Codec froze and then blinked in and out several times. "Did you want to stop for a bite to eat along the way? I know you get cranky when your blood sugar is low."

"Just lead the fucking way, Codec." His form nodded and then turned down an adjacent passage. I took off after him at a steady clip. Codec stayed ahead, distorting and stuttering from one side of the hall to the other, forward and back, as we went. Another explosion thundered against the hull and sent me in a veering slant toward the wall. How much more could the *Albatross* take? I put my hands on a panel and felt her pulse, the heartbeat of the *Albatross*. Whether it was my imagination or her reaction to the damage, it seemed uneven and quick. I pushed off and continued down the passage.

Suddenly, everything went deadly still. The alarm still droned in eerie jangling gongs, and the red lights still pulsed, but the bashing had stopped. I slowed down and looked around as if that small patch of ruined corridor could tell me what was going on. The silence could only mean one thing.

"Codec, are they—"

"Boarding. Yes. Forsaken ships have breached the hull."

I clenched my jaw and stared ahead. "Get me to the command deck. Now."

The passage leading up to the bridge was a shrapnel-laden mess. The panels, which usually illuminated around someone's presence, were dark save for the odd flicker and scarlet probe. The only light came from the far end, and even it was sporadic and strobe-like, casting twisted shadows throughout the corridor. The bodies I stepped over and around were either dead or in the throes of it. The enclosed space, which seemed to get tighter the closer I got to the command deck, flashed me back to only a few hours earlier. The carnage-spattered Stormwater mines and most of my own team entombed there. I shook the thought away as I crept toward the doors, my Tempest raised. I wasn't sure if the boarding parties had breached close by, but I wasn't going to get caught with my pants down. Codec glitched bright blue next to me, but I dismissed him with a wave, so he wouldn't give away my position. I was surprised he had gotten me that far considering how corrupted his programming seemed to be.

"Goodbye, Codec," I whispered. There should have been an urgent flow of crew in and out of the room ahead, but all looked still inside.

Arriving at the doors, I posted up on the right side and took several deep breaths. The dread of what I might find inside shifted lead into my legs. I leaned out slightly to scope the closest corner. All clear. I pulled back and then whipped into the room, digging my rifle deep into the blind corner. Only the lifeless staring eyes of Trig and Black were there. Other command deck personnel I didn't know lay strewn throughout. I swung my weapon around, scanning the room. There!

"Sky!" I rushed over to the far back corner of the command deck, originally obscured by the angle of the main command console, which had been sheared off and lay on its side. Sky and Harper crouched beside Arthur, who was unconscious. Flak sat leaning against the wall.

"Will!" Sky lowered the Warthog she had pointed at me.

"Reach, what the hell are you doing here?" Flak growled. He was hurt bad. The lower half of his left leg was shredded down to snapped bone and looked like it was barely holding onto the rest of his body. It was coated in a thick slather of med gel, which seemed to be staunching most of the blood, but a significant black pool lay beneath it.

"What happened?" I asked. Harper pointed up at the ceiling.

Jesus. A truck-sized hole in the hull led straight down to the command deck. A shimmering pool of water filled the gap, a last-ditch hydro shield sealant for breached sections, like the way the shuttle bay operated when it was open. It was the only thing preventing us all from being sucked out into the cold vacuum of space. Rather not stare at that for too long, I looked down at Sky. "Arthur?" I asked, crouching beside him. His stomach was covered with a large slab of med skin that wrapped around to his back, and his uniform was coated in oily blood around the edges.

Sky shook her head. "It's not good. I put him out to mend his wound, but..." She looked lost. All of them did. "The *Albatross*, it's not—"

"I know." I glanced around the room, seeing if any of the other command staff were still alive. They weren't. "We need to get to the *Swift*. Now. They won't be able to wait much longer."

"The *Swift* isn't even finished."

"It's all we got. The thread drive was completed on Lumen, right?"

"Yes, but none of the weapons are operational."

"We're not fighting; we're running." I looked over at Flak and nodded. "Get to the lifeboats, and detonate the reactor, right?"

Flak nodded slowly. "Will's right. Take Arthur and go."

"Negative. We're all going—"

"That's an order!"

"Then court martial me later. You're coming," I said, glaring at Flak. "Besides, you don't want that little scratch to be the reason you die here, do you?"

Flak frowned at me, then shook his head and chuckled gruffly. "Damn stubborn bastard, Reach."

"And here I was thinking we were finally on a first-name basis." I glanced between the three. "Can you wake him?" I asked, gesturing to Arthur.

"Yes." Sky dug through her medical bag.

"And Sky…he needs to be able to walk, so don't overdo it." She nodded back to me.

Harper's eyes darted around the room at every creak and groan the *Albatross* made. She looked terrified, the kind of fear that took hold deep inside, somewhere between shellshock and a nervous breakdown. I put my hand on her arm, and she looked me in the eyes. I tried to return a steady gaze, instill a sense of confidence or courage or focus or anything that would draw her out of the trauma, even if only slightly. I breathed in and out slowly, and she did the same.

"Where's more med skin?"

"There isn't any," Sky said, gesturing behind her. A large partition had collapsed onto the command deck's main medical supply stowage. "This was all from my personal kit." This was really going to suck for

Flak. Sky readied a stim and held it to Arthur's leg. She hesitated for a moment, no doubt because she knew how much pain Arthur would be in. Ideally, he would have stayed unconscious until we got him to medical. Finally, she injected him, and we watched expectantly for him to wake. For an excruciating few seconds, nothing happened. Arthur didn't even flinch. Sky reached out and took his hand, pulsing some of her own energy into him, a calm green glow between them.

"Come on, Arthur," Flak muttered.

A moment later, Arthur stirred awake, his eyes opening slowly and fluttering. When his sight focused a little more, he stared up at Sky. "Sky…is it…over?"

Sky leaned in closer and tried to offer a reassuring smile. "Not yet."

The corridors were abandoned by all but the dead as we dropped into the midship levels. Our crews were hopefully safe-ish on the *Swift*, the Stormwater civilians jettisoned in the lifeboats, and anyone else still alive holing up wherever they could. It was dark and apocalyptic, the once-pristine hallways of the *Albatross* resembling something closer to ancient ruins or a storm-flooded subway line.

Sky and Harper carried Flak under the arms a little ways behind Arthur and me. Flak was much too heavy for me to support, and Arthur was at least moving a little bit under his own strength. I still felt his significant bulk with each step though. He held one arm across his stomach, the other over my shoulders, and remained silent for several minutes. It was a slower pace than I wanted, but it didn't seem like we had a choice.

Midway into communication with Kilo, our comms were severed by Forsaken jamming, but at least they knew we were on our way down, and I knew they'd wait for as long as they could. I just hoped they wouldn't wait too long if it came down to it.

The command deck had been rendered mostly useless by the damage, which meant we had to work the main reactor access into our route down. There was no other way to initiate the self-destruct sequence without being there. It wasn't just to safeguard the *Albatross's* technology from the enemy but also to hopefully buy us the time we needed to escape on the *Swift*.

"Will…" Arthur said through labored breaths. "The civilians…how many made it to the *Swift?*"

"They—" My voice caught in my chest, not my throat. My guilt didn't live there. I clenched my jaw and focused straight ahead. "We got as many of them there as we could."

Arthur coughed several times, and I saw black blood drip out of his mouth. "Good. Good. Sky—"

Suddenly, a massive impact hammered the ship, knocking us off our feet. Rather than the thunderous booms of before, a sharp ear-piercing metal-on-metal screech reverberated through the halls. Then the passage between Sky's group and Arthur and I collapsed as an obsidian-and-crimson point, like a massive spearhead, drove through the ceiling and punctured deep into the floor. There was an instant rush of air sucking toward it before a rapid gurgling of water sealed around the levels it had cut through. I leaped to my feet and helped Arthur back up, his face contorted in pain.

Looking back toward Sky and the others, I saw the Forsaken boarding vessel had punched almost halfway through the ship and blocked all but a few small gaps in the passage. There was no hatch in the point, and I assumed that meant they were offloading a level or two above us. *Shit.* I leaned Arthur against the wall and ran up to the blockage.

"Sky! Get to the *Swift!* We'll head to the reactor and meet you down there!" I yelled.

"Hurry, Will! We don't have much time!" she called back. No shit. I rushed back to Arthur and hoisted him over my shoulder. He was in a very bad way and muttering things under his breath that I couldn't make out. I quickly double-checked my Warthog.

"Come on, Arthur. We're almost there."

We were lucky. We covered the remaining distance to the reactor access with no sign of the Forsaken and with few detours. I knew they were out there somewhere, but so far so good. Arthur hadn't spoken since we were separated from Sky and the others, and I didn't press him. I imagined every step for him was a force of will. I didn't know the extent of his injuries under the makeshift med-skin patch, but it couldn't have been good.

The access to the reactor's override controls was in a small room off a curved starboard midship corridor outside the massive spherical chamber that occupied much of the central structure of the *Albatross*— the vessel's heart. The room itself, in relation to the size of the ship, reminded me of a fire cabinet in buildings back home, the kind with the sign that said, "Break glass in case of emergency." It was hidden behind a disguised wall panel seemingly in the middle of nowhere with blank stretches arcing away in either direction.

Upon arrival, Arthur placed his hand on the panel, and it slid apart to allow entrance. I ushered him to the console and then posted up at the opening to keep an eye on the passage.

"Program twenty minutes. That should give us enough time to make it to the *Swift*," I said, leaning my rifle against the edge of the door. I double-checked my sleeve display, taking a quick inventory. Full clip in my Tempest but only a half-full backup magazine on my bandolier. Full loadout in my Warthog and two spare clips. One grenade, one jolt shot, and my kite shield. It would have to be enough.

Suddenly, a crimson blast seared inches in front of my face from the opposite direction I was looking and skipped along the passage's wall. I ducked low and spun, returning fire. Three Forsaken strafed sideways, hugging the curve of the corridor. So much for an uncontested evac. Just then another peppering of scarlet shots tore at me from the other side, clipping the edge of the door and ricocheting into the adjacent wall. *Fuck*.

"Arthur! How's it coming?" I stole a glance back. He was slumped next to the console, not moving. "Shit." I rushed back and shook him. "Arthur!" He stirred groggily but couldn't bring himself to fully open his eyes. A shot rang off the entrance and skipped into the upper corner of the room. I dashed back and did what I could to push back both sides of the offensive, my eyes flicking to the rapidly descending ammo readout on my sleeve. I did not love being this close to black on ammo. My energy was also starting to waver. I couldn't keep this up forever. When I was satisfied that I'd forced a pause in their step, I ran back to Arthur, shaking him roughly. I glanced down at my bandolier. I needed the jolt shot, but without Arthur up and running, it wouldn't matter. I snapped it off and injected it into his leg. He woke with a sudden sharp inhale, and emerald energy flaring up his tech lines and into his eyes.

"Will...what—"

"Get up! We need that self-destruct initiated now!" I sprinted back to the door and leaned out just in time to see both sides of the Forsaken push close in. I hammered them back, shredding three in bursts of metal shards and red blood that simmered black midair. It looked like I had bought some time to my left.

To my right, the dark forms filled the passage like a shadow consuming every thread of light. I fired into them, my shots like a cobalt laser putting a stutter into their step. An instant later their obsidian shade was replaced with the fiery blaze of their shields. Each push forward of their line was matched with the thunderous boom of their unified steps. It was just a matter of time now. At least Sarah was on the *Swift*, and they had a chance. At least Frank was out there in the black somewhere. Wherever he was on the *Osprey*, it couldn't be worse than where I was. Sarah, Kilo, Miguel, Megan, Jiro, Seyyal, Cash, all of them, they just needed the chance to get away. Arthur needed just a little more time to get the job done.

I glanced back at him. He was working at the console again. He looked over his shoulder at me, pausing at the controls. I gave him a nod and a sad smile. He had given me so much. Some semblance of order in my mind, some shimmer of purpose. Something I'd never received from my own father, gone too soon. And that had made all the difference in the world. I primed my only grenade, the plasma filtering out from the ports and the orb bursting into sapphire flames in my hand.

"See ya when I see ya."

"Will, wait—"

I tore around the corner, hunched low with my Tempest pulled into my shoulder and the grenade in my other hand. At the crest of the curving path, the Forsaken wall glared back at me. Crimson blasts seared close enough for me to feel the heat on the exposed skin of my face and hands, seeming to stretch past me in slow motion. We'd made the mistake in the mines of trying to throw grenades over their shields, so instead I dove out and threw a hard, low sidearm toss. They tried to lower their shields to deflect it, but the two closest ovals bottomed out on the floor, leaving a small curved triangular gap. The bright blue glow of the grenade just barely tucked between and into the Forsaken line. A moment later the center of their line erupted in a fiery explosion, the chaos sending the onyx armor clattering into the walls. I was back on my feet in a flash and ripped into the remainder. Every fiber was bursting with energy as I gritted my teeth and squeezed the trigger. In a split second, my clip auto-ejected. Before it even hit the floor, I was slamming my last half clip into the side port of my rifle, muscle memory honed to perfection. In my peripherals I saw my raw left hand crack open, dripping blood in a steady flow off the bottom of my forestock, the exposed strands of corded biotech sparking brightly off the metal. A hot round glanced off my shoulder from behind, singeing the hair on my neck. I spun and dropped two more of the enemy along the wall and a third just before he stepped into the reactor access room, his body clanking against the open panel.

A fourth scarlet shot tore toward my face. For some reason, I batted at it with my hand. A bright spark of red connected with blue, and the round deflected into the wall. There was a still pause that was probably only a millisecond. *Holy shit. Did I just block a bullet with my hand?* I fired two more shots back at the Forsaken, who also looked stunned at what I had done. That was close.

I turned back to the main force as a shot swelled in the gap between me and the enemy wall. It seemed to freeze for a second before making contact, as if warning me that it had found its mark. It passed through my hip, spinning me around and dropping me onto one knee. A moment later, the second shot entered the back of my shoulder blade and burst out the front, knocking my Tempest out of my hands and spinning me around onto my knees and my good arm. I huddled there for a moment, sucking in quick short breaths and staring at the floor. My collapsing lung felt like a deflating balloon, accompanied by knifelike pains. I couldn't look down at my body; I knew it was over. I saw what the Forsaken's weapons had done to Jeremy on Stormwater, and this was worse. Bright red blood pooled beneath me. Somehow, I managed to right myself, facing the obsidian-and-crimson wall from my knees. I glared up at the Forsaken soldier shouldering his way past his recovering comrades. Some sort of captain maybe. He towered above me, an obelisk of metal and hate. He stood there, motionless, for what felt like ages, his prism helmet tilted down toward me, his red eyes staring out.

My heart pounded, but my brain went surprisingly quiet. No final smartass jabs came to mind. No "Fuck you" to death, no fear, no anger even. Just…acceptance. Calm.

Amongst the shadowy Forsaken statues, Maria walked with Evelyn holding her hand, each smiling their beautiful smiles. My dad stared out, leaning against the wall. Ali peered from within the dark husks. Other less-focused ghosts pranced around the edges.

I closed my eyes for a moment, and when I opened them, Maria and Evelyn were standing in front of me, smiling warmly. The rest of the corridor was empty, and the pristine white glow of the unscathed Albatross hallways had returned. All the pain seemed to fade away. I was so damn tired. I blinked several times, and between each dark shutter I caught glimpses of the former apocalyptic scene laced over this new dreamland. The Forsaken warrior stepped closer. Maria reached out to me, her eyes sparkling. I reached up to take her hand. As our fingers touched, she vanished in a glare of light, and I was left with the dark reality of the *Albatross* in its current state. My *Gladiator* moment was over. The Forsaken leviathan stood right in front of me, so close he obscured everything behind him. I stared up. God, I could use a drink. Finally, it came to me. I swallowed through an impossibly dry mouth to muster the words.

"In the immortal words of a legend from Earth…Eat my fucking shorts." I smiled up at death and extended the middle finger from my one good hand. *Nailed it.* From one of the enemy's arms, a savage blade shot out with a metallic *shinck* and lit up with red energy. "Yep. That's a bigger middle finger." He raised his arm up above his head. I exhaled slowly. The blade sliced through the air as it plummeted toward me—

PHHT!

The round was nearly silent, but the contact boomed and knocked me onto my back. Half my would-be executor's torso was gone, replaced by the glowing red rough-shorn edges of his armor plating, different fluids gushing out in a gory torrent. He dropped to the floor with a *clank*. The next thing I knew, a heavy salvo of sapphire and emerald was pelting across my vision and tearing into the Forsaken line. I torqued my head around to see who it was.

Sarah. When the firing stopped, she ran to me and crouched down. I saw her jaw tighten as she took in my injuries.

"Hey, beautiful," I said with a grim smile.

"We have to go."

"I gave you an order to get to the *Swift*—"

"Then court martial me later."

I chuckled weakly. "Did I say that to you before? Because I said the exact same thing to Flak earlier." She smiled, but it didn't reach her eyes. There was too much worry there. "I'd tell you to leave me, but I have a feeling you won't listen."

"You're right. I did come all this way," she said, scanning the hallways again. God, she was perfect. I looked back and saw Arthur leaning against the access room opening, his pistol arm hanging low. Sarah looked down at me again, her eyes flickering between my shoulder, hip, and other damage.

"Hand me my Tempest," I said. "You'll have to drag me."

There's a first for everything, I thought as Sarah and Arthur dragged me by my collar. Sarah had spread the last of her med gel on my wounds, but blood still trailed behind us in thick red streaks. I craned my head back. Arthur was struggling. The twisting of his body required to pull me no doubt tore at his injured core. Sarah's arm was wrapped with a metallic med skin patch, and I was amazed she could even keep her grip on me. We obviously hadn't had a chance to talk about Stormwater, but it looked like she'd been through the ringer in the mines. My right arm hung limply at my side, my fingers painting their own bloody path along the floor. I had my Tempest drawn into my left shoulder, ready for anything catching up behind us. It wasn't like there was a bright red trail showing our retreat. We were a shit-kicked lot. I glanced down at my sleeve display.

"Hate to be *that* guy, but we gotta step on it. Three minutes until boom goes the dynamite." I felt drunk and thirsty at the same time. Sarah shot me a death glare but didn't respond, only grunted and did her best to pick up the pace. She was probably doing the lion's share as Arthur struggled. Each of his steps were leaving darker and darker bloody black footprints. I wanted to say something, but we couldn't afford to stop and try to mend him. Granted, I was in no shape to mend anyone.

We turned a corner into a straight shot one hundred meters from the *Swift* access. I looked over my shoulder.

"Come on! Come on! Hurry!" Kilo, Seyyal, and Miguel yelled to us, waving urgently.

"Move your fucking asses!" Megan added.

Just then the Forsaken caught up. Crimson fire skirted around us and glanced off the walls. I shot back, and the others at the airlock laced blasts past us in green-and-blue phosphoric streaks, pressing forward into the hallway. Suddenly, I lurched to a halt.

"Don't stop! Don't stop!" I yelled, thinking Sarah and Arthur had turned to fire back at the enemy. I still felt their hands on my collar. "Go!" Then, almost gently, one of the hands let go. I twisted around to see what the hold-up was and then froze. Everything slowed. The sounds dimmed in my ears to an distant echoey roar. Arthur had reached up to feel a gaping wound at the base of his skull, oily blood gushing out. He collapsed to the floor. I fought against Sarah's attempts to drag me on her own and crawled up next to him. His face was slack against the floor as he stared back at me. He looked calm, and it hit me with a weird flash of déjà vu. It was such a similar look to what I imagined was on my face just before he and Sarah had saved me. Acceptance.

"Love, William. Love will always beat hate," he whispered. I stared, lost to any logical thought. Slowly, with a slight flicker, his eyes closed. It didn't make sense. Arthur was...no...no. No. A slight jerk shook me, and I looked down at my feet. The toes and half of my left foot had been blown clean off, and a small spurt of blood shot up from the stump. I couldn't feel it. I rolled onto my back and stared at the ceiling.

I saw figures step over me, bright flashes of lights, and then the ceiling zipped past. I saw the bulkhead of the doors and heard them close with a pneumatic whoosh. Somehow, I managed to raise my head. I'm not sure when, or even how, but I was holding Arthur's hand, his lifeless form dragged along with me. Or maybe they had dragged him too; I wasn't sure. I let my head thud back onto the floor and roll to the side. Sarah was on her hands and knees next to me, breathing hard. I released Arthur and reached over and held her wrist gently. She looked at me, tears in her eyes.

"*Swift* Command! We're on! Get us out of here!" Kilo yelled.

I felt a jarring drop, like turbulence in an airplane, and then a vibrating hum. Behind Sarah, I saw Kilo pull a small display panel off the wall.

The feed from the *Swift's* exterior flickered onto it. The *Albatross* came into view as we swooped low and away, keeping its floating corpse between us and the nearest Forsaken ship. Large fragments were separated from the body, and jets of oxygen shot out into space. Small bursts of energy and fire erupted out of the intact sections all over and were quickly swallowed by the vacuum. The once-smooth metallic seed shape was pocked and crushed like a crumpled can used for target practice. The *Albatross*. Our home.

In a strange moment, so out of place, a large oak tree from Earth floated past, sucked out of an aviary. The leaves were frozen in rigid form, the bark and stems cracking and splintering off as the water simultaneously boiled and froze out of it. Small icy dots floated away from it, and I had a sinking feeling it was the birds.

I could just make out the small glowing lights of the lifeboats still occasionally jettisoning. The Stormwater civilians' last-ditch effort to save themselves. Each was easily picked off by the large crimson cannons of the Forsaken warships. Each little flare sparked out like the crackle of a firework's end.

Suddenly, a shockwave burst from the *Albatross*, then drew back in. The hull sucked in on itself, one last inhale, like crumpling a piece of paper into a ball. For a moment, everything seemed to freeze. Then…

BOOM!

In a blinding flash of emerald light, it exploded, the debris field rushing toward us. Just before it reached our feed, the panel clouded over to the milky white-grey blur of thread-drive travel. And I passed out.

EPILOGUE

I opened my eyes and stared up at the bright luminescent ceiling. Apparently, I was still alive. At least I thought so. I didn't feel any pain, and I couldn't move, but I could think.

Sky's face appeared above mine. Her mouth moved, but no sound came out. After a few moments, the volume rose slowly, and I could just make out what she was saying. "Will, you're safe. You're on the *Swift*. In the med bay."

In a sudden wave, I remembered everything. Felt everything. Tears burned in my eyes, and I knew my biotech would be igniting all over. Electric-blue tears rolled down the sides of my face in torrents. I forced my eyelids shut and stared at the dark insides of them. Still, the images flashed and burned in the blackness.

I opened my eyes again and by sheer force of will looked to my left through the pain. Sarah was lying in the bed next to me, curled into the fetal position, staring back at me, tears running down her cheeks. A silent sorrow. She still looked beautiful, and I wanted nothing more than to have her in my arms. But I couldn't hold her gaze. I closed my eyes again and rolled my head to the other side.

When I opened my eyes again, I blinked several times, not sure if what I was seeing was real.

"Sky. Is…is…"

"Yes," she said gently, "but barely."

AFTERWORD & ACKNOWLEDGMENTS

The journey of *The Albatross* began about a decade ago when I was wildland firefighting, based in the Southern interior of British Columbia but also travelling all over Canada and the US. I was a crew member and then eventually a crew leader on an elite twenty-person type-1 unit crew. My callsign was Valhalla Bravo 1.

I remember a specific moment where we had to hustle off a fire and board a Bell 205 helicopter fairly hastily. The Bell 205 is the civvy version of the Bell UH-1 Iroquois, a.k.a. the "Huey," the same heli they used in Vietnam. Classic movie WHOOP, WHOOP, WHOOP of the rotor blades and all. I even rode with a few pilots who had actually flown in Nam.

Normally we would stash our bags, chainsaws, and Pulaski axes in the tail boom or where the side suicide seats—"Sueys"—would be, but on rare occasions we'd slide them directly below us under the seats or stash them between our legs or on our laps. Not ideal SOP; but sometimes you gotta do what you gotta do. So, eight of us were crammed in the back of the bird: tired, covered in sweat, dirt, and ash (maybe a little blood); geared up, dips in our lips, radios buzzing, adrenaline pumping, massive forest fire below us, and smoke billowing, thinking the only thing missing was "Fortunate Son" by CCR blasting in the background. The men and women around us were some of our best friends. Folks we'd be with twenty-four hours a day on a deployment that could last two to three weeks; yet they'd be the first group we'd go drinking with on our brief three days off before the next pull. If you can't see that in the crew of the *Albatross*, then I have failed. I was a writer long before my adventures in firefighting began, but work like that taught me all sorts of shit that you can't find in a classroom, which ultimately fueled my storytelling.

The Albatross began as a screenplay, one of dozens I'd finished and let sit on my shelf collecting dust. The difference between this screenplay and the others was that I wrote it as an epic three-hour movie, part one in a trilogy, clocking in somewhere around 200 pages. For anyone who knows the film business, the chances of a screenplay that long being looked at, unless it's written by someone in the upper echelon of screenwriters, is very unlikely. But I didn't care; I had too much I wanted to tell. So, taking as much life experience as I could, some college creative writing and English classes, and inspiration from classics like *The Forever War* by Joe Haldeman, *Starship Troopers* by Robert A. Heinlein, *On Writing* by Stephen King, and a plethora of other amazing books in and out of the science-fiction genre, I took a stab at turning it into a novel. I'd tried before with other ideas that were always put on the backburner for other projects, but this one infected my mind. Every day I worked on it, and every night I dreamed about it. I saw the story, the world, and the characters in near-perfect detail. I fell in love with the voices in my head and knew I *needed* to tell their story. (Spoiler Alert) I'm probably going to be more bummed than you when I start killing so many of them off later...

This is just the beginning. I have a minimum of five books mapped out. The biggest difficulty I can see now is whether I can contain some of those in one book or whether I'll have to split a few in two. Either way, Book Two is already well on its way, so look for the continued voyage of the *Albatross* crew (and maybe another ship's crew) coming soon.

This book would not have been possible without the support of so many people in so many different ways. Chief among them is my family—my mom, brothers, sister, grandparents, and cousins. I'm sure they're happy the books are coming out, so I will finally shut the fuck up instead of talking about them all the time. They've always been there for me, even when I was drinking too much, angry, erratic, remarkably stubborn, fairly insane, or depressed. I'm a fucking writer; what do you expect? For me to be stable? Ha, ha, haaa! Anyway, every step of the way they were there, and I can never thank them enough for that. Smooth seas and rough ones, and you know what Marilyn Monroe said about that…

Sticking with blood, life's a roller-coaster, and I'd be remiss not to also thank my dad. A fallen hero. His memory has driven me in many different directions—good and bad—but all leading to where I am now, which I'm pretty OK with. Hopefully, you can read this book in the heaven, hell, cosmic ether, reincarnated body, alternate universe, or secret WITSEC life in Paraguay you survived to live in that I imagined as a kid. Miss and love ya, Dad.

To my publishing team, for the guidance, editing, designing, promoting, and all matters related to bringing my manuscript from incorrectly formatted Word document to the finished product you see here, thank you.

To all my friends, family, and beta readers—Kelly, Mom, Don, Yvonne, KC, Rogan, Brent, Gord—who read the early rough drafts and actually managed to make it through all the horrible punctuation and give me feedback, I appreciate you taking the time to help me out. Your input was invaluable. Thank you.

Last but not least, to the person who supported my dreams creatively every step of the way and financially pushed them that last leg, thank you. I've always loved the imagery of angels and demons, though I've never believed in them. Either way, you're a goddamn angel, sir.

Connor Mackay

CONTINUE READING FOR THE
PART I PROLOGUE OF

THE ALBATROSS

REQUIEM

BOOK 2 IN THE ALBATROSS SERIES

CONNOR MACKAY

PROLOGUE

The Lost Ones

The shuttle ride had taken about an hour, headed due east of Lumen central. That much I could tell. It had to put us somewhere in the middle of the Candleburn Ocean, but not far enough around that we had crossed into the dark side of the planet—the perpetual red dusk still reflected in the ship's displays. I stole a glance at my forearm band to see if tracking was punching through the jammer, if any blips were registering, or if my Raps had relayed triangulation off landmarks, but no luck. The dark, choppy water stretched in all directions as far as I could see from my side of the ship. My sense of unease grew the further out we went, the more exposed and isolated we became. I would have felt better having Will with us.

"Elora," Kilo said, nodding at the display behind me. I twisted around to see what he was seeing.

A small patch of ground covered in black grasses and navy bushes came into view. Barely large enough to accommodate the shuttle, it extended off the side of a massive, ancient space elevator reaching up to the planetary hydro-shield; which somehow, the pilot had managed to keep in our blind spots—not that he had enabled many of the displays for the trip. Another glance to my band still showed no new information. We landed gently and off-loaded out of the rear ramp. Once we were clear, the shuttle lifted off and sped away over the ocean.

"Hey!" I yelled. "Where's it going?"

The leader of the small chaperone group turned to face me. "It will return when you are ready to leave," he said. "It's best not having it linger around the entrance for long, in case it's noticed." I stared at him for a moment and then glanced warily toward the shuttle rapidly disappearing in the distance. The Lumenarian gestured to the base of the structure. "Please follow me." I primed some energy into my Tempest, double-checking the ammo readout on my sleeve. Full. I knew it was, but I felt it was a good reminder for our "friend." Then, for added effect, I flared the biotech in my eyes a bright sapphire. The rest of my team simultaneously checked their weapons. The leader kept his gaze on me and smiled, then bowed his head and held his arm out toward the entrance.

"No, after you," I said, also bowing my head. "I insist."

As I stepped inside the titanic structure, tense and ready for anything, I was shocked to be greeted by dozens of Lumenarians casually milling about the ground level. Parents with children playing games, the young ones' tails whipping wildly from side to side; ragtag militia eyeballing us and tightly gripping their black-market weaponry, inconsistent sparks of emerald along their tech lines; workers around machinery that looked like it was somehow older than the tower; and elders that seemed to be just leisurely hanging around—there for the show. Ring upon ring of leveled balconies rose higher than I could see, fading up toward the atmosphere within the hollow tower. Onyx vines with deep navy and maroon flowers crawled up the sides, and slits in the walls let beams of scarlet light filter in. Above us, the word had quickly spread about our presence, and thousands of faces leaned out from their levels to observe us. Every surface looked weathered with age and salty ocean grime and gave off the feeling of walking into a futuristic favela. It was not what I was expecting at all. It was a . . . community.

I closed my awestruck mouth and turned to the leader. "What is this place?" I asked.

The leader spread his arms out and spun in place, looking up at the curious inhabitants. "Home," he said with a relaxed smile. "You can wait here. He'll be down shortly." With that, he walked off to the side and spoke with some of the workers tinkering on a beat-up machine that

I'd guess was some sort of water desalinizer or purifier, based on the leaks and piping fed through the walls and into the floor.

I turned to the rest of my team and nodded. "Stay sharp," I said. "It might not look like much, but be prepared for anything." Everyone returned an affirmative nod.

Kilo stepped in closer and glanced at the families playing a game of, amazingly, soccer. "I might not feel good about this," he said. "But I doubt even *they* would risk a fight with children present." I bobbed my head side to side in response. *All the same, no chances.*

"I agree," Miguel said, walking over with Megan and Ska. "Plus, they're playing soccer. That's our game. Can't be all bad."

"Also, I put a det charge on the door when we walked in," Megan said. We all stared at her. She shrugged. "What? Better safe than fucking sorry. Don't look at me like that. Will would've loved my initiative." Everyone went a little stiff at the mention of his name, especially Miguel. The other Dorians, humans, and Lumenarians on the team huddled together off to the side, looking nervous. I couldn't blame them, but after all we'd been through it was surprising that this is what was making them twitchy. Isolated or not, what surrounded us was hardly something formidable.

Suddenly, Miguel's jaw clenched, and his eyes panned up the far wall. "We got something," he said, nodding behind me. I turned and watched a rickety lift descend to the ground level. The doors opened and three Lumenarians stepped out.

The one in the center strode toward us and held out his hand to shake mine. "Welcome, Elora Bhele," he said with a calm, tight-lipped smile. "My name is Mason."

thealbatrossseries.com

@thealbatross_series

@cmackay10

facebook.com/thealbatrosscontact

@cmackay10

CPSIA information can be obtained
at www.ICGtesting.com
Printed in the USA
BVHW072056110920
588618BV00003B/246

9 781525 567285